"Kernan's cre... ...ing
mythology—l... ...can
Lakota my...
...
—*RT Book Re*... ...k!

"*Ghost Stalker* is enthralling with difficult
predicaments and appealing characters."
—*CataRomance.com*

"The twists and the ultimate battle kept
Beauty's Beast a page-turner. The romance between
Alon and Samantha is both sultry and tender, and
doesn't take away from the excitement…a
well-written and exciting adventure."
—*Fresh Fiction*

"The unique story line makes for an exciting novel.
The attraction between Cesar and Bess sparkles
and the story moves along quite nicely."
—*RT Book Reviews* on *Soul Whisperer*

Praise for Sierra Woods

"*The Resurrectionist* is a wildly sexy thriller that
breathes new life into the paranormal genre.
Literally."
—*New York Times* bestselling author Darynda Jones

JENNA KERNAN

Jenna Kernan writes fast-paced romantic adventures set in out-of-the-way places and populated by larger-than-life characters. Happily married to her college sweetheart, Jenna shares a love of the outdoors with her husband. The couple enjoys treasure hunting all over the country, searching for natural gold nuggets and precious and semiprecious stones. Jenna has been nominated for two RITA® Awards for her Western romances and has received the Book Buyers Best Award for paranormal romance in 2010. Visit Jenna at her internet home, www.jennakernan.com, or at twitter.com/jennakernan for up-to-the-minute news.

THE VAMPIRE'S WOLF

AND

THE

RESURRECTIONIST

Jenna Kernan
and
Sierra Woods

HARLEQUIN® NOCTURNE™

Recycling programs
for this product may
not exist in your area.

ISBN-13: 978-0-373-60674-0

The Vampire's Wolf and The Resurrectionist

Copyright © 2014 by Harlequin Books S.A.

The publisher acknowledges the copyright holder
of the individual works as follows:

The Vampire's Wolf
Copyright © 2014 by Jeannette H. Monaco

The Resurrectionist
Copyright © 2014 by Brenda Schetnan

Printed in U.S.A.

www.Harlequin.com

CONTENTS

THE VAMPIRE'S WOLF
Jenna Kernan

For Jim. Always.

To Mick Winjum, a former marine, for his assistance with research for this story. Any mistakes of fact or procedure are the author's. Semper Fi!

Chapter 1

Brianna Vittori peered out the windshield at the wet April snow falling so fast the wipers couldn't keep up. Any sane person would pull over. She kept going because the only thing worse than being captured by the military was being captured by the vampires.

She passed the sign announcing the distance to the Marine Mountain Training Center in the predawn gloom, driving without headlights, because for her the darkness meant only the loss of color from her vision and not the blindness humans endured. She could still see perfectly were it not for the spring storm that sent flakes splashing ice across her windshield. There had been no snow down below in Sacramento. But here in the California mountains spring acted differently. Driving conditions were so dangerous that even the plows and sanders hadn't ventured out. But then they weren't fleeing from vampires.

Was she mad to run headlong toward the only creatures that could stop them? The wolves could save her, if they didn't kill her first.

Werewolves were the vampires' natural enemy, but she didn't know what they thought of Feylings. Her grandmother had not said. Bri thought again of the woman who had changed her world when she was only in high school. She'd told Bri that she was first generation—a Feyling. Now vampires were hunting her. She didn't know why, but they were out there right now, searching.

She might have walked right into their trap if not for her second encounter with another female of her kind. That Feyling had taken a risk to seek her out. The woman was blunt as a dull hatchet with her warning, but without her, Bri would have been caught. No doubt in her mind. They were there at the hospital.

The thermostat told her it was twenty-two degrees out there, and she was only wearing sneakers, jeans and a tight white T-shirt with short sleeves. Brianna gripped the wheel of the rental car and stared out at the night. The snow flew at her like a living thing, blasting against the windshield and exploding against the glass like drops of plasma.

She peered out at the sky, searching vainly for daylight. They didn't like daylight. She knew that much, and she knew what they wanted with her. Bri shuddered.

She glanced into the woods that lined the road, catching glimpses through the snow of something moving there. An elk, a werewolf, a vampire? It hadn't been until she was in elementary school that she discovered every child couldn't see in the dark. Now she wished that she couldn't. She shivered and fiddled with the heat, knowing the cold she felt came from inside. Better not to see what was stalking her.

She'd never run so far or so fast. But she'd outpaced

the one at the hospital and the one in her apartment. It had been stupid to go back there.

She'd known she was different—"special," her grandmother had called her—but she never knew she could run like that. Perhaps you needed the devil on your heels to learn such a thing.

God, she wished she'd never found out about them. Brianna rubbed her tired eyes with her thumb and index finger as she steered with the other hand.

She passed the base entrance with all the floodlights and security. She lowered her head and continued on, anxious to get past this place. She didn't trust the military. The soldiers seemed like drones, mindless and intimidating, while their leaders were more secretive than vampires.

Something stood upright in the road. Brianna slammed on the brakes with both feet, and the car fishtailed. The man stood motionless as a ghost, his white face blotched with huge purple spots. Brianna's heart hammered in her chest as she straightened her arms and braced for the collision, no longer trying to miss him but trying to hit him, because she had realized that the being in the road was no man, but a vampire.

A moment before impact he leaped, clearing the car as her vehicle rushed beneath him. She was now sliding toward the ditch. The back end of the car hit the shallow embankment first. The car skidded sideways, tilting, and then rolled to the driver's side. She careened across loose gravel. There was a shriek of tearing metal and a crunch of collapsing plastic. The impact shattered the driver's-side window, which exploded into a million flying crystals of glass that flew at her like tiny bits of shrapnel. There was a final jolt as the car came to an abrupt halt.

Her heart slammed against her ribs, and her breathing came in puffy, white, vaporous pants of steam. Everything else was silent. Brianna unfastened her seat belt and looked about. The moment she breathed in the air, she noted the sharp scent of the werewolves. They were close.

Where was that thing that chased her? Had she hit it?

The answer arrived an instant later when the windshield exploded and the vampire reached his cadaverous hands inside the cab to haul her out.

She screamed and kicked, but he held on. He shook her to silence as another one grabbed her from behind. Brianna screamed again and the first one let go of her arm to slap her hard across the face. She'd never been struck before, and the sting and explosion of pain in her cheek and ear made her dizzy. She swayed as they dragged her to the vacant road.

Her knees wobbled but she remained standing. She was certain what would came next. Brianna recalled what that strange girl outside her high school had said. She was not to be caught by them. Not ever. For what awaited was a living death. Why did vampires capture Feylings? she had asked. The answer had turned her blood to ice. The April dawn and her panic turned her skin cold. She trembled as the first leaned in. It was the first time she had ever seen one close up, and his appearance made her flesh crawl. He stared with eyes white as milk. He seemed blind, but then she saw the perfect black pupil and realized it was only his iris that had the strange lack of pigment. His wrinkled ears and distorted head made him look as if he had some terrible genetic abnormality. But his eyes terrified her the most.

His slitted nose flared as he leaned close.

Staff Sgt. Travis "Mac" MacConnelly woke to Johnny pounding on his door and then to a female voice screaming just outside his quarters. He shook his head like a dog to clear the dreams from reality and groaned. What time was it? Oh six hundred, he realized. The pounding came again, on his window this time.

"Bloody hell. Johnny, I swear to God, I'm going to chain you up at night," Mac bellowed.

From outside the door, Johnny roared back. John Loc Lam had once been his grenadier, on his first combat assignment under a squad leader also on his first and, as it turned out, his last command. Mac scoured his face with his rough hands, trying to scrub away the grief that clung like tar.

"Fine. I'm up." Since the Marine staff sergeant no longer quartered in the barracks and he had more privacy, Mac slept in the buff. He tugged on his pants and thrust his bare feet into his boots. Then he stood, stretched and felt the familiar twinge across his torso. He glanced at the scars that crisscrossed his chest and right shoulder. There were four long slash marks from the creature's claws and then the punctures and puckered flesh where its teeth had torn open his shoulder. After four months, the battle wounds given to him by that thing had still not completely healed. Mac snatched up a shirt and thrust his arms through the sleeves, covering the worst of the scars, but he left the shirt unbuttoned as he tugged on his cap. "This better be good, Johnny."

He buckled on his holster, tapped the knife down in the sheath and checked the .45 pistol before sliding it home. Then headed out, not dressed for inspection, with his shirttails flapping in the wind. The first thing that hit him was the cold, the second was the unfamiliar scent. Since the attack, he could smell things, tiny insignificant things like the antacids the colonel carried in his left pocket. But now he smelled something new. Enticing. Alive. Something that did not belong in the middle of his territory. He inhaled deeply, bringing the scent to his sensitive nose. Like orchids and the ocean and exotic spices, and then he caught the smell of dank earth, rotting leaves and musty clothing. His body snapped to attention. They smelled different to everyone, they'd said, but the females' scent was universally irresistible and not like humans'. Since the attack, Mac could smell humans and differentiate between them and any other kind of animals, even from a distance. But these creatures did not smell human. They lacked the smell of meat and salt but not the scent of blood. That came through now and grew stronger by the minute.

Johnny appeared around the side of the concrete two-story enclosure that had once been a training site built to resemble the family compounds back in the Sandbox. Now it was their quarters.

John Loc Lam had once been a fine Marine. Now he was a huge wolflike creature, eight feet tall, who easily balanced on his two hind legs as he lifted massive claws and roared a warning, flashing dangerous fangs. His features were not human but neither were they wolf. Instead he combined both: small pointed ears, a long snout, wicked jaws and a face covered with glossy black hair.

"Do you smell orchids and blood?" he asked.

Johnny nodded.

Exactly what he'd been prepped to expect if he ever came upon flesh eaters. They were out late for vampires, because the sun was up. That would make it easier to spot, track and kill.

"Training exercise?" he asked.

Johnny shook his head.

Mac inhaled again. "Bloodsuckers. Males and females. Did you see them or come here first?"

Johnny gave no answer. He couldn't. He could answer only yes-or-no questions, to their continual frustration.

"I thought they avoided our kind unless provoked." He eyed his corporal. "Did you provoke them?"

Another shake of his shaggy head dismissed that line of questioning.

"Why would they come here? Can't be an accident. Got to be hunting us."

Johnny growled.

Mac drew his sidearm. He knew a bullet wouldn't stop them, but he felt better with a gun in his hands.

"Come on, then."

Johnny looked at Mac's weapon and shook his head.

"I'm going to keep it, thanks." Mac released the safety. "A couple in the head will slow them down. The bullets are steel."

Johnny groaned and thumped his chest. He wanted Mac to change.

"I'll turn when we get closer. Don't worry, I'll keep up."

Johnny nodded.

"We have to kill them." He stepped around his gunner. "Capture one if we can. The colonel's wet dream is to have one alive. Might prove we're ready for combat duty again."

Johnny nodded his agreement. He was just as tired of being a lab rat as Mac was. The two of them set off, hunting as they often did, only this time the quarry was vampire. When the scent grew strong, Mac pulled up to disrobe and stash his clothing before summoning the change.

Johnny paused to look back. Mac felt the familiar flash of guilt at his ability. He motioned Johnny on. No reason he should have to watch. Mac slipped out of his boots. Before the change gripped him in that momentary blinding bolt of agony, he issued one last order to his corporal.

"Circle behind them. If they come your way, kill them. That's an order."

Mac recovered quickly from the change, but Johnny had already gone. Mac was faster now, running on two long, powerful legs, his gray fur flashing white in the sunlight that now shone in bright rays from the east. He thought of what might have happened if the vampires had found him in his quarters asleep and wondered if they were inside or outside the perimeter of the training center.

He saw Johnny now, a black shadow running parallel to him through the trees.

Mac recalled what he'd learned in his new training. He needed to get to an artery, a big one. Femoral, brachial or carotid. *Open a vessel and hold the thing down until it bleeds out. Don't let it bite you and don't let it go. It will regenerate any lost body part except its head. Reopen the vessel if necessary.*

Instead of the forest, for just the smallest fraction of a second, he saw his Fire Team around him at the building they had once used for training ops before deployment. He pushed aside the tug of grief he felt at the thought of all the good men who had died in the Sandbox, his men. If he'd known what they faced, could he have kept them alive?

Decisions made in an instant now rolled through his mind with the regularity of the tides. He didn't know, but maybe.

Now he was back in the present facing more split-second decisions that he'd have to live with every damned day. If he told the doctors about the flashbacks, they'd say PTSS and he'd be sidelined for who knew how long. Maybe he and Johnny could prove their worth right here and now. But maybe he'd fuck it up again.

The changing light caused by the breaks in the clouds made it hard to see the things, but he sensed them. Could the vampires sense Mac the way he scented the bloodsuckers? Two males and a female, traveling together.

He saw Johnny drop and realized they were nearly on the intruders. He threw himself down so he could stare through the perimeter fence. He saw two male bloodsuckers dragging a female along the shoulder of the highway beside an overturned car, her feet kicking wildly, uselessly. They seemed oblivious to their company. He glanced at Johnny who looked to him for the signal to charge.

He signaled for him to hold and glanced back to the intruders, gaping, as this was the first time he'd seen the Night Stalkers. The sight sent a shiver down his spine. There were two males and they were hideous, pale and rodentlike, just as he'd been told, with purple-skinned and misshapen heads that looked as if they'd been crushed. Their eyes were milky, and their noses, if you could call them that, were slitted as if they belonged to reptiles. And then he fixed on the woman, struggling against their grasp and making every effort to wrench herself free.

She did not seem of the same species. They'd said the females were lovely, and he was curious to see for himself.

She was tall and lithe, dressed modestly in a pair of faded blue jeans that sat low on her curvy hips. Her struggles showed him both the pink mobile phone that did not entirely fit in her back pocket and also the scrap of white lace undergarment that peeked from above her jeans. Her white T-shirt fit her like a second skin and had hiked over her flat stomach, showing a wide-open stretch of perfect skin and the dark indent of her navel. How long had she been a bloodsucker, and why was she fighting them?

The beams of sunlight chased across the yard, illuminating her to reveal that her hair was coppery-red, shoulder-length, and with ringlets that wound tight, curly as a corkscrew. They bounced as she tossed her head. He wanted to see her face, which was now covered by her hair.

Now what the hell did he do? He hadn't counted on killing a woman.

Not a woman, he reminded himself. A dangerous assassin. The female vamps killed by drawing energy. At least that's what the intel from the Israelis said. The Israelis had captured one but couldn't turn her, so they'd put her down.

She's not human. A killer. *A beauty,* whispered his mind.

He shook his head. This wasn't possible. Her allure didn't work on him. That was what he'd been told. But he still found he didn't have the stomach to kill her. She'd be the capture, he decided. The colonel's prize.

But first he had to get her away from those butt-ugly male bloodsuckers.

The vampire's grip bit into Brianna's wrists. She twisted and kicked, and she worried that she would simply be one more young woman who vanished without a trace.

"Look in the trunk. See if there's something to tie her hands."

The second released the latch and rummaged. "Nothing." He turned to peer at her. "Just knock her out."

"No. Not this one," said her captor, pulling her elbows so tightly that they touched behind her back. "She's special. First generation. Just smell that. I'd like a taste of her now."

Brianna stilled as the terror washed through her stomach and twisted her intestines. She felt dizzy and nauseous as his breath fanned down her neck in a hot blast.

"But you won't," said the one standing before her, just out of range of her kick. "You'll wait for orders or face his judgment."

The vampire behind her sniffed again as if she were some kind of cocaine.

"Still we did find her first. Who has to know? She's not a virgin. I can smell she's not."

"We need to get out of here before someone sees us. It's daylight, Ian. Any human could wander by."

"In this snow? Just one bite. What do you say? She'll heal before we get her to the Lord, and it will be her word against ours."

The one before her cocked his head, staring at her with those creepy white eyes, considering Ian's proposal.

There was a pounding sound, like a horse at full gallop. Both vampires turned, and the one before her shrieked as a black wolf leaped at him, carrying him backward to the ground as the great jaws closed on his neck. A second wolf, this one gray, attacked from the opposite direction, but the one behind her released his grip and vanished before the monstrous wolf got his jaws locked on him. The snapping sound came just behind Brianna's head. She crumpled to the earth as the black wolf ripped out the throat of the other vampire. So this was a werewolf, her first sighting and likely her last.

She saw that the one called Ian had run to the front of her car and then changed direction, circling the vehicle, coming back toward the gray werewolf, which now looked in the direction he had gone. She knew he couldn't see the vampire. But she could.

"To your right!" she shouted.

The wolf dropped and rolled in the direction she pointed, taking out Ian's legs.

The vampire sprawled and skidded as the gray one landed on his back, pinning him to the earth before using a hideous claw to slash at Ian's neck. The blood sprayed across the road like a fire hose turned on for just a moment. Then the blood pumped more rhythmically as the werewolf held Ian down. The vampire struggled as his neck wound sealed and healed. But the werewolf opened his neck again. Brianna held a hand over her own neck and then vomited in the snow. She would be next. Of that she had no doubt.

Ian's struggles ceased. His neck wound remained wide open and the gray wolf rose with his fellow. They turned toward her in unison.

They were huge, at least nine feet tall, and their front forearms ended in long fingers with horrible hooked claws that dripped with blood. Neither had a tail. Their snouts were too short for wolves and too long for men, unlike any creatures she had ever seen outside of a nightmare.

Their teeth were worse than any wolf she'd ever seen, and she got a very good look as they peeled back the flesh from the long white enamel and growled at her.

Brianna scuttled backward on all fours and ran into the undercarriage of her rental. The black one snorted and stared with fixed yellow eyes, and Brianna saw her own death reflected there.

It knew what she was. She sensed that it did. A second low, rumbling growl emanated from its throat. She started to vibrate, preparing to move so fast that even a nine-foot werewolf could not catch her.

They killed the two that took her. Were there others? She glanced about and did not see any.

Brianna lifted a hand to her forehead and recalled thinking that she preferred death to the living horror that came with her capture.

Now that she looked death in the eye, she wondered if she had the courage to accept what came. They would kill her. Why wouldn't they? That was what werewolves did, all they did, if the female was to be believed. Still, she had to try. They were her only hope.

"Help me," she said, finding her voice a strangled weak representation of its former self.

The black one charged her.

"Help me," she said, huddling small and innocent as a fawn against the compact car, which was covered with so much road salt that Mac couldn't tell what color it had once been. She was an exotic bloom growing there in the snow and dirt, beautiful as dawn, as the first golden rays of morning gilded her coppery hair so it shone like flames about her pale upturned face.

Of course it was all illusion. She was as harmless as a heart attack and innocent as a brimming cup of poison. But not to him.

"Please. I have no one else."

She said it as if he were some human she could order about like a mindless slave.

And he would bet a month's pay that up until this very moment no male had ever refused her anything. Human males were easily manipulated by female vamps. Apparently she did not know that her powers didn't work on werewolves.

"They were trying to take me." She began to rise, a blooming rose reaching for the sun. He motioned her to stay down.

Why didn't she disappear, like the male?

"So I came here to find you."

She'd come on purpose into their territory? That was suicidal, he thought, or a brilliant tactic. As to which it was, that would depend on if Mac killed her or not.

Sea-green eyes, pale and lovely as glass polished in the ocean, stared up at him in wide astonishment. Her high cheeks flushed a beguiling pink, and a few freckles lay scattered across her nose, giving interest to the skin that glowed luminescent as a pearl. Yes, she was the most beautiful woman he'd ever seen. But she wasn't a woman.

She covered her face with her hands, letting her fiery hair sweep forward. *Now,* he thought.

As if reading his mind, Johnny charged her. *No,* he thought, but he couldn't order Johnny to halt. Neither could speak in werewolf form and it was too late. She must have heard Johnny for she turned, lifting her startled eyes. But instead of vanishing, she turned her head, elongated her neck, making it easier for Johnny to kill her.

This one was ready to die, prepared for just that.

Mac had just enough time to throw a shoulder into his corporal and deflect his course. Johnny crashed into the rear of the car as Mac hauled the vampire to her feet. She did not resist, as she had with the males of her species. He tugged her forward and she fell against his wide, hairy chest, looking up at him with sea-glass eyes. He had to remind himself that she couldn't affect him, because his heart obviously didn't get that message. Or his skin, for it tingled with a sexual awareness that lifted every hair.

He pinned her wrists against his chest, one in each fist. He realized her jeans and shirt were wet, and he waited for her to slip from his hold like water. But she only stared up at him with wide, frightened eyes. Next he noticed how slender the bones of her wrists were and how silky-soft her skin felt. There was an energy about her, like a static charge that made his skin tingle, as if she were stroking him. He banged her wrists on his chest, and she extended her elegant, manicured fingers so they threaded through the fur that covered his chest. Pink, he realized, like the inside of a conch shell.

Beside him, Johnny growled.

The smell of the breeze off the Gulf of Mexico surrounded Mac. So that was her game. The lure of her person. She'd counted on it to entrance him. That meant either she didn't know he was unaffected or she didn't know that it made a difference. Had she never met a man who could resist her?

Was he really immune, or had the scientists gotten that wrong, too?

If he were immune to her terrible powers, then why was he staring down at those soft green eyes, those parted pink lips? She gasped, bringing air into her lungs. She would be so easy to kill.

Johnny made a huffing sound, and Mac looked his way. The look of consternation was clear, as was the slicing motion he made across his throat. Johnny wanted her dead.

Mac shook him off and threw the vampire over his shoulder. They'd secure her for now and then call the colonel.

He easily vaulted the ten-foot security fence with the woman on his shoulder and ran with her to their quarters, trying not to notice the sweet scent of her skin or the tumble of curly red hair that cascaded over his chest like a silken waterfall. When they reached the yard he thought to wonder if her purpose was to find exactly where they lived. Would the vampires sacrifice the two males and this one to discover their position?

It was possible.

He tossed her to her feet and motioned to Johnny, keeping her wrist imprisoned in his grip. Her eyes widened as he gestured for Johnny to take charge of her. It was only when she saw him approach, teeth bared, hackles raised that she started to struggle. Her strength, though greater than what a human female would possess, was no match for a werewolf's. Johnny clasped her opposite wrist, because he did not want to give her a second to run. Not now that they had her.

How had that male disappeared? Could she do that as well, and if she could disappear, why didn't she when she had the chance?

He needed to transform if he were to interrogate her. But he wasn't about to let her see that. Standing naked and vulnerable before her held the kind of risk even he wasn't willing to take.

He gave Johnny a long look and a slow shake of his head, waiting for the confirming nod of understanding. Johnny would not kill her, though he clearly wanted to.

Was he right?

Mac stared at the beautiful temptation and recognized that he did not want to let her go. He growled. Werewolves didn't moon after vampires. They caught them and killed them. But even as he let her go, he knew what he wanted to do with her and that troubled him.

Chapter 2

The black beast captured Brianna's other wrist as the gray werewolf withdrew, leaving her to her death. Her knees clanked together and then failed to hold her. The werewolf stared down at her with malevolent yellow eyes. She folded like a lawn chair as the black spots spun and danced, like gnats, before her eyes. Bri's head hung down, and she waited to feel the piercing pain of its bite, but it did not come. Instead, she heard the low, rumbling growl as it gave her one reckless shake before dragging her a foot along the cold earth, which smeared mud on the knees of her wet jeans.

"All right, Johnny." The voice was deep, commanding and totally unfamiliar. "Stand down."

The authority of his tone carried an absolute certainty that his orders would be followed. Instantly the punishing grip on her wrist eased, shifted as warm hands grasped her forearms just below the elbows. His hold was firm, but his fingers did not bite into her flesh as the werewolf's had done, and his index finger stroked her bare skin. She gasped at the tiny, intimate gesture.

She lifted her chin to find the black werewolf giving way to a tall, dark-haired man with a military haircut. He knelt before her half dressed in camouflage. The spots swirled into a vivid pattern of light. She closed her eyes, struggling against the darkness that threatened to consume her.

"Just breathe," he said, his words now lower, more personal, and lacking the bite of authority he used on the werewolf.

She did as he said, dragging in a lungful of air through her nose and then another. Her vision cleared and she noted his intent blue eyes pinning her, as surely as his hands that clasped her wrists. His eyes were not friendly; rather, they held caution and a glittering intensity that she could not read. He was imposing and not the least bit concerned by the giant hulking werewolf who stood panting and growling behind his left shoulder like some rabid dog. Where was the other one?

Her gaze flicked back to the soldier. The patch on his sleeve showed a chevron, but she didn't know what rank that was. His posture, his bearing, the rigid thrust of his square jaw and the fatigues all screamed soldier. Bri recalled passing the training center and the fence the gray wolf had vaulted as a child might jump a mud puddle.

The gray werewolf had brought her to this man. Who was he?

His camouflage shirt was all browns and tans, flapping open as he loomed over her to reveal a rising landscape of hardened, contracting muscle. Four long, raised scars slashed across the right side of his chest. They looked like knife wounds, except the marks were evenly spaced and puckered as if a gash, rather than an incision, had caused this damage. One scar missed his nipple by a hairsbreadth. And there was more. Peppered throughout the scars were a series of punctures. What had happened to him?

"Why did you come here?" he asked, his voice no longer holding that calming tone. Now it sounded low and deadly.

The hairs on her neck prickled. She tried to speak, but the muscles of her diaphragm seemed paralyzed.

She lifted her chin to see his pronounced Adam's apple and the dark morning stubble on his throat. The muscles at each side of his neck corded like wings. His clenched jaw looked hard as steel, except for the continuation of the beard that did not mesh with her image of the uniformly clean shave of most army men. His lips showed tight displeasure, making his generous mouth seem stingy at least for her. His long nose had a bump high on the bridge, showing an old break. It gave character to an otherwise flawless slope. His cheeks were high and smooth, above the distinct line of stubble that merged seamlessly into the sideburns of the short, bristled haircut favored by military men and athletes. Bri lifted her gaze to meet his eyes.

She saw the icy blue and decided in that instant she had made a terrible mistake. This man would not help her. He was a soldier, hardened, heartless, and she would find no pity in him.

The hairs lifted on her neck as she looked to the right and left for help. She caught movement and then the large, dark werewolf who seemed to be waiting for the order to attack. She stifled the scream rising like bile in her throat.

"What are you doing here?" barked the soldier.

"I…I'm looking for help."

His thick brows tugged together, forming a perfect bisecting line between them. She noticed another scar now, a thin white line that cut across the outer edge of his left brow, creating a thread-thin territory where no hairs grew. His brows were deep brown. Was that what color his hair would be if he had any?

"Why would we help a thing like you?"

Bri gasped.

"That's right, sweetheart. I know what you are. Surprised?"

Her eyes rounded. "Yes. And you know about the vampires, too?"

He cocked his head as those blue eyes targeted her. Then he gave a slow nod. Maybe there was still a chance then.

"Then can you explain it to me?"

That answer made his head snap back. What had he expected her to say?

"You telling me you don't know?"

"Yes, I know. Bits and pieces. My nana knew they were after me. And a woman came last night to warn me about them." And suddenly one of the things Nana said to Bri suddenly made sense. *Stay single. Keep moving.* She understood now. Nana trying to protect her from the things that stalked her. But why hadn't Nana told her outright? Why hide the threat from her granddaughter? Nana hadn't answered any of her questions until the very end. Only when her grandmother knew she was dying had she revealed the terrible truth, and then there hadn't been enough time.

Keep your humanity, she had said. What did that even mean?

"How did you find us?"

"I can smell…" She turned to the one who waited to murder her, the scent of wet fur and wolf heavy in her nostrils. She could still scent the other, his scent closer, more earthy. She motioned with her head toward the black werewolf. "I can smell them. The werewolves. Scented them last winter and then when those things found me, I remembered what Nana said. So I came back here."

"What did she say?" he asked.

"That werewolves kill vampires."

That stopped him. He exchanged an inscrutable look with the beast and then locked back on her as if he were sighting her through a weapon.

"I hoped the werewolves might protect me from them."

He made a harsh sound in his throat that wasn't quite a laugh, for it lacked all humor. "Them? You must be crazy."

"I had no choice. They would have caught me otherwise."

The soldier leaned in, his nose nearly touching hers. "You had a choice, Princess. But you like to play the long odds. So your plan was to use the werewolves to protect you from the males that are on you like dogs after a bitch in heat?"

Her skin tingled and those gnats were back. This man frightened her again.

He moved in close, like a lover, but his expression stayed hard as iron. She could feel the warmth of his skin and the tang of his soap.

"And when the males were dead, who did you think would protect you from the werewolves?"

His shirt flapped open revealing deeper wounds

on his shoulder. He saw the direction of her stare and tugged the edges of his shirt closed, leaving a long bronze strip of flesh still visible.

"I hoped to find help."

He sneered.

She held his gaze, wondering why her powers weren't working on him. By now he should have been smiling at her. But he wasn't. He was the first man who didn't get that dazed look in his face when at close range. Why didn't they work? He seemed just as cynical and suspicious as when he first set eyes on her.

She tried a gentle suggestion. "Why don't you let me go?"

He curled his lip and actually snarled. That black wolf behind him knelt at his side.

"Don't worry, Johnny. She's got nothing."

The werewolf huffed and rested his hairy knuckles on the dirt before her.

She expected the man to defend her, but he didn't. Just watched her.

Then he thumbed to his left at the black wolf. "You want help from him? He'd as soon kill you as breathe the same air."

"You can call him off," she whispered. "Please."

"It doesn't work on me, sweetheart."

How did he know that, and why didn't it work on him? She needed to understand what was happening to her. This man could give her answers. She felt it.

"Then you could protect me," she whispered.

"Not me, darling." He spun her so she rested back against the hard wall of his chest. His breath brushed her ear, his whisper like a caress. "They send me to kill things like you."

He wrapped one arm about her waist. His other hand threaded through her thick hair, drawing her head to one side, exposing her neck. She lifted her gaze to see the black werewolf snarling, long glistening teeth deadly as daggers. A whimper escaped her lips as she recalled what it had done to the vampires. So it was all for nothing. They'd kill her anyway.

Her body shook and she wished she could pass out instead of facing her death wide-eyed and trembling. Instead she seemed immobilized by the shining yellow eyes of the werewolf.

Mac tried to ignore her perfect body pressed back against him like every man's dream. He had planned to render her unconscious so he could safely secure her without risk of her slipping through their fingers. Instead, he inhaled the sweet floral fragrance as his lips brushed the pure satin perfection of her skin. A tremor went through her.

The bellowing roar came from close by and then he realized it was him, fighting the change, the animal side beckoning, seductive as any mistress. Was that her power, working on his human half? His hands slid from her. Johnny roared and lunged. Mac saw a blur of light as his captive disappeared, then dark fur as his grenadier pursued her.

Mac sprang to his feet too late. Why had he let her go?

He could still see her, legs flashing like pistons as she leaped across the yard fast as a mustang before vanishing. A moment later she appeared on the top of the two-story concrete building.

Damn she was fast as a streak of light.

Not a woman, he reminded himself. Not human.

* * *

"Damn it!" Mac roared, knowing the escape was his own fault. Johnny had lunged only when his grip on this captive had slipped. Mac glanced up at the thing on his roof. He was tempted to get his rifle and start shooting. But that would be a waste of bullets. To capture her, he first had to catch her.

"How'd she get up there so damned fast?" he asked Johnny.

The corporal shrugged, and his silent accusation stabbed at Mac: *Why'd you let her go?*

"Did you see her move?"

Johnny never took his eyes off her as he gave one slow shake of his head.

"So how do we get her down?"

Lam gave him a baleful look and sighed. Then he drew his index finger over his own throat.

"No. We catch her and then we call the colonel."

Johnny growled.

"She used us to kill those bloodsuckers. Now she's got what she wants, she's going to fly out of here. Unless we can stop her."

His corporal lifted one brow, open to suggestions.

"I know. Maybe I should have killed her." Mac rubbed his neck, knowing that even with all his training he couldn't. "They don't affect us, right?"

Johnny gave him a long look as if he'd just shown some sign of madness.

"I know, I know. She's not some damned lost puppy. She kills guys. Guys like you and me, at least like we used to be. I get it, but..."

His silent partner stared him down.

"Damn it!" He glanced to the roof where she stood

staring at them, like an angel with the sunlight pouring down on her as if the light loved her best in all the world.

Reports said they could fly, so why hadn't she? Johnny huffed.

"They've never captured one. Never even seen one close up."

Johnny rocked from side to side in a restless gesture that told Mac he'd had enough.

"You can't kill her. That's an order. Got it?"

Johnny saluted, holding on and forcing Mac to return the damned thing. He thought they'd gotten past this, but the salute was Johnny's way of saying both *I'll do it* and *Fuck you*.

"I'm going up after her. You run a tight parameter. See if there are any more."

Johnny turned and took off at a fast run. Mac knew his gunner could sustain a thirty-miles-an-hour speed for a considerable distance.

Mac returned his attention to the adobe building, which had been used for so many training ops that the stucco was riddled with bullet holes and much of the roof had been blown away.

"Come down," called Mac.

She turned to face him.

"Is it gone?" she called, the her voice ringing with urgency bordering on hysteria.

Mac rubbed the back of his neck and wondered if he should just let Johnny climb up there and scare her back down. But chances were good she'd disappear on him, and he wasn't sure the crumbling roof would hold Johnny.

"That roof isn't stable. Come down before you fall."

She angled her head in a way that told him she wasn't a complete fool. It was an idle threat. He didn't think she could fall, because they could fly or something damned close to it. If she really was ignorant of her powers she might not know that. But then again she might be just playing him, and she had managed to get onto the roof before he could even stand up.

"He belongs to you, doesn't he?" she asked. "He's your hound."

They were more brothers than hounds. He hoped Johnny hadn't heard that. Chances were good that he had because his hearing was excellent.

"Come down or I'll send him up."

She looked about at the crumbling roof. "Not until you promise not to let him hurt me."

"We won't kill you."

"Promise?"

What was he, twelve? He made the appropriate gesture over his bare chest. "Cross my heart."

She regarded him in silence for a moment. Why didn't she just run? They'd never catch her, even in wolf form. But perhaps there were more vampires hunting her. That would be reason to stay.

She nodded her acceptance. "All right. I'll come down."

He waited and she didn't move.

"Well?"

"How do I get down?"

"The same damn way you got up there, except in reverse."

"I don't know how I got up here."

"You flew."

"That's ridiculous."

He pointed to the ground. "Down!"

"Well I'm not doing the reverse."

"Why the hell not?"

"I'm not scared enough."

Which made no sense at all. Mac laced both hands behind his neck and stared up at her. He'd been kissing her neck when Johnny had charged her. Only that had roused him from her spell.

Maybe Johnny was right about her. She was too soft, too lost and too alluring. Everything they'd been taught said that since the attack, he couldn't be tempted by her kind. So why the hell had his body gone into a near seizure of lust when she threw herself into his arms?

Just a potent cocktail of lust and loneliness, he decided. If the colonel found out he'd let her go, he and Johnny would both be back in the brig. Johnny wouldn't give him up. That much he knew. His comrade might be pissed at him. Might disagree with him. Might even want to kill the captive on the roof, but he was first and foremost his friend. They'd walked through hell together, and that made them closer than brothers.

"Probably because you've been out here in the woods too damned long," he muttered.

"Too long for what?"

Had she heard that from way up there? Even her voice appealed to him. And her body—ivory skin, coppery hair, ocean-green eyes. Just the sight of her punched him in the guts. She looked more like a sea nymph than an assassin. He recalled those wide innocent eyes staring up at him and his gut gave another twist. Damned dangerous—very.

"There's a ladder attached to the back of the building. Use that," he called.

She glanced behind her to where he knew the ladder must be, then returned her attention to him. "Call off your hound."

Mac searched the trees, looking for vampires, because he knew Johnny wouldn't disobey a direct order. "He's gone. Come down."

She disappeared. Mac rounded the building. When he reached the base of the ladder, she was halfway down, giving him a mouthwatering view of her ass as she felt her way from one rung to the next. Lord have mercy, he certainly admired the view. It wasn't until she was nearly at ground level that he took his eyes off her backside long enough to see that she was breathing fast and seemed to be having trouble holding on to the rungs. She moved one hand to the next on the same rung, shaking her free hand, as if the ladder itself were too hot or too cold to touch. There had been a dusting of snow last night and an icy slush clung to the shady spots in the yard. He reached out to touch the metal rung, finding it cool and dry.

"What's wrong?" he asked.

"Hot. Burning," she said and shook her hand in the air as if to cool it, then lost her grip with the other.

She was fifteen feet up when she fell. He watched her descent, expecting her to fly away or right herself like a cat, but instead she plummeted, rotating so she would land on her back. Mac raised his arms to catch her. She was small, but the momentum of her descent rocked him, nearly buckling his knees. Somehow he held on.

She gave him that wide-eyed look again. If it was an act, it was a damned good one. His body's reaction was instantaneous. Mac's skin tingled at the contact, and lower down his body went hard. He held her under the knees and behind her back. She felt just right against him. If he moved his hand a little he could feel the swell of her breast. Mac gritted his teeth and set her down.

Her kind needed sex. That was what made them so damned good at their jobs. The longer they went without sex, the more deadly they became. How long had it been for this one? Intelligence said that the vampires had kept some in isolation for years before releasing them on their targets. One night of bliss and then the payoff. A massive coronary, stroke or aneurysm. Simple, neat and undetectable.

Had she escaped them or was this a mission? Who was the target? Not him, certainly. Maybe the colonel. His commanding officer was working with werewolves. If they knew, that made Lewis a target.

"Thanks," she said.

"Anytime," Mac answered, reminding himself that the desire he felt was not caused by her magic. Couldn't be. He wasn't susceptible to her kind. But he was susceptible to this woman. Could military intelligence be wrong?

Mac held her high in his arms, becoming familiar with her weight and the long curve of her neck, the tempting hollow at its base and the riot of red curls that danced about her lovely face.

"Um, you better put me down."

Damn it, he could. Mac looked about for a place to lay her. He was immune to her killing gift, which meant he could enjoy her charms without paying the check.

Mac stilled as their eyes met. It was the very first time since this whole fuck-up that he'd forgotten about his friend, and that was not cool. Johnny came first. Mac's job was to keep him safe and as happy as a man could be who was trapped in the body of a monster.

Now the first female who wandered into Mac's sights made him forget all of it. She wasn't an ordinary female, but still…

He released her legs so fast she startled and pressed against him. He went hard as wood; his body was still on *seek and destroy* even as his mind bugled retreat.

She pushed off his chest with her forearms and tried to step back only to be stopped by his hand, which was still pressing to the center of her back. Mac captured a wrist to prevent a second escape.

He studied her face, concentrating now on those lovely lips, pursed as if for his kiss. The woman lifted her free hand and blew on it. A shiver danced over his skin at the sensual action.

"You need to step away from me. It's not safe for you."

She was worried about him? That was a laugh. But then he realized that she must think he was human because she didn't know he was the gray wolf by the road. He maintained his grip on her and damned if he'd let go.

"Really," she insisted. "You shouldn't touch me."

"I'll take my chances."

She flexed her hands and winced. He tore his attention from her face, glancing instead at the palms of her captured hand. A cold icicle of horror slipped between his shoulder blades. Red-and-pink blisters covered the pads on her hands from fingertip to heel. Some had burst and now wept clear fluid.

He clasped her other wrist and held her hand for closer inspection. "Is that from the ladder?"

"It's a burn. I'm allergic to some metals." She motioned with her head toward the ladder. "That kind, apparently."

Iron, he remembered. It was part of the folklore they had studied. But they'd been told her kind avoided only silver and that it didn't kill them, just pissed them off. It was a way to catch one, a silver pike pinning them to the earth. So that one was true, only iron worked better. Why?

He thought of the steel blade of his knife. That had iron in it, didn't it?

"I've got a med kit inside." Mac held her wrist. "You got a name, Princess?"

"Yes, it's Brianna Vittori. Bri."

His eyes narrowed. "Vittori?"

He glanced again at her milky-white skin, now taking on a luminescence in the sunlight, and that riotous red hair. She looked about as Italian as a leprechaun.

"Northern Italian on my father's side. My mother…" She trailed off.

Yes, they both knew about her mother. A seductress, just like Brianna Vittori.

"Staff Sgt. Travis Toren MacConnelly. Mac," he replied restraining himself from coming to attention though part of him already was.

"Irish?" she asked.

"American," he corrected.

"I meant the derivative of your name."

"I know what you meant."

"Sergeant? So you're an army officer?" she asked.

He winced. *"Marines.* Leatherneck, jarhead, devil dog. You're in our training center."

There were those wide eyes again. "Yes, *Marine* Mountain Training Center. I saw it early this morning."

"This way, Miss Vittori." All business now. If she affected him this way dressed in a modest T-shirt and full-length jeans, what would he do if she stripped out of those wet clothes? His pulse jumped as his heart began a useless pounding. He felt himself engorge. But he wasn't going to need that blood, thank you very much. He clearly wasn't immune to her sex appeal. He hadn't been with a woman since before he shipped out. Now that dry spell was coming back to bite him in the ass. Her fragrance drove him crazy. He exhaled and it was still there.

Wanted. Needed. Couldn't have, he reminded himself.

He'd get her inside. Call the colonel and get rid of her.

The black werewolf came back and Travis Toren MacConnelly sent it to clear the bodies of the vampires from the highway. The black, hulking monster trotted away with hardly a sound. MacConnelly escorted Brianna around the outside of the strange building in a grip that was more custodial than polite. She was beginning to recognize her desperate plan had some serious flaws, because though she had escaped the vampires, she was now detained by werewolves *and* Marines.

Bad plan, she thought. *Really, really bad.*

He'd said he wouldn't kill her. But neither would the vampires. It seemed she had only traded one captor for another.

The high wall around the series of buildings made it impossible for her to see more than the top of the two-story structure she'd found herself standing on. The hated iron ladder stretched up to the top. From up there she'd seen the perimeter wall and an open courtyard surrounded by one-story mud-and-brick structures that fit against the wall like the pueblos she'd seen in New

Mexico. But from outside the eight-foot walls were just exposed cinder block. It didn't fit.

MacConnelly kept hold of her as she pondered how she had gotten up on that roof and why the roof seemed as if it had been the target of a mortar attack. The only solid spot was the one she had found herself on. The rest resembled Swiss cheese. She had stared right down past the collapsed timbers into the floor below.

Bri's ears prickled. She still had that feeling she was being watched.

The Marine glanced at her hands. "How long until it heals?"

So he knew about that, too, she realized. One of her earliest memories was of scraping the skin off her knee and then running to Nana, only to find the wound healed and the redness fading when she reached her. Even her broken wrist had repaired itself within minutes. She'd never been to an emergency room except with Jeffery. Her chin dropped as she thought of him, waking alone in the hospital and wondering where she was. He'd never find her. Never know the danger that pursued her and threatened him, and all because he loved the wrong woman.

He paused to check her palms. The raw skin now looked a healthy pink and the blisters no longer wept.

"You don't spend much time in hospitals, I'd imagine."

She drew back her hand, but he held on, tenacious as a terrier. "And you'd be wrong about that."

They faced off. He ground his teeth. She held his gaze and his eyes narrowed, the threat clear. She bet that was the look he gave his men. It probably sent them scrambling to follow his orders, but she only lowered her chin preparing to fight.

"You're in a restricted area. I'm placing you under arrest."

"Is there anyone else here?" she asked, ignoring that he'd just arrested her.

Mac blew out an angry blast of air. Was she so cavalier because she assumed that she could escape or charm him into doing any blasted thing she wanted? A few things came immediately to mind, and he knew he wouldn't object to her using him as her energy dumping ground for a start. He could take it. Wanted to take all she had to give.

"No one but the werewolf watching the perimeter," he said—his hound, as she'd called him. She was afraid of Johnny and that might be all that kept her here. "Why?"

"Can you speak to the werewolves for me? Tell them I'm seeking protection?"

"Why not ask for *my* protection?"

"Because you're a soldier, MacConnelly, and soldiers follow orders and kill people. I need protection from vampires. Only a werewolf can do that."

"Those things"? She had a lot of nerve.

"It's Sergeant MacConnelly, MacConnelly or Mac. I'm not a police officer."

Bri lifted her gaze to meet his. He was big and broad and tall. She could escape if he'd just let her go. She must have telegraphed her thoughts because he captured her other wrist, dragging her against him.

She made a bad showing at trying to regain custody of her wrist.

"Let me go," she insisted.

He shook his head. "The deal was not to kill you."

Then he turned and continued the way he had come, dragging her along beside him. She dug in her heels, lost her footing and stumbled, but he still kept going. *The hell with this,* she thought and sat down.

He stopped and glared but she held her position.

"You can't detain me. I'm a U.S. citizen."

She didn't like his smile. It held no humor and way too much anticipation. "At the very least you are a trespasser. Federal offense. Now get up."

She didn't.

He stooped, using her captured hand to yank her to her feet. A moment later she was slung over his shoulder. He carried her along the wall just as the gray wolf had done.

"I'll scream."

He laughed. The world jolted as blood rushed to her head. He walked her around two corners and through an open archway to the inner courtyard she had glimpsed from above. The ground was packed earth with not a blade of grass anywhere. Along one wall she spied a huge pile of hay or straw that might have been used to bed livestock, except there was no fencing. He crossed the yard and deposited her on her feet, keeping hold of her wrist. They stood under an overhang. Three doorways lined the porch, each hung with a different color blanket suspended across the opening with a rope.

"It looks like a qala," she said. She'd seen photos in a magazine and read about the multigenerational structures created from this same reddish brick. Beside the doorway with the blue blanket lay a bullet-riddled motor scooter. She felt as if she'd stepped out of the state of California and into Afghanistan. "What is this place?"

He tugged her through the entranceway. She blinked at the sudden darkness. Sunlight filtered through the blue blanket and splashed across the dirt floor. A moment later he released her. She stumbled and fell back to the packed earth.

"I assume you can't walk through walls?"

"Of course not."

"Great," he said and closed the door, leaving her in darkness save for the bright beam of light that shone beneath the door. She reached the opening in time to hear the lock click. She shook the handle and felt the burn of metal again before drawing back.

Chapter 3

Mac headed into his quarters and spent the next hour with a power drill, hacksaw and wooden planking. When he finished his work, he felt like he'd already done a day's work. He studied the results of his labors, satisfied that the barricaded window would hold her temporarily. He paused on the way through their kitchen to grab a cold bottle of water from the refrigerator, then he approached the door behind which Brianna Vittori waited. He paused, listening to her breathing—fast, because she knew he was there.

"Step to the opposite side of the room."

He heard her shuffling away. As fast as he could, he stepped inside and closed the door behind him. The closet was large, six feet by five, but he could still feel the heat of her skin. It took only a moment for his eyes to adjust to the darkness, and when he did it was to find her gaze on him.

Could she see in the dark?

He tossed the water bottle toward her middle. She lifted her hands and caught it easily, answering his question.

"Thank you," she said and released the cap before lifting the opening to her mouth.

His night vision was near perfect if only in black and white. He wondered if she could see colors as he watched her raise her chin and swallow again and again until she had drained the contents. Why did watching her drink make his mouth go dry?

When she drained the contents, she stared at him, eyes glowing slightly in the dark. "What happens now?"

"I'm moving you to my bedroom."

Her eyes went wide and he heard the sharp intake of breath. Only then did he recognize what she must be thinking. He couldn't keep the smile from twitching at his mouth. Not that he wouldn't like to, but…

"There you'll have a bathroom, shower and a bed. I'll bunk with Johnny for now."

"For how long?"

"Not sure. Right now I need to take care of the ones we killed."

Her eyes went wide, the dark pupils impossibly large in her pale irises. "What will you do with them?"

"Turn them over to our superiors."

"But not me?"

"Not yet."

"Thank you."

"Don't. I'm not doing it for you. I'm not convinced you don't pose a threat to my CO."

"What's a CO?"

"Commanding Officer."

"But I would never…not intentionally." Her gaze swept his face. "You don't believe me?"

"There a reason I should?"

Brianna swept a hand through her thick hair as she considered her captor's question. "I can't think of one."

His head gave a funny shake as if her answer was not what he expected and then she remembered. In his eyes she was a temptress, a dangerous seductress artfully using her wiles on him. But the only wiles she knew about were her power of suggestion, which did not seem to work on this Marine. Why was that? She decided to try it again. She stepped silently toward him. His eyes narrowed and went cold, as if this were what he expected. But how could he even see her in here?

"You can see in the dark, too?" she said.

In answer he made a grab for her, and she was too slow to escape. He easily caught her wrist and pulled her out into the light, blinding at first, after the cool dark of the closet.

"Come on. Let's get you to your new quarters."

She followed him at a trot to keep up watching the muscles of his shoulders bunch as he moved.

He led her down a short hall, past a kitchen that seemed strangely out of place in this believable recreation of an Afghanistan qala. Before she could ask, they had crossed a threshold and then another hallway. He paused at the third door. She stepped inside and he followed, shutting them in. He regarded Brianna as her gaze swept the interior.

The one window was covered with rough-cut boards haphazardly screwed to the wall. A full-sized bed frame dominated the adjacent wall, and the bed covers were neatly made in military fashion. There was nothing else beyond a floor lamp, an empty molded plastic chair and a closed footlocker. Draped across the bed was a muddy, wet shirt. His, she wondered, noting his bare chest. There was nothing on the walls and only a small Persian rug to cover the cold concrete.

Her gaze flicked back to the bed and then to her captor.

The Marine stood, hands on hips. Bri's skin tingled and her stomach twisted with uncertainty. He did not look like someone who cared for lost, frightened women. Instead he reminded her of every recruiting poster of a soldier she'd ever seen—rock-hard jaw and implements of killing worn as casually as a woman might wear a bangle bracelet. She suspected he wore those camouflage fatigues to make it easier to sneak up on and murder his enemies. Now *she* was his enemy. What had she gotten herself into?

Her skin flashed hot and cold as she tried vainly to disappear.

She glanced at the scars that slashed across his chest, suddenly seeing a definite pattern. This wound was not random like one made from bits of flying shrapnel. The puckered marks looked like teeth imprints. As if a bear had clamped down on his shoulder as it clawed at his torso.

"What now?"

"Still deciding." He pointed to the bed. "Sit down."

She did, rubbing her palms reflexively back and forth as she waited for what was to come.

He leaned back against the door and folded his muscular arms across his wide chest. She stared up at him, his posture now all menace and might. His eyes were cold as blue glass. A chill danced up her spine.

"How did you get away from them? And don't bullshit me."

"A woman warned me. She showed up out of the

blue and told me that I was like her. The same thing the woman that came to my school my senior year said. Two different women. They looked so different in every way, completely, but there was also something akin about them, other than their stunning physical beauty. When I told Nana about her, she moved us again. And she made me promise not to tell anyone. We were always moving. She died one month ago, but before she went she told me what I am." Bri tried to remember what the woman had said, but it blurred together with her nana's warning to keep moving. But she hadn't. She'd stayed because Jeffery had asked her to stay.

"Who was the woman?" he asked.

"She said she was like me. But she'd been captured by those things."

"By the Chasers. They're the ones who track females like you."

"Yes, maybe. She said they caught her and trained her. She said years. The vampires had held her for years and would kill her if they found out she had warned me. She told me to run and I did. I ran home. But they found me there."

She'd left the strange woman at the hospital—or rather, the woman had left her. Something about her beauty and her earnest tone had terrified Brianna through and through. Her warning delivered, she had said they were coming then vanished right before Bri's eyes.

Of course Brianna had bolted. She'd hurried to the parking garage and run a red light getting home. Only home wasn't safe, either.

Brianna trembled as she told him of her return to the empty apartment. "Someone broke in."

She recalled the sound of a shatterring glass window coming from the empty bedroom across the hallway from hers. If they had entered her room instead, would she have had time to escape? She didn't think so, and the realization of how nearly she came to capture chilled her skin.

Her heart had jumped to piston-firing speed at the crunch of someone walking on a carpet of broken glass across the hall from her bedroom. She'd snatched up her shoes and thrust down until her heels slipped into place. She'd headed for the window as the thing turned the knob of her bedroom door.

"It trapped me in my bedroom," she said to Mac, as she flinched at the memory of the thing hitting her bedroom door.

Bri remembered it crashing into the room. "It had glowing red eyes and a face so pale it was bluish, like skimmed milk. It opened its mouth. It had a scarlet tongue, and fangs like a lion. So I jumped. It was three floors up, but still I..."

She didn't really see the Marine anymore. Her mind had turned inward, seeing that thing charge her and feeling the air rush past as she jumped from the second-story window, screaming, into the night.

"I fell, but I didn't really. I just bounced like I was on a spring. It followed me. I saw it on the apartment roof."

Bri had jumped again, out over the parking lot, down Bell Street, past the Jack-in-the-Box and over the cars that waited at the drive-through.

"I lost him. Then I thought if I kept jumping he might see me over the buildings, so I just ran. I never ran so fast before. Didn't know I could." It wasn't her normal jogging speed. She had been as fleet as Mercury in his golden sandals, and her breathing came swift and easy as an Olympic runner. "I passed a young couple on the sidewalk, but they seemed to be standing still. Neither one even turned a head in my direction." How was any of that even possible?

"And I wasn't tired. I passed a car rental place. I got a compact car. Then I remembered what that woman had said, the one at the high school, about vampires staying clear of werewolves. At the time, I thought she was absolutely crazy. But she said they killed vampires and that I'd know if I was near one. I'd smell it. That it would raise the hairs on my neck, and then I did smell it. Before Nana died, just a few months ago when I was driving near here. I thought if I could find a werewolf before those things found me, it might kill them."

The Marine made a sound that brought her back to the here and now. He had only one arm crossed over his chest as the other cradled his opposite elbow. When had he drawn his shirt back on?

"Did it occur to you that a werewolf might kill you on sight?"

She answered with a question of her own. "Do you know what the vampires would have done to me?"

He couldn't hold her gaze. Oh, he knew all right.

"I'd rather be dead."

MacConnelly's expression changed as if he saw it coming before she did. He took a step in her direction as the tears started, rolling down her face as her breath caught and the hoarse cries came from her burning throat.

"I'd rather die than let them touch me, use me," she whispered in that little voice she hadn't heard since she was a girl standing beside her grandmother's bed begging to sleep with her after a nightmare. Her nana never let her. She'd walk her back to her own room and sit with her until she slept telling her the stories of the little folk, the Selies and the Fairy Court.

All real, according to Nana's deathbed confession. The rambling of a confused mind, the doctors had said, and she had tried so hard to believe them. But they were wrong and Nana had been right.

The sergeant moved to the bed and sat beside her. The mattress sagged. He was big and intimidating and he scared her half to death, but he didn't touch her. The only thing scarier was those things in the woods. No, the thing in the apartment. Bri trembled. Her world had suddenly become populated by walking nightmares, and Sgt. Mac MacConnelly was just one more threat.

"I'm sorry," he whispered.

Her uncertainty grew, swarming in her stomach like a hive of bees.

She didn't prevent him from dragging her to his side, and she found she didn't want to. But she had to. If her nana was right than he must not touch her.

"Don't," she whispered, even though his arms felt so good around her. If she closed her eyes she might believe he could protect her from what chased her. But he couldn't. Only a werewolf could do that. A man, a human man, was just going to die because of her, and that would be her fault, too.

He'd been trained to fight, to mindlessly take orders, to kill innocent men and women. So why were his hands so gentle, his touch so kind?

Her shoulders shook as he held her against his chest, cradling her body to his larger one. She wanted to tell him to move back. That it wasn't safe to hold her, but the tears choked off her words.

He made a hushing sound as he stroked her head, letting his fingers tangle in her curls. The rhythmic caress and soft rumble of his voice made her tears slow, her trembling body still.

"It's all right, now. You're safe now." His voice sounded sincere. "I'll keep you safe."

Exhaustion crept through her now and settled into her joints. She ached to let him take control, and he did. His hand swept up and down her back and his strong arms enfolded her in warmth. It was almost enough for her to ignore the prickling at her neck. But it was there, the warning she'd been told to watch for and had felt last winter. The one that told her a werewolf was near.

How close?

Mac left Brianna's room sure of only one thing. He sucked at interrogation. He had turned to a big puddle of mush the minute she'd turned on the waterworks. When he held her, she had tried to warn him away. Didn't that show she didn't mean to harm him? Or did she know he was a wolf and it was all just a game? Either way he was way, way out of his league. The smart move would be to turn her over before she made him a fool.

His main objective was to get Johnny back to human form and, failing that, get them back in action before either or both of them went crazy.

Where was Johnny now? Had he finished the perimeter sweep?

Mac recognized with increasing chagrin that Brianna Vittori was very good at making people feel responsible for her, even if they were complete strangers.

He'd left the door to the head open and locked the others. If she worked fast and hard, she might pry those boards off. Depended on how strong she really was.

He should go help Johnny and he needed to move the vampire corpses, but he needed a few minutes to think, and he thought best when firing his weapon. So he headed for the narrow trench cut deep into the earth. His private firing range with an upturned stump at one end, to hold extra clips, and a target pinned to the earth at the other.

For the second time in his life, his world had tipped badly out of kilter. Decisions needed to be made, and soon. What if he made another mistake? Mac felt the panic grip his esophagus like a closing fist. The fear quickened his step. Mac walked right past the mobile phone that he should have used to call HQ and instead scooped up his ear protectors, then headed out the door. He didn't stop until he was in the pit, gun in hand. There he flipped the safety off his personal weapon, a new .45, and aimed at the square paper target mounted on the dead tree.

Should he call the colonel? His stomach tightened and he knew he wasn't ready for that. Not yet. But he no longer trusted his instincts. How could he after what had happened in the Sandbox?

He sighted his weapon and then he spotted something moving, low to the ground. *Bloodsucker,* he thought, and swung his weapon at the approaching threat. A moment later the thing dropped into his pit. Mac held fire, tipping his weapon up in a two-handed grip.

A cold finger of fear dragged down his back as he realized what he'd almost done. He tugged the ear protectors down so that they circled his neck.

"Johnny. What the fuck?" The fear now hardened into anger. "I thought you were a vampire!"

The werewolf roared and Mac flipped on the safety and holstered his weapon.

"You can't run around here on your OFP!" Perhaps a shot fired from his .45 couldn't kill Johnny, but that didn't change the fact that Lam had intentionally stepped into firing range. He recalled what they'd told him at the facility, that Johnny was becoming irrational?

Lam dropped back to all fours and growled.

"It's not funny. I could have shot you! I don't need that on my conscience."

This was met with silence.

"Did you scent anything?"

Johnny shook his head.

"Good."

The werewolf held his ground and Mac holstered his weapon.

"We need to clear the road of bodies before some damn civilians see those things."

A rumble sounded in Johnny's throat, not a growl, more an acknowledgment.

"Let me take a few shots. Then we'll go."

Johnny moved behind him.

"Johnny, I don't know what to do with the girl."

Lam cocked his head, a clear question in his expression.

"If she really needs protection, I know the colonel and the medical facility would be the best place. But they're human and, well, she could hurt them, influence them. Plus, what if she's not here for protection? What if she's here on a mission? Maybe to kill the colonel? It'd be easy. Do you think that's why she didn't fly away?"

His only answer was a shrug.

"So do we keep her out of sight for a while or turn her over?"

Johnny offered a third option, made a slicing motion across his throat. Mac felt his body tense as if preparing to defend her even from his closest friend. What was happening to him?

"Twenty-four hours," Mac said.

Johnny hesitated and then gave a slow nod. It hurt Mac every time he looked at Johnny. but he held his gaze as the guilt gurgled inside his belly like poison. It wasn't fair. Johnny was a good kid and a hell of a good Marine, or he had been. Why couldn't he change back?

Johnny had told him in sign and by scratching in the dirt that he remembered the attack. He only recalled Mac shoving him aside that night and then waking in the helo.

That much was a blessing because his own attack still filled Mac's nightmares.

"Prisoner's secure. Just let me clear my head."

Johnny sat behind the firing line.

"Probably give us a medal for catching her."

Mac realized as he said it that Johnny couldn't pin a medal on his dress blues, because since returning from Afghanistan, under heavy guard, Johnny had been just as he was today.

They'd seen action together, too much of it. His first command ended in disaster. Three fire teams gone and only two survivors—himself and Johnny. He glanced back at Lam, wondering if either of them had really survived.

Mac would have given his life to go back to that day. But he couldn't. All he could do now was look after

Johnny. And he would do that, by God, even if that meant protecting Johnny from himself.

Mac squeezed off one round after another, feeling the satisfying recoil of his pistol as the spent rounds bounced to the ground at his feet. He emptied his clip, breathing in the comforting smell of gunpowder as his wrist began the familiar aching. One clip, a second and then a third. Finally he reholstered his pistol, the warmth of the barrel immediately heating his outer thigh.

Mac turned to Johnny. "What will they do to her, do you think?" Mac asked.

Johnny lifted his eyebrows, which were two black tufts of fur with long antennalike hairs protruding from the centers.

"It's just…I don't know what to do." He looked at his gunner. "Do you really think we should kill her?"

Johnny looked away, gave a long sigh then a slow, unmistakable shake of his head.

Mac breathed away some of the tension that had collected in his diaphragm. "Should we tell the colonel or wait?"

He felt the ache settling around his heart, and he knew the answer to his own question. He didn't want to turn her in. But he had to lay it out for Johnny. "Because if we do, they might see what we can do and might give us our first assignment since…you know. Maybe back in the Sandbox. Finally get to see those motherfuckers firsthand instead of on crappy video taken through NVGs." He was referring to the werewolf that got them both, made them the monsters they now were.

Thinking of the video, shot through the night-vision goggles, made Mac queasy. The first thing Colonel Lewis had showed him was the footage of the attack recovered from the camera mounts when the first two Fire Teams went in. Both the grenadier and the rifleman wore one. HQ had six videos. Mac had seen four. Lewis had reserved the ones where Johnny and Mac were attacked, and Mac had not asked to see them.

Mac had watched their routine assignment to clear a route through a crappy little village that was so small it had been IDed only by coordinates. He saw what his teams had seen as they entered that building. Watching the footage from the first team had been hard. Watching the second, even harder. But it was just the beginning. The footage contained the only moving images of werewolves. The Afghanis called them the Devil Dogs, which Mac found ironic, since that was what Marines often called themselves.

But he and Johnny wouldn't be facing the Devil Dogs. They would be facing the werewolves' natural enemies—vampires. Up until today Mac had only seen an image of one, the first footage ever recorded. Today he and Johnny proved they could kill them.

He recalled the image he'd viewed, taken with a high-speed camera, on burst setting at the fastest shutter speed. Even so it had captured only two images, and they were blurry. The guys at MI—military intelligence—said they were moving faster than a human's ability to see them. They also said that the Taliban was using werewolves to fight U.S. troops and to protect against vampire attacks.

Vampires, they'd been told, were mercenaries, selling their allegiance to the highest bidder. Israel had at least one, and the colonel wanted a vampire of his own. He said that the U.S. needed soldiers who could keep their leaders safe, even from vampire assassins. But really, he also wanted the assassins.

Had he and Johnny been lucky today? Vampires could kill werewolves. Their fangs punctured anything, even a werewolf's hide, with the ease of a can opener puncturing a can of beans. And the poison in their fangs was deadly to any living thing, including werewolves.

Mac knew firsthand that werewolves were tough to kill, since his Fire Teams had pumped thousands of rounds into the one they faced and nothing stopped it. Mac didn't know if their skin was like Kevlar or if they just healed superfast. No one knew. But they were going to find out because Johnny's next training regime included getting shot with an M-16.

Mac's skin crawled at the thought and he met Johnny's yellow eyes, so different from the rich cocoa color they had once been. Was this why he stepped in front of Mac's practice today? Had he been trying to get a head start?

Johnny stood on his hind legs as he raised his nose and scented the air. Mac smelled the air, too, but did not find any threat.

His friend pointed to the east.

"Yeah. Let's go move those bodies." Mac removed his holster and laid it on the stump, then stripped.

Once naked, Mac summoned the change, gritting his teeth against the ripping agony that flooded his nerve endings with the upheaval within. He had become faster at changing now, and so he didn't end up on the ground panting with dry heaves.

Once in wolf form, he and Johnny bounded over the uneven ground toward the bodies.

Once at the scene they retrieved the two corpses,

hastily stowed in the woods. The snow had ceased and melted, and everything was wet and cold. He could not see tire tracks on the road, so he didn't know if the accident had been seen or reported. He only knew no one had come yet.

Mac circled his hand above his head, making the signal that all Marines recognized meant helicopter. The old training pad was close and there was an associated storage shed where they could keep the bodies hidden in the short term. Johnny nodded, scooping up the closest corpse.

Twenty minutes later the two flesh eaters were packed away like the sack of blood they had always been. The cold would keep them until they could be retrieved by his superior.

They returned to their quarters together and Mac endured the change, still covered in a cold sweat as he drew on his trousers.

"You want to stay here and watch her or come in with me?"

Johnny pointed to the woods.

"Perimeter sweep again?"

He nodded and took off, leaving Mac to do the explaining. Johnny avoided the colonel whenever possible.

Mac cast one look at the makeshift home and then set off on foot to find the colonel. He wished to hell he was a better liar.

He arrived at the back door to the medical facility, the one custom-made to study and treat werewolves, so new the place still smelled of fresh paint and carpet glue. Once inside he headed to the locker room, where there was always a fresh supply of clothing to cover naked werewolves after they transformed.

A few minutes later he stood outside the colonel's office. The colonel never kept him waiting for long. He swept in with a quick stride.

The colonel still wore a jacket against the morning chill, and beads of rain showed on the shiny rim of his cap.

Mac snapped to attention and the colonel saluted without even slowing down. The eagle marking his rank shone on his sleeve as he removed his jacket, which was instantly swept away by his officious aide. From beneath the rim of his cap, Colonel Lewis's narrow blue eyes peered at Mac. His ruddy, narrow face showed his age, even if his body, still fit and trim, did not.

"MacConnelly, what's going on. They said it was urgent." He'd reached his door, opened it with a push and motioned Mac inside.

Mac stood before the desk and gave a brief version of events that did not include Brianna Vittori. An instant later Colonel Lewis was pushing intercom buttons and barking orders. Mac spent the next two hours re-telling his tale, escorting the colonel to the bodies and then to the scene of the attack. Johnny's absence was noted and the colonel was pissed about it, even when Mac assured him that Johnny was checking the area for more of the bloodsuckers. Johnny had strayed off the compound a few too many times to be ignored. Where the hell was he now?

Mac waited while the techs swarmed over the wrecked rent-a-car. That crappy compact would connect Brianna to the scene. He'd just have to say it was empty when he arrived—which it was, because they were already dragging her off. She'd be reported missing and they might just assume she was a snack for the two dead bloodsuckers. All he knew was that he had to get back to her, perhaps move her to safer quarters, because he could just bet that the colonel or one of his aides would be stopping by unannounced.

Damn, he'd have to patch and cover the screw holes, take down those boards. Now Brianna faced two threats: the colonel and the bloodsuckers. Was he willing to risk everything for her? He couldn't, he knew. He'd have to turn her in or let her go.

Chapter 4

At midafternoon, when Mac was finally dismissed and he returned to the compound, it was to find two new security cameras mounted on trees and pointing at his quarters. Damn, they had so many surveillance cameras every-frickin'-where that sometimes he felt like one of the prisoners.

He'd need to disable them both before he took Bri out. What was he doing, sticking his neck out for her? And then he recalled the smell of her neck and the soft feel of her skin. Lovesick or lonely, it amounted to the same thing. As long as protecting her didn't jeopardize Johnny, he was going forward.

He found Johnny's scent trail but opted to check on Bri first. He crossed the open ground and felt the mud sucking and tugging at his boots before he ducked inside. No need to wipe his feet, as this first room had once been part of a barn, staged for practice operations to resemble a facility to hold livestock. The back third had been walled off and given a concrete floor, converting the former barn into housing for werewolves. He stepped up onto the cold cement into the room that was a combination kitchen and living quarters with satellite TV, couch, recliner and a large futon propped against the wall for Johnny. Dirty, tattered rugs lay scattered over the concrete slab like dry leaves. Nothing but the best in military housing, he thought.

The kitchen, functional and industrial, was centered about the large freezer that held Johnny's food and his. Outside the single high window, the generator hummed, keeping the power on and the meat cold.

Mac continued through one of the stalls, pausing at the newly constructed door and the concrete addition added just for them. Unless she'd managed to get out, Brianna waited there now.

The colonel thought Johnny was scouting for more vampires and that Mac had gone to find him. Just standing here was a violation of a direct order. Or maybe not. He *had* found one, after all.

Opening the door, he surveyed the room. It looked much like a barracks with a large footlocker butted up against his bed. This queen-sized bed had been a gift from the colonel. Since space was not an issue and Mac was a big man, Lewis decided that his sergeant should have a real bed. At first he'd been pleased, but lately the larger mattress only reminded him how empty that bed felt.

He opened the door and slipped silently into her room to find her curled on her side in a ball, knees drawn up to her chest, her breathing soft and relaxed in slumber. She was as beautiful as a fairy princess, he decided, recognizing that his snide nickname was actually accurate. For princess she was.

He moved closer, drawn by her unearthly beauty and the air of innocence. He's seen so much, been through so much, so to meet someone totally separate from all the horror, well, he could not resist stepping closer.

God, the smell of her. It was like a feast to a starving man. He hadn't had a woman since before he'd gone to the Sandbox. His body now reminded him of that with force. The ache settled into a solid pounding south of his belt. He'd joined the Corps, but he wasn't turning over a woman to his CO, no matter what kind of woman she was. He knew the treatment that he and Johnny had received. It wasn't always kind, but they'd volunteered. They knew what to expect, at least up until the accident. Since then things had grown more and more troublesome.

He needed to get her out of here before they found her.

Mac thought of the colonel saying that the Corps had never captured a vampire. The colonel had been pleased to have the corpses, but if Mac and Johnny could catch one alive, then they could study it. If there was a next time, the colonel had asked, could Mac try to restrain himself and bring in one still breathing? Mac thought if he and Johnny could catch one and turn it over to Lewis, they'd be heroes and still keep Bri safe, keep her out of it.

Mac pressed a knee to the bed and then stretched out beside her, carefully sliding his stomach to her back. He draped an arm over her arm and tucked her close. Bri sighed and shifted but did not wake, a testament to how exhausted she really was. He pulled Bri deeper into the hollow of his chest and arms as the need to protect her bloomed inside him like spring flowers from a dying tree. Was he keeping her safe, or keeping her only for himself?

Mac didn't know, but now he wondered what she would say and do when he told her the truth, that he was like Johnny, only unlike him—he could change back.

Immune to her kind, they'd said, but he didn't feel immune, not to her beauty or her scent or her warm, soft body. Oh, no, not immune. Instead, he felt as if she'd taken *him* prisoner.

He knew what the colonel would do to her. They'd all been through mock interrogations. She'd never make it.

He breathed in the sweet, alluring fragrance of spices and orchids and the tang of the sea.

Time to find Johnny. With a sigh, he eased away from her. She made a small sound in her throat, as if she was unhappy to see him go. If only that were true.

He crept toward the exit, afraid of what he might do if he looked back. Her sweet floral scent called to him. But he kept moving, fleeing.

He needed to be careful. If he got locked up, they'd put Johnny back in a cage.

Mac eased out of the room and shut the door, leaving it unlocked. Time to face facts. He wasn't prepared to keep her prisoner or turn her over. Johnny had wanted to kill her. He wanted to keep her. But the safest thing for Johnny was to let her go.

Mac paused outside her door. He felt a hitch in his throat.

"Bye, Bri."

Mac headed out in his human form. He wasn't as fast, but he was still as strong and had the endurance of the wolf. Plus he was carrying his pistol and phone so he could talk to Johnny once he found him. And when he found him, he'd assure him that he still had his back, would always have his back.

Johnny's scent reached him the instant he stepped into the courtyard. Lam was close and Mac had to run only a mile before coming on his friend. Johnny's wolf-ish head turned in his direction at Mac's approach, but he kept his back turned.

"The colonel thinks we are out looking for more vampires."

Johnny drew a suffering breath and blew it out his long snout, glancing over his shoulder at Mac.

"She says a male attacked her in Sacramento and she ran. They caught her here. She also says she can't fly, just kind of run superfast."

Johnny turned his head toward Mac, but still his ears drooped and his eyes stared vacantly at the ground.

"They have the bodies. But I didn't tell them about her."

Johnny met his gaze now, alert, waiting.

"I couldn't kill her, Johnny, and I couldn't turn her in. I'm sorry. I just couldn't."

Johnny lifted two claws before his snout and held them up like fangs.

"I know. I know she's a bloodsucker, but she's also a woman who asked for our protection, for Christ's sake. And isn't that what we do?"

It was a long time coming, but his friend finally gave one slow nod.

"Johnny, I left her door unlocked."

His gaze snapped to Mac's and his expression showed a flash of confusion. He lifted his hands in a silent question...*why?*

"I don't know. Maybe I just wanted to show her that we aren't dumb animals."

Johnny blew out a breath and gave a sad shake of his head.

"I know she'd likely kill us both if she could."

He agreed with another slow nod. Then he made a circle with his index finger.

"I don't want to catch her. I want her to go. We served our purpose. We killed her pursuers. If that's what she wanted from us then she'll disappear and good riddance. She's not our problem, is she? The colonel won't know, and we can go back to the way things were." Mac's smile faded as he held Johnny's gaze a long, silent moment. Back to living like animals in the woods and getting used as target practice as the REMF—rear-echelon motherfuckers—figured out what to do with them.

Johnny stood and offered a hand to help Mac up. His way of trying to cheer Mac up, Mac supposed. But in his heart, the wasteland stretched out like a wide, empty sea. Likely she was already gone.

"You okay with this?" asked Mac.

Johnny stilled, looked back toward the compound and then raised a hand to his eye, making a circle of his fingers and looking at Mac through the hole.

"They set up two new surveillance cameras. I knocked them out so they won't see her leave. But they'll want some answers."

Johnny pantomimed a phone at his ear.

"Good idea." Mac drew out his mobile and reported that he'd noticed a camera down. After a moment he shoved the phone back in his pocket. "They'll have someone out tomorrow to fix it. That should give her time to clear out. You want to scout for any more visitors?" Mac wanted to go back. He wanted it so badly that he knew he couldn't do it. He had to run, hunt and stay away while she cleared out. It was the only way to protect Johnny and protect the girl.

Johnny nodded and rose.

Mac removed his holster and then stripped out of his clothing, laying them in a neat pile. Then he dropped to a crouch, lowering his head to concentrate first on his sense of smell. This unfortunately brought Vittori's scent trail to his expanding nostrils.

Rage was the easiest way to summon the change. Usually he thought of the Sandbox, of that night when the last Fire Team was torn to pieces in that slaughterhouse. But not today. Today he recalled the feel of her in his arms and thought of never holding her again. The helplessness and the fury easily triggered the transformation.

The dizzy rush of power ripped through him as his body transformed. His nails turned to claws, his teeth to fangs, and his skin now sprouted the silvery fur of a wolf.

He looked at Johnny, who waited. Johnny was a bigger werewolf. But Mac was meaner and still in charge. Then they were off, searching for the scent trail of a male vampire heading through their territory at a dead run. When they reached the road, it was to find her car gone. Likely picked up by a patrol. He imagined the techies going over it, finding Brianna Vittori's name on the rental agreement. Had she been stupid enough to keep that with the car? Not doing so would buy her a little time. But not much.

Security was tight at this base, at every base. But they spent most of their energy looking outward. With luck, they wouldn't look inside the grounds for the driver of that car until she was long gone. Johnny could detect what Brianna Vittori truly was and so could he, but to the others, she would appear to be only a beautiful, alluring woman. If she really could run as fast as she said, then she might just get out of here in one piece.

Mac turned to run the perimeter of their territory, the long fence line. He would be certain that there were no other vampires here before he returned to his empty room, and the empty bed and the empty days ahead.

* * *

Mac was pretty far out when he realized that Vittori might not escape, as he'd hoped, but instead she could head right for headquarters where she would find Lewis.

That realization turned him back toward home. Not wanting to frighten Bri any more than necessary, Mac suffered the transformation before he entered the clearing surrounding the qala. He arrived at dusk and hurried into their quarters, pausing only to grab a set of fatigues from the trunk beside the door. Then he headed into their quarters to find his room empty. His gaze flicked to the window, seeing it still barred, and then glanced to the closed bathroom door. He stepped into the room and heard a soft humming coming from the bathroom, low and lyrical and so sweet it made his chest ache. So she was still here. The relief he felt took him off guard.

Why hadn't she left?

The humming stopped. Silence stretched. He hadn't made a sound, so he was quite sure she had not heard him. But what if her hearing was as acute as his? She took a shuffling step, her bare feet whispering across the tile.

"Johnny?" she called, her voice low, cautious.

And then he understood. She could smell him, scent the wolf in him.

"It's Mac," he answered.

"Mac?" The question rang clearly in her voice. "Is Johnny there, too?"

Lie or truth? He took the middle ground. "Close by, I'd imagine." Actually, he didn't know where Lam was, because he'd left him to head back here.

"My clothes are out there," said Bri.

"Yes, I see them." Anticipation curled in his belly. He wanted to see her naked; suddenly he wanted that more than anything else in the world.

He stared at the pile of clothing lying on his empty bed, which he still made each morning with sharp creased corners, though there was no one to inspect it but him. Then he glanced to the orange plastic chair set against the cinder-block walls painted sterile white and windows that were still boarded up tight. Why had he never noticed how empty this room felt?

A bare hand stretched out of the crack in the door. "May I have them please?"

He imagined the possibilities behind that door as he glanced at the pile of grime-streaked garments and then back to his target. "They're all muddy."

Frustration rang in her voice. "Well, they're all I have."

That made him smile.

"I can give you a clean T-shirt."

He waited during the long pause.

"All right."

He opened his footlocker, selecting a white one from the stack of neatly folded T-shirts, and then passed it to her before she closed the door.

"My jeans?" she asked through the closed panel.

"Those you'll have to come and get."

He sat on the bed waiting. The door cracked open and she peeked out at him. He tried to look harmless as the wolf inside him roared to life. He stared at her pretty, flushed face as their eyes met and hers grew wide.

He couldn't keep the smile from curling his lips. "I left the door unlocked." He glanced to the door and back.

She dropped her gaze. "I know."

"I thought you'd be gone."

"Where? I can't go back home. They'll be waiting there for sure."

Brianna Vittori stepped from the steamy bathroom. His T-shirt hung to her midthigh and clung in all the right places. Mac thought that scrap of cotton had never looked so good.

"Did you want me to go?"

He had. But now he was reconsidering. "It would be wise. I lied for you. Told my commanding officer that there were only two intruders."

She stepped forward, crossing the room on slim bare feet, as silent as a summer breeze.

"You have to see that staying here isn't an option."

Brianna halted a few feet away. Was she afraid to move closer or was she afraid for him, if she moved closer?

"My pants?" she asked, extending her hand.

He grasped it and tugged. She tumbled into his lap like a living dream.

"What's wrong, Princess?"

She slid off his lap, her head now hanging low as if the weight on her shoulders was too much to bear.

"Why do you call me that?"

He shrugged. "You look like one, like a princess in a fairy tale. You know, Snow White and Rose Red?"

She stared for a moment to see if he was mocking her. He wouldn't be the first to find her red hair an easy target. But she saw no malice in his pale blue eyes.

"You know that story?"

He looked away. "I have parents. They read to me."

She tried for a smile but got none in return. Instead

his frown deepened. She broke eye contact and glance about the unfamiliar room.

"What time is it?" she whispered.

He glanced at his watch, a giant black scuba-style timepiece. "Eighteen hundred hours."

"What?" Briasked, not understanding. Military time, she realized. Twelve plus the other hours. Eighteen minus twelve. "What time?"

She didn't even know what day it was. She'd left the hospital on Saturday night and arrived here early Sunday morning, but then she'd slept. Was it still Sunday?

"Six in the evening," he said. "In civilian time."

"What day?"

"Sunday."

He walked to the window and tore the boards off as easily as one might draw back a curtain. Outside the daylight still clung to the barren courtyard, but the sun had set. Was Jeff eating his meal, alone in that hospital bed, wondering where she was, trying her phone and...

She scrambled in her jeans pocket and found her phone gone. Brianna drew her legs up before her and wrapped her arms about them, settling her forehead on the tops of her knees.

MacConnelly came back beside her. He sat with his feet solidly on the ground and his hands on his knees.

"You okay?"

She shook her head. "I lost my phone."

He said nothing to that.

"And I need to call someone, someone I had to leave behind."

"Jeffery Martin?"

"How did you know that?"

He reached in the pocket that sat low on his thigh

and drew out her pink mobile phone. "He's left a dozen messages. Handsome guy."

"Is he all right?"

"Sounded good."

She gave an exclamation of indignation as she reached for her property. He handed over her phone.

"You can't call him or turn it on. I disabled it."

Her jaw dropped open.

He shrugged, showing no regret. "At the very least, the police will use it to find your location. But if those vamps have any kind of surveillance, they are waiting for you to call in. Get a new one."

She tucked the phone into her front pocket, wondering why she couldn't turn it on when he obviously had. He'd likely been through every contact, listened to all her messages and voice mail, checked her browser history. Why didn't she ever set that damned password?

"Can I call him on your phone?"

"And tell him what, that you are escaping from vampires? No, Princess. No calls. For now you'll stay missing."

What would Jeffery make of her vanishing?

"Is he your boyfriend?" he asked.

She thought of the image of Jeff on her phone, smiling and healthy. Then she thought of him pale and weak in his hospital bed. When she spoke her words came out in a rush, disorganized and with a breathy quality that showed upset. "Boyfriend. Nana warned me just before she died, but the doctors said her ramblings were the result of the medication. That she was delusional. I didn't know what to believe. But when Jeffery got sick, I wondered…" She raked a hand through her thick, wet hair, combing out the tangles with her fingers. "Nana knew they were hunting me and she knew it was dangerous for anyone to touch me. I mean, I knew I was different, but what she said seemed so absurd…" Her voice got small. "Why didn't I believe her?" She lifted her gaze to meet his. Her eyes were huge and round now as she grappled with her demons. "Do you think they'll hurt Jeffery?"

"No. But they might use him to try to flush you out. I would."

She gave him a look of horror. "But he's sick. He's in a hospital."

"Even better."

She pressed a hand over her mouth as the horror of this struck her. Then she slid her hand away and whispered, "I left him without a word. She said they were upstairs waiting, so I ran."

"They'll find you if you go back."

"I know. But to just leave him. It's heartless."

"Not as heartless as going back."

"Because I might lead them to Jeffery, you mean?"

His mouth went hard and grim as he slowly shook his head.

"He's very sick, and they don't really know what caused it." She didn't look at him as she spoke, and she worried her thumbnail with the pad of her opposite thumb. The shells of her ears glowed pink. "You don't think it was the vampires? They didn't bite him, did they?"

"Vampire bites don't make people sick. It's not like the movies. They rip open an artery and drink. If they're still hungry they eat. Liver, usually."

She shivered and rubbed her hands over her upper arms in a brisk stroke.

"And as for your boyfriend's illness..." Mac pointed out the elephant in the room. "He'll get better now that you're gone." She stilled and met his hard stare, her glimmering eyes a mix of hope and fear.

"Did I do something to him?"

He gave a slight inclination of his head. She bit her lower lip and braced, waiting for him to speak.

"You slept with him Friday night, right?"

Brianna's mind darted back to Friday night when her biggest worry had been whether she wanted to take her relationship with Jeffery to the next level. He was sweet and generous, and she'd been comfortable with him. Not in love but at ease, and they were like-minded on so many issues. She admired him because he helped a lot of needy people. But when he kissed her there was no spark.

Her gaze flashed to MacConnelly. The sparks were flying with him—even if she hadn't touched him. Just one shower of sparks after another. Sexual, male, with an edge of danger she didn't quite understand, Mac was one powerful source of energy. It pulsed from him like sound waves from a radio tower. Invisible, but she could feel them even from this distance and they lifted the hairs on her forearms.

Mac had guessed correctly. Friday night had been her first time with Jeffery. She'd been uncertain, and the sex had been disappointing. Her fault, she knew, because she'd held back. She told herself that it was because she still missed Matthew, but deep down she knew something was wrong and she was afraid.

MacConnelly rested a hand over hers. She glanced down at the connection, their hands sitting one upon the other on his carefully made bed, and then she looked into his eyes. She had his complete attention.

"Princess, tell me what happened."

She slipped her hand away and pressed both hands to her chest. She didn't know why he needed to know this, but she would tell him.

"We woke up together. Jeffery felt off, he said. His stomach was upset. He threw up and then the dizziness started. He wouldn't let me call an ambulance, but then he threw up his coffee, too. So I got him to my car and drove him to the emergency room. They ran tests, gave him fluids. That helped. But then he blacked out. They said he might have internal bleeding and took him to surgery, but there was nothing. Now they think there might be something wrong with his immune system. No white blood cells. That's impossible, isn't it, to be healthy one minute and so sick the next?"

He gave her a long unblinking stare. He didn't seem surprised. Her body chilled.

What if the doctors were wrong? What if everything Nana said was true? No. It's impossible. She dismissed the thought, but a tiny shard of dread remained lodged in her heart like a sliver of glass.

"Nana said I had to leave Jeffery or he'd get sick. She said Matthew had been sick because of me. But that's crazy, right?"

He didn't speak, just continued that assessing stare. Bri looked away.

She could pretend that she was normal, that everything was normal, but it wasn't. She wasn't.

Chapter 5

"Was it me?" Bri whispered. "Did I do something to him." She glanced at Mac.

His mouth was grim. A frost crept through her body. Tears leaked from the corners of her eyes.

"Been any other men in your life, Princess?"

"Yes. One. Before..." Before that woman at the high school showed up and called her sister.

"Tell me about him."

"Matt was my high school steady. We never, you know." She shrugged her shoulders and looked at her hands, now folded into one tight knot of interlaced fingers. "But senior year he proposed and I said yes. My nana was so angry. She forbade me to see him. I thought she was just being old-fashioned. During his freshman year he came home on Thanksgiving break and..." She stared at him as the panic began to rip at her with tiny, sharp claws. *Oh, God, it was her!* "Do you know why this happened?"

"Tell me the rest, Princess."

"He got sick, too. But he went back to school and he got better and then…" The unease was rising to panic. Her heart knocked against her ribs and the sound of her breathing reminded her of an asthma patient in the midst of an attack. "He came home for Christmas."

"He got sick again?"

She pounded her fists on her thighs. "No! He died. Undetected aneurysm in his brain. That's what they said." She met his steady stare. "But that wasn't it. Was it, MacConnelly?"

He cocked his head as those crystal eyes judged her. "You really didn't know, did you, Princess?"

"Know what?"

"How long between Matthew and Jeffery?"

Why? Why did he ask her this?

"I don't know…four years, I think."

MacConnelly gritted his teeth and winced. "Four? He should be dead." His gaze swept her as if searching for answers.

"What?"

"Nothing. Jeffery was lucky because you got more potent with time. Didn't you know that?"

"What are you talking about?"

"Anyone in between?"

She shook her head.

"But you lived with your grandmother. How could that be? Was she like you?"

"No, she wasn't at all like me."

"Then I don't understand. How did she live so long? I read her obit on the internet. Eighty-eight. Died one month ago."

Brianna covered her mouth, trying to force back the grief at her grandmother's passing and the fear that threatened her sanity. "Please tell me what's happening."

She tried to remember all her nana had said. All the nonsense, the doctors called it, just the drug-induced ranting of a dying brain. But now Brianna knew better. Now she could no longer ignore her grandmother's final words.

"Did she know, Princess? She must have known to have lived with you so long. Unless you were just turned. When were you bitten?"

"Bitten? I don't understand." She stared at him in confusion. "I was never bitten. My nana said that I'm a Feyling. She said I was born of the Fey. Born, not turned."

"Feylings? I never heard that." He sat with one leg folded at the hip, half turned toward her now, the stiffness still starching his spine, as if being a Marine somehow came from the inside. "What did your grandmother tell you exactly?"

Her skin crawled at the memory and she rubbed her hands over her arms. "She said my mother was a fairy."

"A fairy?"

Brianna nodded, knowing how crazy that sounded. "That's what she said. She was a particular kind of fairy called a Leanan Sidhe. And that all fairies are real and that my mother didn't really die. She just abandoned me to return to her world with the Fey."

"Is that true?" he asked.

"I don't know. But it is what she said."

"That would make you half fairy."

That thought had occurred to her. It explained many odd things about her, things she'd tried to hide during her childhood and continued to hide now that she was an adult.

"I know," she whispered. "She said a Feyling is one

born of a union of the Fey with a mortal, my father. He was a writer. A great writer."

"We've never known the origin of your kind. Fairy makes as much sense as any other crazy theory I've heard." He scrubbed his eyes with his hands and released a long breath. Then he turned his troubled gaze on her again. "But we have another name for your kind, Princess." She heard a definite note of regret in his voice.

She sat on the edge of the bed, waiting, knowing that whatever he was about to tell her, she was not going to like it.

His gaze had gone cold again. "Vampire."

Bri gasped and drew back as if he'd slapped her. "No, that's what's chasing me."

"Because you are one of them."

"But that's not possible. I don't drink blood. I'm a vegetarian, for goodness' sake. I helped build low-income housing and marched to stop the war. I'm working part-time as a social worker. I'm a good person, not a monster."

"You're one of them."

"But I don't look like them. I'm not...I'm—"

"—beautiful, like all the females. Bewitching, they say." He made it sound like a condemnation, bitten between clamped teeth. "Irresistible to mortal men."

"No," she said, gasping now, her mind screaming denial as her stomach ached like a raw, oozing wound.

He laid out the evidence. "You can fly."

"I can't."

"Well, something damn close. How'd you get up on that roof?"

"I sort of bounced." Why didn't he seem shocked? It was almost as if he expected her to say this. Bri became more certain that he knew things that she needed to know.

His brow knit together. The gesture only added to his good looks. She edged away as another truth hit her, werewolves killed vampires, and she was a vampire.

"I'm going to be sick."

She barely made it to the toilet. Mac waited in the door frame as she finished retching, then offered her a wet towel. She washed her face with the cool terry cloth. Afterward, he gave her his mouthwash and a glass. When she finished she looked at herself in the mirror and saw that her skin still looked flawless and her hair still danced merrily about her heart-shaped face. But her green eyes now looked dead.

She lowered the glass to the sink and faced the Marine sergeant who knew what she was.

"You mean that if I'd been born a boy, I'd be—"

"—like them."

She shivered, rubbing her upper arms with her hands, as if she were standing naked under a shower of ice water.

"You can self-heal, too. I'm sure you know that."

She nodded. It was one of the differences her nana had told her to keep to herself. She was never sick and never injured for long.

"And you suck the life force from any human male you sleep with. There are soul-sucking vampires, too. All female vampires are soul-suckers" He pressed an index finger to the center of her forehead as if sighting the placement of a bullet. "Like you."

She started to deny this and then hesitated. A chill broke over her and she huddled, shrugging her shoulders as the chill ate deep into her bones.

"I killed Matthew. I almost killed Jeffery."

His eyes met hers and he gave a slow nod. She saw it then, the truth. He understood her self-loathing, the disgust at what she had done. What had he done that made him understand? Something bad, it was clear in those sky-blue eyes.

"At least yours were accidents," he said.

Was that some sort of consolation prize?

"So I killed a man I loved and sent another to the hospital, but I didn't mean to hurt them, so that's supposed to make everything okay?" Her voice was nearly unrecognizable, a screeching thing, totally unfamiliar now.

"No. Not okay. It will never be okay. Just, well, we all have regrets."

"Regrets!" Her hands flew up and then dropped down limp to her sides, as she muttered, "Regrets."

"We thought vampires were made, like werewolves, from a bite. But this explains why the males have to chase the females, to hunt them, bring them in, especially if they can't make new vampires through a bite. They'd have to sleep with you."

"What!"

"I've seen the males. So have you. Would you have sex with one?"

She hugged herself. "Never."

"Then they need to catch females in order to mate. Catch them and keep them captive, at least until they deliver. And you escaped because you were warned?"

She nodded, "Twice."

He took hold of her forearm and led her back to the bed, seating her. He sat down beside her again and the bed sagged.

The lump in her throat was the size of a golf ball.

"Now about the woman. Who was she?"

"Which one? There were two."

"The one at the hospital."

Brianna thought back to the lovely woman wearing a long gray cardigan that swept the tops of her stylish boots. The black beret covered most of her strawberry blond hair, but she knew the woman was a beauty with a clear complexion, a generous mouth and startling gray eyes. She had been perfectly lovely. Too perfect, she now knew. When they'd been on the ground floor, the woman had grabbed Brianna's arm and held on until the elevator left without them.

"I'd never seen her before. She stopped me, pulled me into the alcove before the outpatient surgery doors and told me that there were male vampires hunting me. That they couldn't track me until I was grown, but now they had and they were waiting on the fourth floor for me to show up. She told me to run."

"Why did she warn you?"

"I asked her that. She said, 'Eight years. That's how long they had me. No one warned me. No one helped me. Maybe you'll make it, because you're first generation.' But she said that will make them want me more. They won't give up. They never give up."

"What's 'first generation'?"

"I don't know, except that my mom was a fairy. That's what Nana said."

His brow wrinkled and his words seemed more for himself than her. "First generation. What difference does that make?" His gaze snapped back to her. "Then what?"

"She told me what the males had done to her. It was years of abuse. Rape. She was quick, and when she finished she vanished. I was looking at her one minute and the next she was gone. She just glanced over her shoulder and said, 'Run.' Then poof."

"So you left the hospital?"

"No. I *ran* out of the hospital. Then I went to the apartment I share, shared, with Nana. I have it until the end of the month. But they broke in while I was there, so I ran again. But it was different this time."

"Everyone slowed down?"

She fidgeted with her thumbnail. "Yes."

"Tell me about that."

She did and when she finished describing her journey he was silent for a moment as he absently rubbed his jaw. He was clean-shaven again, she realized, unlike when she'd arrived. His smooth cheeks made his jaw even more defined. She watched the rhythmic stroke of his index finger over his face and noticed how the muscles of his forearm corded with the muscles of her stomach. Just looking at him made her twitch.

"Maybe they didn't slow down. Maybe you sped up."

She paused to consider that. "How?"

"Same way you got on my roof."

It all was too much. She covered her face, hunching forward as she wept in long, wracking cries. His big, strong arm came around her, dragging her to his side as she fell against that wide chest. After a time the tears slowed. She sniffed and wiped her eyes, listening to the comforting rhythm of his heartbeat as he held her, giving comfort and asking for nothing in return.

"Nana told me some things before she died, but I didn't believe her. I didn't *want* to believe her. In my heart I knew it was true. But I thought if I just pretended hard enough, if I kept believing that I was like everyone else, I could go on as I was. But it can't ever be that way again."

She sagged against him, letting him hold her, letting him comfort her as she released some of the fear and sorrow in her heart. Then she remembered what she was.

"No!" She extended her hands, pushing with all her might.

Brianna was stronger than Mac expected. Stronger than she looked but not strong enough to escape him.

"You can't hurt me," he assured.

"Yes. I can. I will. Please, let me go." Tears streamed from her eyes as she stared up at him begging for release. "I can't. I won't do this again."

He eased his grip, letting her draw back, but not away. He wanted to tell her, if only to reassure her that whatever happened with human males, it would not happen with him. But first he'd have to tell her the truth.

"You can't hurt me, Princess. I'm like Johnny. I'm a werewolf, too."

She stilled as his confession registered. Her fingers gripped his shirt and her lovely eyes went wide. The sea-green depths, stormy as some internal turbulence made her body shudder. The flush began at her neck and then spread to make her cheeks a rosy pink.

"You're like him?"

Was that fear in her eyes or hope?

He nodded.

"I smelled it. I just thought…but if you're a wolf, then why did you keep Johnny from killing me?"

"You asked for my protection."

"But I'm your natural enemy. I thought I was influencing you, but if it's true…then what I am didn't cause your actions. Werewolves aren't drawn to vampires, except to kill them. That's what I was told."

"But I *am* drawn to you. What man wouldn't be?"

"Why don't you turn me in?"

He glared at her, angry it seemed, over her insistence to keep poking at him for answers. His jaw worked hard as if crushing something between his molars.

"Because I don't know what they would do to you."

"They wouldn't help me?"

"I doubt that very much." He filled his lungs with a great breath of air and then blew it away.

"I don't understand why you are helping me. If you are a werewolf—"

He interrupted her. "I am."

"Well, then. The woman said…she said that a werewolf could kill vampires, but I didn't know I was a vampire then. I knew it was dangerous, but I didn't understand how dangerous."

"If you knew all that, then why'd you come?"

She dropped her chin and her hands fell to her lap. She looked small and defenseless. He kept one arm about her waist and waited. When she finally spoke, her voice was just a whisper.

"Because I'd rather die than go with them." That admission took the roses from her cheeks. She looked pale now to the point of fainting. What did they do to their women that made them ready to run into the open jaws of a werewolf? The hairs on his neck lifted at her words. Rape, she'd said. Years of it.

His CO said the males held the females for indoctrination. But that was all. Did they know what really went on?

She rested a hand on his chest. "Thank you for fighting for me, for lying for me and for sheltering me. You've done so much, but I have another favor to ask."

He lifted his brows, waiting.

"Can you call and check on Jeffery? I'm so worried about him."

His mouth when grim. "Because you love him?"

"No." She said that too quickly and realized with some guilt that it was true. She didn't love him, hadn't, even though she had tried so hard. "I don't. It's because I hurt him."

The tension in his shoulders eased and he breathed deep before answering. "I already checked. Out of the hospital. Looking for you. Back at work."

She pressed a hand to her forehead and sagged. "He'll be all right."

"If you keep clear of him."

She nodded and dropped her hand, lifting her head so she could meet his gaze. "Thank you for telling me and also for telling me that I can't hurt you. That's a great relief."

He gave her a smile that transformed his expression. The twinkle in his eyes made her body buzz with excitement as she recognized something vital had changed between them. His hands stilled their rhythmic stroke of her upper arms and came to rest. He held her gaze.

It struck Brianna that she could kiss him and not worry that she might draw away some of his vitality. The freedom of that realization had her blinking stupidly at him.

She leaned forward, lifting her chin, angling her mouth. His breath caught.

"It won't hurt you?" she whispered.

He lifted his thick brows and grinned. "Let's find out."

His broad hand went about her neck and he drew her toward him. His eyes dropped shut and he angled his head to receive her kiss. She gasped as the anticipation galloped through her. Why hadn't she ever felt this connection with Jeffery? Why was this chemistry stronger with a stranger than with a man she respected, a man she'd almost killed?

She felt Mac's arms go around her, strong arms, capable arms. She could kiss him, hold him and nothing terrible would happen. The freedom mingled with the anticipation hovering like a hummingbird the instant before it perches.

And then his mouth found hers. The gentle pressure increasing as his fingers delved into her hair. Pleasure fizzed in her blood like the tiny rising bubbles in a glass of champagne. A soft moan escaped her as she settled against his chest, coming to rest, coming home, coming alive after a long, long sleep. Her hands grasped, measuring the breadth of his chest and the round sturdy muscle of his shoulders.

Her mouth opened, and his tongue danced and thrust with a skill and confidence that made her go all liquid heat and pulsing need. She leaned close, pressed tight, and he captured her against his chest, the pressure a welcome relief and a tantalizing frustration.

His arms relaxed by slow degrees and still she clung. He gently clasped her chin in one firm hand as he drew her away with the other. She stared up at him, wanting more, needing his touch. She blinked, recoiled at her complete loss of control and then felt her cheeks flame.

"I'm sorry."

"Don't be."

If he'd taken her backward to the wide, inviting bed, would she have gone? Yes, and her shame at the thought made her blush. What about Jeffery? How could she just forget him like that?

"My boyfriend is sick in the hospital and I'm kissing a stranger."

"Your boyfriend is human, and he will get well if you stay away from him. You know that, right?"

"Are you sure?"

"Positive."

She nodded. "What do I do now?"

"Working on that. My colonel would love a female vampire."

She stiffened and leaned back, her expression going tight.

He met her troubled gaze. "And that is why he shouldn't have one."

"I'd be a military experiment."

"Yes."

She gripped his hand. "What do they do to you?"

He shook his head, unwilling to tell her all that they'd been through, were going through, and in that instant he made up his mind. They weren't doing that to her. He'd protect her if he could and help her escape if he couldn't.

He gave her hand a squeeze. "I won't let them take you."

Chapter 6

Mac headed to the lab the next day to donate more blood to their damned research. He supposed they needed it to figure out how to turn Johnny back, but lately he felt like a pincushion. Then he endured another tedious brain scan in both his forms. His mind was on Bri, alone in his quarters. He hoped that if those males showed up, he'd have time to reach her before they took her. He also worried about Johnny, who was now on the firing range getting shot. Johnny said Lewis treated him like a big dumb animal when Mac wasn't there and that worried him. Mac's request to remain with his friend had been denied because they needed more blood. When they finally dismissed him from the infirmary, he got shipped off to the obstacle course, then to the firing range to practice shooting. When they ordered him back to medical, he disobeyed and didn't go. He'd done that twice before and both times over Johnny. Mac had that feeling again, the one he got when things weren't right.

Mac needed to find Johnny, make sure he was all right and then get back to Bri. He found his friend back in the cell they held him in when Mac wasn't around. The air still held the acrid smell of gunpowder, and Mac had the sickening realization that the odor came from Johnny's fur. He scanned Lam but saw no marks on his coat and no blood on the floor. But something was wrong with his corporal; he could tell with just one look at Johnny's unfocused eyes. What had they done to him?

Lewis appeared just behind Mac. Clearly someone had alerted the commander about Mac's failure to report. Mac wondered if this was the moment he and the colonel would go at it. A face-off had been brewing for some time. Mac could take the abuse, but he couldn't stand to see Lam go through it. It was why he hadn't accepted the offer to take a leave and visit his family. He didn't trust them with Johnny.

"We wanted to give Johnny a little time before bringing you in," said Lewis.

Mac's brow furrowed and he dipped his chin, holding back but curling his hands into fist to keep the change from flashing through him like a grenade. "What's wrong with him?"

"He's fine. Just woozy from the sedative."

Mac searched Johnny's eyes, seeing instantly that Johnny was not fine. He could ask Lewis, but that meant questioning a senior officer. He could ask Johnny, but Johnny would just play stupid. His friend had made it very clear that he would not answer questions around anyone, and what first had seemed like paranoia now began to seem wise. But Johnny had made an exception for Brianna Vittori. Why did he let her see his intelligence when he would not show it to anyone at HQ? If they knew he understood, they wouldn't treat him like a dumb animal. But they'd also clam up around him, as they did with Mac.

"He wasn't cooperative when you left, so…"

Mac stepped closer. Johnny's eyelids drooped. "He's not fine."

"No injury from the bullets. We tried the armor-piercing rounds. You two *are* bulletproof. That hide wears like Kevlar. Better. We even used a grenade. No damage."

"Grenade? I didn't agree to that."

Lewis gave him a hard look. "You get a promotion I didn't hear about?"

Mac's nostrils flared as he stood between them, wanting to demand they release Johnny and knowing he trod a very fine line. Still, it took several deep breaths to keep himself from tearing at the bars with his bare hands. He and Johnny together could break through this cage. But instead of doing something so rash he just lowered his chin so the colonel couldn't see the defiance there.

"No, sir."

Lewis draped an arm around Mac's shoulders, gave him a pat and released him. "He's fine. The ME checked him. So did our vet."

"Did you give him ear protection?"

"What? I'm not…no."

Mac felt the rage building inside him like steam in a rusty pipe. Any minute he'd explode.

Lewis's jaw went hard and he made Mac wait. "His eardrums are intact. Might have some ringing for a day or so, I suppose. They said he'd be asleep, but he never went out."

Mac knew that Johnny would do everything he could not to black out while in HQ. Maybe he was right. With growing unease, Mac wondered briefly what they had just done to him when *he* was out. His unease grew, gripping his chest, making it tight and his breathing shallow. He should have been here.

He turned to his commanding officer and stood at attention. "Permission to take Johnny to quarters, sir."

Lewis made a face. "Granted. We're done here anyway. You need help carrying him? I can get a transport."

Johnny hated the transport cage. Called it his circus wagon.

Mac saluted. "I can carry him, sir. Thank you, sir."

"You want the truck or you two going to run?"

Mac motioned for Johnny to stand. He didn't. Mac's stomach twisted. Mac motioned again for Johnny to rise, which he did—then he wobbled and sat down heavily.

"The truck, sir."

Mac helped Johnny board and held on to him as they rode. Johnny couldn't hear him, that much was clear. Through sign language, he gathered that Lam had covered his ears as best he could with his hands, but that gave only minimal protection. It seemed clear to Mac that the colonel had overstepped, which brought Mac back to the same damn question: Was he going to continue to serve his country, or was he going to take Johnny and go AWOL?

A year ago he had never dreamed it possible that he would consider such a thing. But a lot could happen in a year. He'd stayed for months in hopes that the medical staff could find a way to reverse Johnny's condition. Instead they heaved grenades at him. Were they even trying to solve that problem or were they just seeing how much a werewolf could take? If they ran, Johnny would have no chance of being restored to human form. It was a terrible price to pay for insubordination. But no one would be shooting at them, either.

If they ran they'd be AWOL, and God knew the Marines would chase them relentlessly. And Mac would never be able to go home to his family, because that would be the first place they'd look. He thought of the business he planned to join with his dad. Mac's chest ached at the thought of losing so much. He pictured his mom's face as she smiled up at him and then his older sister, Bonnie, now married and expecting her first child. And Sean, who idolized him—what would he think when he heard his big brother was a coward who left his post and ran? Worst of all, he imagined the disappointment in his father's eyes when he discovered that his eldest boy had failed to serve honorably. His father was a vet, and he loved his country as much as he loved his family. His dad and mom had been so proud when he joined the Corps. God, Mac didn't want to have to break his father's heart.

He'd have to ask Johnny. They'd have to make this choice together. Mac would do whatever Johnny wanted. But God, he didn't want to lose his family. His heart ached as he thought of each person he loved and then imagined never seeing them again. It was a sacrifice he'd never considered. He knew he risked his life. But his reputation and his honor and now his family. The decisions weighed him down like stones.

If they ran, where would they go that the U.S. Marines could not find them? And, without the doctors of the Corps, how would he get Johnny back to his human form?

* * *

Mac got Johnny inside their quarters and to the futon, where Johnny collapsed, overcome by the day and the drugs they'd given him.

Mac day had been nearly as horrific, the only bright spot was finding his princess dozing on his bed. Her allure was nearly too much to bear. Only knowing Johnny was right down the hall, sick from drugs and impact injuries and possibly deaf as a result, kept Mac from approaching that bed. Instead he gave a gentle knock on the door and watched her eyes flash open. She stared up at the ceiling for a moment, her brow descending as she oriented herself and turned to face him. Her eyes were red, as if she'd been crying. He remembered their conversation, her discovery of exactly what she was, and he thought that Bri had good cause to weep.

"I fell asleep," she said.

Her warm floral scent filled the air, luring him forward, but he held the doorknob like an anchor against rough seas and remained in place. "Yes. You hungry?"

"What time is it?"

"Eighteen hundred."

She shook her head, sending her fiery curls tumbling over her shoulders. "What?"

"Supper time." He closed the door. Mac couldn't get away fast enough. Brianna Vittori was beautiful on any day, but tousled from sleeping in his bed, with her rosy cheeks and her hooded eyes, she was irresistible. But he had resisted through a strategic retreat. He doubletimed it to the kitchen, surprised to find Johnny up and hunched over the open refrigerator. He knew that werewolves healed fast, but he was still surprised. The

kitchen was Johnny's domain, but he'd been nearly unconscious a minute ago.

"Can you hear me?"

Johnny nodded and glanced his way, his eyes clear
and his expression sullen. Well, he had cause.

"Sedative? Has it worn off?"

Another nod and Johnny returned to the open refrigerator. He lifted a packet of ground chuck and tented
his eyes.

"Yeah, fine."

Johnny turned toward the counter and set aside the
chuck.

"How do you feel?"

Johnny pressed a hand to his forehead and stomach
simultaneously, then pantomimed being sick.

"You hungry?"

Johnny nodded.

"I'll do it."

Johnny pushed him aside and Mac let him.

He glanced back down the hall and hoped Bri didn't
cook, because if there was a turf war, Johnny would
win. Mac thumbed toward his bedroom.

"She was sleeping in my bed."

Johnny paused and studied him a moment then
dragged the buns from the refrigerator and set them
on the counter.

Mac pulled out the condiments, lettuce, onion and
tomato and then turned on the oven.

"You okay with her being here?"

Johnny gave him a peeved look then gave him his
back. He was definitely not fine with Bri being here.

Lam washed his hands and started making hamburger patties, way too big for the buns. Mac tore open a bag of fries and threw them in the oven to bake.

"I told her I'd protect her. You want me to put her out? I'll put her out." As Mac said it he knew he wouldn't and prayed Johnny didn't call that bluff.

Lam gave him a long look and then shook his head.

Mac breathed a sigh of relief and sagged against the counter. "Thanks."

Johnny glared and Mac met his steady stare. He stilled as he became cautious.

"You aren't going to go for her, are you?" There was still the tiniest doubt that Johnny might try to kill Bri.

Down the hall, the bedroom door opened and then closed.

Johnny froze as if suddenly made of wax. Mac went to meet Brianna, wondering if Johnny would be here when they got back.

Bri paused at the first sight of Mac and gave him a tentative smile, full of uncertainty and hope. Her eyes were still red, but it only served to make her look more tragically beautiful. Man, she was a killer in more ways than one.

"Can I meet Johnny now?"

Mac smiled. "If you still want to."

She blew out a breath and nodded. "Yes. I do."

Mac led the way down the hall to find that Johnny had vanished. "She wants to meet you. So come out. That's an order."

Johnny stepped from behind the door frame momentarily filling the space. Bri gasped at the sight of him and went rigid for a moment, but she held her ground. Now Mac could smell her fear, liquid and tart as lemon juice.

Johnny's eyes narrowed on her, sensing weakness. Mac took hold of her elbow and felt her tremors.

Mac walked her across the room and to her credit she kept her chin up and her eyes on Johnny as she moved stiffly forward. He paused to stand between them. Now what?

He cleared his throat. "Corporal John Lam, may I introduce Brianna Vittori."

Johnny continued to glare. Mac kept his eyes on the corporal.

Bri extended her trembling hand. "It's a pleasure to meet you, Corporal. May I call you John?"

Johnny did a double take, looking from her hand to her face and finally to Mac, who found he could not speak for the lump in his throat. Of all the reactions he had expected from Bri, civility was not among them.

John had been in near isolation since their return. He saw the medical staff, all male, and the colonel and Mac. That was it. When was the last time a woman was kind to him or touched him? Mac felt the tension twist his gut.

Johnny wiped his dark, leathery hand on his hairy chest, never taking his eyes off Bri. Unlike a wolf's paw, Johnny did not have pads and toes on his forelegs. His hands more resembled a gorilla's, except the claws were long, curved and deadly. Then he extended his hand to meet hers, taking it gently between his thumb and forefingers for just the briefest instant before quickly releasing her. To her credit she did not flinch or give any outward sign she was frightened or repulsed. Her bright smile held even as he rose up to his full height, now standing like the man he had once been.

She craned her neck and held her gentle smile. "Can I help with dinner?"

Johnny shook his head and pointed to a bar stool. It wasn't the warmest of welcomes, thought Mac. But he'd take it.

Brianna took a seat. "I don't want to be any trouble. Did Mr. MacConnelly tell you that he told me I could stay?"

Johnny lifted his brow and glanced to Mac, likely to see if he had any issue with being called Mister instead of Sergeant. He didn't. He was so damn thrilled that Bri was being kind to Johnny and that Johnny hadn't attacked Bri that he had a lump in his throat the size of a peach pit. He couldn't have spoken if he had tried.

Johnny nodded.

"Is it all right with you?"

He hesitated and then gave another affirmative.

"Mr. MacConnelly told me that you can't change back. This all must be very hard for you. You've made a great sacrifice serving your country, and I'm honored to know you, Mr. Lam."

When he told her what she was, she'd said she was a pacifist, likely an antiwar liberal who opposed everything that he and Johnny stood for. And still she thanked him. Mac's eyes burned. Damned if he wasn't tearing up.

She sniffed. "Is something burning?"

Johnny darted to the stove and flipped the burgers. A few minutes later Johnny had three plates. He ate standing, finishing four burgers while Brianna selected a bun, then made a salad from the lettuce and tomato to go with her fries. Johnny paused between bites to look at her plate.

"So no burger?" asked Mac.

"I don't eat meat."

"Fish?"

"No."

"Why not?"

"People can live quite happily on nuts, grains, fruits and vegetables."

"I can't."

"I'm not asking you to. But for me, it's not necessary to kill living things to survive." Her smile dropped away as she recognized the irony of what she had said. She killed things whether she meant to or not. Mac watched the pain blow over her features like an impending storm as she came to the same conclusion.

"Johnny and I need meat."

"Of course. I'm not trying to impose my beliefs on you."

They lapsed into awkward silence again. Johnny finished first and headed out. Mac was certain he'd be gone all night. He often preferred sleeping outside or in his private quarters.

"That didn't go very well," said Brianna.

"I disagree. He didn't try to kill you."

Brianna cleared the table and Mac washed dishes. Afterward, he made them coffee, and they sat on the dilapidated yellow couch that was draped in a ragged wool blanket.

She sat huddled beneath the blanket in the chilly room with her eyes wide and green as a glass bottle.

"Did you have enough to eat, Princess?"

"Why don't you call me Bri?"

"If you call me Mac."

"All right. I can do that, Mac."

"So, Bri, tell me about your mom and dad."

The smile left her face. She lowered the coffee to the low brass table and half turned, hooking one foot behind her opposite knee. "My father was human."

"Did you know him?"

"No, he died before I was born."

They both knew why. She held his gaze a minute and then she lowered her gaze. "Shortly after meeting my mom. She was my nana's only child."

"That's tough."

"He was a brilliant musician."

"Yeah. They go for the talented ones." He realized too late that he'd said the wrong thing because of Bri's intake of breath.

"Is that so?"

"That's what our intel indicates."

"My mother, well, just before she passed, my nana said that they are called the Leanan Sidhe," she whispered. Then her eyes flashed to his. "The Fairy Mistress. Muses. I mean that's what Nana said. The men they choose live lives of brilliance."

"Short lives of brilliance?"

She glanced away. "Yes."

"Maybe the creative ones give off more juice or whatever you call the energy you drain away. Anyway, maybe your mother *was* a fairy."

"But I'm not, is that what you mean? And I'm not a Leanan Sidhe. But I'm half human, at least." Tears leaked from her eyes and she shook her head in denial. "Half human and half Leanan Sidhe?"

"Yeah, Bri. I think so."

She tried to drink a little coffee but seemed to be

choking it down. He made great coffee, so he figured she was still grappling with all this shit.

"Have any other people around you gotten sick? You don't have to sleep with them, just be near them."

Now she was covering her eyes. "My college friends, yes, Gail and Kerry. They both got sick. God, that was me, too. And we moved again. Now I understand why Nana moved us around so much."

"She might have been trying to keep your friends alive."

Brianna's hand slipped from her face, and she pinned him with those lush green eyes. Her chest rose and fell, as if she were running in full gear. Then her chin started to tremble. "Why didn't she tell me long before then? Why only when she was…was dying?"

He shook his head. "Can't answer that."

Her head sunk to her knees, and her shoulders shook. He draped an arm around her shoulders and after a few minutes she lifted her gaze to meet his.

"I used to see them, when I was a child. Fairies in the woods, little ones, dancing at twilight and at night, when the fireflies came out. Nana couldn't see them and told me I was imagining things. But we moved again, and we never lived in the country after that. Fairies don't like the cities." She wiped the tears from her eyes. "I don't like them, either. The lights and the buildings give me headaches. The air smells so good here." She inhaled deeply, filling her lungs with the mountain air. "I think I belong outside."

"That's probably true."

"But Nana kept us in cities. When she was ill in the hospital, my nana told me everything she knew. I told the doctors a little of what she said and they said it was from the pain medication. Hallucinations. I tried to tell myself that was what it was. But, as you said, I can do things that aren't normal. All my life, she would tell me to shush up, not talk about it. But was she trying to protect me from them or trying to pretend I wasn't a…a vampire?"

"I don't know."

"If she was protecting me, why not tell me what I really am?"

"Perhaps she knew it would be hard."

She placed her hand in his had held tight. Her voice shook when she spoke. "She died of cancer. Do you think…did I do that to her?"

"I don't know. But she was an old woman."

"Only eighty-eight."

"She must have known some way to keep from—"

"—my energy draw? That's what you called it, right?"

"Yeah."

"She never touched me."

Mac cocked his head. "What?"

"Never. No hugs. No good-night kisses. I never crawled onto her lap or into her bed after a nightmare."

"She never touched you?" His insides felt hollow, as he imagined a child with no one to hug her or kiss away the tears.

Brianna's head hung, and her face flushed with shame at her revelation. "I thought it was me, and it was. I knew there was something wrong with me." She stared up at him, anxious to explain, to defend her grandmother. "But I know she loved me. Oh. I knew it then, too. I just never really understood why…and it was hard."

It seemed even breathing was hard for her now.

"So I'm a vampire, like the thing that broke into my apartment."

"The female version. Males drink blood. You feed on energy."

"Energy. I don't feel that. The only thing I feed on is tofu and veggie burgers and nice green salads mixed with nuts. I've never hurt anyone. At least...I never *meant* to hurt anyone."

She met his gaze. It was hard not to look away for the pain she experienced seemed to beat in him as well.

"But I have. Haven't I?" She raked her hand through her hair. "I can't even bring myself to kill a spider in my house. But somehow I can kill people without even trying. So now and for the rest of my life, I can't be around people." She gave a harsh laugh that sounded like a cry. "A social worker who can't be around people." She laughed again and then the tears spilled from her eyes as the laughter collapsed to weeping.

He gathered her up in his arms and she nestled against him.

"But not you," she whispered. "I can't hurt you."

"That's right, Princess." He stroked her head, threading his fingers through the thick curls and angling her tear-streaked face up so he could look into those green eyes, shimmering now like faceted gemstones.

"You said there were two females. One at the hospital. Tell me about the other one."

She nodded. "She was beautiful, too. Not like that thing on the road. I was a senior in high school when she found me. She was a beautiful, strawberry blonde with blue eyes. She called me sister. She said I was a woman now, and that they'd be coming for me soon. I told my nana, and she moved us the next day."

"They'd be coming?"

"That's what she said. Nana acted weird. She wouldn't tell me what was happening. She said the woman knew my mother. I thought maybe the woman *really* was my sister, that my mother wasn't dead at all but just gone. I didn't want to leave school but Nana insisted. That was three years ago. After Nana got sick, she told me that I had to keep moving and that men would be attracted to me but I couldn't…I couldn't ever sleep with them. She said devils were chasing me. That they were pure evil."

"They're not devils. We knew the females were lovely and the males hideous. The fairy part, that's new. I'm not sure about that, but it's possible. The males are an international organization of hired killers."

She squeaked. "A what?"

"They're mercenaries. The females, too, Princess."

Chapter 7

Mercenaries. Brianna's head hung as the implication of his words ate into her bones like acid.

"Is that why they want me? To turn me into a killer?"

He didn't turn away, but continued to meet her gaze, holding it unflinching as he spoke. "They want to capture you, train you and then, yes, use you as an assassin. Human males can't resist you. You must already know that."

"I feel sick," she said, cradling her head in her hands. She glanced up, cast him a forlorn look. "I don't want to hurt anyone." Then she remembered the woman at the hospital. Maybe she hadn't wanted to hurt anyone, either, but they kept her for many years. "She said that no one had helped her. She didn't want me to get caught because she knew what they'd do and why they'd do it. They want me to be one of them." Bri grasped Mac's hand and squeezed tight. "I don't want to hurt anyone."

"But you do. You have. And you will."

"How do I stop it?" she whispered, her gaze pleading.

"You can't. It's what you are."

"But I don't want this. Can you help me?"

"No, Princess. I'm sorry."

Her red hair bounced all around her face, and she released him to push it back with both hands. When she spoke her words sounded dull and lifeless to her own ears.

"That woman, the one who warned me. She said they had her for eight years. Was that to train her?"

"We think that the females are used for breeding during their confinement."

Bri felt dizzy and dropped her chin to her chest until the spots stopped dancing around her as she thought of all the things the woman had saved her from.

My God, could all of this be real?

"My nana used to tell me tales of the fairy folk, the Fey and their court. I thought it was all just bedtime stories, but before she died she said they all exist. The doctors said it was a product of her medical condition and I should just humor her. So I did. I listened and I pretended it was all her mind coming unhinged with drugs and pain. But I knew. I knew it all the time."

Bri recalled all the bedtime stories her Italian grandmother had told her, making sure her Feyling granddaughter understood her mother's people and her roots. Now she remembered all the funny, odd and sometimes terrifying creatures that inhabited the world of Never Never.

"All true," she whispered. "All here on earth and I can see them. I *have* seen them. Now they can also see me."

Her protector fell silent. Was this too much, what she was telling him? Too much for even a werewolf to believe?

"My father died of pancreatic cancer at thirty-three. My nana said that my mother died in a boating accident off Ocracoke, North Carolina, shortly after I was born. Her kayak flipped. She had no life vest, and her body was never found. I still have the article."

"I'm sorry," said Mac.

"I used to wonder if my mother had intentionally left her infant daughter and paddled straight out to sea. It always felt like a suicide. Nana wouldn't talk about it."

"Are you sure she wasn't like you?"

"Not according to what Nana told me in the hospital."

She recalled her nana's words and she repeated them to Mac.

"She said, 'Your father, my son, Vito. He was human. He loved her and he wouldn't leave her, even when she told him the truth. He wouldn't abandon her and she couldn't walk away from him. Nothing I could do to stop them. And then he died.' I asked if my mother died, too. She said, 'Fairies don't die, Bri. I've taught you that. But it killed her heart. She loved him too much to leave him.' I said that that didn't make any sense and she said, 'Love rarely does.'"

"She couldn't leave him?" asked Mac.

"That's what she said. Nana said she begged him to leave my mother, but he told her that he'd rather be dead than live one single minute without her. It was fairy magic, but it was strong, unbreakable on both parts. Once he accepted her, she couldn't leave him unless he found another for her, but he wouldn't even though it was killing him. His death released her, and that was when she left me. It wasn't suicide. Wasn't a drowning at all. My mother is still alive, somewhere." Brianna rubbed the knuckle of her left hand absently with her thumb. "She said that my mother was a fairy, immortal, and she loved me, but I was part human. Nana said that she couldn't begin to know how to raise me. So she left me with her husband's mother and returned to the Fey."

"Do you remember her?"

"No. Not at all. Or my father. He was a composer. Successful, wildly, after he met my mother."

"The muse."

"Yes. He left it all to my nana for me. It's all mine now, or it will be when the attorneys finish settling her estate. Millions and millions, they say."

"Well, that's good."

She snorted. "If I live to spend it. Not looking good right now. I think Johnny still wants to take a bite out of me."

"He'll come around."

"And those vampires, what did you call them?"

"The Chasers. They hunt the females."

"Yes, them. They're still out there. Maybe they know by now that the ones they sent after me didn't come back."

His expression told her he had already thought of that. "Very likely."

"So what will happen?"

"They'll send more to the males' last known location and begin their search from there. If they find you, then I'll kill them, too."

"You think you can stop them?" She held his gaze, her auburn brows lifted in a mixture of hope and incredulity.

"I know it."

She shook her head as if she still had any choice. "This is crazy."

"Yeah. It is."

She wondered about him, realizing all she knew about werewolves came from folklore and the movies. "What about you? Werewolves aren't born, are they?"

His eyes went cautious, hooded, and she realized that she'd broached a sensitive topic.

"Werewolves are made."

"I saw the scars. Did something bite you?"

He answered her by grabbing the sleeve of his T-shirt and tugged it over the rounded dome of his shoulder muscles. His skin was pale, taut and smooth, except for the puckered scars.

"He got me here first. Grabbed ahold with his jaws. Puncture marks," he said, pointing out the result of each long tooth.

Then he lifted his shirt from the hem and tugged it over his head. She sat up straight at the sight of so much muscular male flesh. His defined muscles contracted at his stomach and chest. Her gaze swept up at the tempting expanse of male flesh, and then her own flesh went cold as she saw again the horrible scars that laced his chest and arm. She'd seen them in the twilight when the Chasers had attacked her. Her mind cast back to that time. She realized Mac had been one of the werewolves that had attacked the vampires. Like her, Mac was more than he appeared. She understood now that he was not just a man. Johnny was the black werewolf, so he must be the gray one.

The scars looked different under the unforgiving overhead light. She took in the damage, reaching for him before she even thought of what she was doing. Her fingers grazed the raised, puckered flesh of the slashing scars that sliced across one side of his chest, measuring them with a touch. He flinched as the pads of her fingers brushed white, puckered flesh in a gentle imitation of the attack.

He held his shirt in a wadded ball before him as she circled, studying the punctures on his deltoid and the matching ones on his shoulder blade. It had clawed him and bitten him repeatedly.

"These bites are from the one that attacked you?"

"Turned me. Yes. The last scars I'll ever have. Nothing cuts my skin now."

She was behind him now, her hand caressing his shoulder, and she felt him tremble and saw the blood vessels at his throat pulse. Bri dropped a kiss on the ravaged flesh.

"Tell me about it?"

"Maybe some other time."

Her hands slid over his arms, measuring the strength of those wide shoulders. He turned and gathered her up against him.

"You shouldn't play with wolves," he cautioned. "We bite."

Mac pulled her close. His firm grip and warm hands gave the illusion of strength. Was he really strong enough for her? Would she draw away his energy just as she'd done with the others? She didn't feel anything.

But then she did. There was a tingling excitement that came from the brush of his thumbs against the bare skin of her neck. The gentle cradling of his hands about her upper arms. She could smell his aftershave now and the tang of sweat and soap.

He pulled. She resisted.

"What if you're wrong? What if I draw your energy, too?"

"You can't, Bri. I'm immune to you. That's why they send us to kill your kind."

His head dipped and his mouth pressed to her neck. Her head dropped back as a purr rumbled in her throat. His mouth was so hot, his tongue so thrilling. She turned her head.

"You could be wrong."

"It's all right, Princess. I can take it."

Her eyes narrowed at the challenge, and she tipped forward into his arms. She held on tight, reveling in the bunch and contraction of his warm muscles as he gathered her up against him, cradling her in the safe harbor of his arms.

He tipped her chin up so she could meet his gaze. "You held back with the others. I know you did."

She gasped. How could he know that?

"You don't have to do that with me. I want it all. Everything you've got and then some. I need it."

He slid his hands over her bare back, across her shoulders and down her spine. She closed her eyes, savoring the strength of those arms and the tenderness of his touch.

Excitement buzzed in her belly. She hadn't felt this way in so long. But his touch aroused more than eagerness. There was something about him that was so different from any man she'd ever known. She couldn't explain why. But she could feel the difference. The pull toward him was greater. The desire tugging at her insides was more powerful and the need that even now unfolded and grew inside her was stronger than she'd ever felt before. What if she didn't hold back? What if she released all the passion and need?

"No," she whispered. It was dangerous. Too dangerous, no matter what he said. She had to protect him, keep him safe.

"Yes," he whispered against her cheek.

You know that men can't resist you. Was he really protected, or enchanted like the others?

Fairy dust and moonbeams. Had she caught him like the Fey did, who used humans for their own amusement? Like her mother had bewitched her father?

"What if it's just the glamour?"

"Glamour?" he murmured against her ear and his breath fanned her neck.

"Enchantment. Fairy magic? What if it's like all the rest? It's not me that attracts you, just the Fey part of me."

"I want *you,* Brianna. I haven't had a woman since this happened."

"You could have any woman."

He shook his head. "No. I can't. I have to stay with Johnny. And even if I were free, it's too risky. What if I was with a woman and I changed? What if she saw me?"

She'd never thought of that, but she knew it would be bad. She held his gaze and he went on.

"But you've seen me already. You'd understand."

Was it because she knew what he was or…a different possibility occurred to her and she shivered. "Is it because I can self-heal?"

His answer was sharp and quick. "No. I won't hurt you. I'd never hurt you, Princess, even when in wolf form, and I would never force you. But I want you like crazy."

Mac's fingers delved in her hair and he pressed her against his body, cradling her as if he were her protector instead of a man caught by her appeal. She breathed deep, taking in the newness and making it a part of her.

She believed he could protect her. If only he could also save her from this evil that lived inside her.

He leaned forward, and she let him take her weight. His mouth descended and she knew she wouldn't stop him, because she was as much in his spell as he was in hers. She read a tenderness in his expression, a delicate balance of gentleness and strength that drew her in. She yearned for him now.

This man was special. This man was right. She parted her lips, offering all.

Mac rubbed his torso against hers. Her body reacted instantly to the contact, her breasts setting off a needy ache. She gasped and her gaze shot to his. His blue eyes no longer seemed gentle or kind. Now they blazed with a flame, the hottest of all fires, the blue point of a focused flame. His jaw went hard, and his gaze flicked to her lips. The lust in his expression snapped her from the spell that had threaded between them. He was no different from any man. He was just as susceptible to her charms and just as susceptible to her deadly powers. She pushed off. He resisted a moment and then let her go.

He growled, a deep feral sound of a displeased male.

"What if you're wrong?" she asked.

"I'm not."

She drew back and he let her go. "I have a boyfriend in the hospital. I shouldn't be kissing you."

"He's human. Best thing you can do for him is leave him for good."

Her chin sunk. He was right. He lifted her chin with one finger.

"Do you love him?"

Did she?

"No," she whispered. She knew she didn't. Respected him very much. Admired him greatly. And Mac was right—if she cared at all, she'd leave him.

Some of the tension left Mac's shoulders. "You can't have him, Brianna. If you keep him, it will be just like your mother and father all over again."

He was right. She'd never have any of the things she dreamed of. She'd never delve into a community and make it her own.

"Never have a husband," she whispered. "Never have a big messy house or children."

She crumpled in the middle as if struck by a blow. He gathered her in, holding her as she shook.

"I can't. I can't have any of it. Not ever."

"You can have me."

Her gaze flashed to his and saw the raw desire burning in his eyes.

"I don't even know you."

"That's not a deal breaker."

"Mac, I'm not a one-night-stand kind of girl."

"You are. You just didn't know it because one night with you will kill most men. But not me."

She realized she was considering it. She couldn't go back to Jeffery. She couldn't turn to any friend she ever had. Her world had shrunk to two things: the vampires who wanted to capture her and this man who said he would keep her safe.

"Is that why you agreed to help me?"

His grip tightened and then he released her and stepped back, his expression grim. "No. I'll protect you either way."

Damn, why did he have to say that? It made her want him even more.

"Well, you just think on it, Vittori. We'll be great together."

The attraction between them sizzled. Her skin flushed, her lips parted and she struggled to keep from stepping into his arms. When she spoke, her voice sounded breathy and tight.

"I am grateful for all you've done, but I'm not ready for this."

"Maybe not today, Vittori. But it will happen. You know it will." He lifted a hand and used his index finger to stroke her cheek. "Go sleep in my bed, Princess, and dream of me. You tell me when. I'll be waiting."

There was a roar from directly outside the living room window. Bri jumped, finding herself in Mac's arms, gripping tightly to the fabric of his shirt.

"It's Johnny. We need to run, scout the area, check for intruders. You get some rest. Sleep tight, Princess. We'll watch over you."

He kissed her on the forehead, his mouth warm and full of promise. Her body tingled all over, and she felt herself quickening with need. The pulse of wanting drummed in her chest with every heartbeat. When he drew back, her skin prickled with new awareness.

You can have me. I'll give you everything I've got.

She sighed, leaning into his embrace. The man must be part Fey himself the way he enchanted.

He pushed her gently back. "Stay inside. The surveillance cameras are back on. See you in the morning, Princess. Sweet dreams."

But she wasn't sleepy. Despite the fear and her narrow escape from the Chasers, she felt needy. And he knew it; she could see that in his sparkling eyes and the upward tilt of one side of his mouth. He wanted her to desire him, think about him and not have him.

He lifted his brows and then headed in the opposite direction.

She watched Mac stride away and followed him as far as the door, holding on to the frame to keep herself from going after him.

Chapter 8

Brianna tossed in bed, paced the cold concrete floor and finally gave up on sleep altogether. As she stared at the ceiling from the wide empty canvas of Mac's bed, she thought of Jeff and grieved over her part in Matthew's death. Then she tried to recall everything her grandmother had told her, merging that with what she had seen and what Mac had said. The headache caused her to close her eyes, and the worry finally gave way to restless slumber and dark dreams. She did not hear his approach, but something roused her from sleep as she sensed a presence in the room.

Her eyes flew open to find Mac easing to a seat at the foot of the bed. He held a steaming mug in one hand and two mugs in the other. She inhaled the aroma of coffee, the fresh tang of aftershave and soap and the scent of wolf.

"I didn't know if you liked light and sweet, light or black. So I brought one of each."

"What if I like sweet and black?"

He produced a packet of sugar and wiggled his eyebrows. "Don't add what you can't take back," he said and his boyish grin made her laugh.

"Black," she said.

"Minimalist, eh?"

He offered the mug, and when she reached to take it he said, "It's not free. Costs one kiss."

She hesitated, pushing the mop of hair back from her face and sat up, regarding him with a mixture of amusement and the slow burn of desire.

"All right. But coffee first."

"Deal."

He handed over the mug being sure their fingers brushed in the exchange. God, he was even more handsome in the bright morning light. She considered him as she sipped her coffee. He sat with a relaxed ease that she found very sexy.

"How's the coffee?"

"Strong, like you," she said.

He smiled. "We didn't find any sign of them on patrol last night or this morning.

"Well, that's good."

He watched her with hungry eyes as she drank the coffee. She felt the flush burning up her neck and face. He held her gaze, and she felt her insides heat as she imagined all the things she wanted him to do to her and all the territory she wanted to cover with her fingers and her mouth. She held out the half-finished coffee.

"Done?" he asked.

She nodded and, instead of heeding the voice of caution, crooked her finger to invite him closer.

He set her mug with the others on the wide adobe

window ledge and then knelt over her with one hand on each side of the headboard.

Her heart galloped as he descended to take a long, languid kiss. The man could kiss like nobody's business, she thought, and then she stopped thinking as she wrapped one arm around that strong neck and loop the other about his broad back. She lifted herself up to press against him, gasping at the lovely pressure of his body against hers. He moved smoothly from her lips to her cheek, ear and throat. His touch stirred and coaxed until her senses blossomed into relentless need.

When she clawed at his back and made soft sounds of encouragement, he drew back and cast her a regretful look as if sorry to let her go.

"Did you dream of me, Princess?"

She nodded.

"Have you considered my offer?"

"I did and I have."

"And?"

"It's a generous offer."

"But…"

She wanted to be reckless and brave, but feared the sex appeal that oozed from him like a hive oozes honey.

"But I don't know you."

He sat back down on an empty place on the opposite side of the bed.

"What do you want to know?" he asked a note of caution in his voice.

"Where do you come from?"

"I grew up in Ann Arbor, Michigan."

"Your family is still there?"

"Yeah, Dad, Mom and an older sister and younger brother counting the days until he's old enough to join."

"Tell me about them."

Mac flinched, as if talking about his family hurt him physically.

"Dad owns a towing company. Big-rig towing. Specialized trucks, massive really. I've worked with him since I got my CDL."

"CDL?"

"Commercial driver's license, a trucker's license. I can drive a rig and can tow anything on eighteen wheels. The plan was for me to join my dad after I got my discharge. In a few years my kid brother would come on board, MacConnelly and sons. Once I got out of the Corps, he'd give me a share in the company. But now I'll never be out. They've already told me as much. It's going to kill Dad. But he's still got Sean. That's my kid brother. Then there's Bonnie. My older sister is married to a cop; they live in Ann Arbor, too. She's expecting their first child." He ran a hand over the stubble of his military haircut. "Shit, I won't be there for that, either. But I'll be an uncle soon."

"You can't go for a visit?"

Mac scowled at her and gave a curt shake of his head. His face showed strain and his Adam's apple bobbed.

"We've that in common, Bri. We both had plans that have turned to shit. I won't take over Dad's business. I'll never drive that rig with my name painted in gold on the door."

"I'm sorry."

"I always thought I'd have a life like Dad's. Work a little, fish a lot, find the right girl and fill up a big house with kids and dogs and rabbits and…" Mac looked away and cleared his throat.

"You can still do that."

"I hope so. But not until Johnny turns back. Until then I stay with him."

"That's very generous."

"Generosity has nothing to do with it. I owe him. I'll never be able to make up for what happened." He swallowed hard. "Things change. Plans change."

She placed a hand over his. "I'm sorry."

He stood, withdrawing as he scrubbed his face with his palms.

"It's like I died over there. You know? I went in one way and came out another." His head hung. When he looked at her again his composure had returned but his face still showed high color. "But when they figure out how to get Johnny back, I can go visit. I can see them again. Family is the most important thing. You're nothing without family."

She saw his eyes round. Had he just recalled that she no longer had family? What was most important in his life was nonexistent in hers.

"Sorry," he muttered.

"It's okay. You're lucky to have them."

"I know it. I do anything for them and I miss them." He rocked awkwardly from heel to toe as the silence stretched. Then he said, "You want chow?"

She wanted to talk to him, assure him that she understood his loss and his sorrow, how hard it was to imagine your life one way and then find out it would be another. But his expression had turned hard again. So she only nodded.

He rummaged in his footlocker and then laid out drawstring shorts and another clean T-shirt.

"It'll do for now." He spun and headed for the door. "See you in the kitchen."

She had a quick shower, dressed and headed down the hall. She swam in his clothing but the drawstring kept up the shorts, which were more capri pants on her. He drew out a chair for her at the table and brought her a plate of scrambled eggs and toast. There was peanut butter, jelly and butter all on the table before her. A feast, she thought.

"I cooked the eggs in a separate pan from my bacon."

Thoughtful, she realized. "Thank you."

He sipped his coffee as she enjoyed the breakfast he provided and then thanked him again as he cleared her dishes to the sink.

Johnny arrived, and Bri stiffened at his appearance. He was so big and so fierce looking. It was hard not to flinch around him, hard to keep her face from showing the fear that bubbled inside her.

He slowed as she sat still as a rabbit cornered by a fox and then glanced to Mac.

"Anything?" asked Mac.

Johnny gave a shake of his head and then loaded a plate as if it were a serving platter, heaping on eggs, bacon and toast in a mound that rose like Mount Fuji. Then he signaled to Mac again.

"Her clothes are dirty," he said, as if Johnny had asked some question. "You want to sit?"

Bri tried not to look as frightened as she was and even attempted a welcoming smile but her mouth felt tight and she was sure her eyes were wide as saucers. And somewhere she'd stopped breathing.

Johnny gave her one long look and then shook his head, departing with his plate and no silverware. She blew out a breath and let her shoulders sag. When she glanced to Mac it was to find him frowning.

"He can't help the way he looks."

Guilt flooded through her. She was now certain that Johnny had left because of her cold welcome.

Mac regarded her. "He won't hurt you."

"I believe you. But he's really…"

"Ugly?"

"I was going to say terrifying." She looked to the place Johnny had disappeared. "You said werewolves can kill vampires. Can vampires also kill werewolves?"

"The males can kill anything. Their fangs are poisonous. If they inject enough venom into your bloodstream, it's fatal, that is if they don't suck you dry. The poison is some kind of anticoagulant. Keeps the blood coming."

Bri wrinkled her nose and crossed her arms over herself at the sudden chill that swept through her.

"Mostly they just tear open a vein." Mac cleared the condiments and salt and pepper from the table. She gathered up her coffee mug and followed him to the counter. He took the mug from her. Their fingers brushed. Their eyes met.

"You're cold," he said, his breath just above a whisper. The hushed intimacy of his tone raised her skin to gooseflesh.

"It's cold up here in the mountains."

"I can start a fire. It will take off the chill." He was already in motion.

The efficiency of his fire building impressed her. The smoke billowed outward for a moment and then went straight up the flue. She moved closer, kneeling next to where he squatted and extending her hands as he laid ever larger pieces of wood on the fire.

She glanced up at him and smiled. He didn't smile

back. Instead he stared with an intense focus that made her skin prickle in anticipation.

She found herself wondering again what it would be like to sleep with him. Was she attracted to him because he was so different from any man she'd ever met? She didn't usually go for the warrior type. They were too demanding and too apt to make all the decisions for you. She wanted a partner, not a keeper. She realized with a jolt that she'd never have a partner, because no man could withstand her terrible powers.

"Go ahead, Princess. I can take it."

She startled. How long had she been staring at his mouth? She dropped her gaze and it fell to the white T-shirt that now stretched tight over all that muscle. Her throat went dry, making her words scratchy, as if she had some kind of a cold.

"I don't know what you mean."

"You were thinking about kissing me again. I want you to."

She met his gaze. Considered it. "That's a bad idea. Johnny might come back."

But warrior that he was, he already had his hands on her shoulders, taking what he wanted. He drew her closer slowly. Giving her time to pull back or say no. She should have done either. But she didn't. Instead, she lifted her chin and angled her mouth to accept what he offered. His lips brushed hers in a gentle explora-tion that set off an avalanche of desire surging through her. Her reaction was miles too strong for the simple brushing of lips. She tipped into his arms, falling like a skydiver through space. He caught her up in his arms, holding her, keeping her safe. She opened her mouth. His tongue grazed her teeth. She parted her lips, and his tongue slid against hers, bringing a sweet rush of delight and the taste of strong coffee.

Mac cradled her head as he swept an arm around her, leaning her backward as his chest brushed against hers. An electric storm of desire flashed from the point of contact, tearing through her like a tree struck by lightning. His touch scorched her to the core. A moment later her body tingled and flushed with need.

When her back contacted the rug before the fire, Bri came back to herself. She pushed with both hands. Mac lifted up on strong, muscular arms. He looked down at her, his eyes blazing with need.

"Are you certain I can't hurt you?"

He stretched out beside her. "You're worried about me again, Princess. I could get used to that."

"You're not bulletproof."

"Well, you're wrong there. I *am* bulletproof."

She sat up and he released her. Bri folded her legs, sat and faced him. His smug smile vanished and was replaced by a haunting sadness that tugged down the corners of his mouth and dragged on his handsome features.

He pressed his lips together in a gesture that was more grimace than smile. His eyes measured hers, and she had the feeling he was deciding something important.

"They shot at me. In this form and in my other one."

"Who did?"

"The Marines at the medical facility. Just following orders."

"Why would they shoot at their own man?"

"Testing. No injuries."

"That's not possible."

"I don't believe in impossible any more. Not since I came back from the Sandbox and started sprouting fur."

He rolled to his back beside her and gazed at the ceiling. She tried not to stare at the hard definition of the muscles in his arms and failed. But his words haunted.

"It happened there?" she asked. "In the…"

"Sandbox. Afghanistan." He nodded. "Attacked by an enemy combatant who turned out to be a werewolf. Johnny and I were the only survivors."

She hugged herself tighter, wishing she could go back to the days when she was blissfully unaware of all the monsters that lurked in the dark.

"I'm so sorry." She reached out to touch his arm.

He turned his head to glare at the hand that rested on his. She drew back immediately. This man did not want her pity. That much was clear.

His eyes now looked empty. She stared at this stranger and inched back.

Just a moment ago he'd held her with such tenderness and his kiss had been lush as a rain forest. Where had that man gone?

His mouth quirked in a cavalier smile that turned her cold.

"Why don't you kiss me again?"

"You act as if I can't control myself. I can."

"But you shouldn't. The longer you go, the deadlier you get. After a while you can kill a man without even sleeping with him."

"Is that true?"

He looked deadly serious now as he nodded. "For you, more is better."

Her thoughts went to Jeffery again and the miracle that she had not killed him, too. Even before he grew ill, she had known that sleeping with him was a mistake for many reasons, not the least of which was her mixed feelings. But if she'd had known she was some kind of lethal carrier of energy she never, ever would have slept with him.

Jeffery's sudden, bizarre illness was her fault. She'd nearly killed him.

Bri turned to Mac and held his gaze. "He'll be all right now. Won't he?"

"Should be, if you keep your distance."

If she stayed away from him, he'd recover. The realization that she could never see him again didn't hurt her nearly as much as it should have. Instead her first reaction was relief. Her response surprised her so much she gasped. She had been fond of him, but now she recognized she had never loved him. He'd loved her. She knew it, and she had hoped that would be enough. It wasn't.

His insistence more than her attraction had brought her to his bed. The guilt choked her. She should have known better.

He moved closer, breathing deeply, then gave her a sensual look. The potent mixture of virile male and the edge of danger made her pulse pound. She didn't know if she should step into his arms or run.

"Lucky thing I'm not human. You can't make me sick."

She felt her muscles tighten and her stomach flutter. "I don't think that's lucky. More like tragic."

"You need what I can give you, Princess, and I'll admit I've been without since this happened to me. I miss having a woman."

A woman, as if any woman would do. His words

made her cold and his touch made her hot. For him it was all just filling a need, his and hers.

He placed his hand over hers. She didn't draw back. Her skin began to tingle again. There was no denying the attraction that fired between them. But that was not love, either.

He used his thumb to draw small circles on the sensitive skin on the inside of her wrist.

"I don't have random sex or one-night stands. I've only had two intimate relationships and…" Her eyes flashed to his. He must have seen it, the pain that tore through her, because he opened his arms to her and she fell into them. "I killed Matthew and I put Jeffery in the hospital."

"You didn't know."

She pressed her hands over her face. "It's so terrible. I don't know what to do."

"You'll stay here until they come, and then Johnny and I will kill them. If you need a man in the meantime you take me. Do not go out and find a human. You come to me."

"Yes," she whispered. "I'll come to you."

Mac found Johnny sitting alone on a fallen log five feet off the ground, swinging his legs like a kid playing hooky from school.

"There you are." Mac leaned against the log.

Johnny smelled his nervousness in the sweat that had nothing to do with exertion. He lifted his hands palms up, silently inquiring.

Mac blew out a breath. "I've got to ask a favor. I'm… well, I'm attracted to Bri."

Johnny growled.

"I know, it's just, she's beautiful and I haven't had, well hell, Johnny, neither of us have. But I don't know if it's just that or if it's what she is."

Johnny shrugged his shoulders, unsure what Mac expected him to do about that.

"Can you get close to her, maybe smell her and touch her and see if she does anything for you? I know you don't like her. So if you're attracted it's the vampire in her, not the woman."

Johnny groaned.

"Come on, buddy," Mac urged.

His friend squeezed his eyes shut and then dropped to the ground and cleared the fallen leaves with a bare foot. Then he used a series of twigs to spell out his answer.

"Did that," Mac read.

Johnny collected the sticks and used them again.

"Still…want," Mac read.

Johnny collected and lay out his final three words.

"To…gut…her."

Mac sat back on his haunches. "Really? Well, okay. That's good I guess. But don't. Really, that's an order."

Johnny wanted to say that he didn't like her intrusion. That he wanted her dead and, barring that, he wanted her gone. They killed things like her, didn't they? Instead he nodded his compliance with the order, gave a lazy salute and motioned for them to run.

"Maybe later," said Mac, rubbing his neck and glancing back to the compound where the flesh eater waited. Mac slapped Johnny's arm. "Thanks, buddy."

Johnny loped away. He didn't like having a female in the house. Her scent disturbed him, made him think of all the things he'd lost since the attack, like his mother and his family and his world. He understood that Mac was using her as a lure to draw more vampires, but if she was staying, at least she could be dressed. Johnny had seen her clothes yesterday. They were wrecked, stained, muddy and torn, so his sergeant had given her a T-shirt, a Marine Corps T-shirt. She did not deserve to wear a T-shirt with the Marine emblem, and he determined to do something about that today.

So he left the bounds of his larger prison, crossed into the national forest and ran until he reached the campsite.

There he staked out an RV park. Didn't take long for his recon to find a perfect target. The family had a teen daughter about Brianna's size.

The family of four finished lunch, hamburgers cooked on a gas grill and buns toasted on the charcoal. It smelled great. They ate inside at the large kitchenette, and Johnny wondered why they'd bothered to leave home for the great outdoors. Both junior and the temperamental teen ignored their parents in favor of their electronics throughout the entire meal. Johnny would have given his right paw to see his mom and dad again and to hug his little sister, but these two didn't know what they had. A lump rose in his throat. Someday, maybe. He still held hope that the doctors would figure out why he couldn't change back. It was what had kept him from ending himself. That and Mac.

His squad leader was a ballbuster in-country. But not anymore. Not since the attack. Johnny had changed on the outside, but Mac had changed on the inside.

Mac had a thick head and a warm heart and Mac had stood by him, fought with him and lately fought *for* him getting him out of that cage. It was Mac who understood that in this form, despite the strong urges and the unfamiliar desire to hunt and run, he was the same inside. Sure he was stronger and heard a hell of a lot better, and his sense of smell was outstanding. But he was still John Loc Lam. Back in training, the guys had called him Lock and Load, because of his middle name. He'd heard worse at school in Port Chester, New York, where there weren't a lot of Asian-American kids in the sea of Latinos. But Mac had asked him what his mother had called him. At first Johnny had thought this was just another way to humiliate him, but he'd answered, and from that day forward everyone under the command of Staff Sgt. Travis Toren MacConnelly had called him Johnny or Private Lam. Mac told him later that if anyone was going to bully his men it would be him. End of story.

Johnny stared out from the trees, waiting for Junior to lumber to the car. The girl didn't seem to eat anything and was the thinnest in the group, which was good, because Brianna was a small woman, curvy but small. Of course, most everyone looked small to him now.

It wasn't until the teenager descended from the thirty-three-foot RV that Johnny got a look at her face. Her eyes were ringed in so much dark makeup she looked like a sullen raccoon dressed in black. Steampunk girl, he decided as he watched the family pile into the giant SUV and roll away.

Johnny would have preferred a night raid, but it was as Paul Cummings used to say before the werewolf tore his throat out. He galloped across the open ground, waiting for the screams that didn't come. Somehow an eight-foot werewolf had not been spotted yet. He only needed one hand to tear the door from its hinges, peeling it back like the lid on a can of tuna fish.

He was inside, pawing through drawers and making a pile in the center of the camper. Once he had what he needed he ripped open some of the food containers for show. They had frozen vegetables in neat unopened bags. He added some to the pile, then threw it in a pillowcase and took off.

His exit was not as smooth as his entrance. He nearly ran over a woman wearing boxers and a loose T-shirt who took one look at Johnny, dropped her bundle of neatly tied firewood and screamed like an actress in a slasher movie. Johnny just kept running, and he didn't stop until he got back to base.

When Mac picked up Johnny's scent, he knew he was close. Where had he been all morning? For a few minutes there, Mac feared that Johnny had gone off grounds again. It had been hell to get him the small amount of liberty they now enjoyed. But Johnny still wasn't predictable.

Mac wasn't sure if it was the wolf or post-traumatic stress syndrome. Maybe it was both. God knew, Mac still had nightmares.

Mac admitted to himself that he'd been preoccupied with Bri and turned his gunner down when he'd asked him to run.

Johnny was fast on all fours, but he ran only when Mac was also in wolf form. Now he strode into the yard like a nine-foot shadow monster.

"Where you been?"

Johnny lifted the pink pillowcase and dropped it at Mac's feet.

"What's this?" Mac peered within and scowled. He reached inside and drew out a half-thawed bag of soybeans in the pod and a skimpy pink scrap of silken fabric which now dangled from his index finger. "Johnny! What the hell is this? Holy shit! Did anyone see you take these?" Mac now shook a fist full of brightly colored underwear at him.

Johnny looked away.

"She's not going to wear other women's underwear." He tossed the scraps of silk into the trash.

Mac continued to rummage through the sack. Women's clothing.

"These are good," he said and tossed them into a pile. Next he discovered several small plastic bags of vegetables. All for Brianna, he realized. Johnny had known she had little clothing to wear and little to eat, since both he and Johnny preferred meat, lots of it, and rarer was better. Mac faced his friend and released his anger. "That was a nice thing to do."

Johnny snorted and Mac wondered at his motives. If he didn't do it from kindness, than what?

"How did you know she's a vegetarian?" But he knew the answer the moment he said it because he knew as well. "Smelled it, right? She's sweeter, somehow. Must be the grains." Or the fact that she was irresistible to men.

Johnny nodded.

"If anyone saw you, then we are in deep shit. Did they?"

Johnny shrugged, then motioned his head toward the compound.

"You want to give them to her?" he asked.

Johnny bared his teeth.

"Fine. I'll do it. But don't run off." Mac retreated, stopping briefly in the kitchen to toss six bags of frozen vegetables and one box of veggie burgers into the freezer. Then he returned to the kitchen but heard her down the hall in his room. What was that she was humming? "Werewolves of London," he realized and gave a single sound of mirth. The woman had a sense of humor.

He knocked on the open door, pausing to see her bent over his bed tugging at the sheet. She startled and then straightened as she turned to face him.

"You are so quiet. I never heard you and I hear everything."

"Habit," he said. "What are you doing?"

"Trying to make the bed, but I can't do it like you."

He took in the draped blanket instead of the crisp corners of a tight bunk. Then recalled her bending over and felt his body harden. He lifted the sack. "I've got clothes. Johnny's doing."

She was looking up at him with rapt interest. Her gaze fell to his mouth and his skin burned. He waited and she glanced away. She wasn't ready for what he offered, but she was considering it. He could tell by the pink color of her ears and the sound of her heartbeat, audible to him even from where he stood.

"Johnny and I have to report to headquarters. Stay inside or my command will see you on camera."

"Yes. I'll stay inside. When will you be back?"

"After dark. Eat what you like in the meantime. There's a TV, books and video games, though you don't look like a gamer."

"I'm not. But I do read a great deal."

"Soldier of Fortune?"

Her brow wrinkled, and then she realized he was joking and cast him a dazzling smile. He knew he was outmatched and retreated down the hall.

Back outside he discussed their situation with Johnny. Both agreed that the compound was the most defensible position available. Mac still wanted to keep her appearance secret, and he had no way to explain Johnny's panty raid if that came to light.

Mac made suggestions; Johnny listened, giving his opinion about what to do with their uninvited guest. If more male vampires did follow her, they would have an opportunity to capture one and be heroes. The colonel would see that they were ready to return to combat duty, and that might get them both the hell out of this glorified prison. He was sick of being a fucking lab rat.

Johnny reminded him that they had already captured one.

"I'm not turning her over."

Johnny glared and looked away.

"So I'm leaving you today. You sure?"

Johnny nodded, agreeing to do the training alone so Mac could quit early and watch over Bri. Mac felt pulled in two directions. Because Bri had now become his responsibility.

Chapter 9

The morning at the medical center stretched to afternoon before Mac and Johnny were finally dismissed. Mac paused some distance from their quarters as he smelled lilies where there were none. There were deeper fragrances, cinnamon, soap and the alluring scent of a female's most secret places. He growled at the unwelcome flash of desire as his body reacted before his mind could even process what was happening.

"You scent her?" asked Mac.

His comrade nodded his head. He looked glum after spending an afternoon as a living target. Mac had wanted to leave him, and that was exactly why he hadn't. Instead he'd stayed and watched Johnny suffer from the rounds that bounced off his hide like bullets off Superman's chest and worried about Bri, alone in their quarters.

"Me, too. And I kept thinking about those lacy, silky things you stole and how they'd look stretched—"

Johnny sighed and Mac stopped talking. At least *he* could have a woman. Mac glanced from Johnny to the path leading to Bri.

"So if I can scent her and nothing else, I guess she's all right. What do I cook for the vegetarian?"

They reached the courtyard and then the inner chambers that led to their living quarters to find Brianna standing in the kitchen, a glass of water poised at her mouth. Her skin glowed with good health and the turquoise tee and black yoga pants hugged her curves like nobody's business. Part of the wardrobe Johnny had provided her, he realized. She lowered the glass and cast them a tentative smile.

"Welcome back, Mr. MacConnelly. Good evening, Mr. Lam," she said and stopped to glance from one motionless male to the next. "Did I do something wrong?"

Johnny shook his head, but Mac thought he was smiling. Had he changed his mind about having her here?

"I would have cooked something, but I didn't know when to expect you."

Mac and Johnny managed to chase her out of their kitchen and got her parked on a stool when they cooked steaks and fries for them and macaroni and cheese for her. His gunner was grace in motion but clumsy as a cook, so Mac cooked and Johnny set the table and did KP.

Johnny pushed the salt and pepper closer to the second chair Mac had added and placed a paper napkin where Bri could reach it, folding it once. Then quickly drew back his hand. Now Mac stared at Johnny who gave him a casual shrug. He didn't know his gunner knew how to use a napkin, let alone fold one. Johnny sat on a cushion on the ground and still reached the surface of their table. Mac slid two large steaks onto Johnny's plate and then heaped on the French fries before making himself a similar plate.

Brianna took her seat and gave Johnny, seated adjacent to her, an anxious glance before returning her attention to Mac who carried over a bowl of macaroni and cheese for her to eat. Johnny remained motionless as a dog with a biscuit on his nose awaiting the command for release. Mac stood in confusion. He had never seen Johnny wait before a full plate of food. Was he waiting for their guest? He turned back to the stove to retrieve his portion.

Mac sat and stared at Johnny, who glanced at Brianna.

"This looks delicious." She lifted her fork, grimaced and took the tiniest of bites, then winced.

"Something wrong with the grub?" asked Mac.

She startled and then poked at her pasta, making a show of taking a bite. "No, they're delicious." Her smile faded and she lay aside her fork. "I don't have much of an appetite. I feel a little sick to my stomach."

Mac looked at the metal fork and the aluminum bowl. Was that making her sick?

He took her portion and returned a moment later with a fresh helping on a paper plate. He offered her a plastic fork. She tried them and smiled.

"These taste so much better."

"It's the metal."

She nodded. "Yes. I didn't want to be a bother."

An elephant trumpeting in the room would be less disruptive than having her seated at their table, but he managed a smile. His reward and punishment was that she reached out and squeezed his hand, right there beside his fork. The buzz of sexual energy started in his ears and plunged downward to the usual places. He glanced at Johnny who just gaped at him from over the forkful of meat he'd been about to swallow whole.

"Thank you for helping me," she said.

Oh, he would have liked to do a lot more than help. He managed a civil response. "No problem."

"But I need to get back to my life."

Johnny's fork paused again and he turned from Mac to her and then back to Mac. Did Johnny want him to cut her loose? He felt the tug of uncertainty as he realized he wasn't letting her go regardless of what Johnny wanted and then felt the familiar kick of guilt, low and sharp in his gut. He lifted his brow at Johnny who looked up and to the left as he lifted his tufted brows. Johnny was deferring to him, thank God. Mac looked back to Bri's lovely upturned face.

"You're on their list now, Princess. They know your name and where you live."

She tried to keep her chin up but he noticed a slight tremor there. "I won't go home."

"Or the hospital."

Bri slumped. "But what about Jeffery?"

"That life is over, sweetheart. Gone for good and all."

Mac found himself curious about a man who could keep the likes of Bri without gaining her love, for truthfully, that was just what he wanted. Sex. No strings. That was the perfect relationship. Besides, you didn't bring a vampire home to meet the folks.

"Will they hurt him?" she asked.

"Doubtful. He doesn't know where you are, so they have no business with him. They might stake out the hospital. Hoping you'll turn up. You aren't going to."

Johnny resumed eating like a teenager anxious to get away from his arguing parents.

"Right now the authorities are searching for you. Eventually you'll be added to a list, one of many young women who've vanished and were never found."

She blinked at him and for a moment neither spoke.

"I don't want to disappear," she finally said.

"You don't have much choice. The vampires are searching. And they won't give up. You either join them or you run and hide. There's no middle ground. The males are stronger and faster, and so the females do what they say. As far as we know, none of the female soul…" His words dropped off, but she knew he was about to say *soul suckers*. "What did you call them?"

"Leanan Sidhe. But those are fairies. Full fairies like my mom is supposed to be. I'm half human."

"Maybe all the others are half human, too. Maybe all vampires are descended from fairies."

"From Leanan Sidhe, you mean. Most fairies can't kill people. Except for the Banshee, of course."

He stilled, his gaze flicking to Johnny who lowered his fork to his empty plate and shrugged.

Mac returned his focus to Brianna. "What the hell is a Band-She?"

"It's a fairy that kills by touch. To the heart for death. To the head for madness. It's just folklore. One of the stories my nana told me. A way to explain mental illness, I suppose."

"Or those fucking things are real, too."

Johnny threw up his arms.

"What?"

He spelled out the curse word Mac had used.

"Oh for Christ's…" He met Johnny's scowl and let his words trail off. "What? I can't swear now?"

Johnny inclined his head toward Brianna. Apparently Johnny didn't swear in front of ladies, even ones with powers that could shrivel a man's heart like a prune.

"Well I never heard of those things, but I suppose werewolves can kill them, too."

She drew in a breath and looked at him as if he were her knight in shining armor. Mac held her gaze, wanting that to be the case so much that it hurt.

"How?" she whispered.

"By hunting and killing them, like we hunted ECs."

"I don't understand." she said.

"Enemy combatants."

She didn't raise any objections. Seemed killing farm animals and killing vampires did not fall into the same class for her, which was fine with Mac. He could hear her blood thumping through her veins as she sat perfectly still. Bri lifted a hand to her throat and spoke in a whisper. "Go on."

"Bullets don't kill vampires because they heal too damned fast. If you get lucky and hit one, the holes just heal up. You can spike them with silver, but the minute that silver is removed, zip-zap, they're whole again. Decapitation works, if you use a silver sword and you are damned quick. But if a werewolf tears out their throat or rips open a major artery, it doesn't heal and they bleed out."

"I think iron is more damaging than silver," she said. "It bothers me much more."

Why would she tell him her weakness? Unless it was because it was also the weakness of her enemies. Was she beginning to trust him? He hoped so.

"That's helpful, thanks."

She cast him a wary smile and then glanced to Johnny whose fixed stare was often unnerving.

"So that's what you and Johnny do? You are training to kill vampires?" She was clutching her throat as she waited for the answer.

Johnny held her gaze and nodded.

"That's terrible."

"You'd rather have them out there assassinating world leaders? Because they're killers, Bri. Drink blood, collect millions and kill human targets."

"But they can't come out in the daylight."

He shook his head. "Myth. Most of the stuff out there is wrong. Except the silver part. It's not the cross that deters, its the silver, and if you have a gold crucifix you are shit out of luck. They tolerate gold, I think." He waited for confirmation.

She nodded. "Pure gold, yes."

"Holy water doesn't work. Same for wooden spikes, sunshine, holy ground and coffins. And they don't need to travel with dirt. That's just weird. They mostly go out at night because they are butt-ugly and they can see so much better than humans in the dark."

She shivered, recalling the one she had seen. "That makes a lot of sense. But they have white eyes, like a blind man."

"And purplish skin mostly. It is pinkish after they feed."

Bri pushed her cold meal about with her plastic fork. Finally she lifted her head to meet Mac's stare.

"I don't want to endanger either of you. This is *my* problem."

Mac grinned and met Johnny's eye. "We're Marines, Vittori. Problems are what we do."

"I don't want you to have to face those things because of me."

"That's not up to you. You might not understand

this, Princess. Marines don't just kill things. We protect things. Roads. Towns, positions. Lines in the damned sand. Convoys, cities, countries and people. And as of today, we also protect one female vampire."

"I've never needed protecting before."

"You've been protected your entire life. Otherwise you wouldn't be here."

Her face went pale as that arrow struck home.

"You needed it then and you sure as hell need it now."

Her eyes glittered with tears. "My nana was human and she knew, and *still* she kept me safe."

"She loved you."

Bri nodded, the tears slipping in silver trails down her pale cheeks.

Johnny started signing. Bri watched and Mac put the letters together.

"What is he saying?"

"He's reminding me that you're one of them. But I'll protect her as long as I can." This last part he directed at Johnny who then glared at Bri. Did he have to protect her from Johnny as well? He didn't want to have to choose.

That night Mac and Johnny ran as usual, only they had a purpose—search for sign of intrusion by male vampires. Mac's needs had changed when he had. He needed more food and less sleep, and he needed to run. That was one of the reasons he had to get Johnny out of lockup at the medical facility. He worried that his gunner's trip off grounds yesterday was going to bite them both in their big hairy asses.

After the moon rose they returned to the compound where he could hear Bri's breathing. He took first watch and Johnny relieved him three hours later.

It was a quiet night, except for his thoughts, which kept creeping down the hallway to his bedroom where Bri slept alone. He woke the instant she rose from his bed, hearing her breathing change and the whisper of sheets as she slipped to the floor and crossed on bare feet to the bathroom that had been installed for him. A moment later the shower spray began.

He imagined her bright red hair, now wet and turning a deep shade of auburn while a mass of ringlets danced about her head. Her face would be covered with beaded droplets that would run down her bare shoulder in rivulets. He released his breath into the sofa pillow and crept into his room, moving silently to the bed where he leaned down and inhaled her scent on the sheets. The shower ceased and Mac retreated out of doors to find Johnny sitting watch.

"You still okay with this?"

Johnny gave a reluctant sigh and then a slow nod. Not enthusiastic but he'd take it.

"Thanks, Lam. I want you to know that I still have your back. Nothing has changed there."

His gunner gave his shoulder a quick squeeze then headed inside. They had breakfast before Bri arrived.

"Do you think she'll eat oatmeal?" asked Mac.

Johnny shrugged and Mac heated the water. He added raisins and had the gooey mess ready when she appeared, scrubbed and dressed in tight jeans and a tighter T-shirt. Mac gawked and then glared at Johnny, who grimaced and then covered his eyes.

"Good morning," she piped.

Her hair was indeed a deep auburn when wet, just as he had imagined. But her skin was now glowing pink and fresh as dew.

"I made oatmeal," he said, extending a bowl.

"I love oatmeal." She grinned as she accepted it and paused there, staring up at him as her smile faded and the buzz of sexual energy began again between them.

Mac needed her to get away from him, because he was contemplating marching her back down the hall to that bed. Instead he cleared his throat. "Sugar's on the table."

Mac's phone roared like a Harley motorcycle. It was the ring tone he'd chosen for his commanding officer, Colonel Lewis, and both Johnny and Mac jumped every time they heard it.

Lewis had been in charge of his squad in Afghanistan. The colonel had surprised Mac by leaving his combat assignment to follow him and Johnny to the Marine Mountain Training Center. It showed the kind of concern for his men that Mac had stopped expecting from rear-echelon motherfuckers. Johnny still didn't like Lewis, but he never said why. Just the mention of Lewis made Johnny's hackles lift.

Mac took the call and the order for him to report ASAP.

Mac hesitated before leaving Brianna with Johnny. But he couldn't bring her with him, and they both knew he had to report.

"You'll be all right?" he asked Johnny.

His gunner took his sweet time nodding his acceptance of his new position as babysitter and showed his fangs as a measure of his displeasure.

"Thanks," said Mac.

Mac again felt that pull to be in two places at once, and Bri's assurance that she would be fine did nothing to relieve his mind.

He left Bri reluctantly, lingering for one long look and to give final instructions to stay inside to keep her from revealing herself to the newly repaired Marine Corp surveillance cameras and to trust Johnny if anything happened. All the way to the facility he second-guessed his decision to leave her. Damn, he knew this would blow up in their faces. Only question was when.

At HQ, he reported to his commander's office and to his assistant, who pressed the intercom button at his appearance. He paced, but that made his agitation too obvious. So obvious even an officer might notice it so he stopped, fixing his feet to the floor as if glued there.

Mac didn't like the uncertainty swimming around in his belly like a hungry shark. He knew it was his duty to tell the colonel about Bri. But he knew what would happen if they found her. The possibilities kept him mute. When had he started picking and choosing which orders to take?

Colonel Lewis's assistant opened the door and then stepped aside. Mac removed his hat and entered. He stood at attention, holding is salute.

"Staff Sergeant MacConnelly, sir," announced the colonel's aide.

Lewis stood behind Captain Steward, staring at the computer monitor over the computer tech's shoulder. He glanced up at Mac, frowned and snapped a quick salute. Mac dropped his arm to his side before the colonel's index finger had left his forehead.

Lewis stared at Mac. "You want to tell me anything?"

Mac swallowed but remained at attention, feeling his weight on the balls of his feet as he resisted the urge to change into his wolf form. When unsure, Mac generally feigned ignorance. He held his blank expression, perfected in basic training.

"Sir?"

The colonel didn't know about her. He couldn't. Could he? Still Mac felt the sweat break out on his forehead. If anything happened to Johnny because of this, Mac would never forgive himself.

Lewis spoke to the captain but kept his gaze directly on Mac. "Run it again, Steward."

Captain Steward clicked away at the computer keyboard. The man sat erect with a serious expression that gave the impression of disapproval. He glanced at Mac then back to the screen. Was this about Johnny going off base?

Mac stood motionless until the colonel waved him forward. Mac had the feeling he didn't want to see what was on that screen. Colonel Lewis pointed at the monitor and Mac followed the direction he indicated.

"Our camera caught this on Sunday at zero six thirty. Can you tell me what it is?"

Mac's skin began to crawl as he stared at the blurry, frozen image on the monitor. The shape was unrecognizable.

"I'm increasing the resolution and slowing it down as much as possible," said Steward.

The colonel barked at Steward, "Run it again."

Steward's movements were as crisp and mechanical as any Marine's. He didn't look at Mac as he set to work. Mac's stomach dropped as he saw the image was from the back of his compound. Something swept up the wall, something wispy and white. It showed for an instant and then shot up toward the rooftop and out of frame. The captain clicked a few keys, and a still image of the effusion filled the screen. Mac knew what it was. It was Brianna leaving the compound the first time she'd seen Johnny. She'd moved too fast for him to see, but not too fast for the camera, apparently. Johnny had missed one. Mac calculated the angle and realized the camera was in the woods, pointed at his bedroom window. *Son of a bitch.* His jaw tightened. The surveillance was not for them, but also *of* them.

"You want to tell me what the hell this is?" The colonel pointed at the screen.

Mac moved closer, checked the time stamp to confirm his suspicion and shook his head. "It looks like wood smoke."

"Smoke can't change direction," said Steward, never taking his eyes from the screen. "This thing is moving so fast the naked eye wouldn't see it."

Lewis lifted his busy eyebrows at Mac. "Steward here thinks you're hiding something."

The shark in Mac's stomach swirled in a circle and took a bite of the lining of his stomach. They might be searching the compound right now. No, they weren't. Johnny wouldn't let them in. He knew that, but still his pulse raced.

"He thinks Johnny knocked out those cameras on purpose."

Mac glanced at the captain, who narrowed his gaze. Then he cleared his throat. "If he were hiding something, sir, I'd know."

That much was true.

The corner of the colonel's mouth ticked upward for an instant. He held Mac's stare long enough to make him uncomfortable.

"I told him you are a good soldier and you follow orders. I vouched for you, son. I've given you a lot of lee-way with Corporal Lam. That kind of special treatment comes with strings. I thought you understood that."

Mac's hands began to sweat. He gripped them into fists.

"But Steward here thinks that Johnny can understand things. He thinks he saw him writing something in the dirt. You see anything like that, Sergeant?"

"No, Colonel, sir." His throat went dry.

"We'd want to know if Johnny is showing signs that he remembers who and what he was. You got that, Mac-Connelly?"

"Sir, yes, sir."

"You see anything, you tell me ASAP. That's an order."

"He wouldn't be able to see this, Colonel," said Steward, eyes still glued to the screen.

"That would explain why the sergeant didn't report anything," Lewis said to the captain, but then added. "Doesn't explain the cameras though." He rubbed his prominent jaw and exhaled through his broken nose. "Maybe we need to bring you two in. Our intel suggests that vampires can fly. If those vamps are hunting you, you'll need backup."

"Sir, request permission to remain in our compound, sir."

Lewis pressed his lips into a thin line. "I don't want you hurt, Mac. And I don't want Johnny hurt any worse than he already is. I feel responsible for you both."

Mac understood that feeling and the weight of duty that he lifted each morning where Johnny was concerned.

"Yes, sir. We appreciate it."

Lewis gave him a winning smile. "You do, but as for Johnny, he still growls if I get too close to him."

"He doesn't mean anything by that, sir." Mac needed to speak to Johnny about that, but not near the compound. Too many eyes there. Did they have microphones, too? He recalled his conversations with Brianna this morning and his stomach heaved.

"I expect you two will be fighting vamps in the future. But sometimes the enemy comes to you. You did well against those two, Mac. But it was even odds, and they might have been scouts."

"If there were more, sir, we'd scent them. They can't just sneak in and out of our territory."

"Who the hell knows what they'd do? They are fast, smart and unlikely to come at you head-on. They have a better chance of killing you if you don't see them coming."

"Those two didn't take us, sir." But one nearly had. It was only Bri's warning that told him which way the attack had come. "I haven't seen any evidence of any more bloodsuckers. No scent, no trace. Nothing, sir."

"All right. But eyes open and stay alert. You catch their scent and you haul ass here. You got that?"

"Yes, sir."

"Good. Now report to the lab for testing."

He wanted to go check on Bri and tell Johnny what had happened. Instead he saluted and was dismissed.

They'd caught Bri on video. Maybe the colonel was better equipped to protect her, but then who would protect her from the colonel? Not only that, who would protect the colonel from *her?*

Mac spun and crossed to the exit in two long strides, then looked back at Lewis.

The colonel was still human. Being around Bri might kill him, and if she learned how to use her gifts she could make him dance like an organ grinder's monkey.

But that was not why Mac was keeping his mouth shut. Not for Lewis and not for Johnny. It was that damned kiss. She'd turned him inside out. God damn, he was defying orders.

Mac made it to the door and had his hand on the knob when the colonel called him back.

"Oh, and Mac, remember, Johnny is only out on a trial basis. If I find out he's screwing up he's back in lockdown."

Mac thought of the woman's clothing Johnny had mustered and flinched.

"Yes, sir."

Chapter 10

After three nights here, Bri still jumped at every unfamiliar sound. During the long, lonely afternoons, when Mac was away, Johnny guarded the compound but stayed out of doors, so it wasn't clear to Bri if he was keeping intruders out or her in. Possibly he was just avoiding her. Today, she was more nervous than usual because both Mac and Johnny were gone and all she had for protection was a radio.

She stayed clear of the windows, because Mac said cameras could detect changes in light even though the blinds were drawn. She listened to the rain hit the glass and wondered if it was changing to snow. He'd left on the TV but she was afraid to change the channel and afraid to add wood to the fire. What if the cameras saw smoke from the chimney hours after Mac and Johnny had gone?

When she heard the truck engine, she hid in the bedroom, as Mac had instructed. Finally, she heard him calling for her to come out. She darted from the room but her smile died as she saw him, supporting the eight-foot werewolf who wobbled on legs that seemed unable to support him.

"What happened?" she cried, rushing forward and taking a position flanking Johnny's opposite side without even thinking what she was doing.

"Don't know yet." Mac steered them to the futon in the living room. They almost made it when Johnny groaned and collapsed, taking Bri with him to the ground. She landed under Johnny's massive arm with her chest and head on the futon. That thick pad kept her from any serious injury. But according to Mac, she could heal from all such injuries anyway.

Mac lifted Johnny's inert arm and together the rolled his big body onto the mattress.

"Is he hurt?"

"Drugged. Has to be oral, since they can't get a needle into him. They just snap off."

"Gas would work, or what about his gums? They could inject him there."

He stared at her a minute and then drew back the loose skin of Johnny's upper lip, revealing his fangs and the black gums that matched his skin. Sure enough, there was an abrasion and a small circular bruise around the needle puncture. Someone had done a sloppy job because Johnny's tongue had been lacerated, as if someone had sliced through it with a knife. It was a nasty gash, deep and raw. "Probably used a pole because he won't sit still for doctors or medical techs, and he hates the veterinarians."

"Veterinarians? You can't be serious. He's a soldier, not an animal."

"When you arrived you thought those were the same things."

"Well, I've reconsidered. I never really met an enlisted man before. I thought people who joined up were underprivileged or…" She let her words trail off.

"Or what?"

She looked uncomfortable but she spit it out. "Delusional."

"And now?"

"Well, it's not a job I'd want. But you two aren't what I expected."

That made Mac give a harsh laugh. "I'd imagine not."

She studied Johnny, who was sprawled on the mattress, his head lolling and his eyes rolling back in his head. He looked dead, Mac realized, and he immediately checked Johnny's breathing to find it shallow but easy to discern.

"I think they used him for target practice again."

"Let's make him more comfortable." Bri headed for the kitchen and returned with a moistened dish towel. Then she brought it back and tried to bathe Johnny's face.

Mac held her back. "Wait over there," he said motioning to the far side of the room. "He can be hard to control when he comes out of anesthesia."

She stared up at him, and he thought she might turn tail, but instead she just handed over the cloth and moved where he indicated.

Mac washed the blood from Johnny's snout and then laid the folded towel over his open eyes. A few minutes later, Johnny started to growl. Mac stood between Johnny and Bri. Next his friend roared and bolted to his feet, running blindly into a wall and then scrambling up.

Mac usually met Johnny in his wolf form, but he hadn't wanted Bri to see him for what he now was. Now he recognized his mistake, because his gunner had the advantage of size.

He inhaled, caught the scent of a vampire, turned to Bri and charged.

Johnny barreled toward her, teeth snapping, blood dripping from his jaws as the wound on his tongue broke open again. Mac met Johnny's charge. Together they tumbled and hit the opposite wall.

Johnny rolled from his grip. Mac's heart stopped and an instant later a pulsing burst of fear flooded through his veins. If he bit her, she'd turn or she'd die. Mac called the change, allowing the fury to fill him, take him. As the pain tore through him, the fear beat in his heart. What if during that split-second transformation, Johnny got a hold of Bri?

Johnny wobbled, unsteady as he charged Bri and Mac leaped, catching Johnny before he reached her. She stood frozen in terror. Mac knew he'd never forget the horror etched on her face. As he carried Johnny to the ground, Mac noticed a vibration about her, as if she stood in her own private earthquake. For a moment he thought it a trick of the light, but in the next instant she vanished.

"No," Mac said but the word came out as a roar. But she was gone.

Mac and Johnny crashed to the floor. He held Johnny down as his gunner dropped his head back and groaned. Mac held on as Johnny went slack, coming to his senses Mac hoped.

If Johnny had hurt Bri, Mac didn't know what he would have done. One more mistake to live with. One more responsibility to hold in his heart. Johnny struggled, but Mac held on, waiting for him to come to his right mind. This was the drug, not Johnny.

He knew when Johnny was back, because of the regret he saw shining in his friend's clear yellow eyes.

Mac swung his gaze from his gunner and scanned the room, roaring. Where was she? He couldn't call out to her, not in this form. Was she outside again? Was she on camera right now?

Mac rolled to his feet. Johnny followed, looking about and then made a whining sound that Mac had never heard before. He ran to the window, but when he tried for the kitchen, Mac strong-armed him. He wasn't 100 percent sure that Johnny was back from the sedation and damned if he'd let him near Bri until he was certain.

Johnny scented the air and a moment later crawled out the kitchen window. Mac followed. If she'd gone this way they'd have caught her on the surveillance cameras. He glanced up, noting that the cameras were now housed in a protective cage. It seemed the colonel didn't want any more "windstorms" causing breaks in their surveillance.

They made it to the exterior wall, where her scent trail went straight up. Neither could follow it, so they headed toward the compound exit at a run and ran through the gate as the colonel's jeep arrived.

He couldn't have seen the footage so fast. Could he?

Lewis swung from his seat and marched toward Mac, his tight jaw a ready indicator that they were about to get their butts handed to them.

Lewis aimed a finger at Mac. "Change back, now, Sergeant!"

Mac retreated to the compound with Johnny at his heels. Mac returned less than a minute later, hastily tucking in his shirt while Johnny hung back.

"You said you'd watch him," snapped the colonel.

"Sir?"

The colonel barked at his driver, who hustled around

the jeep, jogging as he booted up a laptop, which he offered to the colonel.

"You do it," he growled, and then to Mac, "Look
at this."

The driver set the laptop on the hood of the jeep.
Mac watched the blurry image that he thought might
be Bri. But then he recognized Johnny running for the
woods on all fours, a pink pillowcase clutched in his
jaws. He actually breathed a sigh of relief until he met
the colonel's narrowing gaze.

"Damn clusterfuck. It's already on YouTube. Calling it a Bigfoot sighting!"

Mac glanced at the screen, saw an RV flash by and
understood. It was the panty raid he'd gone on for Bri.

"You want to tell me what you are doing while Corporal Fido is stealing…" He looked to his driver who
began to rifle off a list ending with "six thongs of various colors and four bags of frozen vegetables."

The colonel removed his hat. Rubbed the bristle on
his head and then jerked his hat back in place.

"If you can't keep him in bounds, he goes back with
us."

"Yes, sir. It won't happen again, sir."

"Your ass if it does."

Mac watched the colonel stride angrily away, forcing his driver to jog back to the driver's side to keep
pace. Once inside Lewis banged the top of the vehicle
with his open hand as a signal to start, and the jeep
lurched away.

Mac scraped his knuckles over the bristle on his jaw
and turned in a full circle. The colonel hadn't seen Bri's
exit. Or at least he hadn't seen it *yet*. The home movie
had been taken several days ago but apparently just hit

the internet or just reached the Colonel's attention. As for the surveillance, Lewis appeared to be about twenty-four hours behind. That gave Mac a few hours to move Bri. But first he had to find her.

Mac felt his world collapsing around him, and all he could think to do was run. He knew it was a mistake to take her in. Because of her, they might lose everything.

Mac turned to discover Johnny already searching for a scent trail. He followed, letting Johnny track, staying in his human form, telling himself it was so he could communicate with Bri. The colonel hadn't yet seen Bri's latest on-screen appearance. What would happen when he did?

Together they raced through the pines, jumping over gullies and dashing up inclines. All the while Bri's scent trail grew stronger. Mac told Johnny that he wanted to move Bri somewhere beyond the surveillance.

A few minutes later Johnny stilled, sighted her first. She sat on a large gray boulder, knees drawn to her chest, forehead on her knees. She was as still as the rock that grounded her. The breeze ruffled her hair and the sleeve of her pink T-shirt.

Johnny pointed.

"Yeah. I see her." He cast his friend a long look. "You coming?"

Johnny shook his head and looked at the ground.

"It wasn't your fault. You were drugged. You'd never hurt her if you weren't coming out of that stuff they gave you."

Johnny looked away. They both knew that he had tried to hurt her the night they'd found her and that he wasn't pleased at Mac's decision to protect her. Mac rubbed his neck.

"Nothing happened. She's fine."

Johnny pointed and then pretended to wipe his eyes. Mac looked at her again and had to agree with Johnny. She didn't look fine. She looked like she was crying.

"Shit," he breathed, his insides already rigging up as he prepared to face this woman in tears. Mac drew a long breath. "Well, what should I do with her? Can't bring her back to our compound. Can't turn her over." Mac raked a hand over his hair. "Shit."

Johnny scratched something in the dirt. Mac tried to read it, but the ground was uneven and Johnny's hand-writing sucked.

"What's My Bacc?"

Johnny tried again.

"My *Place?* You have a place?"

He nodded.

"Where?"

Johnny pointed.

"Cameras?"

Johnny said no.

"All right. We'll move her location. Too much surveillance here anyway. You lead the way. I'll follow your trail."

Mac left Johnny and stepped from cover. If she heard him she gave no sign, just sat dejected with her head bowed and her shoulders hunched. He stood beneath the rock, looking up at her. He could have jumped but he didn't want to startle her.

"Bri?"

She tightened her arms about her knees. He waited and after a few more moments she lifted her head.

Mac's stomach squeezed at the sight of her tear-streaked cheeks and red-rimmed eyes.

"I'm sorry we scared you. Johnny's sorry, too. He didn't know what he was doing."

She unfolded her arms and then she pushed off from her stone island and landed beside him. He didn't think, just enfolded her in his arms. She buried her face against his chest.

"He'd never hurt you."

She nodded her understanding then met his gaze. "What about you?"

"He can't hurt me. I'm already bit, already a wolf." He looked away. "I'm sorry you had to see that."

"What I saw was you protecting me from Johnny. But it wouldn't have happened if I wasn't here. My presence is making it hard for you to care for Johnny."

He couldn't deny it. His life had become infinitely more difficult since her arrival, but he knew that she was also the first good thing to come his way since returning from deployment.

"Maybe he needs your full attention."

"You want to leave?"

"No. But I can't stay hidden in your bedroom forever."

"If you go back to Sacramento, the vamps will catch you."

"I'm not going back. I'll just do what my nana taught me. I'll keep moving. I'll stay away from people."

"That won't work anymore. They are hunting you now and they will find you. If they take you, you'll be their prisoner, underground for years while they use you, brainwash you until you'll do anything they tell you. Your only hope is that *when* they find you, Johnny and I are there."

He guided her back the way they had come using a hand behind her back as he tucked her against his side. She felt natural there, as if that was exactly where she belonged. *Don't get used to it,* he warned himself. He couldn't have her. If he tried, the flesh eaters would just keep coming, tracking her for her entire lifetime or until they killed him.

But he didn't want to let her go. Even if it risked his neck and Johnny's. He wouldn't. But then he thought what choosing her would really mean, and his breath stopped. He couldn't bring her home to meet the folks. She couldn't go out on a double date with his high school buddies. Bringing her into their lives would be like bringing the plague. To choose Brianna was to give up every human connection he had. To protect her and to protect his loved ones, he'd have to choose: Bri or his family.

His breath left him in a whoosh, as if he'd been sucker punched, for in fact, he had.

Was any woman worth that? No. She wasn't. He had to figure out how to protect her and then teach her to protect herself. And then he'd need to let her go.

"You shouldn't have to risk your lives for me."

"Marines are used to risking their lives." He didn't want her to know how important she was becoming. Didn't want to admit it to himself. So he retreated. "Besides, it's not for you. My colonel wants to catch a vamp. You're the bait."

She paused and stiffened. He watched the hurt break across her face.

"I see."

He wished he'd told her the truth. That he wanted her safe and happy, but most of all he wanted her here with him. He thought of his parents and felt guilty for his need for this woman.

She moved away and he let her stray a few steps before pursuing her. He wished he could lift that sadness that hung on her like a cloak.

"What now?" she asked.

"My commander saw you on surveillance cameras a few days ago."

Her hands shot to her cheeks and her face went pale so fast, Mac grabbed her elbow to steady her.

"Just a wisp of smoke. But he's suspicious. And there is a good chance they caught your exit today."

"Oh, no!" She wrung her hands and glanced about as if expecting tanks to come barreling through the forest at them. She started to vibrate again, and he saw the distortion of light that had preceded her last disappearance. He grabbed her arm and held on.

"Wait. Don't run."

She looked back at him, her green eyes huge and round but she nodded and the vibrations ceased.

"Listen now. There are more cameras up. We can't go back there. But Johnny says he has a place where you can hide. We're going there now." Mac followed Johnny's scent trail, catching a glimpse or two of him. Johnny had kept just ahead of them and out of Bri's sight.

Mac and Bri walked together in the quiet woods. When he was with her, it was hard to remember that this was a training facility. That just a few miles away from them, men were crawling under barbed wire and practicing various assaults.

Chapter 11

It was twilight by the time they came to Johnny's place, as he had called it. Mac recognized it as a supply drop used in winter maneuvers. Now, in early April, it was all but abandoned and as far as Mac could tell from his recon there were no cameras in the vicinity. Johnny had torn off the lock and gathered supplies, much of the supplies that the colonel insisted that Johnny had been stealing from various outfits and of which Mac had denied having any knowledge. Johnny had sleeping bags and blankets and mattresses and crates of food padded with more mattresses to make a raised seating area. His gunner had made his own man cave. *Or wolf cave,* Mac thought.

"It's nice in here," said Bri. Then she turned to the woods. "Thank you, Johnny."

He must have heard her, but he did not appear. Mac and Bri moved outside. Bri sat on a crate while Mac got a fire started in the fire pit before venturing into the woods to find Johnny, but his gunner could not be convinced to join them. He indicated he wanted to run. Mac warned him to stay in bounds this time, and he nodded his understanding before departing at a lope.

Mac returned to find Bri warming her hands. The evening air held a chill as the temperature began to dip with the approaching night. Bri untied the hoodie from her waist and slipped into the tight-fitting sweatshirt as he rummaged through the crates for MREs, meals ready to eat, choosing the mac and cheese for her because it was vegetarian and not as terrible as some of the others. For himself, he chose the beef stew, which was pretty bad, but he was hungry enough that it wouldn't matter. He heated them in a pail of water from the stream, keeping the little packets sealed as the water came to a rolling boil.

Bri divided her time between watching him work and watching the woods. "What if they come when you aren't here?"

The vampires or the Marines? he wanted to ask. But instead he told her that he'd get the radio but he feared that he'd never get back here before they took her. She seemed to know it as well, for she held his gaze for a long moment and then nodded, flicking her gaze to the fire.

"I can run. I outran them once." She glanced to him. "You really think you can stop them?"

"Bloodsuckers? Already did. Do it again, with pleasure."

"Then what?"

He met her gaze. "Then I catch them if I can and kill them if I can't."

"After that?"

"I'm going to teach you to defend yourself. Teach you how to kill them."

She hugged her knees tighter and glanced away. "I'm not a killer. I might run, but I don't think—"

"You'd be defending yourself. There is no moral dilemma."

"Maybe not for you."

"You'd rather be captured?"

She rested her chin on her folded arms. "I'd rather be human and still unaware that monsters are real."

"That's not going to happen for either of us."

She met his gaze. "Yes. I know. But even if I do survive this, I will never be free." She watched the sky now. Did she see the stars beginning to twinkle to life, visible as the daylight released the earth to darkness? "It's strange to have your whole life seem like one thing, and then it tips on its axis and you get a new perspective, and you realize it was something altogether different all the time. I thought I was helping people. I thought I was a good person. I thought my nana was just very stern and the fairy tales were just stories. But I'm not good and she wasn't cold and it's all real. I'm like Typhoid Mary. Everyone I touch gets sick."

He moved closer, forcing her to shove over on the crate.

"Not everyone."

"What will Jeffery think when I just disappear?"

"He'll look for you, I suppose. But he'll get better and he'll move on. There's no other way, Bri."

She blew out another breath. "He's a chemical engineer and has been working on some big research project. They've been stuck for months. But the team he's heading just had some big breakthrough. He was so happy. Management made him their golden boy, and he said I was his lucky charm. But I'm not."

Mac's ears pricked up. Maybe she was. He thought of what she had said about her father: a brilliant musician, famous, wealthy. How often did that happen? What had the website called her—a muse? A suspicion began to form in his mind.

"What did the other one do?"

She stared at him. "What other one? Do you mean Matthew? He was a writer. Mostly freelance for various magazines. He wrote feature stories."

"Did that change when you two met?"

"Yes." She paused and her brow furrowed. "He took out the novel he'd written in college and completely re-wrote it. I read it. It was marvelous. He got an agent, and then two publishers bid on it. It will be published soon." She dropped her head and her shoulders rounded.

"So it's true then."

She stared at him, her face golden now in the fire-light and her hair blazing more brightly than the flames.

"I looked up that fairy name, Leanan Sidhe. It says that they're a fairy muse. That when she chooses a man, she kind of makes his energy burn faster or more brightly. I don't really know which. She is like fuel to his talents, feeding them."

"While killing him."

"The price, yes. The site said that their chosen ones lived brilliant lives, but short ones."

"But I'm not a Leanan Sidhe. My mother was. I'm a soul sucker. Isn't that right?" She lifted her trembling chin.

"Maybe you don't draw energy. Maybe you make a man's life run faster. Make his brain run faster, too."

She shivered at this, and he wrapped an arm around her. "I don't know why you agreed to help me."

"You can't hurt me, Princess. That's what they tell me. It's why we can get up close and personal with bloodsu…vampires."

He realized that he wanted to help her, he *could* help her. She was not like his squad, now planted in Arlington. Bri was alive and in danger. It gave him hope again, because unlike Johnny's issues, she had a problem that he might actually be able to solve. Up until this very minute he never realized how much he needed that hope.

"But Johnny needs you, too," she said.

He let his arm slip from her shoulder and moved to check their meals. She was right about that. And his family—what about them? Was he prepared to drop off the planet for this woman? She was beautiful and alluring, but really she was just a woman.

"It's hot." He tore open one of the packets and offered it to her. "Just wait until it cools and then tip it up, like you would if you were drinking out of a milk carton." He handed her a bottle of water from Johnny's larder and a tube of crackers.

She did as he instructed and for the next few minutes they ate in silence. When they had finished, he burned the containers, watching the plastic twist and shrivel on the logs, writhing like a living thing.

Bri cleared her throat and then spoke. "Do you have a sweetheart, Mac?"

He wondered why she cared. Was she considering his offer? His body twisted like the collapsing plastic on the flames.

"No. Had one. Cut her loose when I signed up. She's engaged now to someone who will stay put."

"I'm sorry."

"My choice."

She nodded. "Have you had contact with your family since…?"

His smile turned to a grimace. "They think I'm still in-country. Made a few video calls. My dad had some trouble with his heart. Seems okay now. But…" He shrugged and then went cold as he thought of what meeting Bri might do to his father's narrowing arteries.

"They must worry."

He rubbed his jaw. "Yeah."

"And you must miss them."

"Well, I can see them online, call them every week, but…" He glanced toward the scent trail that threaded through the dark woods. "I have responsibilities."

"Johnny." She squeezed his hand. "Will you tell them what happened?"

"Can't. Top secret."

She took the hand that rested on his knee. "Then will you tell me how it happened?"

For just a moment he thought that her appearance and the vampires' attack were all just a setup to learn about how he became a werewolf. But then he remembered the intel they got from Israel. The vampires knew how to kill werewolves. But they preferred to run rather than face the chance of dying. That made them as smart as they were ugly.

He poked at the fire with a stick, recalling the night he turned and not wanting to go back to that dark place in his mind.

"Mac, I'm half fairy and I'm some kind of a monster.

Surely if anyone can understand what you are going through, it would be me."

"It's rough," he warned.

She nodded her acceptance of that.

He sat across from her, fixing his gaze on the flames as he traveled back to the Sandbox in his mind and recalling the distress call he'd received from his second Fire Team. Sometime in the remembering he began to speak. He described the mission, to clear the road and perimeter so they could use the route for transport to the combat outpost. The COP had been cut off by heavy engagement, and they were low on everything. They'd pushed their enemy back, but not before the retreating force had littered their escape route with improvised explosive devices. The IEDs and mines were being handled, but in the meantime a new road was going in and the buildings along the way needed to be cleared of the enemy. They could permit no snipers on the rooftops taking shots at their guys.

Staff Sgt. Travis MacConnelly stared through his infrared goggles at the ground before them. The lifting of his forearm and the closing of his fingers signaled his men to halt. No light spilled across the small courtyard inside the enclosure on the moonless night. But he could see everything clearly in green and black. Kabul, Afghanistan, at zero three hundred, and nothing stirred not even the hot wind that deviled them, blowing sand into all their gear. But appearances were deceiving, because his first two Fire Teams were already in position, one clearing the building and one standing by.

Mac waited with the men of the third and final Fire Team for the agreed-upon time. His heart jackhammered in his chest as the silence seemed to collapse in on him. Too damned quiet. His first command since his promotion to staff sergeant, and now the responsibility of all twelve souls in this squad rested with him. They were good Marines, and he was proud of them already.

His watch ticked off the seconds.

At zero two fifty-six his sharpshooters neutralized the watchmen on the roof, and his teams moved in. His first Fire Team used silenced .22s to take out the guards at the front entrance, the only noises their footsteps and the next round being chambered.

His team moved inside the wall. He watched the first team enter the building in tight formation. Now the way was clear for his third team. Their grenadier was a corporal named Lam. Hell of a name for a Marine, but his team respected him, and from what Mac had seen he was more lion than lamb.

His Fire Team leader checked his watch and then glanced to Mac, who nodded. He signaled his men and they ran the distance to the entrance.

Lam was the first man in. By the time Mac cleared the archway, Lam was dropping a body on the foyer. The man's blood made a dark pool against the pale tile floor. The first team had missed him, so he wasn't here when they came through. Mac signaled for them to check the ground level, knowing the first and second team had the higher two floors.

Systematically they searched each room and then hit the corridor still in formation, his men searching for targets as they climbed the narrow stairs. A shooting gallery for anyone above. The quiet was deafening. Where were the gunshots? With three guards so far, there had to be more.

From above them came the first report of gunfire, a spray of bullets and then the shouting of his men. More gunfire and shouts followed. Then high-pitched screaming echoed down the narrow stairs with frantic shouts to pull back. Fire Team One requested backup, and Mac sent them the second team. They could then hear the second team charging up the stairs ahead of them.

An instant later, the howl of agony seemed to vibrate from the walls. Why weren't they firing?

The screaming diminished and then stopped. Lam looked back to Mac, and he gave the order he would live to regret.

"Double time," he yelled, and his men responded, eager to come to the aid of the first two teams.

They reached the west wing and met with silence and an open door. Lam stepped into the room first followed by his team: the rifleman, Towsen; the assistant light machine gunner, Barbari; and the light machine gunner, Gonzalez. They fanned out, backs to the wall, as Mac cleared the door and stepped into the large room. For a moment, he made a perfect target against the opening. Something streaked forward. Robert Townsen, Lam's point man, managed to squeeze the trigger of his M-4 before something tore him off his feet. His scream came a moment later and died in a liquid gurgle.

"Get down," called Gonzales as something clasped his ankle and dragged him off his feet.

Mac swept the room and his heart went cold. Bodies littered the floor like trash bags. His first two Fire Teams, he realized as the bile rose up in his throat. What the hell was going on?

There was something here, something big as a bear. What was this, a half-assed zoo?

A creature ran straight at them on all fours.

"Fire," Mac yelled.

Barbari and Lam both opened up, and they continued firing but the thing kept coming— slashing at Gonzalez and tearing his innards out despite his Kevlar vest and body armor. Then it turned toward him. Lam stepped in front of Mac, swinging his weapon at the beast's head as Mac drew his knife.

That wasn't a bear, he realized, but he'd never seen anything like it. Huge, with massive forearms and claws that still dripped blood from its attack on Gonzales.

"Kill it," shouted Lam, striking the thing in the forehead with the butt of his weapon. Mac raised his knife as Lam was tossed across the room.

Mac aimed for the jugular and sliced across the creature's neck. Nothing happened. No laceration. No blood. The thing stared at him, seeming to grin. Had this one thing killed his first two teams? In that instant, looking into those yellow eyes, he knew that it had.

Mac fired his personal weapon until it was spent, and the monster just stood, as unaffected as a tank being struck by rocks. What the hell was this thing?

Johnny came back, charging the monster like a lineman on Friday night. The creature turned.

"No!" Mac shouted. He couldn't watch another man killed by that animal. Mac moved to intercept Lam, shoving hard, knocking him off balance as he took the hit intended for Johnny. Fangs punctured Mac's shoulder. Top and bottom jaws clamped on to him as the creature tore him from his feet. His weapon clattered to the ground as he lost control of his arm. Pain seared through him, and his stomach heaved. As abruptly as it grabbed him, the monster let go, using its claws to flip him and then toss him. Mac sailed across the room and crashed into a concrete wall. He lost his goggles and with them his sight. Now he was blind in the dark, seeing the world only in short blasts of machine gunfire.

Towsen, he realized. Where was Barbari? Was he alive? Was Lam?

"Fall back," Mac ordered. "Fall back, damn you. Get the hell out of here." The smell of blood filled his nostrils and he slipped on the viscous fluid, unable to regain his footing. "Get out and call it in."

His shouting brought the thing in his direction as he'd intended. It grabbed him again and shook him like a terrier with a snake. Mac's arms flailed, his jaw snapped on his tongue and his vision blurred. It shook so hard Mac thought he'd lose his arm, but instead he'd only lost his humanity. He hadn't understood at the time, but that was the moment when everything had changed.

Mac blinked until he could see the fire again and Bri seated beyond, still and pale as carved ivory.

"I told him to fall back," Mac whispered.

She'd wrapped her arms about herself, though whether from the cold or the horror he could not tell.

"I woke up in a medevac. Johnny was there with me, right beside my stretcher. My memory is bad here, because I remember him telling me to hold on, but he couldn't have, because they said he was in worse shape than I was. I think he was in wolf form before we touched down." Mac pushed the guilt down deep and rubbed his hairline, feeling the raised scars that threaded over his head. "It also tore my scalp. They said it was flapping like a toupee. Collapsed a lung here." He hiked his shirt to show her the puncture mark in his ribs. Mac pointed at the scars as if displaying a road map. "I have these because I was still human. Nothing scars my skin now. It's better than Kevlar."

Bri nodded, having seen the scars before; he was still impressed that she didn't look away.

"They must have hurt."

Not as badly as how much he hurt inside. At the time they were a welcome distraction from his anguish. The pain and the pain pills both gave him the only respite he knew from the haunting memories. When he closed his eyes he still heard those screams. Marines, screaming like animals in a slaughterhouse, for they were.

"They shipped us both stateside. But not to a hospital. They sent us here. When I was allowed out of bed, I went to see Johnny. He was all that was left of the team. They'd already buried the rest." Mac felt the air leave him as he recalled writing a letter to each family.

He pulled a stick from the fire and used it to poke at the dirt until the flaming tip extinguished. Then he threw the stick, watching the glowing ember spiral until it hit with a tiny explosion of sparks.

"They said he was…like he is, because he'd been attacked by two of those things. They knew because of the separate bite marks. The shape of the canines were different."

"There were two?" Bri asked.

He shook his head, not trusting his voice to hold steady. Mac clamped his hand over his mouth as if that could hold back the self-loathing. For just a moment he thought he was going to puke.

He was supposed to protect his men. He was supposed to keep them safe, for Christ's sake. He damned sure wasn't supposed to attack them.

"Mac?"

He dragged his hand from his mouth and held up one finger. "Just the one that attacked us and then me. *I* attacked Johnny. They said the teeth marks matched. Lam did his best to protect me and I turned on my own man. I don't know how many I killed. Which ones. I don't remember. Towsen, probably, and maybe Barbari, too. They wouldn't show me those videos and I didn't ask. But they said nobody else got out. Me and Johnny were the only survivors." Though part of him had died with them. The best part. He kept going to see Johnny through this nightmare. After that...he didn't know.

He wanted to go home to his family. Pretend none of this ever happened, lock it down so deep and so tight that he forgot everything. But he already knew that wouldn't happen because of the nightmares. They just kept coming.

He pressed the heels of both hands into the sockets of his eyes. And then she was there before him, kneeling at his feet, her slim arms slipping about his middle and her soft breasts pressing against him as she held on tight.

"Did you hear me?" he whispered.

"I heard."

"My own men."

"Shhh, now," she cooed.

"You should be running the other way."

"No. I'm staying."

"Might turn on you, too."

"I don't believe that."

"I'm dangerous."

"Yes. And so am I. Maybe that's why we are together."

Mac looked into her eyes and saw understanding. It

drew him in, captured him more surely than any magic spell she might be able to cast over human males. But this was stronger, this bond they shared, this parallel of being different, being dangerous and hurting those you cared about.

"We have that in common," she whispered. "You and I are not human. Before she died, my nana told me she wanted me to hold on to my humanity. I think I understand now what she meant. She wanted me to be like my father, passionate and full of life. But I've been like my mother, attracted to those who have that life instead of generating my own. When I'm with you I feel alive inside, Mac. Sometimes I'm afraid and confused, but always very alive."

He felt that, too, not the mindless infatuation he'd heard described in a briefing of the only known survivor of a female vampire attack. The victim was saved by werewolf bodyguards, who recognized the female before she got too close. Even after he knew what she was, he was ordering off his bodyguards, who ignored him, of course.

Mac's attraction to Brianna was also physical, but there was more. So much more he didn't want to dwell on it. But he knew that she did understand his sorrow and the loss of so much of his life. She knew what it was to be other among your own friends and family and to have hurt those she loved.

"With anyone else I have to live with the knowledge that whether I draw their life away or make them burn it up like gasoline, I don't bring my own flame. It's different with you. I feel my own passion burning now. When I'm with you, I feel my own life force instead of yours."

"Because I block your powers."

"And you are certain that it's safe for me to let go. I never have. Even before Nana told me, I knew deep down it was dangerous."

"It's not with me." He ran a hand up the long muscles of her back and then wrapped his fingers about her slender neck, controlling her. "You can't draw my power. We're opposites, I think, or perhaps we are just the same."

"Are you sure that I can't hurt you?"

"Not in the way you mean. Not physically." But she could do a job on him emotionally if he let her get too close. This had to be just physical. It was his only protection from the inevitable loss. Once Johnny was human again, Mac could leave here and return home, at least to visit. He might always be a Devil Dog, but he could reclaim some of what he lost, unless he chose this woman. He couldn't do that, not without losing everything and everyone else. But he could have this moment.

Bri still looked unconvinced. "How do you know I can't hurt you?"

"Lewis told me. For years the Israelis have had werewolves acting as bodyguards for political officials. Recently they added a female vampire. She works in their intelligence operations. They've done studies. Placed the male werewolves in close quarters with her. They found that werewolves are on a different frequency or something. I don't understand it exactly, but my brain doesn't respond to your mojo."

"This werewolf was all right?"

"Even after he slept with her. They checked cell growth and division. All normal. They said that vampire-werewolf teams were safe and that werewolves would make natural colleagues for working agents, as the vampires wouldn't have to worry about killing their partners."

She stared in silence as the ramifications of what he told her sunk in. Could it be true? Hope fluttered in her chest but she held it in—afraid to accept the possibilities he dangled before her.

"He wasn't attracted to this woman?"

He shook his head. "He reported he was no more attracted to her than he would be to any beautiful woman, and all her attempts at persuasion failed."

Bri tried to say something, but her heart was pounding so hard in her chest that it hurt her ribs. He wasn't drawn to her.

"Bri, do you understand what this means? It's safe. Lewis showed me the report. I read it. Female vampires emit power is a high-frequency electrical wave that increases brain activity in humans. It stimulates the, oh shit, I forgot the name." He lifted his hand and scratched his head. "It's the part of the brain that is responsible for creative thinking. It also damages growing tissue and interferes with cell replication."

She understood what that meant. "Cancers."

"Yes and bruising and nosebleeds and loss of hair. Damage to reproductive organs. It's like radiation, sort of, or that's how they explained it to me. Your body gives off this energy all the time, but on occasion, the emission is much higher. High enough to kill." He held her gaze as her cheeks burned. They both knew what kind of occasion caused this high emission, as he dubbed it.

"But you are part human."

"So are you. Now come here."

She closed her eyes as he tipped her head and lowered his mouth to hers. The first kiss came sweet as cane sugar. His warm mouth pressed to hers, filling her with a honeyed lethargy. He used gentle pressure to encourage her to open her lips for him and stroked her tongue with his own. The contact set off electric charges of excitement through her body. She leaned against him, and he took her back to the earth, pinning her with one strong leg as he sucked her tongue. She gave herself willingly, knowing that with this man she could burn away her passion without stealing his. She had always been afraid of what would happen if she ever allowed herself that ultimate release. It had been a sore spot with Matthew, and since she had been with Jeffery only that one time, she didn't think he realized she had not reached her own fulfillment. Both men thought she was reserved, shy. But she was none of that. Instinctively she had felt the danger and had kept her response tamped down deep inside herself.

Mac pulled back and gazed down at her. "You taste so sweet," he whispered. "I want to taste you all over."

She closed her eyes and made a sound that most resembled a purr of anticipation. Yes, she wanted that, too. She wanted all of it. She wanted to plunge into passion and open wide to all he offered.

Bri stretched out beside the fire, the flames warming one side of her as the night air cooled the other. Above her, Mac stared down, his face half gilded and half in shadow. Just like the man, he was half apparent and half mystery. But she felt she knew him better now, understood how he became what he was.

Bri pushed off the ground and lifted the hem of her T-shirt and outer sweatshirt, drawing them both away in one graceful sweep. His eyes went to her breasts first, made more tempting, she knew, by the turquoise push-up bra that Johnny had collected. The A cup did not quite fit her, and so she spilled over the top. Mac used a thumb to brush the exposed top of one breast and Bri trembled. Ah, yes, she thought, this was what she'd longed for and never had—until now. Mac offered himself like a banquet to a starving woman. She wanted to touch every square inch of him and take everything he had to give.

She captured his big, warm hand against her breast, savoring the sweet aching pressure at his touch.

"Now you," she whispered, releasing him.

He reached up behind his neck, grasping the T-shirt with one hand and yanking it with a violent tug that made her stomach flutter. He was her warrior, violent and dangerous. He was also part wolf, feral, driven by instinct. And now his only ambition was to have her. Her gaze devoured him, both the hard muscles and the raised white scars that had made him what he was—hers.

The edge of danger that clung to him aroused her in ways she did not want to consider. She let her eyes gobble him up, rising to explore the hard planes of his muscular chest. Was this what they meant by body armor? He certainly had muscle to spare, hard, defined, ripped. Her fingers swept up his torso, and he inhaled sharply through his nose. The pads of her fingers registered the change in texture from the satin of his skin to the puckering nubs of his nipples and then the leathery white scars where the werewolf had torn him open.

"I haven't had a woman in a long time," he said.

"Dry spell's over," she whispered and kissed his chest.

Bri patted the place beside her, and he rolled onto

his back, wrapped an arm possessively around her hips and brought her flush against him.

She wiggled away, feeling the need to go exploring. Bri leaned forward to kiss those scars. She let her tongue follow them like a river, down to his nipple, where she sucked. He gasped, clasping the back of her head and holding her there. She didn't mind. She used her tongue to flick over his taut nipple, feeling her heartbeat quicken in anticipation.

His fingertips danced over her shoulders and down her spine, raising a tingling awareness and stoking her internal furnace. He held still for her exploration, but she felt what his stillness cost him in the tightly coiling muscles. He did not grab at her or hurry her, as Jeffery had done. He let her do as she liked, letting his body be her playground. The sense of power elated her. She knew that he was the stronger, but for this moment she held the power. Bri glanced up at him and saw her intuition was right. His stillness was a thin facade. He watched her like prey, his mouth grim and his eyes blazing with emotion. He was waiting for her to finish, waiting for the signal to advance. He held her gaze and his mouth quirked as his eyes issued a challenge.

"Go for it," he whispered.

"You think you can take it?"

"Oh, yeah. Take it all."

Her fingers danced down his ribbed abdomen but she paused when she grazed the top of his fatigues and found his erection there beneath the wide waistband.

She gasped in surprise at the length of him. He took the opportunity to sweep down and capture another kiss. This was no gentle caressing or quiet exploration. He plundered as he brought her head back, his fingers grazing her neck as his tongue invaded her mouth. She gasped at the thrill of desire bolting through her middle and streaking down to her core, and felt herself go hot and wet. He moved from her mouth, the stubble of his cheek grazing her sensitive skin as he took her earlobe between his teeth and bit down with just enough force to make her startle in excitement. Mac pushed the straps of her bra down until the lacy undergarment encircled her waist. His hot tongue stroked the ridge of her ear before dipping inside. She trembled and clung to him as excitement shuddered through her. With each kiss and caress she grew wet until she shifted her hips impatiently. She wanted out of these clothes.

"Take off your jeans," he said as his gaze roved over the long length of her.

He must have read her mind.

Her fingers trembled as she released the rivet fastening of the adolescent, straight-legged, low-riding jeans and sat back to peel them off, turning them inside out in the process. He shook out his T-shirt and laid it down for her and then lifted her onto it with frightening ease. He smiled at her surprise.

"I'm stronger than I look."

"Apparently."

"It's part of the whole wolf-thing. I'm just as strong in either form."

"Good to know."

"I keep the strength, hearing and sense of smell while in human form. You smell delicious, by the way, all musk and smoke. I can't wait to taste you."

Was he talking about her…? Bri flushed with embarrassment and anticipation. She met his steady stare, swallowing as a trickle of fear rose up inside her. In many ways he was still a stranger, and she was about to place herself in the most intimate of all vulnerable positions. But that wasn't what gave her pause. What if this was as good as she hoped? What then?

"You're looking at me like I'm the big bad wolf," he said and smiled, showing straight white teeth.

"Aren't you?"

He dropped his smile. "No. Not with you. I'll only bring you pleasure, and I'll stop when you say. For me it's just about the sex. You good with that?"

It sounded good, so good her body vibrated from a deep internal need that rose up like an orchestra crescendo.

"Yes," she whispered, taking what he offered with both hands, greedy as a hungry child.

He had her permission to do as he liked, and she had his permission not to hold back. She held his gaze as his sensual smile made her stomach flutter. He still frightened her, but not because of what he might do. He frightened her because of what he made her feel.

Just sex, she repeated, knowing it was a lie.

Chapter 12

Bri sucked in a breath of air at the first contact of his tongue to her abdomen. He licked and stroked, using his mouth and his hands with feathery-light touches that brought all her senses buzzing to dizzying arousal. She shifted beneath him, anxious for more.

"Are you sure you're safe?" she whispered, some remnant of her thinking brain still fighting for control above the flood of sensation, still afraid to allow her release.

"Yes, Princess." This time when he used that nickname, it was like a caress. "Relax. It's safe. And good," he whispered. His tongue dipped into her navel. "So good."

His voice went all gravel, the male equivalent of a purr, she thought and let her head drop back to the earth as she lifted her hips to meet his descending mouth. He stroked the sensitive skin of her inner thighs, moving ever closer to her most needy places. She could have him, enjoy him, let him enjoy her, and there would be no price to pay.

There's always a price, came the voice in her head.

She pushed it aside. No, his touch was magic. He was so good at this. A gasp escaped her as his fingers delved into her tight curls. She glanced down, aroused by the picture he made, his short, dark hair contrasting against the white of her thigh, and his long, tanned fingers laced into the thick orange hair as he separated the folds of flesh to reach her clitoris. His mouth descended, her eyes fluttered shut and she arched at the first contact. His tongue swirled and he sucked. The tension built inside her, jumping and climbing to heights that made her dizzy. She lifted her hips and he clasped her bottom in his strong hands, bringing her to him again and again.

Sharp threads of tension, pulled tight within her, taut now to the point of breaking. And still he kissed and sucked and caressed. The threads vibrated as a web of nerves fired all at once. Bliss.

The contractions surged outward with her cry. He didn't stop. His fingers delved inside her, prolonging her first orgasm. The echoes of pleasure retreated like a sound wave, leaving her body relaxed and weak. And sated. She'd never felt so perfectly at peace. She gave no resistance as he continued to kiss and stroke, moving up her hips with slow progress, as if bent on kissing every inch of her. The floating sensation of peace ebbed, replaced by the rising need to have him inside her. She groaned as her body begged for opposing needs.

He lay at her side and then pulled her over himself, so that her head lay on his shoulder and her back was pressed to his stomach. His erection now slid between her legs and along the slick folds of her cleft. He used it to stroke her without entering her. The sensation made her shudder. She now lay open to him like a banquet. He stroked the soft outer mounds of her breasts and then worked toward the peaks that budded at his touch. A gentle tug and squeeze sent pleasure rippling to her core, and she shifted as the arousal grew, building with each skilled stroke. He kissed her ear and neck, whispering of her beauty and the exotic taste of her. She lifted her hips, clamping her legs about his arousal and stroking the long, tempting length of him. When she tried to take him inside her, he stopped her. One moment she was lying across him and the next he had spun her so that she straddled his thighs. His erection stood at stiff attention before her. She glanced at him to see his knowing smile and the invitation in his eyes.

"I'm all yours," he whispered.

"Permission to come aboard," she said.

He laughed. "Navy talk. Granted. Marines don't ask permission. We just take the ship." He reached for his trousers, retrieved his wallet and then came away with a condom in a small green packet.

"Always prepared," she said, lifting a brow.

"That's the Boy Scouts."

She plucked the foil packet from his fingers and took her time as she slipped the thin sheath over his magnificent erection.

She rose to her knees and admired the view of Staff Sgt. Travis MacConnelly stretched out before her, willing and able. She took hold of his erection in one hand and guided him into her soft, wet folds. He rolled his hips, and she sank down upon him inch by inch, savoring the friction and slick slide as he filled her. She straddled his hips and he smiled up at her.

"You're a wonder," she whispered.

And he was so hard. She lifted up. His hands settled on her hips, guiding her but not allowing her to break this new connection. With downward pressure he sped her descent. The glide of his erect flesh on her yielding folds was magic. She wanted to move faster, but he kept her from galloping along. One hand left her hips, and he moved to finger her again, his stroking only hurrying her ascent and increasing the urge to move.

"Faster," she said.

The muscles at his jaw bulged. "Just a few more minutes."

She threw her head back and tried to hold on, but the tension inside her built and she felt her control slipping, allowed it to slip, because she could trust him to survive her need.

"Now," she cried. "Please, now."

She was on her back an instant later and Mac was over her, his eyes glittering with passion as he drove into her with strong, smooth strokes. Each one bringing her closer. He moved fast, so fast, a steady marvelous pounding that shook her deep inside and brought her second orgasm.

Bri cried out his name, "Travis! Oh, yes. So good!"

He never slowed as her contractions broke, rolling outward to her fingers and toes. She was dying, the pleasure making her weak. And then she felt his control break with the last great thrust. His cry mingled with hers as another orgasm swept through her, milking his erection as he began to slip from inside her.

"Look at you," he whispered.

She opened her eyes and saw a shimmering sheen of gold, like a heat mirage, only this came from her skin.

"What is that?" she asked.

"Damned if I know. But it's beautiful. *You're* beautiful."

He straightened his arms, drawing back to watch the shimmer.

"Do you feel all right?" she asked.

He grinned. "Spectacular. Don't worry, Bri. I'm fine." Slowly the glimmer faded, like a lamp turned low.

Mac fell back to his elbows, grasped Bri and rolled until he lay on his back and she rested in his embrace. "Does it happen every time you come?"

"I don't know."

He lifted his head to give her an incredulous look. "What do you mean, you don't know?"

"I never...I didn't...I never looked for it."

He tipped his head. She looked away but still felt his stare.

"That's not what you were going to say." There was a pause. She kept her eyes down. "You were going to say that you never...Bri?"

Her skin went hot and her ears tingled.

"You've been engaged and you have a boyfriend or had one. This wasn't your first rodeo. But...was that your first orgasm?"

Bri went slack against him and nodded, feeling somehow ashamed and inadequate.

He stroked her head. "Why?"

She swallowed, trying to regain her voice past the fingers that seemed to now grip her larynx. "I was close a few times but I got scared. I don't know why. Or I didn't know why at the time. But I felt it was dangerous. My nana said I shouldn't ever sleep with a man. I thought she was just being old-fashioned. But it wasn't only her warning that stopped me. I felt something inside myself, something dark."

His hold tightened. "It's not dark."

"Dangerous, then." She found the courage to look up at him, and when she did Bri was relieved to find his expression held no condemnation, but rather gave an impression of sympathy.

He stroked her cheek. "You were trying to protect them."

She nodded. "But it didn't matter. I still made Jeffrey sick, and Matthew. I killed my fiancé."

"It wasn't your fault."

She pushed off him, coming to a seated position beside him. "It was *completely* my fault! Why didn't my nana come out and say it until her death bed?"

He met her glare with an open gaze. "Maybe she hoped your human side was stronger than the other part."

"The female vampires you are supposed to hunt and kill. That's what you said. Mercenaries. Assassins. That's what you said. And you are supposed to capture one."

"No. Capture and kill."

She inched away. "So you've captured me. Why haven't you turned me in?"

He dragged a hand over the bristle that was his hair and pushed up to his elbows. The position was so enticing she gave a quick sweep of his body, tucking the memory away for later consideration.

"I guess it's the same reason you haven't run away. I know you could. And I could track you but I doubt very much that I could catch you."

They sat in silence for a few moments, he with his thoughts and she with hers.

"What's going to happen now?"

"What do you mean?" he asked.

"Well I can't stay hidden here forever. Your commander will surely find out."

"I'm working on it. For now, I keep you out of sight and I keep Johnny out of trouble."

She wrapped her arms about her knees and rested her chin on her folded wrists. She liked Mac, and she wanted to help him and Johnny. They were the first people she'd ever met who understood what was happening to her, and they were different, just as she was. What would he do if she told him that she didn't want to leave them even if they did kill the vampires? His words came back to her: *just sex.*

She closed her eyes and groaned. How could she be so stupid?

Mac eyed her cautiously. "You okay?"

She forced a smile and nodded. "Perfect."

"How long have you been able to go into supersonic speed?"

Bri gathered her panties and gave them a shake, then slipped into them. "I only did it once when I was a girl. I got called to the office and they told me my grandmother was sick. That they took her to the hospital and that I would be going to stay with a neighbor. The next thing I knew I was at the hospital. The school was searching for me for hours but I found my grandmother. She had an intestinal blockage and had to have surgery. But she was fine afterward." She wound a lock of hair around her index finger and then let it slide away. She thought of something she hadn't before. "Do you think I caused the blockage?"

"I don't know."

Honesty, she realized. She appreciated that.

They stared at each other in silence as each wrestled with their demons. Hers were too dark, so she turned to his.

"When did you find out what happened to you back there?" she asked.

Mac drew on his boxers and trousers and sat up. "A few weeks later, maybe."

She nodded her acceptance of this and motioned for him to go on.

He rubbed his temples, and when he spoke his voice carried a weariness unfamiliar to her. "I was pretty chewed up. I don't remember much of evac or the hospital over there. Maybe I was sedated. They said my lung collapsed and I lost so much blood that I flatlined. When I finally came around I had healed, so I thought I'd been out a long time and that I'd been hallucinating. But then the memories started, first in my dreams and then when I was awake. I started asking questions. They showed me Johnny." He pressed the pads of his fingers into his eyes as if trying to keep himself from seeing.

Bri rested a hand on his leg. He lowered his hands and she caught a glimpse of the unfathomable sadness that hung heavy inside him.

"They had him in a cage. Like the kind they keep tigers in at the circus. I didn't recognize him. I thought it was the thing that attacked us." He shook his head at the memory. "I tried to kill it. My brain stopped working and I tried to kill it with my bare hands. Only they weren't my hands. They were dark with long claws and gray fur. I started screaming but it was just a howl. That was the first time I changed. They used a tranquilizer dart on me. Had to hit me in the mouth to break the skin. When I came around they told me what happened back there and that it was Johnny and he couldn't change back."

Bri rubbed his shoulder.

"I'd do anything to change him back," he whispered.

From somewhere far off a wolf howled. Mac straightened and his muscles grew tense.

Bri rested a hand on his shoulder.

"He's out there all alone," she whispered.

"Running the perimeter to keep you safe." Mac stood and dusted off his backside. He glanced toward the dark woods and then back to where she sat huddled beside the fire.

"Go on," she said.

And in a moment he was gone.

The instant Mac left Bri, he broke into a run. The howl came again. Johnny needed him. He glanced behind him at the retreating campfire. Bri needed him. He wished he could cut himself in two.

He and Brianna had been so good together. He'd been with women, more than a few. But never had he felt so in sync and so moved by sex. Because it wasn't sex. It was making love. Now he understood the difference. And on some deep level that he did not quite understand, he knew that it was the woman that drew him, not the part of her that was fairy. Finally, he realized he was in way over his head.

He was deep in the pines before he realized that he was heading back toward Bri instead of tracking Johnny. He scented the air for signs of threat and found nothing but the sweet smell of the damp earth and the alluring fragrance of her skin.

Mac shook himself like a wet dog and turned to search for Johnny's scent, hurrying now with this task that now seemed a burden. He wanted to get back to Bri, back to her warmth and her smile and her sorrow. Back to the welcome of her arms.

Damn it. Before her arrival he knew his duty. It was to his country and his family and to Johnny. But now…

He concentrated on his fury, letting the emotion break through him with the wave of pain, tearing him apart from the inside. He endured it, dropping to his knees briefly before rising in his wolf form to follow his gunner. He could change quickly now, in the blink of an eye. But it still hurt like hell. He ran Johnny down, finding him on the east side of their territory. His friend heard him coming, because he was waiting, tongue lolling, as Mac loped up to him.

Mac suffered the transition back to human form. Naked now, he dropped to his haunches, covering his privates as best he could. After three months, he and Johnny had few secrets.

"Why were you howling?"

Johnny roared and swung an open hand through the air. His claws made a whistling sound as they lashed out.

Had Johnny seen him with Bri? Mac stilled at the possibility, knowing instinctively that his friend would be pissed. Now he wished he had bathed. Bri's scent was heavy on his skin along with the aroma of sex.

Mac stayed downwind as Johnny motioned to the east and then signaled him to follow.

"Wolf or man?" asked Mac.

Johnny used his fingers to simulate upright walking and Mac followed at a jog.

After a few minutes Johnny pointed to a tree. Mounted on the trunk was a surveillance camera.

"Son of a bitch," said Mac.

Johnny sighed.

"Any near your place?

His gunner shook his head.

"Do you think they caught us moving her?"

Johnny shrugged.

"Bri can't come back to the compound. She has to stay at your place."

Johnny nodded.

"No more writing in the dirt. No more sign language around the compound. Only out here."

Johnny nodded his agreement and looked about as if searching for more surveillance cameras.

"How long do you think we can keep her secret?" Mac asked.

His friend gave a slow shake of his head and then breathed a deep sigh.

"We can't leave her unguarded. One of us needs to be with her from now on."

Johnny used an open hand on his chest. He'd take the first watch.

"Twelve hours each?"

Johnny nodded and set off toward his secret hideaway.

"I'll see you at noon. Do you think I should go explain it to her?"

Johnny huffed and kept going. Mac wondered what Bri would think of her new guardian sleeping opposite her at the campfire.

The two male vampires finished checking the apartment where the female and her grandmother lived before the old woman's death and Vittori's escape. They found nothing to indicate where she might have gone and no trace of the two sent to apprehend her. The elder, Burne Farrell, stood on the balcony looking out at the empty street below. The hours between two and four in the morning were usually quiet in human neighborhoods, and he felt at his best then. His lavender skin held no purplish cast because of his recent meal, but the artificial lights made his veins prominent. He stared at his hands, seeing the twisted bluish ropes beneath his transparent skin. Beside him stood one of his best Chasers, Hagan Dowling, flipping through the loose paper in a file folder. Beneath one arm he clamped a battered red leather journal. A younger vampire by two decades, Hagan's skin remained the unnatural cadaver white of his birth, but that would change in time as his veins bled through. Eventually they all ended up looking like ripe plums.

Hagan had scored a hit, one of the females that had eluded them for a decade. Unfortunately he had sent two of his less experienced men to retrieve her and they had failed. Vanished, really. No report, no location. Just gone. It made Burne angry, for he expected better from his Chasers. They had better both be dead, because if not, he'd kill them for disobedience.

Now he understood why this female had been so successful at remaining loose.

"She had a protector," said Burne.

"Yes. Her grandmother knew what she was and she knew exactly how we check each quadrant. Her moves were methodical, from one cleared territory to the next. It was almost as if she was chasing us."

"How did she know?"

Burne lifted his gaze from his hands to look at his

Chaser. Hagan's lips were the color of blood and his fangs had grown so long that they no longer fit in his mouth. The faded color of his irises made his eyes look milky, instead of gray, as if he were staring at a corpse. The effect was deceptive because their vision was perfect, far better than the humans.

"According to this, the human learned of our methods from a Leanan Sidhe. The female we seek is the human's granddaughter, Brianna. She's not like us. She's first generation."

"First?" Burne blinked. "Are you sure?" The most pure vampires he knew were fifth generation. Many were tenth or more. To capture a first-generation vampire might change everything. They might even have children by her that were not so abhorrent. He might even have a son who could walk among humans.

"Her father was human. Her mother was a true Leanna Sidhe."

"How do you know?"

He held up a battered journal. "The old woman kept a record of everything. Where they were, where they should go next. Instructions dictated to her by Brianna's mother. Photos of her mother." He flipped open the journal and withdrew a snapshot, handing it to Burne.

He stared down at the face that could have been an angel's, she was so lovely. Flowing red hair, crystal-blue eyes and skin smooth and pale as cream. Burne felt his heart pitch and his loins tingle. "Where is her mother now?"

"The best I can piece together is that after Brianna's birth, she returned to the Fey."

"She was afraid her power might kill her child."

Burne stared out into the night. "Does her daughter look like this?"

Hagan handed over another photo. Brianna's eyes were leafy green, and her skin was more pink than ivory. But in all other regards she resembled her mother. Hagan held out his hand for the photo. Burne tucked it in his vest pocket.

"Do you think that is why your man failed? Is she more powerful than our females?"

"She might be very fast and her draw stronger than our females, but she has no training. We could give her that. I volunteer, sir, to train this one."

Burne snorted. Of course he did. Anything to get close to a first-generation vampire. Perhaps impregnate her in the process. "First we catch her. Then we worry about the rest." He forced a smile for Hagan's benefit, felt the sharp tips of his fangs graze his lower lip.

"Yes, sir."

"I want three Chasers on this. The first is to return to the area we just swept and begin again. If she follows her grandmother's pattern, we will find her there. The second is to begin a search of increasing circumference from this spot."

"And the third?"

"Follow the direction of your men's last check-in. All teams are to contact me at any sign of our target. I want this one, Hagan. Bring her to me."

Chapter 13

After Mac left her, Bri spent an unpleasant night tending the fire and jumping at every rustling sound from the forest. She could see past the orange flames of the campfire, and though the light gave her a certain comfort, it also made her very easy to find. It was for this reason that she left the fire and moved deeper into the darkness. At first she thought her perception was a trick of the night. But the longer she sat away from the flames, the greater her visual acuity became. She could see everything down to the creases in the bark and the tight new pinecones clinging to the upper branches. Her vision wasn't that funny green night-goggle thing, either. It was a perfect gray, like a black-and-white movie. Why couldn't she do this before?

She thought back and could not recall one single time in her life when she was away from streetlights, away from a city. She breathed deeply.

Another rustle brought her head swiveling about, and she spotted a small rodent, a mole or vole, perhaps, scuttling along in the pine needles and sounding like an elephant. Bri sighed and rubbed her tired eyes. How long until Mac came back for her?

She settled against a pine and drew her knees up for warmth and comfort. Her head rested against the trunk of the tree, and she rubbed her legs to try and sweep away the gooseflesh there. Bri caught some movement out of the corner of her vision. She turned in that direction and saw something big moving between the trees. She gasped as she came to her feet, then covered her mouth as a tiny squeak emerged from her throat.

Vampires!

The rush of energy surged through her and she bounded away, seeing the tops of the trees before coming back to earth. She looked back and saw the creature running toward her. She jumped again but this time she heard a howl. Bri froze. She knew that howl.

"Johnny?" she whispered.

There was a huffing sound and then she saw him clearly. He stood on his hind legs, arms at his sides, the long claws curled slightly as if he cupped something in his palms. His shoulders sagged and he lifted his furry, dotlike eyebrows as he met her stare. He made a whining sound and then a huff.

She didn't know what to do. Mac trusted Johnny, but she'd never been alone with him in the woods. On those few occasions when he guarded the compound he had never approached her. And she knew he had been against Mac taking her in. Then there was his recent attack on her. Mac said it was the drugs. Was it?

Suddenly a more frightening thought struck her. What if something had happened to Mac? What if he couldn't come back? Her worry for Mac overcame her fear and she hurried toward Johnny.

"Is Mac all right?"

He nodded and then motioned back to the supply depot she had left.

"Is it safe?"

Another nod. She hesitated only a moment and then joined him. They walked back side by side. He was so tall that her head only reached his elbow. She could feel the impact of his footsteps on the earth as they continued along. When they reached Johnny's personal hideaway, he added more wood to the fire and then dragged a rug from inside for her to sit upon. Through a series of questions and Johnny's scratching words in the sand, she discovered that she must stay here for the time being and that he and Mac would take turns as her bodyguards.

He held her gaze until she stopped shaking and gave him a nervous nod. Then he continued his slow scrawl in the sand. More cameras had been found in the woods; plus, they had replaced the cameras at their quarters and added new ones. Bri felt cold right through to the core at this revelation, and her inclination was to run again. Johnny must have sensed her need for flight because he gripped her at the elbow. She trembled and he gave her arm a squeeze before releasing her.

Bri thought about the risk that Johnny and Mac took for her, a stranger, an enemy, a defenseless, soul-sucking vampire. Her chin sank to her chest with shame.

"Maybe I should go before you get into more trouble."

Johnny growled. He clearly didn't like that idea. Bri nodded her understanding, and Johnny motioned to the rug, lifting a blanket and pillow. She accepted the offer and nodded off to sleep with her werewolf bodyguard keeping watch.

Bri's life fell into a pattern from then on. Johnny watched her during the day and Mac returned at night. The only deviation was when Headquarters wanted Johnny for tests. On only one occasion was she alone. Since this supply depot was her home for the foreseeable future, she gained Johnny's permission to do some decorating. She arranged the oriental rugs and ammo crates and the low Moorish furniture into a living area inside the concrete shelter. Mac brought her a mattress, bed frame and bedding, helped her fix meals using the MRE packets and stocked the firewood. She felt like Rose Red living in the woods. At least here there were no cameras. And though the shelter was less comfortable than the qala that Mac and Johnny used as their quarters, she still preferred it because even though it had no electricity and no kitchen, it also had no surveillance. So she had the freedom to walk in the woods here, as long as she didn't wander too far. Johnny accompanied her on daily walks during his shift. Mac kept her distracted with stories about basic training, but he never spoke of his squad again. After supper they retired to the compound, where she fell easily into Mac's arms. He was a gifted and generous lover—inventive, playful and intense. She'd often fall asleep in his arms, but he never slept, at least not in her bed. He was holding back, she knew. Keeping their relationship sexual. But sometimes she caught him staring at her and felt the longing in his eyes echoing in her soul.

Tonight, after making love, Mac sat on a folding chair, drawing on his boots while she remained in bed, now dressed in his long T-shirt, which she used as a nightshirt. Johnny would be here soon, with the changing of the guards at midnight.

"When do you think they will come?" she asked.

"I don't know. I expected them to have tracked you already. Seems they didn't know your pursuers' exact location. They're backtracking, circling until they find your trail. That rental, for instance."

Bri tried to push back her anxiety and pretend she was safe, and that Mac's protection came from something more than keeping the only known she-vampire safe and sound.

The nights they spent together were magic, but knowing that this was a "no strings" relationship poisoned the sweetness of their joining. She knew that when they parted she'd miss Mac. Chances were good she'd never meet another man who could resist her energy draw, and so she faced a terrible choice. Spend her life alone or kill the one she cared for. It was no choice at all, really. She'd have to remain celibate, but that would make her more dangerous to be near, if Mac's information was accurate. So even if she didn't sleep with a man, just being near a human—any human, male or female—would be toxic.

Bri had once thought to have a family, settle in one place and be like other people with a job and a mortgage and toys underfoot. She'd lost all that when she'd discovered what she was. She couldn't love a man without risking his life. *Except one man.* But he didn't want strings.

Mac was an escape clause in a life sentence of solitary confinement. She still held stupidly to the hope that he might find her more than physically attractive.

But Mac was a Marine. He had a mission—to look after Johnny—and he wanted an active combat assignment. Beyond that he wanted what she could never give him: a house filled up with kids and dogs and rabbits. Bri stifled a sob and covered her mouth with her hand as she ached for that life.

He'd be a fool to choose her, though he was opportunist enough to take advantage of the situation at hand. And what more could she expect? He protected her and satisfied her and then left her at midnight like some male Cinderella, reverting back to a soldier.

And what did that make her? Bri sighed miserably and hugged herself, sitting up on the single bed that Mac had provided her. She hated these nightly partings. His arrival at midday was always joyous, and the afternoon would fly by. Then they would have sex, and he would leave her like a married man hurrying home to the wife and kids. Bri wondered if they were protecting her or just using her as bait. Perhaps she was naïve. Perhaps Mac wasn't keeping her safe but just keeping her. If she tried to leave, would he let her, or was she more prisoner than guest? After they caught a male vampire, if they could catch one, what was to stop him from turning her over to his supervisors? Wouldn't it be better to bring in a male *and* female?

That evening she asked him about her situation again.

"Even if you catch the ones that are tracking me, there are more of them. Aren't there?"

His silence was answer enough.

"You can't hide me in the woods forever." But a small part of her wanted just that. "How will I keep them from finding me, Mac, after you have your prize?"

He leaned forward, elbows on knees, hands relaxed

with fingers before him. "We have to teach you to use your powers. Tactics, hand to hand combat. Practice. Just like basic training, so that you'll be ready if they find you and ready when the time comes to defend yourself."

And there it was. The implication in his words. *I need to defend myself so I can survive after he leaves me.*

She nodded woodenly. He was right. Her nana had protected her without her even knowing. Mac and Johnny protected her now. In their way, both Matthew and Jeff had tried to protect her. She'd allowed others to jeopardize their lives to guard hers. It was too much. She needed to start taking care of herself.

"Yes. I want to learn."

Bri spent the next week practicing her bounding. At first she was clumsy, faltering between her human speed and her vampire one. It was difficult to summon her power when she was not frightened out of her wits. At first, Johnny provided the scare, leaping out at her unexpectedly. One day it just clicked. She switched to her vampire speed without being afraid and bounded away so fast that even Mac, in werewolf form, couldn't keep up. She shot straight up to the top of a pine tree and watched him run in circles trying to find her. Unfortunately her laugh gave her away. Then she found she couldn't get down. That scared her so much that she gained her power again and made the jump to ground.

"It just keeps cutting in and out like a bad wireless signal. Like dropping a call. One minute I have four bars and the next, nothing."

Mac gave her shoulder a squeeze.

She looped her arms about his neck and smiled up

at him, then gave him a quick kiss on his furry snout. "You're right. I'm getting better."

She let her hand slide off Mac's hairy shoulders. He captured one hand and held it for a moment longer. She looked up at him. "What?"

His fingers dropped away and he sighed.

She wanted him to change so she could make love to him right here in broad daylight. Then at least she wouldn't see the shimmer. She and Mac didn't talk about it since that first time. But they often saw the golden glow, the wispy tendrils that emanated from her skin when she found her pleasure. Neither knew what it was.

"Phew! I'm tired. All this running and jumping. I feel like I'm in boot camp."

Mac grinned showing rows of sharp white teeth. Then he scooped her off her feet so fast it made her head spin. She shrieked and laughed as he set off at a run, carrying her in his arms as they returned to her new home. His jarring gait forcing Bri to wrap her arms about his neck.

"Mac! Put me down. I'm not that tired!"

He sped up and she laughed again as the wind whistled past them. Mac skidded to a halt. Bri turned to see what had stopped him and found Johnny.

Mac released her legs and she swung down to his side, her arms slipping from his neck as she reached the ground. Mac kept one hand on the center of her back. Bri stepped away. Johnny's dark expression and rigid posture made her cautious. He stood with hands on hips glowering at them both and finally fixing his glare on Mac.

Johnny growled.

"I said I was tired and Mac just…"

Mac had taken a defensive pose. He'd lowered his head and bared his teeth.

"No," she said, stepping between them. "It was just a joke. We were laughing and—"

Johnny lifted a finger to his lips and pointed towards their new quarters. Brianna went still. Was someone here? Had they come at last?

"Vampires?" she whispered.

Johnny shook his head and then patted his ears.

"Too loud?"

He nodded.

"I'm sorry," she said. "It won't happen again." He turned to Mac. Her silliness had put them both at risk. Thank God it was only Johnny that heard. "Thank you, Mac, for helping me down from that tree." She addressed Johnny. "I'm getting better, but I poop out sometimes."

Johnny gave them one last look of censure and then disappeared back the way he had come.

Mac took her back to the compound, his mood no longer light. Once there he left her, going into Johnny's refuge to change shape and dress. She didn't have long to wait before he returned, in wrinkled khakis and a rumpled olive-green T-shirt. Mac's shoulders slumped and his chin dipped. For just a moment he looked defeated.

"What's wrong?"

When he spoke his voice held a deep sorrow that struck Bri like a blow. "You made me forget."

"Forget? Forget what?"

"Everything. This place, the danger we're in, your attackers, Johnny…my duty." He stared down at her with blue eyes that glittered with emotion. "And I can't forget. Not any of it."

She nodded her understanding. "You have a duty."

"Yes." He scrubbed his face with one hand. "I have to stay. The colonel and the med techs are working to bring Johnny back. Trying to find a way to make him human again. It's terrible, but they need my blood and they need more time."

"I understand."

He glanced at her. "All I can do is follow orders and pray they figure out how to bring Johnny back soon." He took hold of her shoulders and drew her in front of him. "I need Johnny's cooperation and I need him not to give up."

"And you've been neglecting him because of me."

"Yes. But I think he enjoys spending time with you, too."

"I'm asleep most of it."

"He says you talk to him at breakfast."

She smiled. "Yes. Sometimes I sing. He likes that too, I think."

Mac nodded. "He misses his mom and his sister."

"I didn't know he had…" She stopped. Had she really been about to say that she didn't know he had a mother? Or family? She realized she just never thought about who Johnny was before. "They must miss him terribly."

"They think he's MIA. They don't even know he's alive."

She gasped, pressing a hand to her chest. "That's terrible."

"For them and for him. It eats at him. But he can't visit or call or write. He can barely hold a pen."

"I could write it for him."

"No. No contact. They can't know. Not ever. It's for their protection as much as his."

She held his gaze and then recognized the truth. "You're hoping that they fix this and he can reappear."

He didn't deny it.

"But what if that doesn't happen?"

"It's a military secret either way. But if he can't change, he stays missing." Mac rubbed the back of his neck. "Anyway. He says you remind him of his sister."

"What's her name?"

"Joon—Julia, they call her."

"I'm making things harder for you both."

"Yes. And easier. We both miss home."

How was Mac's family? Had he been in contact with them, made his video calls when he wasn't in her bed? "How is your sister?"

"Bonnie? She's good. Getting big. She says it's a boy."

He rubbed the back of his neck and glanced away, as if anxious to be rid of her. She sensed that he didn't want his world and that one colliding and why would he? She could kill them all by just spending the weekend.

He'd mentioned his father; heart trouble, she recalled. She briefly considered what her appearance might do to him.

"How is your dad?"

Mac actually flinched. "On a new diet and grumbling about it." He forced a smile.

Bri felt the sorrow well up inside her like floodwater. She missed her nana. Johnny missed his loved ones. Mac couldn't see his family except on a computer screen. Suddenly it all seemed too much. She wanted to be independent, but instead she'd let Mac and Johnny risk their lives for hers. "Maybe I should just go."

"You aren't ready to defend yourself. Though you are a damned good runner."

"Are they close to a cure for Johnny?" she whispered.

"Damned if I know. All I can do now is hold on and hope. But it's hard. Really hard."

Mac started a fire in the brazier after supper. He was damned tired of sitting on the ground in these freaking qalas. He wanted to go fishing in his bass boat or sit in a recliner, preferably with a beer and a remote. He wanted to watch a Detroit Tigers game with his dad while his mother made pot roast and Yorkshire puddings.

He wanted to go to a bar with his squad and laugh and tell lies. But his squad was buried under the sod at Arlington, and he couldn't leave Johnny or Bri to visit his family. Mac jabbed at the embers and watched the sparks fly into the metal pan. He readjusted the pillow behind his back and sighed.

Bri appeared from inside Johnny's storage depot carrying two mugs. The aroma of coffee reached him an instant before the intoxicating scent of orchids. She gave him a smile, and he knew she was worth all the trouble. Bri didn't make demands. She accepted that their relationship was physical. The problem was, he was having trouble accepting it. This attraction between them only seemed to grow with each passing minute he spent with her. And he liked her. He enjoyed talking to her nearly as much as sleeping with her. That had never happened before.

He'd told her that when she could defend herself, he'd let her go. But now he saw two problems with that. First, she might not ever be ready to defeat a pack of hunting male vampires. And secondly, he didn't want to let her go. But how could he keep her? The woman killed people just by showing up.

"Here you are." She passed him one of the mugs.

He took a sip. She made damned good coffee. She also managed to spruce up those MREs with the fresh vegetables he brought her to make some really good grub. He was getting used to having her around, and that was a problem.

Why couldn't Bri have had a difficult mother or a brother in prison or a kid or some shameful secret in her past like other women? Why did he have to go for a fucking vampire?

Mac raised his nose to inhale the scents on the breeze. Her coffee came to him first. But then he scented the rain, coming from the west. There had been no sign of vampires. MI said that they smelled like blood, which was true, but they also smelled like rot. Apparently they didn't just drink blood; they cannibalized their victims. Unlike the myths, being bitten by a vampire did not insure immortality—but death.

Mac sipped his coffee and stared at the fire. It kept him from looking at Bri, which was what he wanted to do. He failed to keep his attention on the flames and glanced her way.

She wore a white T-shirt. The stretchy cotton molded over her breasts revealing the shocking turquoise lace bra beneath. None of her clothes fit her, since they weren't her clothes. He wondered what she wore before coming here. Likely not skintight blue jeans, extrashort shorts or tops that was gauzy and as transparent as a bridal veil.

Their usual routine was to finish their coffee, move inside and make love, sometimes more than once. Then Bri would fall asleep, and he would move outside to await the dawn and Johnny's appearance to relieve him.

The physical intimacy sated his body, but he wanted more. He wanted to know everything about her. He'd been trying to resist, instinctively fearing the intimacy while craving it.

"What did you do back there before this happened?" he asked.

She paused with the edge of the mug against her full lips and then lowered the coffee. She brushed the hair back from her face. Her eyes sparkled when she talked, and her nose moved when she smiled. He felt a tug of desire and pushed it aside.

"I just finished my bachelor's degree. It took me five years, because we moved around a lot and because I was working to pay for it. I just started at Social Services in Sacramento. Nana didn't like it. She said social work was for saps. We argued about it. She was getting ready to leave again, and I was planning to stay put. She hadn't told me yet and…"

Mac held her gaze. Bri looked away.

"That's how they found me, isn't it? Because I wouldn't leave when she told me to."

"Do you think your grandmother knew how to stay out of their way?"

"She must have. I never saw one until after her death."

He drummed his fingers on the mug, wanting to know how to keep her safe. Needing the knowledge that her grandmother had. "But she never spoke about them or how to keep away from them?"

"Not until she knew she was dying. She kept a journal, but it's still at my apartment. It was as if she thought keeping her secrets would keep me safe. But I knew I was different. Like when I'd ask about my mother, Nana would just say she was a bad mother, abandoning her child. I didn't think she died on purpose, but Nana would get angry, so I just stopped asking."

"Did your grandmother ever see you run?"

"No, but she knew about my metal allergy. She made sure the bathtub was fiberglass in the apartments so I didn't get a rash, and she used ceramic knives. She mostly cooked casseroles in Pyrex. We ate with plastic cutlery."

"Metal just makes you itch?"

"Break out, itch, a nasty allergic rash. I get headaches, symptoms of an allergies, runny nose. Only we both knew it wasn't pollen. I'm a mess. I get carsick even when I'm driving and airplanes…" She shuddered. "The worst migraines ever. But now that I'm away from the wires and cars and well everything, I feel so much better. Stronger. And I can see more clearly, especially at night."

She described her new night vision which was much the same as his own. "Sense of smell?"

"Yes, always better than…humans."

"And you don't know how to intentionally draw energy?"

"No!" She turned back to the fire and her mug of coffee. Her posture told him she was upset.

"You don't want to learn how to use that power?"

"Only if I can learn how to shut it off." She stared at him, her eyes luminous and shimmering.

"It might save your life."

"I don't want to hurt anyone. I'm a pacifist. I'm a good person…or I thought I was. Now I discover I'm—I'm this." She swept a hand over herself. "Mac, if we get through this and you catch your vampire and, we part ways…well, I'm not really free to go anywhere, am I?"

He inclined his head. "What do you mean?"

"I can't go back among them. Humans, I mean. Not knowing what I can do to them. I can never do that again. So where will I go?"

He was silent as he considered that problem.

"I've spent my whole life trying to help people. I've put my energy into social causes. I've marched, petitioned, rallied, worked in the trenches. Well, not the kind of trenches that Marines work in, but I've tried very hard to make this world a better place. But I haven't. I'm a fraud. I'm not a good person. I'm a killer like you."

"No. All my kills were intentional." The instant he said it he knew it wasn't true. He still didn't know if he'd killed any of his own men, because he couldn't remember what happened after the werewolf attacked him. He'd tried several times, but there was nothing. But Lewis told him he'd attacked Lam.

She lowered her gaze to the flames and her words came at a whisper. "Mine wasn't."

Her fiancé, he recalled. His obituary said it was leukemia. That was a hard thing. He knew something about living with regret.

"You can't change it by reliving it. Going over it and over it will just drive you crazy."

She stared at him a long moment, those lovely green eyes shimmering. She looked at the contents of her half-empty mug. "But if my grandmother had explained it to me earlier—"

"Would you have believed her? If you didn't see that vampire coming for you, if you didn't jump out of that window, would you have believed any of this?"

She sniffed, and the tears that had hovered on her

lower lids splashed down her face. Damn, she was even beautiful when she wept. "I don't want to believe it now."

"We are what we are. All the tears in the world won't wash that away."

"You're the only one I can't make sick."

Her glamour didn't work on him. He knew it. So why then did the thought of letting her go fill him with a kind of creeping panic? The only thing more frightening was losing his family. He ground his teeth together and met her gaze. "Me or another werewolf."

She set aside her mug and clasped her arms around her knees. She looked small and helpless. An illusion, he knew. She was powerful, more powerful than she knew. If he were not able to tolerate her, would he be able to resist her? He didn't think so.

But he knew that Bri was getting faster each day. Fast enough to outrun them, he believed. After he caught his vampire, he'd have to let her go, because he knew he was growing too attached to her. He felt it, those tendrils that bound him more tightly to her. The intimate moments and the realization that each day he wanted her more, instead of less. This had never happened before. He wasn't bored, distracted, restless. The only restlessness he felt came from thoughts of their parting.

But he'd have to let her go soon. He'd send her on her way for her own good as much as his. He and Johnny could go back to the way they had been. The med techs could find a cure for Johnny. Then maybe he could visit Mac's family, see with his own eyes that his dad was all right. Hold his nephew. Oh, damn.

What if they didn't find a cure, and what if they couldn't go back to the way they had been?

Her chances were worse without him. He knew it.

But she was safe now. He'd put himself against any vampire to protect her; he relished the thought. He anticipated the encounter more than he should have, and that made him think he was in the right profession. He wanted to fight. Needed to.

Bri sniffed, and he found that her suffering cut him as deeply as his own. He reached out to her, wrapping an arm about her shoulders. She sagged against his side, molding to him as he stroked her back.

"Come here," he said and turned her so he could brush away the tears that now glistened on her cheeks. "There have to be others like you. Ones the males haven't found yet."

"I could join them."

He nodded, but he didn't want her to join them. He wanted her to stay here with him forever.

He kept thinking what it would be like to have her in his life. It wasn't a pretty picture. To have Brianna, he'd have to give up his commission, possibly go on the run, because he just couldn't picture military intelligence letting one of their two werewolves and the only one who could change shape, just waltz out into the general public. So he'd be a wanted man. They'd be coming after him and Johnny, because he wasn't leaving his friend behind.

Even if they did remain free, Mac would have to be on constant guard for the vampires who hunted her.

Then there was his family. He couldn't introduce Brianna to his mother or his father. His sister was pregnant. Mac thought what horrors Brianna could bring to a fetus or newborn, and winced. And while he was on that topic, what about kids? He wanted them, a pile of them. Her children would be vampires, and his...

He lifted one hand and used his thumb and forefingers to rub his tired eyes.

He couldn't have the life he led or the one he imagined and have Bri. He would have to choose.

Chapter 14

Mac watched her as she left the brazier's warmth and swept inside toward the room they had arranged for her to sleep in. He let her have a few moments' privacy, but the pull was there, urging him to follow her. His skin itched and he could no longer sit still. He poked at the fire. He paced. Still the need built inside him. He could hear her removing her clothing. Hear the whisper of sheets as she pulled back the covers. Her scent lingered in the air, growing weaker by the second.

He needed that scent, needed to touch her soft skin. He balled up his fist and pressed it to his forehead. Mac didn't remember leaving the fire or walking across the clearing. Instead he just found himself at her door.

The door she had left open.

To him.

He drew himself up, tightened the muscles of his shoulders and torso. Even if he went in there it would change nothing. She wasn't his. Couldn't be. He could sleep with her, but eventually he'd have to let her go.

Her scent came to him with the rustling sound. His body went cold, then hot, then ready.

The flickering light told him she'd lit a candle again, instead of the kerosene lantern. She said she preferred the soft illumination, and the lantern was mostly metal. Likely it burned her to turn the knob.

Did she know how lovely she was by candlelight, her hair all ablaze and her skin gilded?

He stepped into the doorway. She stood beside the bed straightening to stillness at his arrival. The tension between them tugged like a rope stretched to its limit.

The bed stood between them with the covers turned back so that the top sheet lay half over the blankets. She'd centered the two pillows, one at the headboard and one where her hips would be when he kissed her there. He lifted his gaze to Bri, seeing first her long, taut legs and the scrap of blue lace that hugged her like a second skin. Her wide hips narrowed at her bare waist, and he studied her belly button, the small, enticing indenture. She didn't wear a bra or tank this evening. Her lovely, full breasts hung like ripe fruit, soft, perfumed and inviting. Her large rosy nipples tightened under his scrutiny. He took a step closer. She lifted a hand to her throat, her fingers splayed. He watched her hand slide down to cup one breast.

He closed his eyes and listened to her approach. He heard everything she did, whether it was brushing her hair or rubbing on moisturizer. She glided across the room on bare feet, pausing so close that he could feel the heat of her skin in the cold room.

"What's wrong?" she asked.

He shook his head. How could he explain that even with her right in front of him, he already missed her, grieved their parting as if it had already come? Dreaded it as one dreads the phone call from the doctor with the test results. His mind scrambled to find a way. How could he keep her and not lose everything and every-one else?

Mac reached for her, letting his hands slide from her waist to the enticing curve of her hips. Then he tugged, bringing her against him. He'd take her again, know-ing that each time he did he only wanted her more. He wasn't immune to this woman, because it wasn't her vampire gifts that drew him. It wasn't just her scent and her lush body. It was her kind heart and her brave spirit. She was too idealistic. Too gullible and too trust-ing for this world. She was his opposite, his perfect fit. She needed him. He needed her.

He could protect her, satisfy her. He wished he could offer more.

Her hands slipped under his shirt. Fingernails raked his back as she removed the garment and then lifted her chin, silently demanding a kiss.

He swept in, the passion rising in his blood, in the melting of their bodies. She stroked his neck, and one hand caressed his head, but his hair was too short for her to find any purchase there, so she wrapped her arms about his neck and clung as he walked to the inviting bed. She fell backward and he landed on top of her, tak-ing enough of his weight on his arms that he did not hurt her, but not so much that she was not pinned be-neath him. He relished the contact of their mouths and the pressing of his hips to hers.

She made a sound deep in her throat. He loved that sound. It held anticipation and pleasure, the cry a sweet blending of need and the purr of contentment. She wrapped her long legs about his hips and locked her ankles, pressing against the ridge of engorged flesh as she rocked. Mac released his breath in a whoosh. He'd wanted to go slow, but she was giving all the signals of needing a more aggressive engagement.

He drew back, arching up onto his extended arms. "What have you got in mind tonight, Princess?"

In answer she clamped her long legs about him. She lifted up again, bouncing against him and then falling back on the bed.

"I want what you always give me."

"And what's that?"

"Mind-blowing orgasms and…" Her words drifted off.

He lifted his chin, urging her to go on.

She bit her lower lip. He watched the plump pink tissue slide between white teeth and felt his mouth go dry as hunger surged and thundered inside him like an avalanche.

"When you're here with me, I'm not scared anymore. I forget what's out there hunting me. That's the best part. I make it through the day knowing that you'll be here with me at night."

He wished he could be there forever. His smile faltered. When had he stopped wishing to go back to that day, the moment before he'd ordered his men into that building, and started wanting Bri? There was so much he wanted to forget. So much he needed to remember, and Bri was confusing him. His hands stilled.

"Mac? Did I say something wrong?"

"No. Nothing." He slipped out of his trousers and Skivvies, dropping them on the floor. Then he stretched out beside her.

That was when he realized that she did the same thing for him. When he was with her, he wasn't back there reliving that night, fighting against his guilt and anguish. She freed him from that pain.

He rested on his hip to stroke her side, starting at the soft junction of her arm and torso down to the scrap of lace that didn't quite hide her charms. Expertly he swept it down her slim legs and tossed her panties to the ground. She settled back on the bedding, sliding one hand behind her head and smiling up at him. She was letting him decide. He liked calling the shots.

He started at her wrist and worked to her neck. All the while the scent of orchids and musk surrounded him. She was so sweet, he wanted to take a bite. Mac let his teeth score the skin of her collarbone. She gasped, and her fingers danced over his shoulders, kneading his tired muscles and scoring his skin with her sharp nails. By the time he reached her breasts she glowed from within, that strange, alluring golden shimmer that he was now certain was not a trick of the flame but just her reaction to arousal. The skin of her stomach was the softest, softer even than her full breasts. Here he had to pull back and take a breath. Her arousal fired his own, and the need became nearly too sharp.

She was close. He could see it in the moisture on her skin, read it in the shimmering color of her green eyes and hear it in the soft, needy sounds vibrating in her throat.

He stroked her most sensitive flesh and sucked in a breath through his teeth. She was so damned wet and ready. He'd bring her to orgasm and then come with her on the second round.

Then she did something new, sliding two fingers

inside her cleft. He watched her move her hand in and out. He stopped breathing. Then she reached with her wet fingers until she had a hold of him. Her hand was slick as she moved her palm along his shaft. He closed his eyes and rocked to his back. Sensing his momentary confusion, Bri pursued like any good warrior, lifting a leg and throwing it across his hips. She straddled him and brought his erect flesh to her slippery folds. Then she dropped down on him until her hips collided with his. He groaned at the rush of pleasure that shot through his abdomen.

No you don't, he thought. *Hold on, soldier. You are not coming. Not yet.*

He gritted his teeth and glanced up at her. She sensed victory, because her eyes widened and glittered dangerously.

Oh, the hell with this.

He rolled her to her back and thrust. This time she gasped, her eyes rounding.

"You want it like this?"

She nodded and rocked her hips. He slipped farther inside her. His eyes closed as he grappled for control.

"Faster," she whispered. "I'm so close, Travis. Please. Faster."

Orders received.

He slipped out and then came back hard. She arched, lifting to meet each thrust. He forgot to breathe as she made her final climb. Wisps of golden mist rose from her heated flesh. He felt her so close in the tightness of her passage and the frantic thrusts that met each long descent. Her breathing changed. She cried out once and then again.

"Travis! Oh, God, yes!"

He loved the sound of his name on her lips. Her contractions gripped him and he relinquished control. They came together for the first time. She threw back her head and then felt his last thrust. She opened her eyes and stared up at him, her face flushed and her expression filled with wonder. He watched the pleasure roll through her as it fired along every nerve ending in his body.

Her eyes drifted shut as he fell beside her. Their bodies came to rest. Breathing fast, they lay inert.

His limbs now heavy and clumsy. God, he'd never felt anything like that and knew he never would again. He didn't deserve her.

He closed his eyes and his body went slack. He didn't deserve this peace. Not after what he'd done.

How fast the guilt closed in. He squeezed his eyes shut as the faces of his men rose up to haunt him.

He could hear their voices calling to him for orders, and then the sound of gunshots and the cries of agony. When his first two teams went silent, why had he sent in the third? He was like those miners in West Virginia running into a mine shaft filled with methane trying to save their fellows and ending up just as dead.

They'd all run in. Every damned one of them. And they'd all died. All but him and Johnny.

Why had he sent in the second team and then the third? If he'd waited, they'd all be alive. Nothing could have saved his first Fire Team. He accepted that. But he should have held at least one team back. Any squad leader worth his salt would have done so. But not him.

His first command. His last command.

Mac bolted up. Bri groaned and then followed him, stroking his back.

"Will you lie here next to me?"

It was the one pleasure he denied himself. To sleep in her bed, in her arms, would be too much like what he longed for with Bri. For many nights now he had wanted more than sex. More than the brief pleasure of release before parting.

"I have to check the perimeter," he said and grabbed his discarded clothing.

Wouldn't that just be fine if he waltzed out of here with Bri? Turned his back on the colonel and Johnny and just took off.

He had too much honor to do that. He was a member of the Corps, so he'd see this through to the end.

Bri would have to understand. He wasn't free to do as he liked.

He slipped into his skivvies and trousers in one motion, rising to his feet as he fastened the waistband. He stooped to retrieve his shirt and had it on when he reached the door. He turned back, allowing himself the pleasure of seeing her there on the bed they had just shared.

He left her to sleep and went outside, running a perimeter and checking for any sign of intruders. He made two sweeps, one close and one farther out. There was nothing but the scent of where Johnny had passed on his way back to their compound. He wondered how long before Headquarters asked him why he wasn't spending nights in his own bed. He was going to say he wasn't sleeping well, which was true. They'd probably draw more blood. Damn, he already felt like a one-man blood bank.

When he returned to the storage depot, he listened for the sound of Bri's breathing. Instead he heard a sound that stopped him. The sniffling and the choking were unmistakable. Was she crying?

Now what did he do?

He hesitated. He was no good at comforting women. He only knew one way to go about it. If he went in there, he knew what would happen. Mac blew out a breath.

"Damn it," he muttered and then marched into hostile territory.

He gathered her up in his arms and she clung to him.

"I don't deserve this," she cried. "Not after what I've done to other men."

That stopped him. Survivor's guilt, they called it. He recognized it, because he'd seen enough shrinks and knew all about how it was normal and blah, blah, blah. But looking at Bri now was like looking in a mirror.

"It's wrong, isn't it? Shouldn't I be suffering, doing some penance for Matthew?"

"It won't bring him back." That's what they had told him again and again.

She drew away. "So I just forget what I did? Just pretend it never happened?"

"If you figure out how to do that, let me know, because I've done worse."

She stared up at him.

"Besides, you didn't know your own power."

"And you didn't know what was in that building."

He used his thumbs to wipe the tears from her cheeks. "At least you can keep from doing it again. Now that you know, I mean."

"So what am I supposed to do? I can't touch them or let them touch me."

"You could have children if you wanted. I know you can."

"Not without hurting someone, and then my babies would be like me."

"Not exactly. Not as powerful, because they'd be second generation. Each generation is less potent than the previous one."

She drew away to sit on the side of the bed, head bowed and hands pressed flat on her knees. "I wanted children. But it's like having a genetic abnormality. It would be wrong to pass this on."

He released a sigh, and he realized afterward that the emptiness he felt yawning in his chest was not sympathy but sorrow. She wouldn't have children from him or anyone else, and he was certain that she would have been a great mother.

He drew her down to the mattress, lying still as she curled against him. He stroked her shoulder and arm as her breathing went from ragged to steady.

"How do you live with it?"

He stared at the ceiling. "Wake up each morning and try to make amends. Try to fix what I can."

He lived it every damned day and it didn't get easier, but he wouldn't tell her that.

"I don't think I can ever forgive myself for what I've done," she whispered

"Maybe we shouldn't."

She lifted her head, gazed up at him with eyes streaming tears and nodded. "You're right."

Bri didn't know exactly what woke her as she startled upright in the empty bed pushed against the side of the far wall of the former storage depot. She listened while searching the dark room for any threat. Everything seemed still and calm, but her heart jackhammered.

"Johnny?" she called and then heard a roar.

There was a thump that shook the building.

Bri sprang from the bed as the door flew open and several men charged inside. She raced around the small room moving smoothly into her top speed, but an instant later the windows were blocked from outside and she found no escape. It was clear that none of the four soldiers in the room could see her. She knew now that she was moving too fast for them to perceive. But it was also clear that they had barricaded each window and the door of the supply depot before she could escape. How long could she keep her momentum up and flash about a room from which there was no egress? Would they shoot her?

The Marines held their automatic weapons ready, barring the door and only exit. She glanced at them as she passed by again. From her point of view, each stood still as a gray statue, their square jaws the most prominent feature visible below their helmets.

The adrenaline poured through her, but the room was secure, as Mac called it and she was caught like a lobster in a grocery store fish tank. Where was Mac? What had they done to Johnny? How long could she run before they saw her, shot her?

She raced on but now her legs burned with fatigue. She paused at the window to try again to force the barrier back and failed. One of the Marines swung his rifle in a slow arc in her direction. The action must have been split-second to him, but she was gone before he had time to point the barrel at her.

She kicked at the door and then considered trying to take the weapons. She grabbed one of the rifles and pulled. The Marine held on. She lifted a foot to his chest and yanked, using a tactic Mac had taught her. The weapon slipped from his grip.

Great. Now she had this heavy rifle to lug around and three more weapons to take. The metal began to burn her hands. She looked at the men's belts and saw grenades and knives and sidearms and God knew what all in all those pockets and pouches. She'd never get all the weapons, and even if she did, four Marines did not need weapons to capture one exhausted female.

Where was Mac? What had they done to Johnny?

She called to them, shouting their names, praying they would hear and come in time.

Then she realized with a sickening jolt that she wanted them to fight their own fellows for her. No, she wouldn't. If she was getting out of this, she would have to do it herself and without hurting any of these men. The rifle fell from her hands. Bri slowed. One of the three soldiers who still had his weapon appeared. Everything sped up, the four men sprang at her and Bri sprang away, coming to her feet once more before darting from them again.

Mac had trained her to use her speed and told her about how females were said to used their gifts of attraction.

They seemed frozen again in the place she had just been, but she could see them straightening now, their movements slow but discernible as she reached top speeds. After several more minutes of running she heard more men outside. Did they have instructions not to open the doors or windows until she was captured or...

She looked at the strain on the faces of the young men sent inside to capture a vampire. This wasn't right. None of this.

Bri stopped.

One of the soldiers blocked her path. She collided with him and fell. Two Marines seized her by both arms as a third clasped her legs. Where was the fourth?

She felt a needle prick and then a rushing sensation as her mouth dropped open and her head lolled back.

Chapter 15

At eleven hundred the following morning Mac's radio crackled to life. He'd just left the medical facility, but already the command wanted him back. They said that Johnny had broken perimeter. But that didn't make any sense. Johnny was watching Bri, and Mac knew Lam wouldn't leave her unless he scented a bloodsucker, and even then Lam would come straight to him. Unless there wasn't time.

Bri.

Mac headed out of the qala. He'd find Johnny's trail or he'd find what was happening.

His phone chimed again with another text message adding to the three missed calls. The colonel wanted to see him ASAP.

Did the colonel already know about Bri?

Mac had that sick feeling in the pit of his stomach.

He acknowledged that he was obligated to report to the colonel. But some part of him had changed after the attack, and not just the furry part. Mac wasn't the good soldier any longer. He'd recognized it for a long time. Bri's coming just made him accept what his heart already knew. Mac didn't want to follow orders and he knew Johnny didn't, either.

Was it time for them to go? Past time?

He felt the tug of loyalty to the Corps pulling against his duty to his friend and to Bri.

Mac headed through the courtyard and paused at the sound of a jeep. His heart sunk. He glanced toward the adjacent wall knowing he could leap it, then his eyes trained on the surveillance camera fixed to the tree just beyond.

"Fuck," he muttered.

"MacConnelly!" It was the colonel's voice. He hadn't expected to see his commanding officer waiting for him outside headquarters. "Get your ass out here."

The moment Mac appeared the colonel started shouting. "He's off base again."

That didn't make sense. Johnny was on watch. He was guarding Bri.

"Sir, I—"

The colonel interrupted. "You said you'd watch him. You said he listens to you. Tech Support tells me you two don't even share the same quarters anymore. What the hell is going on?"

Mac stood at stiff attention. Why had Johnny left his post? "I don't know, sir."

"Clearly, you can't handle him, so I'm shutting you down. Johnny comes back into custody as soon as we catch his furry ass."

Mac lifted his gaze to meet the colonel's. Mac hesitated. He had to get to Bri.

"You are a Marine, MacConnelly. You swore to follow orders, and you are about one step away from the brig. I saw something on that video. You know what it is. So you tell me or we sweep the area with orders to kill anything that moves."

They'd catch Johnny, but Bri might get away. Was he willing to bet her life on her ability to control her unpredictable speed? Was he willing to toss Johnny back in a cage for her sake?

Mac stood before the colonel, motionless against the current that swept beneath his feet, dragging him under. He recognized the danger of this darkness and realized that if he let it swallow him up then he would be of no use to anyone. Not Johnny and certainly not Bri.

"All right, then." The colonel lifted the radio off his belt. "Lieutenant, call the MPs. We're taking MacConnelly into custody." He leaned toward Mac and glared. "And Johnny goes back in that cage, and this time he doesn't come out."

Sweat popped out on Mac's brow. Johnny hated the cage. It would kill him.

"No, sir, please. I can track him. I'll bring him back." Were there bloodsuckers near? Was that why Johnny went outside perimeter?

"We're past that. Get in." The colonel pointed with his radio to the backseat, behind his aide and driver.

Mac hesitated.

"Direct order, son. Don't be stupid."

Mac took a step backward, then turned, leaped over the fence and galloped away, hurtling through the forest at speeds no human could match. He had not gone far when he heard Johnny's roar coming from his right. He slowed. The next sound was one of feral pain. Johnny again, howling as if mortally wounded.

Mac needed to find Bri. But Johnny might be facing those bloodsuckers alone right now. He headed toward Johnny, tearing up saplings and slashing at greenery as he blazed through the woods only to come up short as he flung himself from the forest onto the jeep trail.

He glanced around trying to make sense of it. There was a flatbed truck with two cages bolted down tight. A jeep held two large speakers on tripods and the agonized scream came again from the speaker.

Mac felt a wash of panic make his knees wobble. A diversion. They didn't want him going toward Bri.

They knew.

The minute he slowed he saw the Marines moving in behind him, closing him in a circle. He knew they couldn't stop him, but instead of rifles, they held sticks, each tipped with a metal dart. Did the colonel know that if he bit any of these men, they'd turn?

Was that exactly what he wanted?

Mac waited as they closed in, weighing his options. He wasn't getting darted in the gums. That was certain.

Colonel Lewis's jeep appeared and stopped just outside the perimeter of Marines.

"I gave you a chance to come clean, MacConnelly. We already know about her."

Her? Mac's stomach dropped.

The colonel continued on as Mac wrestled to control the urge to vomit.

"I just didn't know how long you've had her. Female vampire. That's what they tell me from the lesson we caught in the woods. You teaching her how to use her tricks, Sergeant?"

Bri was in trouble. He turned in her direction.

The howl came again from the speaker and the colonel covered his ears. "Turn that shit off."

The cry ceased, and Mac now heard only the shifting of nervous soldiers awaiting orders.

"That was Johnny during the grenade study. We tape them all. I was afraid you wouldn't follow orders. Women do cloud a man's judgment. Though she's not a woman. You know that, right?"

Mac roared, the change already on him.

"'You are getting in that cage and coming in to base right now, soldier."

The pain at transformation lit through him like a flame to gasoline. His clothing shredded as he lowered his shoulder to sweep away the closest Marines and their silly pointed sticks. A moment later he bounded away but the colonel's voice followed him.

"You're too late. We got her already."

Bri came awake, drifting in and out of consciousness and finally recognizing that the bright light above her was a large, rectangular fluorescent fixture in the ceiling. She was groggy and weak. She turned her head, but felt stiff and awkward. Medical equipment stood behind her to the right. Numbers. Her blood pressure, she realized, and heart rate. On her left a metal stand held a clear plastic IV bag, but the writing on the bag was too blurry to read. With slow deliberation she turned her head to stare down at her arms, carefully arranged on either side of her hips, above the thin cotton blanket that covered her. She wore a hospital gown, blue and white.

Where was she?

Bri stared dumbly at the IV needle protruding from the skin of her right hand and secured with clear tape.

The vein ached from the intruding metal. How long had it been there? How long had *she* been here?

She tried to move her hand and the throbbing ache intensified. Inside the clear tubing a thin line of dark red blood flowed. Were they giving her blood or taking it?

She tried to turn her head and her vision swam. She found her body slow and sluggish as if the world had sped up and she had slowed.

But she managed to look back at the plastic bag on the metal stand. The IV fluid was clear. She glanced back to her arm, seeing the second IV disappearing beneath medical tape at the crease of her left elbow. Here the tube was filled with clear fluid.

They were taking her blood and replacing it with whatever was in that bag.

She reached with clumsy fingers, her muscles slow to respond to her command. Her hand halted as the circle of metal jangled against the bed rail. Bri stared at the handcuff. The skin on her wrist was puffy, red and itched. Her heart pounded; she glanced up at the machines and watched her blood pressure climb.

Bri tried and failed to sit up as tears streamed down her cheeks. She wondered if she deserved this treatment as penance for what she had done to Matthew and Jeffery.

The curtains drew back with the scrape of metal on metal, and there stood a tall, slim man in his late forties with startling blue eyes and a weathered face. This Marine had spent most of his life out of doors, she thought. His uniform looked like Mac's: the same tan color, crisp folds on the pockets and an identical belt that circled his hips. Only in place of the chevron she'd seen on Mac's sleeve, there sat an eagle with wings spread wide.

"I'm Colonel Noah Lewis," said the officer with the eagles on his shirt. "I run this show."

The officer glanced past the curtain to someone Bri could not see. She looked at the two-foot gap between the curtain's hem and the sparkling white tile floor, and she saw another pair of legs sheathed in a similar pair of creased trousers and the distinctive shiny black dress shoes. A moment later the man stepped into view and cast her a smile that clashed with the predatory glint in his eyes. He was younger, African-American, with light mocha skin and pale green eyes. He wore a white lab coat over his uniform and stepped right as the other went left.

"So, she's awake at last," he said. His voice held a very distinctive drawl, and he spoke as if she wasn't there or could not understand him.

The man's smile held charm, yet it froze her to the spot. She was afraid to even draw breath.

Bri eased back to the pillows as a chill settled in her lungs like ice crystals.

Lewis motioned toward the man in the lab coat, who loomed across the bed from him. "This is Dr. Sarr. He's been overseeing your care."

Dr. Sarr gave her a bright smile. "It's a pleasure to meet you at last, Brianna. Let me bring up the bed. Make you more comfortable. You'll feel a little dizzy. That's normal. Nothing to be concerned about. That's the anesthetic wearing off. Hopefully we won't need to sedate you again."

Again?

How many times had they sedated her so far? How long had she been here—hours, days? She realized that she had no idea. Her insides turned icy cold, and she tried to draw up her legs to roll into a ball, but they only twitched and her feet lolled to the side.

"Paralysis will also abate. Just be patient."

Is that why they call us patients? she wondered, as a wave of dizziness rolled through her. She couldn't think straight.

Dr. Sarr inched forward as if drawn and repelled all at once. "My, she is a beauty. Intel certainly got that right."

Bri jerked her hands reflexively toward her body and found them both cuffed to the raised rails.

There was a whir of a motor as the bed rose, lifting her into a semireclining position. She didn't know if it was his overzealous smile or his tone, but something about this guy sent a chill right up her neck. She shuddered and recoiled from the horror of this nightmare.

"You'll be thirsty. Let me get you some water." Sarr spun sharply away.

She'd be thirsty because they were stealing her blood. How much had they taken? Mac's words came back to her.

The only way to kill a vampire was to drain them of all their blood. They healed too fast to kill any other way.

Were they killing her now—taking all of it? But then why give her the IV?

"We know what you are, Brianna," said the Colonel. "Don't be alarmed. We aren't going to hurt you. Just running some tests."

"You can't keep me here," she whispered.

"Legally, I can, since you're a threat to national security."

"I'm not."

"Perhaps not intentionally. But I've looked into your past. There was a Mr. Matthew Solomon."

Bri hunched at the mention of her fiancé. The colonel lifted a brow and waited. When she said nothing he continued.

"And then there's Jeffery Martin. Mr. Martin is out of the hospital, by the way. He's made a miraculous recovery since your departure. I'm sure you're not surprised. But you overstayed your welcome with Mr. Solomon."

The air left Bri's lungs in a whoosh. Her skin crawled as she lay impotent—trapped. She tried and failed to draw up her legs as her breathing grew erratic.

Lewis's smile broadened at his victory.

Dr. Sarr returned now carrying a small blue plastic cup of water in two hands, as if the contents were a precious gift and then offered it to her.

Brianna lifted a hand reflexively to accept it and was restrained by the handcuffs again. Her raw skin throbbed at the movement.

"I'll do it," said Dr. Sarr, holding the cup to her lips. He grinned at her, a foolish smile that she'd seen on the faces of many men in her lifetime. She'd even seen this stupefied expression on the faces of total strangers. Men, mostly, but women as well. She never understood it. Now she did, because Mac had explained her power. She was irresistible to them—humans.

They all found her appealing. At least now she understood why.

Delight flashed in the doctor's eyes as he continued to grin at her and slipped one hand behind her to cradle her neck.

She started to lift her head and then that little voice

spoke in her head. Was she crazy? No way was she taking anything to drink from this guy.

She turned her head away.

"No?" said the doctor. "I'll set it here. You just let me know if you need anything." He hovered, keeping his gaze on Brianna as if he could not or would not take his eyes off her.

She lay on the bed, restrained and nearly naked, as she faced the two sharply dressed, confident Marines and was unable to keep her body from quivering. Her teeth tingled and her jaw clacked. She clamped down, gritting her teeth to prevent them from seeing her utter terror.

Helpless, she realized. They could do whatever they liked to her and she could do nothing to stop them.

The colonel's tone was conversational and his smile genuine as she lay before him cuffed to the bed. "We need to learn more about your kind," he said.

Her kind. The words fell hard. She was not human. Not like them. She knew it, had known it for some time but still the words pierced her like thorns. She was other, outside. Bri's chin sunk to her chest and her words were a whisper. "What are you going to do with me?"

He didn't answer. She lifted her chin and met his gaze and held on as if the contact of his eyes might somehow keep her from drowning. By slow degrees the colonel's features softened, but he did not look away. Something was happening. She felt it in the tingling of her belly. Bri remained still and alert. The colonel began to speak.

"I don't know what Sergeant MacConnelly told you, but we have had some trouble with vampires. The males are nearly impossible to neutralize, though my werewolves succeeded with the two on the road, confirming they make effective bodyguards. I have a theory that they were after you."

Bri glanced away.

"Yes, I thought so. The males have proved impossible to capture. This has pressed us into the unenviable position in the past of being forced to hire them."

She recalled Mac saying that she needed to look at a man to be most persuasive and so glanced at the doctor and found he was sweating in the cool room. He reached for her and then froze, his hand hovering there in midair for a moment before he redirected it to smooth over his short brown hair. After which, he shoved his wayward hands into his pockets as if to trap them. Bri turned her attention back to the colonel to find he had inched closer to her side. Dr. Sarr now stepped hastily away from her bedside, backing toward the curtains.

The colonel paid Sarr no mind, nor did he seem to note his odd behavior as he continued. "We'd much prefer to have our own unit. I dislike dealing with mercenaries. You will be our first operative and the mother of all the rest."

Bri's eyes bulged and her words were barely audible. "What?"

"Your cooperation on the first part is necessary. But not on the second, surprisingly. We can harvest your eggs to use in vitro and then implant the fertilized egg to a surrogate. Do you have a preference?"

Bri's head swam and she closed her eyes at the horror of what was happening. Whatever she deserved for her past mistakes, this was not karmic justice. In that instant she made up her mind to fight back.

She tugged at the handcuffs, feeling the burn of

metal and knowing she could not escape. They had imprisoned her to this metal bed. She needed to get out of here. But how?

"I can't," she whispered.

"Oh, you can. You're young and healthy. It's a minor procedure. Surrogate might be better. You'd be free to train, and it'd be a shame to spoil your figure."

She blinked away the hot tears that rolled to her hairline and saw Dr. Sarr had reached the curtains that ringed her bed. Sweat now rolled down his face. He stepped outside her line of vision. Bri looked to Lewis to find his smile bright, as if he had just brought her flowers instead of his terrible plans. He seemed elated and slightly mad. The colonel's smile widened, euphoric now. From beyond the curtain Dr. Sarr cleared his throat. Lewis looked annoyed.

"What is it?"

"Should you be telling her that, sir?" asked Sarr.

"Telling her what?"

"Your objectives?"

The colonel scowled at Dr. Sarr, whom he could obviously see from his position, then his eyes widened. He rubbed his face with both hands. Then he glared at her. "God damn it!"

He hadn't intended to tell her anything. She'd influenced him, just as Mac had said she could. A tiny spark of hope tingled inside her. She could do this. She could get out of here.

Lewis spun and retreated, dragging the curtain closed behind him. "No one goes in there," he ordered.

"I have to remove the IV from her right arm." That was Sarr, she knew. If he looked at her, she might persuade him to let her go.

"Sedate her first. And figure out a way to sedate her from out here. Don't let her look at you."

"Yes, sir."

Her hopes withered. She couldn't influence anyone if she was unconscious. She shook her wrists against the bed rail as panic welled inside her. She glanced to the red tube where her blood drained away, and it was all she could do to keep from screaming.

"Colonel! Colonel Lewis. I have to talk to you." Her voice held a definite edge of panic.

Next came the sound of those boot heels striking the linoleum tiles as the colonel retreated. The footsteps came again and she shook her head in an effort to clear the fog that still captured from her brain.

The curtain drew open.

"Colonel." But it wasn't Lewis. It was Sarr. The doctor approached carrying a needle, his gaze fixed on the IV.

Mac raced over the uneven ground, the vegetation blurring as he reached top speeds, and still it wasn't fast enough. The colonel's words echoed in his mind. They had her already. Did they? What had they done to Johnny, because sure as shit Lam had not left his post. To get to Bri, they would have to have gone through one pissed-off werewolf.

He and Johnny were still leathernecks. *Semper Fi.* Always loyal. But now they were loyal to each other.

He jumped the trunk of a downed tree, staying low, building speed. The worry made him stomach sick. What were they doing to her?

Maybe they wouldn't even be able to catch her. She was fast. So damned fast.

Run, Bri. Run like you never ran before. Remember what I taught you.

He hoped she'd get away and that made him a traitor.

Mac had acted like those fucking rear-echelon motherfuckers, calling the shots and doing a shit job. Disobeying direct orders, he thought. Shit. He never would have believed…but he never would have thought that vampires were other than monsters. Still, if he was no longer a Marine, what the fuck was he?

Johnny was close now, he could smell him.

Mac couldn't decide if he should stay in his wolf form or switch to human. Why didn't he hear anything? No sound of struggle, no roar of fury. Just the sound of his own breathing and the pads of his feet tearing into soft earth.

He caught sight of the supply depot. The door lay hanging open, and the barricades were still braced against the windows on either side. Mac scanned the area and found him. A big black mound of fur lying on the ground. Bits of dried leaves and grass stuck to his glossy coat. Why hadn't they taken Lam in?

Mac ran past Johnny and into the depot. The furniture, boxes and supplies lay strewn about, showing signs of a struggle of some kind.

He roared for Bri and was met with silence. They'd taken her. Mac retraced his steps, checking Johnny and finding him breathing, but out. Mac retracted his gums and found no stab wound. How had they done it?

The answer to his questions came a moment later when he heard a familiar *thunk*. He knew it. Grenade launcher.

They'd left Lam as bait and were about to use on Mac the same weapon they'd used on him. Percussion grenade? he wondered, as the unfamiliar canister rolled into view.

Mac's training was to dive for cover, but instead he hoisted the nine-foot werewolf onto his back and made use of his speed, running in the opposite direction as the grenade exploded behind him in a great plume of smoke.

Gas, he realized, closing his mouth and plugging his nose with his free hand. His eyes burned and he could not see where he was running, but he stayed on his feet. To fall was to go down, and if he breathed that gas he would not get up.

Now he understood how they had stopped Johnny and how they had taken Bri.

The smoke began to clear. He could see the ground, but he kept up the pace, his lungs burning, demanding the air he withheld.

Not yet. You don't know what they used. It might still take you out.

The Marines were nearby. They'd have more gas, might be aiming at him already. He changed course, veering off as a new canister of gas exploded in the direction he had been running.

He had no choice but to breathe, drawing one long desperate breath, and he instantly felt dizzy. Johnny shifted against him and groaned. Mac patted his leg and used some of his precious oxygen to growl. Johnny relaxed and Mac charged on. He knew these woods and made for a culvert that would be good cover and difficult for Marines to reach with any equipment. Not that this would stop them for long, but he only needed to get Johnny up again.

He slid on his ass down most of the incline, happy to

disappear into the wild rhododendron bushes that lined the stream. Once at the bottom, he rolled Johnny to his back and flopped down beside him, gasping and spent.

Johnny threw a hand over his eyes and groaned. Mac rolled to one side and threw up. Lam tried to rise and fell back down. Mac grabbed him by the elbow and tugged. His gunner went still and Mac listened for signs of pursuit but heard none.

Then he called the change, gritting his teeth as his body contorted. Now he was naked, which was awkward, but at least he could speak to his friend.

Johnny turned his head in Mac's direction and groaned, panting now.

"The gas made you sick."

Johnny nodded and pinched his eyes closed.

"They used a recording of you to lure me away. By the time I realized, I was too far off to help."

Lam groaned and tried again to push himself up.

"They took her."

Johnny's head dropped back to the ground.

Just saying it out loud hurt like a body blow. What the hell were they going to do now?

"She's gone."

Johnny threw back his head and bellowed, rolled to his hands and knees, swayed dangerously and then began writing frantically. Mac squatted beside him and read.

What do with her?

It was a question he couldn't answer. "I don't know. Study her, maybe, like they are with us." Mac felt sure he would puke as the fear for her safety attacked him.

His friend held his gaze, and Mac saw sympathy in his friend's dark eyes.

"I disobeyed a direct order coming back for you both. Lewis wants you back in a cage and me beside you. Smartest thing for you to do is take off before they find us."

Johnny wrote, *You?*

"I'm going after her."

Johnny nodded and then studied Mac's face. Finally he wrote, *I go 2.*

"No. If they catch you, then you are in that fucking cage for good. I won't have it."

My choice.

"You take orders from me, Lam. Don't forget it."

Johnny shook his head and used his fingers to pantomime walking. He was coming, too. Following him into another goddamn building, only this time what awaited them was worse than a fucking werewolf—it was the entire U.S. Marine Corps.

"Johnny, I can't stand it if something bad happens to you, something else, I mean. And I can't stand to think what they are doing to her right now."

Mac fell forward onto outstretched arms and bowed his head. He couldn't draw breath. A wave of dizziness rocked him. What if they hurt her? He covered his mouth with one hand to stifle a cry. Then he dragged his hands up over the short bristle of his hair and laced his fingers together behind his head like a captured prisoner of war. The truth struck him hard.

He loved her.

That was why he slept with her. Not to scratch her itch or because she had a cute ass or any other damned excuse he fed himself.

"Johnny, I think I'm in love with her."

Johnny held Mac's panicked stare and gave a nod.

"I have to save her," he said to Johnny.

His corporal pointed back toward base.

"Yes. After we get her, you know we'll have to go AWOL."

His friend did not hesitate but gave another slow nod. Then he extended his hand. Mac took it. When had they both stopped being soldiers and become a tribe of two?

Mac focused his energy for the change and braced as the pain swept through him like acid. They were a team again, both focused on one goal. Recapture Bri.

They were Marines. They'd improvise.

They started toward the medical center, knowing that Bri was there in the underground facility.

As they ran, Mac considered what he was doing. It was just like the night he'd ordered his Fire Teams into that building. Then, he knew he'd made a critical error. Only this time he had a chance to make it right.

Chapter 16

Bri struggled, and the metal handcuffs clanged against the stainless steel rails as she shrank away from Sarr. Her eyes fixed on the needle he carried and the clear fluid within. Sarr never looked at her and never touched her as he lifted the clear tubing.

"No, wait," she said.

He injected the liquid into a juncture in the tubing. A moment later her vein burned. An instant later her skin tingled. She tried to remove the IV but the restraints stopped her and then there was a rushing sound as everything went black.

The next thing she knew she was shivering violently, curled on her side and huddled in a tangle of sheets and thin cotton blankets. The smell of bleach and disinfectant reminded her of the nursing home where she'd once volunteered.

My God, she thought, had she hastened the deaths of any of the elderly there? No, she realized, because she had been younger then, not as dangerous as she was now that she had become a woman. That was what her nana had told her.

Her head ached, and she lifted her hands to cover her eyes. The light was too bright. It felt as if the fluorescent bulbs were burning the tissue behind her eyes. There was a steady pulse of pain that accompanied each beat of her heart. And the waves of nausea told her she was either touching metal or was too damn close to it.

Where was she?

"Mac?" she whispered.

She panted as the pain grew worse and the memories fell upon her like a pack of hungry wolves. Her capture, and then the colonel saying he'd use her eggs to create more of her kind.

He couldn't. She had to stop him. Had to escape. She lifted one hand from her eyes and peered out squinting against the ripping pain that traveled through her skull. But she could see a blurry image of the bed. A metal hospital bed that had been slightly elevated to lift her torso. A thin mattress separated her from the hated steel. Was she still in the medical facility, or had they moved her? Her eyeballs seemed to pulse with her heart, but she could make out the bedding—white cotton sheets again. She used one hand as a visor and kept the other one pressed securely to her opposite eye as she glanced down at the blue-and-white hospital gown.

Had she had surgery?

She slipped both hands over her abdomen and found no pain, no bandages, but she wasn't sure how eggs were harvested. Could they have taken one or more? She didn't know. Bri then extended her gaze beyond the bed. Even this slight movement made her stomach pitch. The sour taste in her mouth warned her to move gingerly.

Bri stilled as a realization struck her. They had not cuffed her wrists to the bed rails. She lowered her arms and endured the avalanche of pain from the blinding light.

Opposite her bed was a gray metal door with a brushed nickel latch. The white walls to either side were cinder block and lacked the customary light switch that usually sat just inside a door. A chill that had nothing to do with the thin blanket lifted the hairs all over her body. This was a prison cell.

She was alone, but she felt as if someone were watching her. Bri tried and failed to sit up. That was when she heard the whirring sound. She opened her eyes and glanced toward the door. The whirring stopped.

Bri listened. Nothing.

Then she lifted her gaze to the ceiling, squinting against the bright lights. And then she saw it. Her gaze flicked to the small black dome of plastic. A camera mounted in the corner where the walls met the ceiling. There was another behind her in the right corner.

Bri grabbed the hem of her hospital gown and tugged it down to cover her hip.

"Colonel Lewis? Are you there?"

There was a click and then a reply, slightly distorted by the speaker she could not locate.

"Yes, Brianna. How are you feeling?"

She ignored the question. Anger flared inside her, sharp as cut glass.

"You won't get away with this."

His voice came back, calm and filled with smug superiority. "Feel free to write your congressman."

"Mac will get me out of here."

The colonel's chuckle filled the room. "Werewolves

are immune to your kind. He's not your puppet. He's a Marine and a damn fine one."

"He'll come."

"Extremely doubtful, since he is the one who turned you in."

"Turned…" The shock of his words hit her like a slap. She fell back to the mattress. Was it possible? Could Mac have abandoned her, or was this just a lie? "I don't believe you."

"No difference to me what you believe."

Uncertainty tugged. Had Mac betrayed her? No, she wouldn't believe it. She lifted her chin and stared at the camera. "He'll come."

"I hope you're right. Now just relax. We're prepping the OR for you."

Mac paused in the woods beside the stream to collect a rumpled, musty set of clothing from one of his drops. Lam stopped beside him and cast an impatient look as Mac tugged the sweater over the rumpled T-shirt and then zipped his pants.

The stark reality of his choice loomed large. It was a decision he had already made, but he did not have the right to make it for Johnny.

"When I go after her, it's over. You understand? I'll have to go AWOL."

Johnny gave a slow nod.

"If you come with me, we'll be on the run. All of us, and they'll never give up trying to bring us in."

Johnny's nod showed he knew this as well.

"But if you stay behind, then they won't blame you. You'll still have a chance."

Johnny growled.

Mac's head sunk. "Johnny, I got you into this mess. I ordered you into that building and I…" He couldn't finish that. He swallowed back the guilt. "But I always thought…think…that they'll find a cure. I couldn't have gone on unless I believed that. But if you go, you're stuck like this. For good, you understand? Stay here. It's your only chance."

Johnny glared.

"It's an order."

Johnny shook his head, apparently also done with taking orders. He lifted his hands as if gripping something. Bars, he realized.

"They'll lock us up. Yeah. Sure as shit."

Johnny held his position and Mac understood. "They'll lock you up either way?"

It was true. A truth they both understood.

Mac glanced away and then back to meet his friend's gaze. "If I could, I'd trade places with you."

Johnny exhaled in a long blast and then gave him a rough pat on the shoulder, hard enough to buckle most men at the knees.

"I'll never forgive myself. And I won't give up until we find a way back for you, too."

Johnny pointed at the road.

"Yeah. I just…I don't know…Johnny, I don't want to make another mistake. What if this is another bad idea? What if…" Mac hunched with his hands on his knees like a runner after a race. He blew out a breath and spoke to the ground. "If she dies or you die…"

Johnny pointed toward the medical facility.

Mac hesitated. "I can get her out. There is no reason for us both to throw everything away."

Johnny inhaled and then his head snapped up. An

instant later Mac smelled it, too. The scent was sweet and metallic, like blood, but there was more, a deeper cloying fragrance of blooming jasmine and beneath that the musty stink of a carnivore.

The hairs on his neck lifted. *Vampires!*

Johnny's ears flattened back. Mac stripped from his clothing and changed to his werewolf form as Lam stood guard. Mac followed his comrade, who went after the scent on all fours, not because he had to, but because it kept his nose to the ground and his body low and out of sight. They were heading back to the place where Brianna had been taken. Before they reached the building they found what they were tracking.

Flesh eaters. Six of them.

Mac's hackles rose. Johnny dropped down into cover.

The vampires' skin was pinkish, like the skin of a newborn rabbit, but their eyes were rimmed with crimson. Their misshaped heads resembled humans but for the slitlike noses and prominent fangs that protruded over thick, liver-colored lips.

The males had found the place where Brianna had been.

He and Johnny were outnumbered three to one. To kill them, Mac needed to hold one long enough for it to bleed out. That would be challenging with two of its fellows attacking him. How long did it take to bleed to death?

Depends on the size of the hole, he decided.

"Too many," he said to Johnny.

There was no choice now. The vampires would track Bri to the medical facility and even the heavy guard would be useless, because once the flesh eaters went to top speed, the Marines would be helpless as toddlers against them. "We have to get Bri, now."

Mac ran with Johnny on his heels. How fast could a

male vampire travel? He thought of Brianna, moving so quickly she disappeared, and ran faster.

Mac cut through the woods, the shorter path for someone running. If they could catch the colonel before they reached the facility he had a chance of retrieving her. After that…

Mac ran faster.

Would he have to kill his fellow soldiers to take her?

Mac felt something snapping inside himself as he recognized that he would do whatever it took to get to Bri, and he'd kill anyone who stood in his way.

"Bring her out," said a male voice.

Bri tried to relax her clenched jaw as the footsteps approached. Her bed moved. She peered through her eyelashes as they rolled her into the corridor. They paused at a locked door and were buzzed through. The bed began to roll again, into an elevator. The doors swished shut.

"She out?" asked a voice behind her.

"Not sure," came the reply.

When the doors opened she found an escort of four armed Marines.

"Secure the prisoner." The voice was deep with a Texas twang and was wholly unfamiliar. She saw the glint of handcuffs and bolted, running blindly.

"Where'd she go?" asked one of the men from the elevator.

She ran in a circle around the entranceway, pausing to try the two doors. They opened with a key card, like hotels, she realized.

"There she is."

Bri turned to face them. There was no way out. They

were on her a moment later, strong hands gripping her, dragging her back to the gurney. It took the men no time at all to handcuff her to the raised bed rails and wheel her through the door. Her wrist began to burn. Blisters formed, broke and wept. But she welcomed the pain, because it helped her fight the drug that threatened to gobble her up. Bri watched to see who had the plastic key card as they swept through the next set of doors, and she noted where he kept it. Unfortunately the Marine with the key card remained behind with the other three as she continued through the open door with her original two escorts.

This corridor was wide. She passed several rooms that looked like operating theaters. She rattled against her restraints as she repeated one word—*no*.

"What'd she say?" said the one behind her.

"It's the drug," said the one at her feet. "Will you just look at her?" He grinned, his smile making him look younger, less threatening.

She recalled Mac telling her that her influence was stronger if she stared into the man's eyes. Apparently vampires and snakes had a way of mesmerizing a victim. Then, according to Mac, she only had to tell them what she wanted and they'd do it. But these were trained Marines, not weak-willed or easily influenced. Still, she saw no other hope.

Bri cleared her throat and forced a smile at the orderly. Her ears continued to buzz as if she had thrust her head into a nest of hornets.

"Could you take off these handcuffs, please?" she asked.

He gave her a "be serious" look. But she just held his gaze and gradually he reached in his pocket.

"What are you doing?" asked the one behind her.

"She wants them off."

"Yeah, and…?"

"So they're coming off."

He slipped the key in the lock and twisted it. Bri tipped her head up and glanced at the man behind her.

"I can't get away," she said to him and watched his expression soften, as if he was staring at a helpless kitten instead of a tigress.

"That's right," he said. "You can't."

"So it's all right if my wrists are free." She held her breath, expecting to be cuffed again. But both men just continued down the corridor to the last room as she tried to contain her astonishment. Large, imposing machines circled the bare stainless steel operating table. A huge light shown down on the silver surface so brightly she had to squint. Then she saw the metal stirrups fixed to the end of the table. Bri's heart rate climbed and sweat broke out on her forehead. She trembled so hard that the gurney shook.

"Easy now," said Dr. Sarr, stepping into view and smiling down on her. Seeing him in blue surgical scrubs only added to her terror. He glanced to her escorts. "Why isn't she out?"

"Maybe the dose is wrong. We figured on her weight, but she's not human."

Bri blinked as she realized how close she came to being completely helpless.

"Let's get you prepped," said Sarr.

Bri swallowed and fixed her attention to the doctor who returned holding an IV needle. He grasped her hand, turning her wrist to study her skin, searching, she suspected for a plump vein for that hollow-tipped steel needle.

He loomed and Bri tensed. If she didn't do something quickly he'd press that plunger and it would be all over.

She had no choice. To escape, she would have to become the very thing she had denied.

Chapter 17

"Dr. Sarr. I'm not quite ready for that," said Bri, eyes fixed on the terrifying needle. Her voice sounded funny and the buzzing in her ears had grown worse. "I need to speak to you."

The IV needle glinted. Bri forced her eyes up to meet the doctor's and fixed a smile as her mouth went dry as clay. His gaze locked to hers. The wrinkles on his brow eased.

"I have a schedule. Make it quick."

Her periphery still saw the needle but she looked into his eyes, seeing his pupils enlarge with each passing second.

"I don't want those Marines to hear," she whispered and pursed her lips.

Sarr ordered them out.

"Could I have some water?"

Sarr poured her a cup and hurried back to her then handed the water to her.

"Is there something you could give me to counteract the sedative?"

"That's not wise before surgery. You need to be relaxed."

"I am relaxed. Just being around you makes me relaxed. But I'd like something to make me more alert." She kept her gaze fixed on his.

Sarr mentioned something.

"Yes, please."

It was all she could do not to pull away as he used a syringe to puncture her vein. A moment later he was injecting a clear fluid through the rubber cover and into her bloodstream. If her influence hadn't worked then it was game over.

But almost immediately she felt more alert.

"It's a mild stimulant. How are you feeling? Ready to begin?" he asked.

"Almost." She stared deeply into his watery gray eyes and wondered if she could pull this off. "You seem tense, Doctor. Why not give yourself something so you can relax?"

He turned to the counter and rummaged through drawers. "What about this?"

"Will it put you to sleep?"

"If the dose is right."

"Perfect."

She watched while he injected the drug into his bicep. The ease with which he did as she asked gave her a chill. How simple would it have been to ask him to inject a lethal dose?

"I need your exit card."

He passed it to her.

"Will this get me out?"

"I'm sure they'll stop you. There are cameras everywhere. Whoa. I need to sit down."

"Here." She patted the mattress. "Lie beside me."

Sarr scrambled up as Bri slipped off the opposite side of the gurney, her bare feet contacting the cold floor.

The doctor yawned. Bri turned to go and then asked for his surgical scrubs. He struggled to comply, getting tangled up as his pants caught on his shoes. Thankfully his white boxers remained up. Bri helped him and received a smile in return.

"Did Travis MacConnelly really turn me in?" she asked.

"No. That was a lie. Standard procedure—turn allies against each other."

His words brought sweet relief. Mac had not betrayed her.

The doctor slipped out of his scrubs to reveal a muscular torso with some extra flab encircling his middle. She accepted his top.

He grinned at her. His words were slurred. "You're so pretty."

Bri unfastened her gown and dropped it to the floor. Sarr's gaze swept over her and he licked his lips. She stepped back and into Sarr's trousers tugging the drawstring until they fit her waist. Then she dragged on the blue V-necked top that hung on her but at least she didn't feel a breeze. She tucked the plastic key into her breast pocket. On the way out of the door she grabbed a head cover to conceal her coppery hair.

The urge to run twitched against the need to know what happened to Mac and Johnny. She glanced at the door and then to the man who might have answers to the questions that troubled her.

"How did Mac and Johnny come to be werewolves?" she asked.

"Mac was bitten."

"Accidental?"

His laughed was the kind one used as a weapon to make someone feel small. "Lewis knew. He sent the squad into that hot zone." Sarr lifted a hand to speak to her from the side of his mouth, dropping his voice in a confidential way. "He knew about the werewolf. That was his objective. Not securing the building. Not securing the werewolf. Lewis wanted a survivor. One squad, thirteen Marines. And he got two survivors. Mission accomplished." Sarr yawned and closed his eyes.

Bri's breath hissed through clenched teeth and then gave Sarr's jowly cheek a little slap. "The colonel sent them in on purpose to be butchered?"

"To face the werewolf, yes." He patted her arm clumsily and let his hand drop to the table. "I can tell you one thing, those things are vicious. I saw the surveillance tapes."

"Mac said that he attacked Johnny. Is that true?"

"Hell of a thing."

Bri's mind reeled. Mac hadn't made an error in judgment trying to take the building. He'd been sent in there like cannon fodder.

"Did Mac attack John Lam?" she asked again, feeling her opportunity at escape ticking away with the seconds.

"We haven't succeeded in generating any new ones. In vitro doesn't work. Fetuses are normal, no werewolves. Just regular little human babies, more's the pity. We've tried with both Lam's and MacConnelly's sperm. I think werewolves have to be made instead of born. That's my theory. Just can't replicate what happened to MacConnelly. But we will."

"You... Do they know that?"

The doctor frowned and shook his head. "Need to know." His eyes drifted closed. "I wonder what would happen if we mixed theirs with yours?" he muttered, dropping into a doze.

She shook him awake. "How do I get out of here?"

He explained the route and told her where she'd meet armed Marines. The stimulant was now humming in her blood like a double espresso. Her fury and the fear only added to the mix. She knew she could run fast. But she'd have to pause at doors to unlock them, and there she would be vulnerable.

Time to go.

Brianna took the surgical mask from around Sarr's thick neck and secured it over her face. Then she tucked her hair into the blue cap and headed through the door. All Dr. Sarr told her spun in her mind like a cyclone.

She made it out of the operating wing without discovery and slipped unnoticed into the adjoining corridor past the signs indicating the recovery room and the pre-op area. She glided past the nurses' station at normal speed, keeping her head down and her feet moving. Bri used Dr. Sarr's key to slip out of the secure area and ran right into Colonel Lewis. He apologized and stooped to retrieve her key card. She didn't wait for him to hand it to her but snatched it from him as she broke into a run that transitioned to a full-out dash. The nurses in the corridor seemed to slow and came to a standstill as she streaked past.

With luck she'd be out of this damned building before they could sound the alarm.

Then where?

Bri paused to let herself out of the medical building and then bolted across the yard on bare feet, losing her cap. She could see the ten-foot perimeter fence, the razor wire rolled on the top, glistening with spikes. She'd have to jump it. She could. She knew it. But her gaze fixed on the razor wire and fear washed her cold.

Her panic was roaring inside her, making her movements spastic. Was the stimulant wearing off or was the sedative growing stronger? Whatever the reason, she saw the Marines pouring from the buildings like red ants, their movements sluggish, but discernible. She was slowing down. She could hear their shouts now. See them pointing—at her.

She'd never make the fence before they cut off her escape. Bri sprinted forward, but her legs grew heavier with each step. She leapt and hit the fence midway, clinging to the chain-links like a gibbon monkey. The metal seared her flesh. She reached and pulled, scaling the fence. Below her the wire shook as men climbed after her.

She'd never have another chance. She felt it in her marrow. Her hands burned, blistered, and still she clung. *You'll heal. Keep going.*

McConnelly and Lam approached the perimeter fence that ringed the medical facility and headquarters. The evening air had turned cold, but warmth still clung to the damp earth. Above them the sky was a midnight-blue carpet casting the trees in dark silhouette.

It was hardest to see at this time, when the light had faded, yet the sky was still too bright to see with his night vision. Colors faded to black.

They stared across the stretch of open ground before the medical facility, which squatted like a toadstool with much of its structure belowground.

What were they doing to her right now?

A moment later they heard the siren and saw Bri running across the open yard toward the fencing. He could see her clearly, despite the fact that the spotlight had not yet found her. She wore pale hospital scrubs, like oversized pajamas, and her wild red hair flowed out behind her as she galloped across the ground barefooted. She was moving fast, but nowhere near her super vampire speed. Bri ran and they chased—a dozen Marines charging after her. He watched her awkward gait. Something was wrong with her. They wouldn't catch her before she reached the fence. But they'd reach her before she cleared it. Their bullets wouldn't kill her. She'd heal no matter how many bullets they put in her, unless she bled out.

Mac forgot the plan. He forgot every blessed thing except getting to Bri as he streaked to the fence, determined to tear it down with his claws.

A sharp sting of pain ripped through her upper arm and Bri lost her grip. Her opposite hand reflexively squeezed tighter, taking her weight, until she recovered enough to lift her left arm again, reaching to clutch the hated metal wire once more. Her palms burned as if the metal were molten hot, but she clung, tenacious as a barnacle, knowing that to release her grip was to fall back into the hands of that maniac Lewis and his evil doctor, Sarr.

She caught movement beyond the fence and trained her gaze on the creature, recognizing him instantly. Huge, gray and running on all fours. Mac! He bolted straight at her on the opposite side of the fence. Behind him, some fifty yards back, Johnny followed, as always.

Bri clung as Mac reared up on his hind legs and slashed at the barrier that separated them. The metal links popped open with a ringing sound as his nails sliced through steel. No wonder his squad had stood no chance against the werewolf.

Behind her came the shouts of men and an instant later the pop of gunfire. Bullets sparked on the metal beside her head, and she dropped to the ground as the fence buckled and Mac leaped through. He gripped her upper arms and dragged her to her feet. Before she could run through the gaping hole, he lifted her and ducked out the way he had come. Bullets whizzed past them, and she knew from the way Mac arched that more than one shot had found his exposed back. But he crouched around her, protecting her from the flying bits of lead.

As bullets drummed against his hide, he didn't slow, just kept running over uneven ground, shielding her from harm as he carried her closer to the line of trees and the protection of the forest. Johnny passed them, running into fire as they fled. He moved so fast he was a blur of black fur, but she heard him howl a challenge to anyone foolish enough to try to follow his sergeant. She looped her arms even more tightly around Mac's neck and clung. An instant later a ripping pain lanced through her arm as if she'd been stung by a hornet. Her arm dropped from Mac's strong neck as the pain changed to a burning. A glance told her she'd been hit again because blood now ran from her upper and lower arm and stained the front of her scrubs. Mac looked down at her, spotted the wound and placed one hand on her head, covering her further as he increased his speed.

Behind them the gunfire continued amid Johnny's roar. She knew Johnny held back their pursuers, gaining them precious minutes.

She and Mac reached the woods and Mac slowed, stopped and then howled. The sound shivered over her skin and iced her blood. Mac dropped to a knee and turned the way they had come. He set her gently on the mossy ground and looked toward the compound behind them.

"Go get him!" she shouted to be heard above the din.

Mac ran back toward Johnny. She was alone. Bri stood on shaky legs. Her skin flashed hot from the blood and cold from the night air. The palms of her hands looked as if she had been branded, but even as she stared the red welts and burns faded. She gingerly held her left wrist with her right hand, supporting her injuries and taking a more careful look. The blood that had poured like water from a pitcher, now oozed from blackish wounds. There were two holes for each bullet. Entrance and exit, she realized and she also realized the bullet had shattered at least one bone in her upper arm. That was likely why she felt nauseous. Her stomach pitched and kicked. Bri folded and lost the contents of her stomach. The dizziness came in waves as she stood with her forehead resting on the trunk of a tree. At last she could open her eyes. The gunfire had stopped.

"Mac? Johnny!" Bri straightened and instinctively moved toward the two men who had protected her and risked everything to get her out. What would they do to them?

Bri made it half the distance to the open ground beyond the trees when Mac leaped into view. Johnny dove into sight behind him, and they both landed gracefully amid the undergrowth. She could see them perfectly in black and white, and she knew they could see her just as clearly. But still Bri gasped when their glowing predatory eyes fixed on her. Together in their wolf forms, they were a formidable pair.

She stared in awe, taking in the differences. Johnny's coat was pure black and Mac's the mixture of gray, white and black hair that she thought a more traditional color for a wolf. They looked neither man nor wolf, but some corruption of both, and the combination unsettled her.

Mac's gums were black and he had the upright musculature and carriage of a man, but the fur, face and eyes of a wolf. The claws that jutted from his fingers did not belong on a wolf, but more resembled something from a horror movie.

Bri was used to seeing Johnny like this but not Mac. He had seldom shown her this second self. Then as now, he had little choice.

He was terrible and fearsome and she was so happy to see him that she threw herself into Mac's arms, hugging him fiercely. His hand cupped her head and he let her cling for a moment before setting her on her feet. She stood staring at Mac and looked to Johnny, who shifted from side to side, his eyes on her.

"Thank you for coming for me." She held Mac's hand and then reached toward Johnny. "Thank you, Johnny."

Johnny looked at the hand she extended and then took it in both of his, bringing it to his cheek for just a moment before releasing her. If Johnny had resented her at first, he had apparently changed his mind and now meant to protect her. She did not know if it was for Mac's sake or for her own, but she was grateful.

"Are you both all right?"

They nodded. Mac clasped her injured arm. His nostrils flared as he sniffed at her wound. She trusted him. She trusted both of them. So she offered her injured arm for their inspection.

"It hardly hurts now," she whispered, noticing the holes now scabbing, the blood drying. "Healing, so fast."

It was the most serious injury she'd ever sustained, and the bone did not even hurt now.

Johnny cocked his head toward the compound and then signed something to Mac. Johnny took the lead.

She fell into step with them, and for the first time since her capture she felt safe.

After a few minutes the sounds of shouts and curses died away. But they were back there. She knew it, because the colonel would not give up his prizes so easily. And what would happen to Johnny and Mac now?

She felt shaky again as she realized what this rescue would cost them. Did they understand what they had just done? The weight of their sacrifice dragged at her. She didn't deserve such loyalty. All she had ever done her entire life was use and hurt people. Why would they help her?

Chapter 18

Bri looked around them and saw that her night vision had begun to pick up color. It was nearly morning. Mac slowed to a walk. How far had he run with her in his arms?

The silence of the forest enveloped her like a cloak and she could hear nothing but her own heartbeat and Mac's labored breathing.

The fur that blanketed his face did not quite cover the upper and lower canines that jutted dangerously in opposite directions. She wasn't used to seeing him like this, and she thought it would take some getting used to. But this was part of him. Just like her powers were a part of her. Welcome or not, they just were.

Her excellent eyesight made it possible to see his restless eyes and the way he rubbed one hand over the other in an anxious motion.

Bri stepped forward and stroked him from shoulder to elbow. He tensed but allowed it.

"It's soft, your coat."

Mac glanced behind her. She turned to follow the direction of his fixed stare, listening for Johnny.

"Is he angry with me because of this?" she asked.

Mac shook his head and lifted a hand to point. A moment later she heard the approach of something tearing through the undergrowth. She knew it was Johnny, because Mac waited with a casual ease that should have reassured, but Bri still found herself inching closer to Mac and taking hold of his thick, muscular arm. It was hard to forget the first time she saw Johnny. The night of her arrival. The night he'd tried to kill her.

Mac glanced at her and then back in the direction of the noise as Johnny broke from cover and then made a graceful stop. Only his heavy breathing and the lolling pink tongue indicated that he had exerted himself.

Johnny had scouted in front, and now he and Mac engaged in a series of hand gestures that Bri did not understand. It occurred to her that they should both learn sign language and then realized they had invented one of their own.

"Is it clear?" Bri asked.

Johnny huffed and nodded.

"I never would have gotten out without you two."

Johnny grinned and then looked to Mac who motioned in the direction that Bri surmised they would be traveling.

"Wait. I need to tell you something. Something Dr. Sarr told me."

At the mention of the good doctor, Johnny's entire body went rigid and a low growl emanated from his throat. The hairs on his body lifted until they stood out making him look even more deadly.

"Yes," she said. "I feel exactly that way. But I remembered what you taught me, Mac, and tried my persuasion on Sarr. He was very easy to control. At my suggestion he injected himself with a sedative and gave me a key card."

Mac and Johnny now both more resembled owls as their eyes went big and round as they exchanged a look.

"It's how I got out."

Mac recalled telling Bri just that the same night he had assured her that her talents would not sway him and that her energy draw would not weaken him. He had told her purely for his own self-interest. Telling her the truth had been the simplest way to get what he wanted—her.

Only he wasn't really immune to her. Not really. But it wasn't the magic or her power that drew him. It was something much more alluring—her spirit, her empathy, her kindness toward Johnny and her optimism that things could be better.

Now he was willing to risk all their necks for hers. Brianna Vittori was the one female in the world who could understand him. What it was like to be different, outside. And she could understand what it was like to have hurt the ones you love, because she had done the exact same thing. And something else, something he couldn't do for himself. She had forgiven him for the critical error that brought death to his squad.

He loved her for all that and more. Mac had acknowledged the truth when he realized he'd lost her, but his heart had known far before that.

She was speaking again. Something about making humans do what she told them. He tried to focus on her words while listening for any sign that the colonel or the vampires he and Johnny had seen had found them. They needed to move.

Bri shook her head. "It feels weird to say that—'humans'—because it forces me to admit that I'm not one of them anymore, at least not completely." She laced her fingers together and then twisted her hands one against the other as she stared up at Mac. Her gaze did not hold the accusation he deserved but something he thought might be anxiety.

"I have to tell you something I found out about how you two were turned."

The moment she said the word *turned* Johnny set his teeth with a snap and Mac spun away. This was a topic they did not speak of—ever. In all the months since their return, he had never told Johnny how sorry he was for doing this to him. He had tried to show him day after day, but to say it aloud? No. Mac squeezed his eyes shut and thought he might be sick.

She began speaking again. *No. No. He did not want to hear this.* It took all his restraint not to clamp his hands over his ears like a child to shut out what came next.

Bri touched Mac's shoulder, her fingers threading through the hair that covered his back. "Sarr told me that Lewis knew there was a werewolf in there and he sent you in anyway. No, not anyway. He sent you in *specifically because* there *was* a werewolf in there."

He spun to face her now, his lips curled back to show the long white teeth capable of tearing her to ribbons. She drew back her hand and clamped it over her throat. But she did not run. Bravery, he wondered, or trust? How could she know the hatred blazing through him was not for her but for Colonel Lewis?

Bri turned to Johnny, extending her hand and stroking his upper arm. "Johnny?"

He motioned for her to continue. Mac braced for her next words. Could it be true? Had his commanding officer known what was in that building?

Bri nodded and cleared her throat, her gaze darting between them as they loomed like twin nightmares.

Her voice was tight and trembled when she spoke. "Lewis knew the werewolf was there and he sent your squad. He didn't expect you to capture that building or clear the roof or whatever he told you to do."

Mac stood stupefied by her words as his version of reality collided with this new one.

Bri continued her voice a dirge. "Sarr said that the objective was to have at least one survivor. Instead, Lewis got two."

Mac stumbled back as if she'd punched.

Could it be true?

The solid surface of a tree trunk was all that kept him standing as the dizziness flooded through him. Half of him was relieved because it made it easier to go. The other half was mad as hell at being used.

He glanced to Johnny to see how he was taking it and saw his Lam's eyes narrowed as he turned in the direction they had come. Mac knew his gunner's intention was murder, so he moved to stop him and a scuffle ensued that sent Bri retreating behind a sturdy tree. Mac held Johnny. Johnny broke free. Mac caught him again. They thrashed and tumbled, but Mac never lifted a finger or fang and neither did Lam until Johnny raised a hand to call a halt.

Bri knew her words were triggering something dangerous. But instead of retreating as anyone with sense might have done, she waited until the two werewolves had ceased their struggle and then continued on in a rush as if speed might somehow help in the delivery of her words.

"It was Lewis. Not you. *His* decision. Not yours. None of this was your fault."

Mac's heartbeat thundered in his ears so loudly that he feared he could not trust his hearing. It was like a windstorm roared within him as the forest all about sat still and calm.

"There's one more thing."

Mac didn't think he could stand one more thing. He shook his head and pointed at the trail. They needed to move. He needed to move.

Bri held her ground and launched in as he reached for her, intending to carry her if she would not walk.

"Sarr said that Lewis planned to lock up Johnny either way."

Her words brought him up short.

"But worse, terrible." She covered her hand with her mouth and drew a long breath through her nose. Then she shivered as if trying to toss something vile from her skin and he and Johnny stood rooted like the trees that surrounded them.

What had they done to her? Mac flexed his claws and lowered his chin, wishing for a chance to pay Dr. Sarr and Colonel Lewis back for all their attention.

"Lewis had plans for me, too. He wanted to harvest my eggs and breed his own vampires. I escaped from the operating room."

Mac forgot he could not speak. His words came out as a howl of outrage, an explosion of fury.

Bri didn't cringe or brace, she just continued on. "And they harvested your sperm as well. Johnny's, too. They've already tried to impregnate women with them.

Sarr said the fetuses were normal. Do you know what that means? Mac, your children will be normal. You can have them, lots of them."

The two Marines looked at each other in stunned silence. The horror of being attacked had been hard. Knowing it was his fault had been agony. Now Bri had added the knowledge that he had been attacked twice. Once by the werewolf and once by a man he had respected. The treachery of Lewis's action seeped into his skin like poison until he burned from within. The government they had sworn to protect had betrayed them.

And there was fallout: he and Lam might have children out there very soon. Normal children. He squeezed his eyes shut as the relief and sadness gripped him.

When he opened his eyes, there was no doubt, no more uncertainty. Mac believed Brianna's words and felt in his heart they were true. It all made perfect sense. Mac had to get them away.

Mac didn't remember setting off. But he found himself carrying Bri again, loping over uneven ground with Johnny at his heels.

His feet moved methodically and he scented the air for any spoor that indicated threat. But his mind stuttered and wobbled as he tried to absorb what Brianna had told him. He'd been set up, tricked, betrayed because he followed orders.

Semper Fi. Always Faithful.

But how could he be when those he trusted had betrayed that loyalty?

Before he had turned wolf, he had never disobeyed an order. Now he didn't know how to follow one. So what was he now if not a Marine? *A monster, that's what. And a man.*

He'd heard it said that there were no ex-Marines. No retired Marines, no former Marines. Once a devil dog, always a devil dog.

Was it true? Because his world had now shrunk to include only two people: Bri and Johnny.

Protecting them no longer ran in two opposite courses. They all needed to escape this place and the commander who did not understand the Code.

Duty, Honor, Country. Lewis had no honor, and so Mac held him no allegiance. He still loved his country and was still willing to make the ultimate sacrifice to protect her from all enemies. But he wouldn't be used like a zoo animal. No, that he would not do.

Mac was still a Marine. It was Lewis who wasn't. He didn't deserve to be. And Mac would make it his personal mission to see he was held accountable.

My God, they've taken our sperm and used it, too.

For now, Mac ran. They didn't stop. That was the thing about his second form—he could run tirelessly. When Mac did draw to a halt, it was because he had reached his first objective—an isolated home with a female occupant who hung her laundry on a long line.

He set Bri on her feet, and she stretched and rolled her neck as if stiff and sore from being jostled for hours. She could run faster than either of them, but to do that was to leave their protection. And she stayed, making her choice to trust him. He promised himself to be worthy of that trust.

He had to tell her about the vampires they had scented. She needed to know that they faced two threats.

But for now he was mute. He motioned to the little

square of grass cut into the forest by human hands. The lawn was dotted with weeds and scattered with a collection of discarded and rusting automobiles in various stages of disassembly. Between the white Thunderbird on blocks and the unidentifiable truck seats lay the clothesline. He pointed, and she understood what he wanted. She crept into the yard. He watched from cover, ready to protect her if she was sighted, but knowing it would be far better for the homeowners to catch a glimpse of her than him.

She began by removing an old comforter from the line and laying it beside her on the grass. Into this she tossed a pair of men's jeans, a wrinkled white T-shirt and an old blue-and-gray plaid flannel with elbows worn so thin he could nearly see through them. She turned to go, then glanced at her green scrubs and added a few more items to the pile. Then she looked toward the house as she bundled them all in the bed covering and returned so fast that he lost sight of her for a moment. An instant later she was beside him, extending the offering, but he didn't take them. Instead he lifted her and the bundle and set off at a run. This time Johnny took point, pausing only to check the air for any scent of the vampires.

At first Mac had no direction. His objective was only to put as much distance as possible between them and the colonel and to stay in the cover of the forest. But as he ran, he began to consider options and formulate a plan. He knew the colonel would set up a perimeter. He needed to be outside it and in a vehicle large enough to carry two people and a nine-foot werewolf.

Mac knew that the colonel would anticipate his objective and therefore watch the motor pool. Mac needed his move to be unpredictable. He considered and dismissed several possibilities before he finally settled on a strategic risk—the local ghost town, Bodie. It was isolated, but several of the area businesses drove tourists up there. Most of the tour companies had vans or small buses. He thought the drivers might not be too careful about the keys, but it would be easy to take them by force, if necessary.

The trouble was the location. It was exposed with no good cover for miles in any direction. Lewis would expect him to stay in the forest. That was why he needed to leave it. Mac did not trust his intuition. That was why his breath caught and his skin tingled. He glanced from Bri to Johnny praying he was doing the right thing.

Could they stay ahead of the vampires? His preference was to take on those bloodsuckers one at a time and not fight them on open ground.

He'd tested the theory that a werewolf bite was the only kind of wound that a vampire could not heal. Was it also true that only a vampire's fangs could pierce a werewolf's thick hide and that their venom was lethal?

Mac feared he might soon find out.

As the night slipped quietly into morning, they crossed a road and continued into the woods on the opposite side. The light glimmering through the trees told him they were on a course paralleling the river. At midmorning the sky had clouded over as they skirted well around the town of Bridgeport in the Toiyabe National Forest. By late afternoon the rain swept in, muddying the river and making the unpaved roads a quagmire.

Good, Mac thought. That will slow down the search. Then Bri began to shiver. The warmth of his arms was no longer enough to protect her. She needed a fire. He motioned to Johnny, who understood and took off on a recon. Johnny found an abandoned miner's cabin that looked to have been forgotten since the 1849 rush. The roof had collapsed on one side, and the remaining portion was thick with moss, but it was dry inside because the miner had set the cabin into the sloping hillside. The subterranean back third was protected and dry. The stone fireplace chimney had fallen, but the hearth remained and the gaping roof would vent the smoke, while the rain would make it invisible. Once inside, Mac saw that someone had more recently used this shelter and left behind several articles, including a rusty lantern half full with fuel oil, aluminum pots and pans, candles and a stack of dry wood tucked against the earthen wall on the backed dirt floor, along with kindling and newspapers from the 1980s.

Johnny left them to search for something to eat. Mac knew he could run down anything on two legs, with the possible exception of Bri, and he felt sure Johnny would not come back empty-handed.

Mac began the fire by splashing kerosene on the newspaper and using an iron spike and a stone to throw sparks. Bri huddled, watching, and Mac noted that her toes where all white from frostbite. He needed to get her warm.

By the time he had a flame started her jaw was clacking like a set of chattering teeth.

He retrieved the bundle of clothing to find that the comforter had kept them reasonably dry. He offered Bri the female things she had gathered, motioning for her to get dressed. Then he called the change, enduring the shift and then lifted a bare foot into the denim jeans still warm from Bri's touch. After much tugging, he found the pants too snug, the flannel too loose and the wrinkled white tee just right. He untucked the tee so it covered the fact that he couldn't fasten the top rivet of the jeans and left the flannel unbuttoned, flapping over his ass so Johnny wouldn't make fun of how tight the jeans were. He hadn't worn civilian clothes in so long, he wasn't sure how they were supposed to fit.

When he turned, it was to find Bri still in her wet clothing, clutching the ones he'd given her and staring at him.

"That bad?" he asked, wiping the sweat from his brow with the soft flannel of his sleeve.

"No, no. You look fine. I'm just not used to seeing you in real clothes."

Mac wasn't either, but he supposed he'd have to get used to it.

"How are the bullet wounds?" asked Mac.

Bri lifted her pale arm and touched the flawless skin at her forearm and then bicep. "Perfect," she said, the astonishment evident in her voice. "You'd never even know."

"Fast healer."

She lowered her arm. "What about you?"

He lifted the shirts to show her his back, which looked perfect, though the ache was still there from the bruising underneath.

Her smile was weak, pained.

He motioned a finger at her clothing. "Get out of those."

She quickly stripped out of her sodden surgeon's outfit.

Mac felt his skin flush at the sight of her, but Bri was quick to drag on a pair of jeans that swam on her and a woman's purple turtleneck that was wet in only a few places.

"I wish I'd taken socks."

He glanced down at her dirty bare feet and set both pots under the stream of water running from the holes in the roof, determined to offer her hot water. Outside the rain poured down in gray sheets.

Soon he had the water heating, and Brianna was no longer shivering.

Bri dipped a finger in the water and grinned. "Warm enough for a bath. How long do you think Johnny will be gone?"

Long enough, thought Mac.

Chapter 19

"I was so frightened," Bri said, sinking easily into his arms.

He gathered her up, comforted by the floral fragrance of her skin and her small body, molded perfectly to his. He wanted this, wanted her, but not just for an hour or a night. No, that would not be enough. Would a lifetime be enough?

He didn't think so.

Bri drew away and dragged off the turtleneck. Mac tore a patch from the hem of his stolen T-shirt and dipped it into the warm water. He used the wet cloth to bathe her stomach and chest. Driving off the chill and washing her clean of the mud that splattered her arms and face. As the water ran in rivulets down her pale skin, she dropped her jeans. He knelt at her feet, bathing first one slim leg and then the next. She sat on the comforter as he washed her feet, admiring the perfect toes and fit of her foot in his large hand. Her skin was no longer unnaturally white. Now they glowed pink with good health and warmth.

"They're still tingling," she said.

He wanted her entire body to tingle. He offered the flannel, and Bri dried what the fire's heat had not. Then she stretched out on the comforter and waited for him to come to her.

"We don't have a condom," she said.

"I can work around that."

She grinned as he started at her toes, nibbling and licking up her calves to her knees. She made a sound of satisfaction and settled back as he stroked her inner thigh with feathery caresses. Her hips were satin smooth as he slid his hands up to the soft skin of her belly, his hands the scouts for his mouth. He dipped his tongue into her navel, and she writhed beneath him. He cupped her breasts, stroking the soft mounds as he dropped kisses straight up the center of her body then veered along the fragrant ridge of her collarbone. The yielding tissue was trapped between his mouth and the bone beneath. At her throat he felt the bob of her Adam's apple as she swallowed and then the purr as she gave her approval of his caresses. The outer shell of her ear tasted sweet as nectar. Mac reached between her legs to stroke her there and found her body already wet with need. She wrapped her hands around his neck and pulled. He allowed her to bring his mouth to hers. He wasn't sorry, for she gave him a kiss of fire and promise that stiffened his already hard body.

She moved her hands over his chest with quick, needy strokes that trailed down his torso and to the skin of his abdomen, which twitched at her caress. Finally she grasped the root of his need. Her eager fingers wrapped about him and she tugged, allowing her fingers to slide over him with just the right amount of friction.

He was so grateful to have her safe and here in his arms, so grateful for the rain that sheltered them and to Johnny, who gave them these few stolen moments of privacy. He drew her hands away and sunk between her legs, grasping the two round cheeks of her pear-shaped bottom and lowering his mouth to her clitoris.

Bri moaned and writhed. He sucked as she lifted to meet his mouth and he licked her as she bucked against him. Her breathing grew erratic. Small needy mewling sounds came from her throat as he increased the speed of his kisses. The now familiar shimmer of gold rose from her skin and became a brilliant aurora of light. She placed her feet solidly on the ground and lifted to meet his ministrations. Her stomach tightened and he recognized the sounds she made. She was close, so close. The urge to thrust into her welcoming body roared like a living thing, but he pushed it back. There was no protection, and Bri did not want a baby.

A baby… He had once wanted to fill a house with kids and dogs and rabbits and any critter his kids dragged home. Now he only wanted her.

She came against his mouth in a sweet flood of sound and moisture. When her body stopped trembling and she relaxed back to the earth, Mac scaled her slim body and gathered her against him. They both needed sleep. But Bri was not done with him.

She wriggled from his grasp and sunk down to take him in her mouth. She used her hands to toy with his balls as her tongue danced along the ridge of engorged flesh, stroking him from stem to stern. Sweet Lord, the sensation of her mouth on his body. He groaned and threaded his hand through her hair, encouraging her with a gentle pressure on her head.

He drew her away just as the need grew too strong. But she wrapped her eager fingers about him and brought him the rest of the way home. He came in a sweet rush of pleasure and liquid. Bri held him a moment longer, then drew away to cross to the heating water and gingerly retrieved the cloth, returning to wash him clean.

They lay together in each other's arms, dozing. Sometime before Johnny returned, Mac slipped into his clothing and helped Bri into hers. He nestled with her beside the fire and drifted toward sleep.

"I love you," he whispered.

He thought he felt her stiffen, but then she relaxed and he dozed.

The birdsong woke him before dawn and they found Johnny roasting a shank of elk for Mac and cattails for Bri.

They ate and washed, and he changed to his werewolf form before they were off again. Bri was unusually quiet all morning, which Mac attributed to worry and fatigue. He and Johnny remained watchful for pursuit by either Lewis or the six male vampires they had sighted.

Last night's rain and the morning fog condensed on the needles and leaves, dripping down onto them as the sky lightened in slow degrees.

By sunrise they reached the higher elevations and left the timberline, crossing into open country. Mac knew the chance they were taking. In broad daylight with nothing but the rocks and sage to hide them, Mac felt as exposed as a miner with the seat torn out of his britches.

In the afternoon Bri asked to run and he agreed, provided she stay close. She kept up easily, vanishing and then reappearing up the trail. Somehow they reached their destination without seeing anyone, though that did not necessarily mean they were not seen. He hoped he had guessed right, that the very thing that made this course most dangerous for them would also make it the least likely place the colonel would search and a place the vampires would not wish to journey, for they had good reason not to be seen in daylight. The open ground would also provide no opportunity for the bloodsuckers to come at them unawares. Unless, he reminded himself, they came at them fast. Not even he could see a vampire moving at high speed. But Bri could. He'd need to count on her for that.

They crested a high rise of exposed rock and strawlike grasses and sighted their destination.

Below, the defunct stamp mill clung to the hillside like a big, ugly wart. The ore-crushing plant was by far the largest structure but was by no means the only surviving building. Despite boom and bust and several fires, much of the town remained, with wide spaces between buildings like the gaps between the teeth in an old man's mouth.

The dirt road wound down the valley and threaded through the town that once bustled with miners, gamblers and businesses at the peak of the California Rush. He'd taken the tour. "Bad men from Bodie," they'd called them, and with three killings a day they'd earned their reputation. Now managed by the California State Parks system, the desolate heap attracted curiosity seekers, history buffs and two werewolves escorting a female vampire.

They needed to get to the cover of the buildings before the tourists arrived, so they cut straight past the mill. Mac kept alert for attack from within the hulking three-story structure with wooden trestle, which once held the track from which the ore cars ran from the mountain to the top floor of the stamping plant. Mac recalled that the plant once crushed stone into dust to extract the ore. Inside, he recalled, lay rusting pistons, flywheels, camshafts, and other equipment. Could Bri sense all that iron? Was that why she leaned away as he descended the mountain where the building perched?

They made it past the stamp mill without incident. Mac felt a mixture of relief and unease at reaching the relative cover of a sagging shed and tilting house that seemed to be losing the battle with the winter's heavy snows. Beyond, a bellows with dry, rotted leather and fallen timber told that the blacksmith's shop had given up to collapse. Before them the town of Bodie waited.

Mac instinctively moved toward cover, checking the interior of a charred outbuilding and finding nothing but dirt, weeds and piles of gravel. He called a halt.

He glanced at Johnny and found the familiar look of agitation. His gunner felt it, too. The town was too quiet.

Mac stared down the empty road to the series of ramshackle buildings, and a chill stole down his spine. What was it that set him on edge?

He listened to the creak and groan of the wind whistling through the abandoned buildings but found no threat. The smell of dust and decay clung to his nostrils, but it was the decay of dry rot and moldering wallpaper and charred wood. Not the sweet, sickly stench of vampires.

What, then?

He could see nothing that threatened. Yet both he

and Johnny were crouching in the dead grass, uneasy as steers in a slaughterhouse.

He listened and surveyed their surroundings. The wind and snow had scoured all paint from the planking, leaving the entire place the universal gray of driftwood. Portions of the wooden walkway stretched beneath overhangs beside the false fronts of a few buildings.

Bri hunched down beside him, her gaze flashing from the empty town below them and then back to him.

And then he realized what made his insides swirl like water down a drain. He had not realized how much this stretch of century-old wreckage resembled the rows of buildings recently abandoned by the Afghani outside of Kabul. Now daylight streamed down upon the town. Back then he had seen the world through infrared goggles. But it felt exactly the same as the night he had led his men to their doom. Then as now he did not know what awaited him inside. Then as now he needed to secure a building for the safety of others.

Which building should he choose? Mac gazed from one to the next, knowing he must find cover but fearing another mistake.

Bri again offered Mac the rumpled clothing that she had stolen for him. This time he accepted them.

He left her with Johnny for only as long as it took to call back his human form because he couldn't bear for her to see him writhe and contort again. The transformation bathed him in sweat and left him sick to his stomach, but he knew the weakness would not last. Besides, in werewolf form, he couldn't sit behind the wheel of the vehicle he planned to steal.

He dressed quickly and returned to Lam and Bri.

"We have to get down to the center of town. The

tour guides leave their vehicles in that lot and walk."
He pointed and she followed the direction of his raised
finger.

Mac stared down a sagging row of buildings. "The
church. We can see approach from both sides and it's near
the parking area." He glanced at Johnny. "That sound
right to you?"

Johnny's ears went back. His corporal was still uneasy
with his squad leader asking his opinion. Well, things
had changed. Mac waited. Lam hesitated before nodding his agreement.

Mac glanced at the sky. "Park offices should open
soon, and they'll unlock the gates. First tour probably
left Bridgeport by now. We better go."

The feeling of unease grew as he approached the
abandoned town. He could hear nothing but their footsteps as he took point, leaving Johnny to guard their
backs. He couldn't tell if he was sensing danger or just
reliving it. His senses were all tangled like a ball of
barbed wire. He couldn't trust them. He couldn't trust
himself.

Mac made a quick march through town, avoiding
the roads but walking in a beeline from the stamp mill
past two foundations and across Main Street. They hurried over one wooden walkway past the false front that
looked straight out of a John Huston movie. The peeling sign announced the establishment had once been
Sam Leon's Bar. From there they cut past the sawmill,
the circular blade visible through the bowing boards
and missing timbers. When they reached the church—
Methodist, according to the State Parks sign—Mac
was relieved to see it secured with only a flimsy wire
mesh fence across the entrance. He peeled it back with

ease and entered first, turning immediately right. His training caused him to hug the wall. A moment later Johnny was nudging Bri out of the door as he hugged the wall on the opposite side of the doorway. The quiet yawned. He scanned the empty room. Dust coated the wide floorboards and the pews. Midway down the row against the right wall, a cast-iron stove still squatted. Rusty with age, it must have once been a welcome relief from the snow and cold of the Sierra Nevada Mountains. The altar had gone, but the commandments remained painted on the wall above the raised dais. *Thou shalt not kill*. Mac wondered if he'd get through the day without breaking that one again.

Johnny returned the wire fence to place so it almost looked undisturbed. Mac motioned and Johnny crossed down the center of the pews, his feet raising dust and leaving unnatural prints on the floor. Mac signaled to Bri to follow him then turned toward the door, backing after them.

Johnny reached the front of the church and looked out the small door to the right of the dais. Then he motioned for Bri, who came at his bidding and waited where he indicated. With luck they could go out that door after the tourists left their van and before they toured past the church. Then Johnny joined Mac at one of the long segmented windows that gave them a view of the road and the parking area.

"Can Lewis track us?" she asked.

"He doesn't know where to look."

"They could use dogs or something. Helicopters, maybe."

They'd use both, he knew.

Johnny cocked his head and glanced to Mac. He heard it, too.

"The van," said Mac.

The sound reached her ears, a low hum of an engine and the bounce of struts on uneven ground. The first tour group had arrived.

"What if they see Johnny?" she whispered.

"We'll wait until they clear the vehicle and then we'll go."

Bri stooped on the pew below the window, crouching now to peek out of the glass pane rippled with age and streaked with grime. The white van rolled into view. A magnetic sticker on the door advertised *Gold Rush Ghost Tours, Badmen from Bodie*. The van swung in perpendicular to the warehouse, pulling up to the hitching post in the same place as older tire tracks. The gears creaked as the driver shifted and stopped. Then he exited to the dirt square designated for parking. He was dressed in a wide-brimmed cowboy hat and period clothing, including red suspenders that stretched over his faded cotton work shirt.

"Okay, folks, here we are. This way for a brief overview and a story of a public lynching that happened back in the day."

The van door slid open and a teenage boy unfolded first. His ball cap advertised he was an Angels fan. Behind him came a pretty blonde woman, followed by a tall man who quickly gathered her elbow as if fearful a ghost might spirit her away. The woman checked her camera as he stretched his back. A heavy middle-aged couple groaned and heaved their way from the back of the van and then joined the teen, who ignored them.

Mac stood beside the window looking at the group. Johnny held the opposite side of the frame. He was so big he did not need the pew to gain a view from the window.

What came next happened so fast Bri did not even have time to scream. Below them six male vampires rushed in. Each captured one member of the tour group. Bri pointed and fell back. Mac caught her and set her on her feet. Mac and Johnny looked at her, scrambling backward with one hand clamped over her mouth and the other pointing to the window and looked again. Couldn't they see?

She knew the moment the vampires became visible to them. Johnny growled and Mac tensed but the vampires already had hold of their victims.

A scream came from the parking lot, high and thready. Bri leap back to the pew. She saw them, the vampires each with their teeth clamped on the exposed neck of a tourist. They held them from behind as blood poured from the exposed wound at their necks. This was no sensual puncture and romantic draw of the force of life, but a ripping of vessels and a slurping of the hot gush of blood. Bri could not look away. She stared in horror as one after another of the tour group went slack and were discarded in the dust with the rest of the rotting, decaying town.

Mac acted first, surging toward her and gathering her against his side as he rushed to the side door. Johnny ran past them and leaped out. He rolled to his feet in the yellow grass that dotted the backyard. Mac tossed her like a football to Johnny, who snatched her from the air and threw her over his shoulder.

The world blurred as Johnny ran. She caught glimpses

of Mac beside them. There, then gone. A door slid open and they rushed inside a building. Mac drew the door shut.

Johnny set her on her feet, and she saw Mac throw off his two shirts as he shifted into his silver werewolf form. Instantly she felt sick. A glance around told her why. They'd retreated to the stamp mill. All about her, rusting iron machinery seemed to pulse with lethal energy. She stared at the lattice of iron cam shafts and tappets, power wheels that once spun, driving the iron stamp shoes down to crush stone to dust. She swayed.

"Too much metal," she whispered.

Mac glanced back at her, pointed to the long rows of metal pistons and then to the door.

She understood. Mac had chosen the one place they might have an advantage over their attackers. All the iron that affected her would also affect them. That did make sense. Her stomach pitched. Johnny slid the door back a crack and peeked out.

"He can't see anything," she said. "Because they move too fast for you to see. I should be lookout."

Both werewolves exchanged a glance.

"They're coming," she whispered. "I feel them. God, I hope the metal weakens them the way it weakens me."

Johnny left the door to stand back to back with his squad leader. She saw the vampires rush through the door but Mac and Johnny did not. They still turned their heads from side to side, searching for the invisible.

The fear poured through Bri like an exploding geyser as she left them to charge the first vampire. This one she knew. This was the same thing that had nearly caught her at her apartment. But since that day she had learned how to run and how to fight. Thanks to Mac.

She was past her guardians before they could move. As she charged she felt herself changing. Not just speeding up but preparing for battle in a way that was new. Her teeth grew in an instant so they jutted past her gums. Her fingers stretched into claws, horrible talons as she assumed her second form, the one she had taken only once and never even tried to show Mac, for if he saw her like this could he ever love her? And despite her knowledge that she could never have a life with Mac, she still wanted his love.

Bri slashed at the first vampire, taking him by surprise. Her blow cut across his neck and blood sprayed her face. Was it the blood he had just stolen from those poor people? He fell to the ground and Johnny grabbed him, clamping on to his neck like a pit bull as he used his strong arms to twist. The snapping of the creature's spine sent a shudder through Bri. Johnny jerked his neck, leaving a raw tear over the jugular and blood vessels of its neck. Two vampires grabbed her but Mac was there. He didn't stare at her in horror or shrink from the sight of her. Instead, he latched on to the closest creature and tore open its throat with his jaws. Bri's stomach heaved and she fell to her knees, only to be lifted by her hair by a third attacker. Two held her now and dragged her toward the exit. The remaining two vampires engaged Mac and Johnny, staying clear of their jaws and long reach while delaying them.

Bri twisted and snapped her fearsome teeth but could not break free. She clawed at their arms, tearing flesh to ribbons. Johnny lunged at the legs of his opponent and managed to grab hold. A swipe of his claws opened the vampire's chest. A moment later the creature was airborne as Johnny tossed him into the stamping mill.

At the contact with the iron mortar box the vampire screamed, writhed and twisted, trying to escape the wide stretch of metal even as his flesh seared, sizzling like meat in a hot skillet. He bled from his wounds, growing weaker with each passing moment. He fell still as Mac managed to get hold of his attacker. Bri's captors dragged her toward the door as she heard the screams behind her. Was that his opponent or Mac?

Chapter 20

$\mathbf{M}$ac gutted the vampire and then used his claws to tear something vital away. Johnny's opponent struggled weakly on the top of the stamp press. The two remaining vampires dragged Bri toward the exit as he and Johnny bounded after them.

The vampires released Bri to face them. It was a mistake. She bit the shoulder of the closest one, lacerating the thing's muscle and exposing the blue pulsing blood vessels that threaded beneath its stark white collarbone.

The creature howled and slapped her, sending her to the ground. Johnny leaped and landed on the vampire's chest. There was no escaping Johnny's jaws that latched hold of its throat and held on as its blood drained away.

Mac charged the remaining vampire, but before he could reach it, the male vanished. Mac turned in a circle expecting it to come at him from behind but the seconds ticked by and nothing happened.

Bri rose to her feet, a large welt now marring her perfect skin. The creature she had been had vanished, the gaping jaws receding to the straight white teeth that brightened her smile.

For a moment there she had looked like the males except her skin had never turned to that bruised mottled color. Had she known she had a second form?

"It's gone," she said looking out toward the door and pointing at the air.

He glanced at the empty space beyond to the horizon and then fixed his gaze on her. He used his index finger to circle his face and then pointed at her lifting his hands into claws. He was sure she understood his question because she glanced away and her pretty face flushed clear down to her neck.

"I don't know. It only happened once before. We had a break-in and…I don't really know how I do it. It just sort of is. When I'm really, really angry I can feel it coming. When I saw it attacking you, I…"

Mac squeezed her shoulder and nodded his understanding. Then he and Johnny checked the other five vampires. Their wounds did not heal. Methodically Mac moved from one corpse to the next to be certain they had all bled out. In death their skin turned an even more hideous plum color, and their cloudy eyes turned opaque and white as marble.

Johnny climbed up on the stamping press to check the last body and Mac saw it move. Johnny growled and lifted his claws.

Bri felt something cold touch her neck. A heartbeat later it began to burn. She turned and found herself captured against a hard male body. One hand grasped her hair, the other held the long silver blade to her throat.

She opened her mouth to scream but no sound came.

"Hold tight," came the whispered order from behind her captor.

Bri recognized the voice. It was Lewis.

Her gaze darted to Mac and then Johnny, but they were watching the stamp press where a vampire, who was still alive, held their attention. From the change in his posture, Mac seemed to sense disaster first.

Johnny and Mac turned in unison as the Marines poured into the large open room of the stamp mill like ants, their boot heels drumming on the thick wood planking.

And here it was, Bri realized, Mac's decision coming to him in the worst possible way. To rescue her, he would have to attack his fellow Marines.

"One move and I slit her throat," said Lewis to Mac. "It's iron, Sergeant. Just a twist and the wound stays open."

Mac held his position as his gaze flicked from one Marine to the next. His breathing showed his upset and the locking of his long dangerous jaws. Finally his gaze swung back to Lewis.

"Get down from there," the colonel barked.

Both Johnny and Mac eased off the large iron block. Behind them smoke rose from the vampire's burning body.

"Check them," said Lewis. "See if any are still alive."

Several of the Marines fanned out, moving from one vampire to the next and then dragging them into a line at Lewis's order. Two of the men climbed up to check the final vampire still on the mortar box.

Johnny shook his head. Lewis saw the gesture and smiled.

"Missed one, did you? I hope so. I need a male and female to insure the next generation. Be stronger if both parents are vampire. You both did well in your second engagement. I knew you could do it. Been at each other for centuries, according to MI." Lewis stepped forward. Mac and Johnny followed him with their eyes. "I wonder how long sperm lives after the body dies." Lewis turned to the assistant flanking him. "Call Dr. Sarr. Get him up here in a chopper, ASAP. And bring body bags and ice. Lots of ice."

The metal touching Bri's throat seared her skin and she set her jaw to keep from whimpering. She was scared down to her toes, but she couldn't call her second form. Why did it only come when she was angry? Now, when she needed to change, it eluded her.

"Captain," barked Lewis. "Check the bodies."

The Marine moved down the line performing some ghastly version of an inspection of dead vampires. He stepped from one body to the next, nudging them with his foot.

Lewis watched his progress. "Look at those wounds. Spectacular."

One of the Marines on the pressing mill called out, "This one's still breathing."

"Breathing?" said Lewis's aide. "I thought vampires didn't breathe."

Lewis gave him a suffering look. "Breathe, fart, working kidneys. They even die of old age. That undead crap is bullshit. These things aren't human, but they *are* alive." He snapped an order. "Drag him down."

The two men on the press handed down the limp, smoking form of the living vampire to another Marine, who dragged him before the colonel.

Mac growled and the colonel glanced his way, the grin of supremacy broadening on his face. "Got one."

Mac shook his head. Lewis held his gaze and that was why he did not notice that the vampire's body no longer smoked. The wound that Johnny had given him bled, but his burns healed fast.

Lewis squatted before the inert form as he spoke to his aide. "Bring in the steel cage and lock up my wolves. No more liberty for you two."

The aide spun away barking orders. Bri leaned against the man behind her trying to put some distance between her neck and the burning blade. But the soldier just pressed harder.

"It burns," she whispered.

"Hold still," he growled.

She breathed in short little pants against the pain, dropping her gaze to the ground. That was when she saw the vampire's eyes pop open, meeting hers. For what seemed an eternity he held her gaze, those cloudy, dead eyes on hers. Then, in a move so fast that she was certain only she could see it, the vampire was on his feet and behind Lewis. It took one vicious bite from the side of the colonel's throat. Bri heard the vampire's teeth click shut. Blood sprayed from Lewis's neck as he dropped to his knees. Men moved in slow motion now as the vampire charged her. He knocked the blade from the Marine holding her and kicked him backward. Bri imagined the Marine must look to the others as if he was suddenly flying. The vampire grabbed her wrist and dragged her out of the stamp mill. He ran her past the Humvees and jeeps, dashing up the road with her in tow.

He was taking her to the others. She knew it, and she knew Mac could not stop him. If she was to escape, it would be her fight.

Bri wound up and punched the vampire in the stomach as hard as she could and heard a satisfying *oooff* sound as the air left his lungs. Her feet touched the ground and she hit him again, this time in the face with the heel of her hand. He staggered, recovered and reached for her again.

"You don't belong with them. You're one of us."

She hit him in his bleeding shoulder.

He covered the wound with his opposite hand and glared at her.

"We'll come back." His words were not threat, but promise.

"And I won't be here."

Her grandmother had evaded them for years. She could, too. But for how long now that they knew of her existence?

"We will find you."

When she spoke her words were not threat or bravado, but also a promise. "And when you do, I'll kill you."

She meant it. Mac had been correct. Given the right circumstances, anyone could kill.

The vampire stepped back and then back again before turning to race away. She watched him crest the hilltop an instant later and then disappear. Behind her came the sounds of gunfire.

She turned to see Marines fleeing the stamp mill as yellow smoke poured from the interior. The men outside quickly donned their gas masks.

But Johnny and Mac were still inside.

Mac and Johnny hit the floor the instant the first canister went off. The gas did not smell like the caustic smoke designed to send men fleeing from buildings and right into enemy fire.

The gray smoke billowed out and Mac knew that it was something to either kill them or render them unconscious.

Mac's lungs burned. He could not hold his breath much longer. Through the haze Johnny motioned toward the back. They both knew they had no choice. The Marines outside would fight, and he and Johnny would defend themselves. *My God,* Mac thought, *how many will we have to kill to escape?*

He had to get out and find Brianna before that thing took her where he'd never find her. He recognized then that he would make any sacrifice to have her. He would even give his life for hers. He had to survive this, had to live to save her so he could tell her that what he wanted most in this life was her.

Something moved before him. Who was stupid enough to enter a building consumed with gas?

Then he saw her. Brianna crouched low, feeling her way through the swirling smoke—a gas mask fixed on her head—as she swept the ground for them. She'd come back for him. He was elated and furious in equal measures.

"Mac!" Her words were muffled by the plastic shield that covered her face.

He grabbed her ankle and she gave a yip of fright then sank to her knees offering two masks. They didn't fit over their faces.

Mac forced his change, writhing on the floor as his bones and tendons collapsed into his human form. The moment he went still, Bri slapped the mask over his face. Ten seconds later he was holding the mask on Johnny, who had fallen to his back.

"I'll get one of those Hummer thingies." Bri pointed and disappeared before his eyes.

Mac tore the breathing tube from the mask and shoved it into Johnny's mouth then pinched his nostrils shut. Johnny roused slowly, his eyes tearing as he blinked up at him and shook his head as if fighting off the lethargy that stalked him.

The crash brought Mac to his feet. Bri had taken out the closed barn door. Red lights glowed in the toxic mist as Mac lifted Johnny and ran with him to the backseat of the Humvee and then tore the wooden door from the grill. Bri shoved over as he climbed into the driver's seat, naked, the vinyl hot on his bare butt cheeks.

"Go, Bri. We'll be right behind you."

She hesitated a moment, pressing her lips together. Then she nodded and vanished an instant later.

He decided to break out through the side of the stamp mill, hoping the plants were as dry-rotted and weak as they appeared. He knew that once he tore free, he'd have only seconds to avoid whatever obstacles lay beyond.

The side of the stamp mill exploded in splintering wood as they crashed through. Mac turned hard left before he saw the circle of jeeps that ringed the buildings. He aimed between the closest two and floored it. The Humvee swept the two smaller jeeps aside with a crash and the screech of twisting metal. Then they were bumping over rough ground. He'd gotten out without killing anyone. It was a miracle.

At least he didn't have to worry about IEDs out here. He steered for the town and fishtailed onto the wide dirt road, roaring past the Marines who guarded the entry by veering around their portable plastic roadblock. Next he passed the abandoned van surrounded by the dead tourists scattered in dark pools upon the ground.

His rearview mirror told him two things. The Marines were on his ass, and Johnny was still out.

Mac tore off his mask at the same time Bri reappeared in the passenger seat. Mac startled and gripped the wheel.

"Holy shit. You can jump into a moving car?"

"It moves slower than I do," she said and swung the door closed.

Mac motioned to the rear seat. "Check him."

Bri scrambled into the back and hoisted Johnny's massive head onto her lap and began patting his slack cheek as she called his name. Mac focused on gaining top speed in their vehicle. If they could stay ahead of pursuit until Johnny regained consciousness, maybe he wouldn't have to kill anyone.

"How did you get away?" Mac asked.

"I used what you taught me and punched him in the stomach." She slapped the heel of her right hand and grinned.

"That's my girl."

He focused on the road and getting Bri and Johnny to safety. Johnny needed to be able to run. The Marines were good, but they'd never be able to track a vampire and two werewolves once they got to cover.

In the backseat Johnny groaned and pulled the breathing tube from his mouth. He coughed and choked while Bri rubbed his hairy back and murmured encouragement.

"Careful. He wakes up hard."

"No, he's fine. Aren't you, John?"

When Johnny straightened, he hit his head on the roof. Mac caught his eyes in the mirror.

"You guys ready to run?"

Johnny nodded and Bri's eyes went wide before she gave a nervous series of nods.

They descended from the high deserted plains with the Marines following close behind. Once below the tree line Mac knew they were in territory where the humans could not follow. He swerved from the road and zigzagged through the sage and tufts of yellow grass. Even the Humvee couldn't climb the incline of rock that stretched before them. But he and Johnny could.

"Can you climb this?" he asked Bri.

"Better. I can jump it."

He scrambled out from behind the wheel and then helped Bri. She took a moment to let her gaze sweep over his nude form before she hurried after Johnny, who had already reached the incline. Behind them vehicles screeched and men shouted orders. In a few minutes the din they made faded away. Mac shifted and followed Johnny. Bri had vanished, but not too far, he hoped. There were at least two males still out there. Johnny ran and Mac followed. Before they'd reached cover Mac heard the helicopters. Take cover or run? he wondered.

"Bri! Get to those trees." He pointed to the timberline several miles below them.

Her voice came from far off. "Okay."

"Meet us there."

She appeared, giving him a view of her already at the tree line, and then she vanished. He and Johnny charged one of the birds. The helicopter spotted them when they still were five hundred yards out. It started firing at one hundred. The high-caliber rounds did not break his skin, but they knocked him around, as if he was the sparring partner of some heavyweight champion.

Johnny went down and Mac helped him rise. They made too damned big targets. Just fifty feet to the trees and then they'd vanish just like Bri.

They reached cover. Above them the treetops exploded as branches were cut to ribbons by the gunfire.

They hadn't gone far when Bri appeared carrying running shoes, shorts and a turtleneck. Mac noted she now wore dirty white tennis shoes. Mac accepted the clothing with a questioning look.

"Backpackers," she said thumbing over her shoulder. "A few miles that way."

"Stay close now. Those vampires might be hanging around."

Her eyes went wide, and he realized she hadn't thought of that.

They moved quickly through the forest and did not stop until evening. There was no sound of pursuit. He still didn't have a vehicle, but now he thought that staying in deep cover was best. They could travel east to Nevada or all the way up the Sierras into the Cascades. With luck they would reach Canada without ever leaving the woods. They couldn't put a roadblock in the forest. Their first night's camp, he did not risk a fire.

Bri stood a little way off, hands folded before her and a troubled expression on her face. She seemed worried. Was it the vampires, the Marines or had she heard him say that he loved her?

Mac intended to find out.

Johnny curled up to sleep and Mac took the first watch. Bri must have been exhausted, but she came to sit beside him, her back to the downed log and her knees drawn up to her chest.

"You came back for me," he whispered.

She made a humming sound of agreement. He looped an arm around her shoulders and pulled her close.

"Mac, stop." She cut him off and slipped from beneath his arm, rising to her feet.

He followed feeling a sense of approaching disaster

from her tight expression and the way she would not meet his gaze. It was bad.

She crossed one arm over her middle and pressed the opposite hand to her mouth, as if she was trying not to be sick. The dread grew in him. His flesh began to tingle.

"Mac, you've taught me how to take care of myself. It's time for me to go. Past time, really."

The shock rendered him momentarily speechless, when he found his voice it was thin and strained. "No. We're staying together."

"I can't. I'm not going to hurt one more person I care about."

"Please, Bri. I love you."

"I know you do, and that's precisely why I have to go."

"That doesn't make any sense."

"My being her, my staying. I'm keeping you from what you want, Mac."

He gave her a look of utter confusion.

Her chin sank to her chest. "I've thought a lot about this, about what will happen next. Even if we get away, even if there were no vampires chasing me and the military didn't want to put you and Johnny in a cage, what kind of a life would we have?"

"We'd be together."

"What about your family?"

He looked away.

"Are you going to bring me home to meet the folks? Your mother, your younger brother. He'll fall in love with me. You know that, right? He'll be crazy with jealousy and try to spend every waking minute taking me from you. What about your father? You said he has a bad heart. How much of my company can he stand?"

"I'll tell them about you. I'll make them understand."

If he chose her, he'd lose them. The truth hung about them like smoke, how much it would cost to love her.

"Even if you picked me, sooner or later you'd grow to resent me."

"Never. Bri, I love you. We will make it work."

"You deserve a life filled with love, and children. And those children deserve doting grandparents and holidays with their big loving family. You can have that Mac, have it all. I can't. They'd be hunted and they'd be killers. Just like me." She lifted her gaze to meet his, her eyes pleading. "A family. That's what you said you wanted. I'm giving you that—by leaving."

"Is this because you don't love me or because you do?"

He waited with his heart pounding in his throat.

"I love you. And that's why I'm going."

Bri knew the moment that Mac recognized what would happen next because the color washed from his face. He opened his arms. But she would not let him touch her because if he got hold of her, he might not let go. But even worse, she might not have the strength to leave.

"Bri, no," Mac said, already reaching for her. "I can protect you."

Yes, he could protect her and he would never leave her. Just like her father would not leave her mother even to save his own life.

Her power would not kill him, not in the way her mother's had killed her father. It would be a different kind of death, one that stole away each person he loved. She saw it all repeating. His devotion and her willingness to take everything he offered because she could not imagine her life without him.

She gave him a smile that hurt right down to her heart.

"I can protect you, too, Travis. Take care of Johnny." Bri blew him a kiss and then ran. He dove at her, but she was too fast. In an instant she had left them behind. She didn't look back, because she knew what she would see, Mac changing and moving too slowly to catch her. Mac howling as she put a mile between them and then two.

As she ran, she ignored the crushing sensation in her lungs and the quavering ache that vibrated from her beating heart. Was this why her mother stayed, to keep from feeling this terrible pain? Was this what her grandmother had wanted, for her to protect the ones she loved?

"Did I do it, Nana? Did I keep my humanity?"

Brianna reached the paved road and continued along in her bounding run, galloping up the miles with no destination except away. Away from Mac. Away from Johnny. Away from the life Mac offered—a life of sweetness and sorrow.

She wondered if he would ever forgive her. Wondered if she'd ever forget him. Did her mother still love her father from her place in that other world? Did her mother ever think of her daughter?

Bri wished she could have gone with her to the Fairyland instead of being condemned to a life apart from the rest of humanity.

The road stretched out before her, long and lonely and dark. But she ran it because she had no other choice.

Chapter 21

Mac followed Bri's trail, with Johnny on his heels, until well into the moonrise. But she'd taken the highway, knowing, he supposed, that Johnny could not follow.

He had to find somewhere safe for Johnny. Then he could go after Bri. But even if he found her, how could he convince her that he wanted a life with her?

Mac suffered the change as Johnny watched glumly. Once in human form he told Johnny what he planned to do. Johnny agreed to wait but he wasn't happy.

Two hours later Mac had found Bri's old apartment. Her scent hung about the place, but it was an old scent. But then he saw something move inside the upper apartment and went to investigate.

By sunrise he pulled the compact car to the shoulder closest to the place he had left Johnny. He exited the vehicle dressed in an assortment of clothing from Bri's grandmother, slip-on shoes, black sweatpants and a sky-blue turtleneck that fit a little too well.

Johnny stood waiting then lifted his head at the car's arrival.

"Bri's grandmother's, according to the registration. Keys were in the apartment."

Johnny waited.

"No sign of her. But she had company. Another one. I killed it."

Johnny drew a long breath and blew it out. Mac knew it was his concern come to fruition, that he would find himself outnumbered because he had asked Lam to stay behind.

"Just one. I handled it. Also got some money and a few sacks of food. Her grandmother kept a well-stocked cupboard."

Johnny motioned for paper. Mac rummaged in the glove box and came up with a stubby pencil and the back of a receipt for an oil change. He handed them to Johnny. The pencil disappeared into his hand as he scrawled across the page.

Followed her trail. Lost it. She's gone.

Mac felt his heart drying up inside him. Johnny wrote, his handwriting all but illegible. *What now?*

Mac wondered the same thing. "I'm not giving up."

Mac combed their trail again and found no trace of her. He backtracked and followed every lead to a dead end. After three months of seeking Brianna, fall had arrived and he was still wondering what he and Johnny should do.

The summer months had been lush and the cover excellent. Now with the seasons changing again, he'd found a series of cottages on a lake far to the north but still in California. They seemed to be used only in the summer. He and Johnny established a residence in one in early September. He left Johnny to search for Bri but found no sign. Then he visited his family, careful to avoid the military surveillance. He spoke only with his dad, told him everything and arranged a way to get in touch. Then he returned west, taking a job with a local lumber mill clearing trees from private land. He was at a job site on 314 acres, working on a tree he'd just dropped, when a small, mud-spattered pickup pulled up and out stepped Paul Scofield, Mac's drill instructor from basic training.

The Marines sent the right man to confront him, likely one of the only men whom Mac still respected. Scofield was a tough old leatherneck, but every man under him knew his aim was to give them the skills necessary to stay alive.

Mac let his chain saw idle. It wasn't an automatic weapon. But it would do in a pinch.

"MacConnelly," said Scofield as he slammed the driver's-side door of the mud-streaked black pickup, which was not standard issue.

The DI looked thinner in civilian clothing, and his bald head was not covered with his familiar headgear but a cap advertising the brand of truck he drove.

"Drill Sergeant." Mac started to snap a salute and then stopped himself.

"You look as comfortable with that chain saw as you did with your M-4."

"Less recoil," he said and waited.

"They want you back, son. Both of you."

Mac said nothing to this. He knew Johnny was nearby, listening. Waiting for a signal from him.

"They asked me to tell you that Lewis and Sarr went off the farm. They never had clearance for any of it. I know what they did to you, son. And I know it was outside the orders of their superiors. Colonel Strangelove and Dr. Mengele, there, were out of bounds. *Way* out of bounds, and I'm sorry for what happened to you and Lam."

Suddenly Mac's throat felt tight and he had the urge to tell Scofield how betrayed he felt. Then he shook himself and held on to his anger. That, at least, had never let him down.

"You better go," Mac said.

"They replaced him with a man they think you can trust. He's overseeing the operation now and he is on board with helping fix Private Lam's, uh, issues."

"I don't trust anyone but Johnny."

"That wasn't their first choice, since he's still on a UA."

Unauthorized Absence. Mac knew that was a lesser term for what they were—AWOL.

"What asswipe do they think I'd trust enough to come back in?"

Scofield scratched beneath his cap. "That asswipe would be me."

The two men stared at each other.

"It will be different, MacConnelly. You have my word. You'll be in the loop on everything because I'm appointing you my second in command."

"I'm only a sergeant."

"Not if you come in, you're not."

"I'm trying to find someone."

"Yes. Brianna Vittori. We found her, but we thought you might like to be the one to ask her to come in."

Mac switched off his chain saw but his heartbeat seemed to be revving at the same speed. "You found her?"

Mac sat in the helo beside Maj. Paul Scofield and listened intently as he reviewed their intel on Brianna Vittori.

Below them the tops of the aspens shone a brilliant gold in the October sunlight.

Bri's new place lay in a remote area in the mountains outside Taos, New Mexico. Off the grid, solar powered and heated by woodstove. She had no neighbors and had moved twice since Mac had seen her last.

"She spends four hours each afternoon in a cubicle at the public library working online helping nonprofits with grant preparation, project planning and the creation of skilled volunteer programs," said Scofield.

Mac smiled at this as he realized that she'd managed to find a way to help people even as she avoided them.

"Small income, but she gets by. Does all her banking online. That's how we track her. She rides a motorcycle which she could easily abandon if attacked."

"I don't want her to see the helo," said Mac.

"We'll drop you and wait for your signal."

"I appreciate that."

The bird touched down and Mac disembarked holding a map and a cell phone.

"Good luck, Captain," said Scofield, using Mac's new rank.

His throat felt suddenly dry. What if she wouldn't come back?

Bri took the last quarter mile on her motorcycle slow. October's cold had gilded the aspens and the cottonwoods a lovely red, but the afternoons were still sunny and warm.

Bri pulled to a stop and cut the engine. She had already lowered the kickstand of her bike and removed her helmet when she noticed her front door lay open.

She stepped away from the motorcycle knowing she

was faster on foot, faster than anything human and everything half human that she'd met so far. She'd already outrun the vampires twice.

"Who's there?" she called as she eased backward, letting her power tingle through her like a shower of sparks. She was ready to run. Ready to disappear again.

Something moved from the darkness beyond her door. A man stepped out.

The heels of his shoes slapped loudly upon the large stone step. She stared at the familiar blood stripe on the royal-blue trousers above the shiny black shoes and the midnight-blue coat of a Marine's dress blues. He held his white cap, clamped under one arm by the shiny black brim, perpendicular to the midnight-blue belt that cinched his trim waist. Fixed in the center of the belt's buckle was the gold emblem of the Marines, the anchor, eagle and globe. As he moved into the sunlight of the yard she saw the flash of his gold buttons and two parallel silver bars on his shoulder. Bri took another step away, but the possibilities kept her from running. Could it be?

Mac!

She recognized him now beneath the pressed midnight-blue jacket festooned with bars of color across his left chest. The instant his blue eyes met hers she felt that familiar rush of excitement and the tingling awareness that only happened with Travis MacConnelly. It was all she could do not to rush into his arms.

Oh, nothing had changed in three months, except now she wanted him even more. Somehow she held herself back.

"Bri." He replaced his hat to his head, the brim now shielding his pale eyes against the bright afternoon sunshine and then extended a hand toward her. "I'm alone. Don't run again. Please."

She swallowed back the emotion that choked her. It took all her willpower not to rush into his arms. Her eyes drank in the sight of him as she trembled with the sheer joy of seeing him safe and whole.

"How's Johnny?" she asked, her voice a whisper.

His brows tented, disappearing beneath the brim of his hat. "The same."

She nodded her understanding, absorbing the sorrow that the news brought to her bruised heart.

He kept one hand out like a blind man feeling his way along as he inched toward her. She watched his approach. Each step brought an new urgency to her pounding heart.

"How did you find me?" she asked.

"Military intelligence. They've had you pinned for two months."

She glanced over her shoulder at the empty road. Her escape.

"Don't," he said, his voice tinged with anguish.

When she turned back it was to find him too close. Her skin tingled and she knew she should go, but she couldn't make herself do it. Instead, she stood there gobbling up the sight of him. She could see the blue of his eyes now and the intensity of his stare. If she let him grab her there would be no escape. How she wanted to let him.

"Stop," she ordered.

He did, holding up his hands in surrender. "Okay. Just don't run."

She agreed to this with a slow nod. "I've only been here two months."

"A little more. Boulder, Colorado. Then here."

Her jaw dropped. It was true, then.

"But if they knew, then why wait?"

"Because now I'm in charge of the unit that studies vampires."

She didn't understand. "You're what?"

"The brass had no idea what Lewis was doing, which isn't really surprising considering the stupidity of those rear-echelon motherfuckers."

She glanced about to check if they were really alone. Something about him was very different than when they had parted, and it wasn't just the shiny shoes and new badges on his chest. There were circles under his eyes and a weariness that clung to him like a heavy cloak.

"Bri, I've missed you," he whispered.

She absorbed the sharp thrust of pain in her heart at his words. She didn't respond in kind. What was the use?

"I want to take you back with me. Major Scofield has a position for you."

She stiffened. "Who?"

"My commanding officer. He's a good man. I trust him, Bri. What's more, Johnny trusts him."

Johnny didn't trust anyone but Mac and with good reason. Her heart tugged at her and she wanted so much to believe everything he said.

"Johnny trusts him?"

Mac touched his tongue to his upper lip and nodded. His eyes earnest and his expression hopeful. "The whole operation has changed. They court-martialed that rat fuck Sarr and six others."

That was welcome news. Still, it changed nothing.

"Do you remember saying that I couldn't have the life I deserved if you stayed?"

She flushed.

"And you were right. Because if you stay, my life will be more than I deserve."

She opened her mouth to object but he lifted a hand and she fell silent.

"It won't be the life I envisioned. That's true. But it will be different only because it will be so much better. I can't picture a future that doesn't include you. Bri, I'm miserable without you. If you want to protect me from loss and sorrow, you have to stay with me."

Had the last few months been as terrible for him as they had been for her? Yes, she realized, seeing the truth in his sad, tired eyes. And she knew he was right. They needed to be together.

"What about your family?" she asked.

"I told my parents everything, about me, about you, about us."

"You what?" Astonishment rolled through her. Was he even allowed to tell them this?

"They are waiting to meet you in Taos. I flew them out."

"But it's dangerous. I—"

He held up a hand. "Princess, you keep thinking of what I'll give up, but the only thing I can't give up is you. It's time to forgive ourselves. It's time to take what life offers—the love and loving." He removed his cap and tossed it to the ground before capturing her hand. Then he dropped to one knee in the dust beside his cap and fished in his pocket, then drew out a black velvet box, which he flicked open and extended to her.

"Brianna Vittori, I love you. Please, be my wife."

Inside the folds of ivory fabric nestled a pale green ring. The band had been inset with diamonds.

"Yes," she whispered, extending her hand, accepting the forgiveness he offered with the love.

Her hand trembled as Mac slipped the ring over her knuckle. She waited for it to burn. But it never came.

"It's jade and diamonds. No metal."

Bri stared down at the beautiful ring. "It feels just right."

She cradled her left hand over her heart and then extended her arms to her fiancé. He pulled her close. She rose on her tiptoes to hug him, pressing her cheek against his. Bri locked her hands about his neck as Mac swept her off her feet and carried her in a slow circle. She was breathless with joy and dizzy with hope when he set her back on solid ground and gave her a long, languid kiss.

Mac laced his fingers through her thick hair, gazing down at her. "I love you, Bri. And I always will."

She wiped the tears away and gave him a trembling smile. The lump in her throat was so big she didn't know how she spoke past it.

"I was terrified that I'd keep you from happiness."

"That can only happen if you leave me." He gave her hand a squeeze. "Don't ever do that again, Bri. Promise me."

"No, never again," she promised.

He kissed her again. When they broke apart he was grinning and looked years younger. "Ready to meet my parents?"

"Is any woman ever ready for that? What do they think about me?"

"Curious, of course. Bri, I showed them what I am. They know I will not be leading an ordinary life."

"You…"

He nodded.

"Where are we going?"

"Taos first. They're waiting there. Then on to Oahu."

"Hawaii?"

"Yes. Deep cover for Johnny, a defensible position and a specialized research facility for us."

"Hawaii?"

They exchanged grins.

She clung to his elbow. "I'm ready."

Bri stooped and retrieved Mac's hat, dusted it off and offered it to him. He set it expertly on his head, then lifted a phone from his pocket and spoke into the unit. A moment later she heard a loud *womp-womp-womp* that vibrated through her chest.

"What's that?" she asked, covering her ears as she turned toward the sound to see a large military helicopter sweep in from the east.

"Our ride," he shouted. "Unless you'd rather run?"

She shook her head as the dust rose all around her. "No. No more running for me."

The helicopter touched down and Mac assisted her into the compartment. As she took her seat beside Mac, she felt her grandmother smiling down on her for Bri knew that she had found forgiveness and love. That was the best way to keep one's humanity.

* * * * *

SIERRA WOODS

Sierra Woods grew up in the heart of the Appalachian Mountains where folklore, mysteries and superstition surrounded everyday life. Sierra's interest in the paranormal began in her childhood and hasn't stopped yet. Today she works in healthcare, where interesting and unusual situations may be taken and used in her fiction writing. She lives in New Mexico, in the foothills of the Sandia Mountains. If you'd like to drop Sierra a line, she'd love to hear from you at sierrawoodswriter@gmail.com.

THE RESURRECTIONIST
Sierra Woods

This book is dedicated to the victims of crime who can no longer speak for themselves.

The inspiration for this book was yet another news story about a murder for which the motivation was pitiful. I so wanted there to be justice for this victim whose killer was caught in just a few days.

My wish is that all victims find justice for crimes committed against them.

Resurrectionists are a breed all their own. Some are born into it, some are called into it and some are murdered into it. Resurrectionists have been a constant presence on the earth plane since humanity learned right from wrong. During ancient times, superstitions forced resurrectionists to remain hidden, secretive and fiercely protective of their rituals. Over the centuries, superstition battled religious fervor, and resurrectionists remained underground.

Teachings passed from one generation to another, then the information was destroyed for the safety of all. Zombies and witches took much of the blame for the good deeds of resurrectionists, who only sought to right the wrongs humans committed against one another. With no support for their efforts, resurrectionists stayed hidden.

In this century, technology, the Age of Aquarius and an opening in global consciousness have enabled a few gifted resurrectionists to forge new trails, bringing their fight for justice into the light.

Albuquerque, NM
September
Office of Dani Wright, Resurrectionist

Chapter 1

"I'm not going to have to walk around with a bullet wound in my forehead forever, am I?" Betsy Capella looked at me, her eyes not quite focused. After being deceased and in cold storage for nearly a year, it was understandable. The senses take a little while to warm up and remember what they're supposed to do.

"I don't think so. It should fade as you recover more fully. These things take a little time." Not exactly a lie, not exactly the truth, and I hope I interjected enough sympathy into my voice. I don't know the answer to her question, as I've been performing resurrections for only a year or so. Not long enough to come up with a stat sheet. Each resurrection is different, just as each death is different. The state and success of recovery depends on how long the deceased has been gone, and on whether we've stored the body or it was buried in a traditional manner. Embalming is not a good thing if you intend to return to a living state. Yeah. Cremation is a bad idea, too. Way bad.

Betsy sat more upright and smiled, the corners of

her mouth a little tight and dry. "I'll bet some makeup will help."

Yeah, and a spackling trowel to slap it on with. "Give it a go. I hear there are sales on this week." Looking down at the contract she signed, I added the date. Having been dead and on ice, she wasn't up on current events. "Do you want to go with us to the 'yard? You don't have to, but if you'd like to, someone can drive you and follow us to the site."

"The yard? What's that?" A frown of confusion made the bullet wound between her eyes pucker. *S-o-o* not attractive.

"Graveyard." Where the life-swap rituals are completed, sending killers where they belong. A one-way ticket to the nebula. Looking away, I tried not to focus on her wound, like a deadly zit on her forehead.

Before answering, Betsy put away the compact someone had given her. Most newly resurrected have a difficult transition at first, which is why I don't keep mirrors around the office. Let 'em get used to the idea of being awake and alive again before they wonder what they look like. Sometimes it ain't pretty.

"No. I just want to go home, see the kids and take a shower." Rubbing her hands on her arms, she shivered. You go a year without a shower and see how you feel. I'd recommend a good exfoliant, like steel wool. Maybe I could come up with a gift bag for the newly resurrected. Steel wool and a mild bleach solution. That would be good PR, wouldn't it? I should write that down.

Betsy looked at her ex-husband across the room and dismissed him as if he meant nothing to her. I suppose that's the best attitude. He's the one who put her in the ground, so she obviously meant nothing to him. In my book, turnaround is simply justice, served neat.

She rose from the chair and wobbled a little, then got her land legs again. I don't know quite what to call it when they've been in containment. Grave legs? Jeez. This job just gets freakier all the time. Every day is Halloween around here. We just need some candy; we've already got the nuts.

Betsy's family was weepy and gathered around her, then pulled away. A few wiped their hands on their pants, grateful for, but at the same time repulsed by, her condition. If her body hadn't been found and put in containment quickly, none of this would have been possible.

Without my death and the death of my child, it wouldn't have been possible either. The cramp in my chest that I refuse to acknowledge surfaced, but I shoved it back as I always had. This was not the time to renew the grief of my past. This was the time to kick the ass of the guy responsible for putting my client in the grave.

Some newly resurrected have a hard time remembering what happened to them, and that's probably for the best.

I, however, will never forget.

Three years ago my husband's lover stuck a butcher knife in my belly and cut my child out of me, leaving me to die in the desert. Fortunately for me, there were forces at work in the universe that took exception to that act of atrocity and rescued me. It's made me what I am now, and I can never go back to my previous life as a nurse, a wife and almost a mother.

That debt of honor can never be repaid.

Returning from the dead definitely has had some unforeseen consequences. Like the other-siders wanting something in return. Like learning how to raise the dead and performing life-swaps. Simple stuff like that.

Many of my resurrections involve women who, like me, married the wrong man and didn't live to tell about it. Other life-swap cases I handle include cops killed in the line of duty, and kids murdered by their mothers' new boyfriend, who just happens to be a pedophile. Fortunately, I was sent back to right the wrongs done to others just like me. It's a living as well as a mission. There are other resurrectionists out there, but we are a small force trying to bring our abilities to the public without getting ourselves killed. Our country has already had one giant witch hunt. We don't need another.

It was my turn to stand, and I got up from behind the desk. I'm tall, but I usually wear cowboy boots with heels. Gives me the height to look down on these assholes so they know a woman is the one putting them in the grave for good. I have long black hair I wear straight, past my shoulders, and skin that appears perfectly tanned year-round. Not my choice, but my mixed ethnicity. It's my eyes, though, which are an odd shade of muddy green with yellow flecks, that give me the advantage over the nut jobs I deal with. Some say it's like looking into hell when I give them the right stare. Frankly, I don't believe in hell anymore, so I don't know what they are talking about.

"How you doin', Rufus? You ready for all this?" He was a weasel of a man, not much to look at. Dark brown eyes too closely set, a short, wiry frame and the disposition of a rabid coyote. Probably has a dick the size of a baby dill, too. I've discovered the meaner a man's disposition, the smaller his dick. Hmm. Wonder why?

"Fuck you," he said and spat at me.

"Sorry. I don't fuck dead guys." As if.

"You're gonna pay for what you do. Someone's going to take you down." He made the sign of the cross as well as he could in shackles. Kinda tough, though.

The guards on each side of him just laughed, and that makes me smile. As close to a warm fuzzy as I'll ever get. I'm not warm, and if I'm fuzzy I need to shave my legs.

"Really? Well, it ain't gonna be you." I let my eyes wander over his hot pink jumpsuit. I took a cue from that sheriff in Arizona who makes the inmates wear pink underwear and live in tents outside no matter how freakin' hot it is. Unfortunately, pink is not a good color for most men, unless they're gay or less than three years old, and Rufus was neither. "Let's go, boys. We don't have all night."

The guards are equipped with a bulletproof, four-wheel-drive van. One drives, one rides with a shotgun trained on the life-swapper, and I mentally prepare for what I'm about to do. My main man, Sam Lopez, is unavailable tonight, and I actually miss his strong, hunky presence at the 'yard. He has secrets I can't penetrate even if I wanted to, and I suppose he's entitled to them. I don't own him, and he isn't obligated to have share-time with me, but his presence at the graveyard gives me strength I didn't know I needed until he said he couldn't be here. Each ritual takes a lot of energy, and I'm usually too wasted to drive safely back from the 'yard. Maybe it'll get better the more resurrections I perform, but for the time being, I have guards. Men like to drive anyway, so I don't mind having them cart my ass around once in a while.

* * *

The next morning, I felt as if someone beat the hell out of me when I wasn't looking. Obviously, I hadn't had enough meat yesterday. This girl needs loads of protein just to function in a normal manner. Well, my normal anyway. My stomach roars to life the second my eyes open. Dammit. I am so ruled by my appetite.

The life-swap had taken way longer than it should have last night, and as a result I was more ragged out than usual this morning. Having Sam present for the rituals obviously makes a difference, so I'm going to have to make sure he's not out dancing naked under the full moon for the next one. My energy stores last only so long and must be replenished frequently.

After a shower I put on some jeans and a black T-shirt. The crystal amulet on a chain never leaves my neck (a little gift from the other-siders), so I tucked it inside the shirt. They didn't give me direction on the crystal, but just said it was a source of power. Maybe it wards off bacteria, too, 'cause I haven't been sick since I began wearing it. I tugged on scarred black cowboy boots I wouldn't give up for anything and shoved a pair of sunglasses over my burning eyes. When I'm depleted of nutrients, my eyes turn funny colors. Scared a waitress half to death the first time that happened, hence the shades.

Coffee sustains me in my hour of need, which is every bloody hour of the day, so I swing by the coffee shop for a couple of those gallon-size coffee boxes. I keep one and share the other with the cops in the office.

They love me.

And I love 'em right back. They're the good guys in blue. Entirely too many of them have lain down their lives for others and not been returned to this plane. My never-ending project is getting a few of them back on the force and sending their killers to the nebula instead of a cushy jail cell for twenty-to-life. Two good cops had been killed a few years back by a psych patient, and it's been a high-profile case ever since. The venue for the trial had to be changed several times because there was such a public outcry on both sides. Fortunately, the cops have been on ice in my cryo lab since their deaths in anticipation of future resurrection, but I don't know when, if ever, it's going to get straightened out. Figuring out the legalities of this case still gives me a headache.

Can the mentally ill who murder be considered for life-swaps? Do they have real quality of life as they exist now? If not, then I'd like to play swap-a-cop for this particular bad boy. But how is one to know?

That's the part that has always given me pause and a lump in my gut that won't go away with an antacid. Truly mentally ill people may or may not be held responsible for their actions, no matter how heinous. If that's the case, then I could not in good conscience perform a life-swap with this afflicted man and the two cops, no matter how much people begged. My personal moral code wouldn't allow me to proceed. As far as I know, there are no *Resurrectionists Guidelines* to refer to in this kind of case.

Psychiatrists will fight to the death to defend either side of the fence, which leaves me sitting in the middle of it with splinters up my ass. So that's where we sit until someone more important than me makes a decision. I've been trying to get the court to pass some new legislation that will speed up the decision, but so far I'm having no luck getting them even to look at it.

These are the issues we resurrectionists ponder every

day. They may never be solved in my lifetime, however long that is, but I've got to try. Something won't allow me to walk away from a situation I might be able to help with. Maybe it's the way I'm made or part of being a resurrectionist. Others in my situation have few answers, either. Those of us who have heard the battle cry for resurrections always feel alone, even though there is a small group of support available.

"Hey, Dani." A deep voice that gives me shivers at night got my immediate attention. Though I could have just sighed and listened to him talk, I have a reputation to uphold. Tough chicks aren't just born. They're cultivated.

It's a lot of work.

"Hey, Sam, what's up?" I usually leave the door propped open with a large piece of petrified wood, about the size of a bowling ball, I had found in my yard. Here in the desert, the stuff's everywhere, and someday when he's being a butt head (and you know he will be no matter how hot he is now), I'll probably have to clobber him with it.

"Just reviewed your notes on the cop-killer case." He held several files in one hand that contained my attempts to outline the legislation. In his other hand was a cup of coffee I'd brought. See? Bringing coffee is a good thing, no matter what it costs my budget. Makes for good relationships with smart men who carry big guns. Here was one with a 9 mil on his hip, and he ain't afraid to use it. That's yummy, in my book.

"Take a seat and tell me what you think." Although I have my suspicions, I want to hear it from him. My powers don't extend to mind reading, but I know Sam pretty well, and he's giving off a negative vibe. Could be his years as an army Ranger, though. He's one tough dude. That makes him a good resource for me, but he's hell on relationships.

With a sigh he sat and parked the files on my desk. "I'm not a lawyer, but I don't think they're going to make a decision. At least not yet. The public isn't ready for it."

"Yeah." Running my hands through my hair is a habit, and one I engage in now. One I'll probably regret down the line when I experience androgenic alopecia and there's more hair in my brush than on my head. "I wish there was a way around this. It could be the start of something big here. I hate waiting for New York and California to set the bar, and then we catch up later." I wanted this, bad. Not just for me and setting a precedent in New Mexico, but setting one for all resurrectionists. We need to know. The families of those we resurrect need it, too. I tried not to think of how badly the families of the cops needed it.

Sam's dark, dark gaze roamed over my chest and lingered for a second before his attention returned to my face. Not that I dislike that sort of attention, especially from him, but we have bigger things to focus on than the bumps under my shirt.

He pushed the files back to my side of the ugly desk that was a recycle from the precinct. "Sorry, babe."

You know, I'm a fully liberated woman, but for some reason, I don't mind him calling me babe. Mostly because he does it with affection, and knows that if he ever gets in my pants we'll set the desert on fire. If anyone else tries it, I'll rip their tongue out. Sometimes the sparks between Sam and me are visible at night. In a graveyard. Woo-hoo. How romantic is that?

"Thanks for taking a look at it." Trying not to be disgusted and impatient, I shoved the file into a drawer.

"Did you get any sleep last night?" He's got dark, dark eyes that don't miss much. Of course the bags under my eyes are probably as big as *sopaipillas* and just as puffy.

"Some. I never get enough." Never, never enough rest. Someone needs to invent a pill to replenish lost sleep. I'll buy stock in the company.

"Did you eat this morning?" He was starting to get bossy, which I didn't like. I'd gotten out of a controlling relationship with my ex-husband. I didn't need a lecture from Sam. Having been born the oldest in a house full of women, he was born bossy. They let him get away with entirely too much and ruined him for any other women, hence his track record of disastrous relationships.

I shrugged, noncommittal. Something I learned from him. "Yep. The usual."

Sam grinned. The man has a smile that could set me on fire. I must resist. "You're the only woman I know who has steak for breakfast."

"Is that a bad thing?" Hardly. I know better, but can't resist teasing him sometimes, and my irritation disappeared. There's so little joy in my life, I have to take it where I can get it.

He rubbed the back of his neck as if it ached. Having known him for a year or so, I picked up on little nonverbal signals, and this was one of them. Something was up that he didn't like and didn't want to talk about. Wonder what it was? He'd eventually talk, but until then, he'd stay clammed up. I should start calling him Sam-The-Clam.

After getting up from the chair, he strolled around

to my side of the desk and leaned a hip on the edge. Hmm. Our flirtations over the past year have always been restricted to arm's length. This was new. Wonder if it had anything to do with that neck issue of his and the one growing between my shoulder blades? There was either something coming, or my gallbladder was having an attack.

"You need more sleep." He ran a finger down the side of my face. "The rings under your eyes aren't going away."

"I don't wear much makeup, so they're easier to see." Maybe that makeup sale was still on. I could pick up a spackling tool on the way back.

"You're beautiful with or without makeup, but you're also damned tired. I can see it every time you walk in here that you're burning out. Can you take a week off and get out of town? Relax on a beach with a fruity drink and a book somewhere?"

"Could you?" As if. We're both chained to our work.

"Is that a proposition?" There was that damned grin again and a new tingle in my stomach to go with it. Interesting, but it ain't gonna happen.

"Hardly." I shoved him off my desk. When he's too close to me I get distracted, and sometimes I think that's what he's after. "Go arrest someone, will you?"

He took a step away and rubbed the back of his neck. "No rituals tonight?"

"None so far."

"Make sure you call me if anything comes up." That dark, guarded look was back in his eyes. There was something behind it. Something he hid that crept out at times despite his efforts to bury it.

"You're taking the bossy thing to a new level today." I glared. I didn't need a babysitter.

"It's my job, babe." Serious now, he held my gaze as if he wanted to say something else, but held back. Yeah, he was a man of secrets, and I wasn't likely to penetrate that barrier he erected every time I asked him a personal question. Sometimes I just can't help myself and must ask. Just makes my day to irritate other people.

"So what's going on with you today? I'm getting a weird vibe from you." I raised my brows and waited for the answer I knew wasn't coming.

"Nothing." Slam. That door in his eyes closed, but I knew something was bothering him.

"You're lying, I can see it. If something's up, I need to know. If you don't share, dude, then neither do I." That broke all the rules of my agreement with the P.D., but right now I didn't care. Something was up.

Narrowing his eyes, he tried to stare me down, but failed. I know his tricks, and he sighed. "There's something I can't get a hold on. Something in the air."

"In the air? Could you be vaguer?" My turn to frown.

He stood and spun away. "Never mind. If anything concrete shows up, I'll let you know."

"If you've got a feeling about something, I want to know, even if you think it's nothing."

"Like I said, when it's concrete, I'll let you know." His hand drifted to his neck again, but I kept silent. Miracles do happen. Sam gave me a crumb.

He's my assigned protector from the P.D. I've been through private training like you wouldn't believe. I know a thing or two about guns and how to protect myself, but when I perform the rituals my focus is internal. That's when I'm vulnerable and need someone to watch over me. A big, bad, hunky cop like Sam will do. Sometimes I resent that I need one, but it's become obvious I do. The security guards offer some protection, but there's something about Sam in particular that needs to be there. I don't know what yet, and it's pissing me off.

"Like I said, it's my job." He gave that tight little smile he has when he has to do something he doesn't want to. Talk about control issues.

"Yes, I know. You're the liaison, blah, blah, blah." I get so tired of the blah, blah, blah sometimes. "But you're off your game, and that affects me whether you know it or not." Well, I guess he knows now.

"Yes, I am. One of these nights we're going to have more trouble than we bargained for." Concern emanated from his eyes and a little something twisted between my shoulder blades. That's my signal something is wrong.

I hope it isn't an omen. Not that I believe in them, not seriously, but I sort of wish for a bit more protection at times. Something small and inconspicuous, like the Spear of Isis. That's all.

With a nod he left, and I tried to return to the work in front of me, but it didn't keep my attention.

I'd had a sense of foreboding for a week now and didn't know why. Maybe that's what I was getting from Sam. He has senses finely tuned from his military service that I'll never get close to, but he's so damned closed-mouthed sometimes, I just want to strangle him.

I must resist.

Chapter 2

The sound of a skateboard on the sidewalk always gets on my nerves. I never know whether I'm going to get run down by a herd of teenagers, or if there is a message from my mentor, Burton. This time it was Burton and the muscles in my back tensed. I'm going to need a painkiller by the end of the day if this keeps up.

"Where you been, *chica?*" He knows that any reference to my ethnic backgrounds will get my immediate attention. When I went to nursing school, I applied for scholarships based on my three ethnic groups, but was denied two of them. Bastards.

"Oh, get off it, Burton. What do you want?" Sometimes I have no patience for the man. Sometimes I want to cuff him just because he's such a piece of work. Any spiritual entity that's four thousand years old shouldn't be such a smart-ass. There's just something wrong with that.

"Just wanted to make sure you're okay."

"Okay? I'm fine." I narrowed my eyes, immediately

suspicious. Him, I never quite trust. "You've never asked me how I am before. What's up?" That niggle between my shoulders was aching again.

"The other-siders have a sense something's changing in the universe. They want to make sure you and other resurrectionists are unharmed."

"Unharmed?" Maybe that was why Sam and I had had uncomfortable feelings we couldn't name. "Who would want to harm us?" Aside from the obvious.

"The Dark."

"What the hell is that?" As if I needed something to screw up my life more. The judicial system was enough.

"The entity who has disrupted the balance, and grows larger and more dangerous every time evil wins out over good. It is a congealed group of dark souls that has banded together from the deepest part of the nebula. They had been banished for their misdeeds while earthbound and have gathered to form a darker, stronger being. It's made a declaration to stop the resurrectionists, but most especially you."

"Me? Why me? What about the others out there?" He said it as if this thing had challenged me to a game of checkers. Was he serious?

"Of that we are uncertain. They ask that you take no unnecessary risks until the threat has passed."

Jeez. Could they be more nebulous? Unnecessary risks? What the hell was that? Every day I take on a case, and the risk I take with my body and my life to send killers to the nebula is a huge risk. What about that seems unnecessary? I thought they were out there to help me. And I know that most threats generally don't just pass by without slapping you upside the head.

"Uh, how will I know when that happens?"

"That is unknown. At this time we are offering the warning to all."

"Well, that's some comfort, I suppose."

"Do not underestimate the power of this entity. It has been dormant for millennia and now seeks its vengeance." For a moment I saw every one of his four thousand years revealed in his eyes, and a chill rose over me as the full effect of his warning got to me. Then the moment was gone, and the teenager with a goofy grin returned. "Man, this is just too much fun." Hopping on his board, he was off in a flash and a whoop of delight. Too bad more people aren't pleased so easily. I'm certainly not, though a big gun and a frozen margarita come close.

"I don't understand what you see in that kid. He's nothing but trouble." Sam was right behind me, and I nearly jumped, but I controlled the urge to clobber him. My instincts are finely tuned, and I could have given him a bloody lip just then, or driven his testicles up into his eye sockets, but I restrained myself. Turning, I gave him a glare instead, but the sunglasses made it less effective. Sometimes I'm just too nice.

"What are you doing? You shouldn't sneak up on people like that." Especially now with universal warnings of doom and gloom on the horizon.

"I know, but with you?" The shrug said it all and his army Ranger training proved it. He liked to live dangerously around me. "That kid's trouble."

If he only knew. "He's harmless. He's probably just like you were at that age." Yeah, right.

Sam glared down at me, and I was surprised his shades didn't melt. "Don't ever compare me to that kid. Ever."

O-o-o-*kay*. An unintended arrow hit a tender spot I hadn't known existed. "Why not?" I just had to know.

"Don't go there, Dani. It's none of your business."

"You're the one who made it my business by giving me a bone with nothing on it."

"Forget it. I heard him mention not taking any risks right now. Is he threatening you?" Sam stepped forward, violating my personal space and trying to pressure me into telling him something I don't want to. Won't work on me. I'm immune to that sort of pressure.

I almost laughed. Burton? Threatening me? *Pfft*. But this new thing? Had me thinking. "It's fine. See you later." Some secrets are mine to keep, and I don't have to explain them to anyone. Not even the man who watches my back.

"Dammit, Dani, if something's going on I need to know about it. If I'm to protect you, I need to know what's going on." He followed me at the pace I set.

"You need to trust me, that's what you need to do." I won't be controlled. After one disastrous relationship like that, I was never doing another, not even with Sam.

He said nothing because he knew I was right and wouldn't admit it. He didn't trust anyone. Me more than most, but not enough to sit down and have share-time over coffee. That pissed me off, so this conversation was over. We were at a stalemate on the issue, but at the moment it didn't matter. I knew he had his reasons that were related to his military service and probably his life growing up in the *barrio*. These were areas of his life he spoke little of, and I respected that, but I didn't like it. "Catch you later."

As I walked away I felt Sam's eyes watching my ass, *not* my back, so I put a deliberate saunter in my stride and took a quick look over my shoulder. There he was, feet spread apart, arms crossed over the chest I'd like to spend some time crawling across. Seriously, there ought to be a cartography class for women who want to map out a man's geography to remember fondly later. Then, I caught his gaze over the rim of my sunglasses, and there was nothing except complete male appreciation in those eyes. The look said he'd have me on my back with my feet in the air if he thought he could do it without getting his jewels crushed. That made me laugh, and I turned around again, leaving him with his tongue hanging out.

It's good to know that there are some consistencies in life I can depend on and for some men to behave like men. That thought made me smile a little bigger, and the tension of the day eased a bit. Sam was nothing if not dependable.

There's only one thing I hate worse than weepy women, and that's weepy men. Today, I had 'em both. They're manipulative, whether they mean to be or not. People come to me all the time to resurrect their loved ones, but if it isn't for the right reasons, I won't help them no matter how much they cry. I *hate* being manipulated.

A young couple, Juanita and Julio Ramirez, sat across the desk from me in my office. The pain in her eyes reached out to me. "Please, please, Miss Wright. You have to help us."

"But this isn't what I do. You need a psychic, not me. I come in at the end when everything is settled. I don't find lost people." I charge in on my white steed and send the bad guy away, but not till all the shootin's done.

"No one else can do it. He's our only child, and he's gone!"

That did it. I was on the job, whether it was normally my job or not. I couldn't not help, even if all I did was offer comfort.

I have an unfortunate kinship to these people, but they'll never know it. My personal loss must stay buried in order for me to work successfully with others like me.

Before I could move away, Juanita took my hand in hers. Unable to remove my hand from her grip without looking totally stupid, I had to sit there while she cried onto my skin. My nerves are raw and the sensations I pick up are extreme. That's why I don't touch people very often. I pick up their vibes, their emotions, and their life force if I'm not careful. The skin reveals a lot in the sweat, the texture, the nerve endings that send out little pulses, and we just don't realize it. If people knew others picked up all of that information, we'd never touch each other. Don't get me started on the bacterial transmission.

With Juanita hanging over my arm and sobbing on the desk, I had no choice except to ingest the energy she put off, and I tried to resist it as much as possible. It was like being simmered in *menudo*. A greasy soup of animal parts you don't want to have identified.

"Juanita." I tried to focus and push away the overload oozing out of her. She was a terrified mother, and I felt every emotion, every pulse of her terror knifing through my head. I had to get the woman off me or we were both going to be on the floor sobbing and nothing would get done to save her son. "Sit up and tell me what's going on."

After one last wail, she sat and released my arm. Oh!

What a relief. I could breathe again. I couldn't think without having her emotions bleed into my brain. It was sad enough in there. It didn't need any help.

Juanita was one of those unfortunate women who were too caught up in appearances. At around age twenty-four or so, she was truly beautiful, her skin flawless, her hair shoulder length and a thick, dark brown. It was the makeup that killed the effect. She'd shaved off her brows completely and drawn them in with a pencil in an unnaturally high arch on her forehead.

Maybe she thought it looked good. Maybe Julio liked her that way, but the effect made her look overly alert, as if she were questioning everything you say.

"Well." She looked to her husband, who had yet to say a word. "Our son, Roberto, has been missing for two days. Two days! The police are too slow. He's out there by himself." The implication being that if he weren't found immediately, he was going to die. The bigger implication was that he was already dead. I recalled hearing something about this case and feeling the urgent energy of the cops, but I tried not to watch or listen to the news too much. It overwhelms and depresses me.

With trembling hands, she slid a picture of an engaging-looking, happy little boy, about the age of six or so, with one front tooth missing. I didn't touch the photo because I was certain I would end up on my knees in pain. I don't like to do that in front of clients. Kinda puts people off when the expert loses her mind.

"When did you last see him? Is it possible he's simply run away?" The truth is, if the cops don't find a kidnapped child right away, the kid is probably already dead or out of state and unlikely to be recovered.

"He didn't run away. He didn't *come home* from

school. My cousin, Filberto, was to get him because I had a dentist appointment, but Roberto never came out of the school." She covered her face with her hands. "He's gone!"

Never came home, my ass. If I had hackles they'd be standing straight up. You didn't need to be a resurrectionist to smell something foul in the story. "Was Filberto questioned by the police?" Something in me sizzled when I said his name, and I jumped as if I'd been stuck with a cattle prod. Bad sign for Filberto's team.

"Oh, sure, I know what you think, but he'd never hurt my baby. Never." Wiping her eyes with a tissue, she was careful not to disturb the black mascara topping off her wide-eye look.

The skin on my back began to itch and crawl, as if maggots had already begun to eat my flesh. Not a good sign, either. Everyone has a sixth sense; some are just more highly developed than others.

Mine was on fire.

"I need to meet with your family. Can you set that up for tonight?" I looked at my watch. It was almost 6:00 p.m. "In a few hours, please. We have to move fast." I was fairly certain it wasn't going to be fast enough.

"We'll do anything to get our baby back."

Leaning forward over the desk, I focused on Juanita, cupped my hands around her face, and held her gaze for a few seconds. At first she was startled, but then she held my gaze. That's not easy. I'm a little scary sometimes. She was true, and I released her. "Are you certain you'll do anything to find him?"

"Yes." She hadn't blinked and neither had I. You'd be surprised what shit could happen in the blink of an eye.

"I'll see you around eight." I slid a piece of paper across the desk. "Write down your address."

I walked them to the door with a mental sigh. It was going to be a long night. Calling Sam occurred to me, but after our conversation this morning I was feeling ornery. Besides, I wasn't doing a resurrection. Just information gathering, so technically I didn't have to call him.

I just love technicalities when they work in my favor.

I arrived at the Ramirez house a few minutes early. I like to watch a house for a little while before walking in. Opening the door for a person I didn't know got me killed once. It ain't happening again.

Instincts on full alert, I approached the door. Letting my senses reach out, I felt for imminent danger, but found nothing, so I rang the doorbell. Burton and the other-siders had to be mistaken. There was no big, bad darkness out to get me, just a missing boy who needed to be found. Looking overhead, I saw no threat. I was just a simple resurrectionist doing a job. I wasn't any threat to a universal force.

But I kept my right hand free to grab my gun, anyway. I carry a 9mm semiauto. I also tuck a derringer in the top of my boot, but that requires a little extra maneuvering to get to. Most people aren't used to women carrying weapons openly, so I wear a light blazer over my shirt and shoulder holster. Basic black, goes with everything. And hides the dagger strapped to my left wrist too.

"Miss Wright, please come in." Julio opened the door and ushered me in. Here, everyone says Miss, not Ms., but it means the same thing. "We're here, like you said. Tell us what we need to do."

Oh, he might not like what I was suspecting he had to do. "Thank you. How about I just talk to everyone, and we go from there?"

"I don't know if it will help." He swayed slightly as he held on to the door, and I detected the faint odor of tequila leaking from his pores. After what he'd been through, I couldn't begrudge him a shot or two of fortitude.

"Someone knows something." He shrugged, but led me to the kitchen table, which was the hub of the family activity. This was a typical Catholic-Hispanic household with crosses of various sizes around the house and a small shrine in the living room. My grandmother's house is nearly identical, except she has a shrine to Buddha. No matter, same deal.

"We're here because I believe someone here may have information about Roberto they haven't told the police. On his own he's not going to survive for long."

"You think he's still alive? After all this time can he be alive?"

This question was posed by one of the family matriarchs. Although only two days had passed since his disappearance, I was certain it felt like an eternity. Anger and grief warred for control in her eyes. She was afraid to hope, afraid to believe he would be found, and terrified something she didn't want to think about had already happened. I wanted to help this family, but I knew I was going to bring more bad news. That part wasn't my problem to deal with. Recovering a child was. I hoped.

"That's what I'm here to find out."

"Are you a *curandera?*" she asked, watchful and suspicious.

That's the Hispanic version of a witch-woman or a healer, depending on the interpretation. Not my gig, but most people, especially the highly superstitious, are more comfortable with that term. "No. I'm a nurse, not a healer in the way you mean." Once a nurse, always a nurse. We're kind of like the marines that way, but without the firepower and snappy haircuts. "Tonight I'm here to see if I can help find Roberto." I looked away from her and the grief pouring out of her. That kind of energy messes with my mojo. "I need everyone to go outside and form a circle in the yard."

This family understood the need for ceremony and rituals, so there were no complaints. I entered the circle the family created. Turning, I moved toward Roberto's parents and held my hands, palms out, toward them.

I don't have the power to see energy or auras that other resurrectionists do. I feel them, sense them, and almost taste them if they are strong enough. Not very palatable, but it's not as if I have a choice. I'll brush my teeth later.

The little charge of energy that flowed from Juanita and Julio was clean. I don't know how else to explain it, but it wasn't tainted with evil or deception. I guess I have an evil-ometer in my hands. I have to be careful of whom and what I touch because my senses pick up things when I don't want them to. One of the undisclosed perks of coming back from the dead.

I focused on the present and the possibility of finding this child. Alive or dead, I wasn't sure, but at least we could find out what had happened to him.

I moved around the circle with my radar on full alert. It was as if I had a bubble of energy around me with tendrils that reached out for information and drew it back to me. Kind of like an electrical octopus feeding information instead of fish. I felt the vibrations flowing around and over the bubble and absorbed some of the energy. Not unlike static feels when you rub a balloon against your hair. Assuming you have hair. You know what I mean.

One of the women shivered as I approached her and made the sign of the cross, then rubbed her arms. Whatever makes you feel better, I guess. She wasn't my target, and I moved on. Women were rarely the perpetrators of crimes against children. Sure, you got the ones who murdered their entire families, but those people were mentally ill. They had to be or I couldn't sleep at night. I was in search of a male. And I had found one. Possibly abused himself, but had never dealt with it.

My hands nearly glowed with golden light, and I began to sweat. Damn. I hate being right sometimes. "Filberto?" I asked. Fear and shame oozed out of this thin young man. In his early twenties, he still carried that uncoordinated stance of a teenager who hadn't quite found his place in the world. Filberto was going to find his place in the world, and it wasn't going to be to his liking.

The hairs on my arms stood up, and my evil-ometer went nuts. This was the guy. I knew it. Looking into his eyes, I knew that he knew that I knew it, too. He stepped back, scared shitless of me. My eyes must have been going wild again. I'd have to work on that.

"Get away from me." He backed up. I stepped forward.

"What did you do?" I didn't want to touch him and see every blasted detail of it in my mind. I wanted him to confess to these people. Making him tell of his crimes was so much more powerful on the universal scale. It wouldn't balance the scale, but at least it would help add a stone or two to the side of justice. There needs to be equal parts of good to counter the evil in the world.

Gasps and screams filled the air and broke the circle apart. Juanita wailed the way only a wounded mother could, and the sound set my nerves on edge. I had made that sound once. But now I couldn't let it or my memory interfere with what was going on in front of me. Filberto continued to back up until he stepped against a large cottonwood tree. "Get away from me. Witch!" he cried and held out his hands. *Pfft.* As if that was gonna stop me.

I stepped into his personal space, and we both began to glow. From my feet all the way to the top of my head, I was encased in a golden light. It was both healing and protective. Filberto, however, glowed sort of a dark green. Bad news for him. So maybe I'm seeing auras after all.

He broke into a run. Shit. That meant I had to chase him. I hate running in boots. Fortunately, all of the yards in Albuquerque have some sort of fencing. To keep things in or out, I was never sure. So I had to chase him only a few feet and caught him as he was trying to climb over the fence using the trumpet vine like a ladder.

I grabbed him by the back of his jeans and yanked. He came flying, and we landed in a heap. Screams and hysterical Spanish, most of which I didn't want to have interpreted, landed on us as the family descended. Filberto was ripped out of my hands, and I was left in a heap all by myself. That's sort of hard to do, so I got up and went after them.

I had to stop them before they killed him. We needed information, not another murder. That wouldn't be justice for Roberto, and it wouldn't balance the scale, giving evil more weight. The Dark's been growing enough from what the other-siders have said. "No! Wait." I squeezed through the mob and landed on my knees. Crawling forward, I maneuvered myself closer and stood again. How could I stop this before they killed the only person who knew what had happened to Roberto? I could shoot my gun into the air, but in this part of town it probably wouldn't get any attention.

Fortunately, my years of martial arts had given me some muscle, and I used it now. Elbowing my way through, I nearly fell on top of Julio, who was pummeling his fists into Filberto's face. The men of the family, some of whom were certainly armed, stood in a protective half circle around the two and let Julio wale on Filberto.

"Stop it!" It was like talking to a couple of pit bulls who had their teeth into each other. I tackled Julio. What else could I do? We fell to the ground, and Julio pulled back with an elbow that landed in my chest. That was gonna hurt later. "If you kill him, we'll never know where Roberto is." I didn't say I thought Roberto was already dead and we needed to recover the body, if possible, for a resurrection and life-swap.

Julio stood abruptly, then I realized he had help. Sam had yanked him to his feet and shoved him into the arms of his cousins. "Hold him." He pointed to two of the larger men. Without question, they complied and held on to Julio. Now, why don't men react like that to *my* direction? That's just disgusting. Machismo at its finest.

I grabbed hold of Filberto's shirt, yanking him to a sitting position. He was bloody, and his eyes were swelling shut. Most of his wounds appeared superficial, like a fat lip that bled as if he'd bitten through it, but who knew about what was going on in his brain. He could have damage I couldn't sense.

"Don't touch me," he cried and put his hands up like a girl.

"Oh, please, give it up. You're caught, so just can the innocent routine." I hated touching him, even by the shirt, but had to.

"What are you doing here?" I asked Sam, who glowed with his own sort of angry-red aura.

"I followed you." Sam moved closer to me. "You were supposed to call me if something came up."

"Had a late case come in."

"What did you do to my son?" Julio cried and strained against the arms of his cousins. Though he wasn't the biggest man in the yard, he was fueled by the need for vengeance and to tear something apart. That's different from the need for justice, which is where I came in.

"Where's my son?" Juanita collapsed on the ground at his feet, sobbing. The night was alive with cries.

"Yeah, Filberto. What did you do to Roberto?"

Chapter 3

Filberto swayed back and forth. Sam and I had to hold him upright. He might be more hurt than I first thought. Although I had not been gifted with X-ray vision, I was a nurse, so I could keep his ass alive long enough to get some information out of him. He wasn't really hurt. Not hurt like Roberto. I shook him. "Where's Roberto?"

"Gone."

In that word, I knew everything. Just once I'd like to be disappointed and have a happy ending, but that's apparently not my karma this time around. "Dammit." Focusing, I heaved out a sigh, then took a deep breath and steeled myself against the pain that was going to saturate me the second I touched his skin. I placed the heel of my hand on Filberto's forehead and let my fingers fall over the top of his head. This was the only way I knew to access another person's memories. It hurt me to do this. Physically, emotionally and spiritually I would suffer for days, trying to get the stench of someone else's mind out of mine, but I had to do it. For this family to recover their loved one, I had to do it.

After a glance at Sam to link myself in the present, I closed my eyes and let it wash over me.

Flashes of light hit me first. Then I sort of saw a slow-motion movie playing, and I was the only one watching it. Filberto had picked up Roberto at the school. They got into a car and drove away. Filberto sweating and cursing himself all the way as memories of his own molestations filled him. So many years, so many hidden secrets and lies had finally bubbled up out of him. He couldn't help it, or that's what he told himself, as he choked the life out of Roberto's little body and tucked it away at the edge of a rock outcropping. Then he raced away and returned to Albuquerque before he was missed.

Pulling myself out of the memory, I gritted my teeth against the impulse to pick up where Julio had left off. My stomach cramped, and I wanted to vomit.

"I know where he is." I removed my hand from Filberto's forehead, then wiped my palm on my jeans. They were going in the washer as soon as I got home.

"He's alive?" Julio asked, the fragile hope in his voice staggering.

"I'm sorry, Julio." I hated this part, but it had to be done swiftly if there was to be a chance of recovery. "No. His body is out in the lava fields between Laguna and Grants." There was little hope of us finding his remains, but we could try. Many people had been lost out there and never recovered despite massive search operations. How was little ol' me going to find him? *Help?*

"Where's my baby?" Juanita screeched and raced at Filberto with a knife in her hand. Before I could think of moving, she reached out and struck Filberto across the face, blood spattering from the wound. "Where's my son?"

Sam and two others tackled Juanita and divested her of the weapon. I grabbed a fistful of Filberto's hair and held his face up as anger, hot and bright, coursed through me. "You look at these people, at that boy's mother, and tell us what you did."

"I killed him." He squinted through eyes already narrowed to slits by the beating he'd taken. I wanted to reach into his head and pull his brain out through his nostrils. "I didn't mean to, but I had to."

"What do you mean, you *had* to kill him?" I asked, really not wanting to know the answer to that, but pretty certain I was going to be sick once I heard it. A quick image of The Dark flashed in my mind. Could this be the influence Burton had talked of? Could The Dark have made Filberto act when he wouldn't have otherwise?

"He would have told. He would have told!" Filberto breathed through his mouth, as his nose was most certainly broken, if the swelling was any indication.

"Did you hurt him?" I knew he had, but I wanted him to tell the family.

Sobs made Filberto's head wobble, and he cried, feeling sorry for himself. Not what I wanted to see, but confession was supposedly good for the soul. I'd just rather hear the story than have all the blubbering along with it. "I couldn't stop. I couldn't stop myself."

"Did you touch Roberto in a way you weren't supposed to?"

"Y-e-s."

Anguish as you've never heard ripped the night to shreds. Sam and I looked at each other as we were shoved out of the way. There was no reasoning with an angry mob, and certainly no reasoning with a family who was rightfully justified in tearing apart one of their own.

"We have to stop this." I held on to Sam's shirt. He tried to put me behind him, to protect me. He's such a guy. But I hardly needed protecting. After dying once, I learned what to really fear, and these people weren't it.

We shoved into the group. We needed to get to the middle of this, where the action was, and prevent them from killing him.

Dropping onto my knees, I was able to crawl through and around the others. Not as dignified as I would have liked, but I got through and pulled my weapon. "Stop it." Sam joined me, on his feet, and drew his gun, too.

"We need him alive," Sam said.

"He doesn't deserve to live! He killed my baby." Juanita dissolved into a puddle on the ground. The women surrounded her and held on to her. The atmosphere in the yard was changing, becoming darker and malignant. A dark cloud or mist appeared overhead, but failed to manifest into anything I recognized.

Julio's fists were a mess of blood and raw flesh. He breathed heavily as the murderous light finally left his eyes.

"Julio, see to your wife," Sam said and motioned him back with the gun.

"I will see this done now. I don't care if I have to die for it. He'll pay for what he's done to my son!"

"We need him alive if there's any chance to bring Roberto back." I didn't tell them I wasn't sure I had the skills to do it, whether it could even be done, depending on the amount of decomposition that had begun, let alone animal involvement. Ew. "If you kill him now, there's no chance, and you'll die, too." I reached out to Julio and touched his shoulder. I tried to resist the vibrations coming off him. I was contaminated already by Filberto, so what was a little more? "Do you want that? Your family needs you now."

He collapsed beside his wife, and they wept together and clung to each other. I was unable to offer any solace.

Reaching out to Sam with my hand, I nearly fell face-first into him. He would have liked that too much, so I settled for dropping to my knees from fatigue.

After things settled down and a small plan for recovery took shape, Sam led me to his truck parked down the street. I got in and let him drive to the nearest diner we could find. "That was damned stupid." Anger crackled off him, nearly lighting the night around him.

Yeah, yeah, yeah, I know, but I didn't need to be reminded. I survived, and no one died in the process. Bonus. "I got the information I needed." Filberto had taken a beating, but he deserved it. Almost instant karma.

"At what cost?" he asked. "I've never seen you so wasted, Dani, not even after a tough life-swap." Sam was never outright angry; he's too controlled for that. What he does is simmer. It's not brooding, because that's too much like a pout for a man. But he simmers, and stews, and makes me wonder what's going on in that mind of his. I might have to do a mind-meld someday, but not now.

Right now, I didn't care. I needed flesh and lots of it. For whatever reason, it's what I need to keep going. I don't need just blood, though I do like my steaks rare. It's not just protein, either. I tried plenty of whey protein shakes and granola bars at the beginning, and they didn't do squat. I now despise granola. But something in a good, bloody steak does it for me. Who am I to question it? Maybe it's in the chewing and grinding of the food in my mouth that makes it work, or part of the digestive process. Do you know what's going on in your stomach when you're not looking? I don't know and don't care, as long as it fills up whatever is depleted.

We inhaled the meal and headed out the door. This was a fuel stop for me. I was so depleted of energy, I'd have chewed my own leg off soon. We had to get to the lava fields near Grants. About an hour away, depending on who was driving. I could make it in forty-five. We had to try to recover the body tonight. Preventing further decay was essential to a successful resurrection, but as always to fully restore the body would require some sort of blood sacrifice, and there was no way to know how much blood the ritual would require.

I didn't know if I had enough. I was exhausted enough already. However, Sam had volunteered for this duty. I didn't want it to be his sacrifice either. Perhaps our combined forces would be enough to get the job done. There was something special about Sam that helped make the resurrections successful.

The unmistakable sound of a skateboard approaching made me step back into the doorway, into Sam, and his hands were on my hips to steady me. What I wouldn't give to be able to really reach out to him, but I couldn't. Touch, skin to skin, made me feel things I wasn't prepared for, so I hung on to the wooden doorway and gasped for air.

"Hey, you okay, *chica?*" Burton asked and flipped his board to a stop beside us. My little mentor. At first I was always surprised to see him, but then I figured he knew things I didn't and let it slide.

"Yeah. I'm good."

"Don't you listen to anything I tell you?"

"Huh?"

"I just told you not to take any extra chances. Maybe your brain is going bad or something."

"Hardly. But I couldn't not take this case, you know that." Or at least he should. "Go away. I'm fine."

"Cool. But heed the warning." He tossed the skateboard onto the sidewalk and leaped onto it, disappearing into the shadows as only he could.

"That kid drives me crazy. How did he know you were here? We didn't even know we were coming here." Sam stepped up beside me to watch Burton zip away.

"I don't know. I think he has some sort of radar." Yeah, four-thousand-year-old radar.

"Has he been following you?"

"What, like you did?" Bingo.

Sam didn't answer, but just stared down at me with a perturbed glint in his eyes. As a rule, I do *not* enjoy being looked down upon, but with Sam, I make the exception. When he looks down at me, I almost feel petite and feminine. I need to avoid that feeling. I'm not petite or particularly feminine. I'm strong and in charge of myself. Softer feelings aren't in my job description and could get me killed again if I allow them.

"I tell you that kid is trouble."

"How can a kid with his pants halfway down his ass be trouble?" I mean, really. Who takes a person like that seriously?

"You do have a point," Sam said and watched as Burton skateboarded back to us.

"Later, dudes," he yelled.

"See ya, Burton. Pull your damned pants up!" I

called over the rush of the night. He raised his arm and flipped me off. Typical teenager. "He's harmless."

Sam shook his head, not convinced with my judgment of character. If he only knew how far I'd come, he wouldn't question me now. "If you say so, but that's the future of this country riding away on a piece of wood."

If he only knew. Burton was a piece of the past trying to hold on to a future for the entire universe, and I was helping him. No wonder I was tired all the time.

"Let's go."

Two nights later we were back in Albuquerque. We had searched for two days before finding Roberto's remains. It was a shame, too. All I could do was put what was left of this young boy on ice and see if we could figure out how to bring him back. The reverence that surged through me as I touched the small bones, placing them into the little cooler that would become his temporary coffin, surprised me. I pulled back and closed the lid as a wave of unwanted emotion washed over me. There was no time now for emotion.

The balance in this case was only partially restored. The crime had been committed, the criminal caught and the body recovered. Filberto was in a coma on life support with a significant brain injury and not expected to survive. I suppose that made my job easier. This was one case where a life-swap was certainly warranted, but the method by which to create the swap wasn't in my hands yet. Paperwork and red tape. It all came down to who could argue better, your lawyer or theirs. I was betting on Liz, my little Chihuahua with the heart of a Rottweiler. All I had to do was wait.

I hate waiting.

* * *

Sometimes, I simply don't understand the universe. Today is one of those days. Before I left the house, I spilled water three different times and in three different ways. That either meant something significant or my kitchen was more cluttered than I thought. But I made it in, coffee in hand, ready for all of the really important stuff I do around here.

I sat behind my desk trying not to laugh at the plight of the poor woman sitting across the desk from me. She could have been anyone's auntie or grandmother, sitting there all prim and proper with her Sunday best on, and her glasses shoved pertly on her nose. There she sat, with pictures of Fluffy, her four-legged canine companion. Recently deceased. This wasn't boding well for an improvement in my day.

"I'm sorry, Mrs. Chapman, but I simply can't help you." Not entirely certain I would, even if I could. I wasn't trying to be mean; it simply comes out of me that way sometimes.

"But you can do it. I know you can." She held out a flier I had mistakenly made when I first started out. It was somewhat unclear, and I now regretted ever putting those pages together. One came back to haunt me now and then, and this was one of those times. Maybe this was where the spilled water came in. An omen. "It says so right here." She shoved the thing across the desk to me.

"I know what it says, but this is old and the wording was poor. It doesn't say that we life-swap animals."

"It doesn't say you don't, either. I want my Fluffy back." She was on the verge of tears, and I pushed a box of tissues toward her. Here we go again with the tears. "I'll give you every last penny I have. My entire savings, if you'll bring back my dog!"

"Please calm down, Mrs. Chapman, and take a few breaths." I didn't want to have her stroke out right in front of me, 'cause then I'd have to go back to nurse mode and do something heroic. I wasn't in the mood. "Even though we know who killed your dog, in this case, Cesar, the Doberman next door, and you've kept Fluffy in your freezer, that doesn't change anything. I simply don't perform canine resurrections." That was to the point and not quite as tactful as I could have made it, but the woman was wearing me down. I should have done it just to get her out of my office.

"It was my neighbor's damned dog." Her lips pressed tightly together. No love lost there. She'd run him down if she got the chance.

"Yes. Weren't there numerous noise complaints made by that particular neighbor about Fluffy's incessant barking?" I had the file in front of me and pushed that toward her, too. Not that she picked it up. She knew what was in it.

"It doesn't justify murder. Fluffy was a terrier, and it's part of the breed. Anyone who owns terriers accepts that." She said it as if everyone in the world ought to know that terriers are barking maniacs. As everyone knows that fast food makes you fat. (Everyone knows that, right?)

"Yes, I know, but it doesn't mean your neighbors do. And it still doesn't give me the power to bring him back." I stood. Fortunately, Mrs. Chapman took the hint. She gathered her tote bag against her middle as if it were a priceless object. The bag was about the right size for... Oh, gag. The smile on my face melted as another thought occurred to me. If she had Fluffy in there, I was gonna puke. After the last night I had, it wouldn't take much. I was still trying to clean Filberto out of my brain. "If our conditions change, then I'll be in touch." I patted the file, indicating I had her contact information. I was going to shred it the second she left.

She nodded, didn't say thank you, because she had nothing to thank me for. I wish she'd just go to the pound and get a replacement dog.

Kind of like boyfriends were for some women. When you lost one, you just went to the pound (the bar) and brought another one home. He could make you happy for a while, but may have a straying problem and some were better trained than others. There was just that pesky neutering issue...

I sat and dropped my head into my hands, closed my eyes and groaned.

"Tough day?" Sam asked from the doorway.

I didn't even have to look up, but I did. "Understatement of the century."

"Wanna go shoot something?" There was a grin hiding behind that well-controlled expression of his. There was a little secret behind his eyes, too, and I definitely wanted to know what it was. The temptation of having him around for so long was beginning to wear on my defenses.

"You got a new toy?" He'd mentioned something about it.

A twitch of the brows was all I got. Intriguing.

"Get me outta here before I shoot something I'm not supposed to." I stood and grabbed my bag that was equally as large as Mrs. Chapman's, but there was no frozen dog in it.

* * *

The firing range was a great place to let off some steam. It was a safe environment where no one was going to shoot back, and you could pound the hell out of a flimsy paper target. I love that.

Sam got out his new toy, and it was a doozy. A forty-five millimeter with a nice weight in the hand. I love a man with a smokin'-hot piece of...*steel* in his hands. Makes me shiver all over. Not that I'll let Sam know that. Too many times in my past I let a man have control over me, and it is never, *ever* going to happen again. Control is something that is mine and mine alone. I don't care how illusive it is. Denial has gotten me through many years of my life, so I don't see a reason to stop using it now.

Now, I've gone through a number of weapons training courses, so I've shot many different kinds of weapons. Never stopped me from salivating over a new one, though. Kind of like some women are over shoes. It's all about the accessories, right? Mine just happen to be loaded.

Sam looked at me through that sexy, protective eyewear in a bold, jaundiced color and raised his brows. He really didn't even have to ask, but I *so* appreciated it.

"Hell, yeah, I want to shoot that thing." He grinned and handed me the weapon.

"Give it a whirl."

"Where'd you get this thing, some online shooting shop?"

"Yeah, right."

He knows I want his contacts and insulting him is one of the ways I'm trying to pry the information out of him. Not subtle, but then, I'm really not known for it. I tried the direct route for a while by just asking politely, or as polite as I get, but he just dissed me, so I was reduced to insults.

He went over a few specifics before I loaded the thing, then leaned against the wall beside me. I think he likes watching me shoot. Probably gives him a hard-on. He didn't stand behind me or try to put his hands around me or treat me like a girl, which I totally appreciated. I am *so* not a girl.

Without a word, I squinted through my equally sexy eyewear and popped off one shot, just to get a feel of it before I unloaded the clip. "Recoil's a bitch."

"Did I forget to mention that?" The man had wrists of steel, so recoil meant little to him.

"Uh, yeah." Squinting my left eye, I focused on the target again and squeezed off five shots.

"Nice, Dani. Very nice," he said, admiring the way I so sweetly took out the target.

I returned the gun to Sam and shook out my hands. "Gonna have to work up to that bad boy." Not that I was weak, but my wrists were tiny compared with Sam's. I had supernatural powers, but not supernatural strength. Maybe I could put an order in with Burton, but I doubted it. He'd just laugh.

We picked up our spent shell casings and cleared the way for someone else to shoot. There was never any shortage of cops, P.I.s or gun fanatics practicing at the range. After we left the shooting area, we removed our ear protection. He used an over-the-head earmuff type, and I used the squishy things in my ears. They were cheap and didn't mess up my hair. A woman's gotta watch out for these little issues in life.

"That's a nice piece," I said and meant it.

"Feel better now that you've shot something?"

Oh, the man knows me too well. "Yeah. Sometimes the grind of the job just gets to me, and I want to kill something. Better a target than a person, ya know?" Since I came back from the other side, controlling my anger has been an issue. Kickboxing and margaritas help keep it under control, depending on the situation. They are *not* interchangeable coping mechanisms.

"So, you want to tell me what's really bugging you?"

We headed outside into the parking lot on the south side of the big square, cinder-block building out in the middle of nowhere. Guess the desert has its perks. There are a lot of open spaces that no one wants to build on, so this was perfect.

I told Sam about Mrs. Chapman and the stupid dog she wanted resurrected.

"My grandmother would have loved that one." Normally, Sam is your typical, well-controlled, serious cop-type guy, but now, he wiped his eyes beneath his reflective sunglasses. He was laughing so hard, it brought tears to his eyes. I'd never have bet money on that happening.

I tried not to smile, but couldn't help it. Laughter is nearly as good as sex as a tension reliever. There has been little of either in my life of late, but then sex was what got me killed in the first place. Not mine, my ex-husband's. He's the one who couldn't keep it zipped. "Did she have a dog like Fluffy?" I asked. I knew his grandmother had passed into the beyond, but other than that, I knew little about her.

"No." He shook his head and put his hands on his hips. The laughter was still with him, and it was good to see. I love police officers, and our men in blue have little to laugh about on the job, so a snicker here and there does them good. "Oh, no. She'd have never had a dog like Fluffy."

"She liked big dogs then, like the killer Dobie?"

"No."

"Then what?" I couldn't see what was so funny now.

"The irony of the underappreciated. Like you. Like her. I never told you, but she was like you," Sam said, and all humor between us came to a screeching halt.

My smile faded. "What do you mean, just like me?"

"A resurrectionist." Sam removed his sunglasses. I saw his eyes, so I knew he spoke the truth. "That's why I volunteered for the liaison post with you. I have some experience with it."

"Are you kidding? Why didn't you tell me?" I yelled and slugged him in the chest. Touching people gives me too much information about them, but now and then I put up with it if I get to punch someone. Like now.

"What was the point? She was gone already, and I don't know how to do that stuff."

"The point was that…well, hell, I don't know, but I would have liked to have known."

"She was gone, Dani, years ago."

I sighed, not satisfied with that explanation. It was as if he had insider information and had kept it from me. "I would have liked to have known, that's all. Maybe you could have helped me in the beginning. Maybe you could help me now get some things figured out." I know there are others out there like me, but finding them is not easy. It's not as though we have an online newsletter or a blog like other, more populous states do. I'm going to have to work on one for New Mexico, because no one else is doing it.

"I don't know anything about what goes on during the rituals, other than what I've seen you do."

"Didn't she raise you?" As if that meant he knew everything about her life.

"Yes, but she kept that part of her life very secret when we were kids. It was only by accident that I found out."

Sam put his glasses back on, and we walked to his car. It was an unmarked police vehicle, and it looked like one. In the dark, no one would know, but in the daylight it screamed *cop car*. Just needed a cherry on top. The dashboard was outfitted with more technology than a small plane, and the two hundred antennae on it was a dead giveaway. It looked like an insect on steroids. But I got in anyway. I had to unless I wanted to walk back to the office, some forty miles away. I didn't. "How did you find out?"

"She didn't think my sisters and I were old enough to understand. Our family and the neighborhood were very superstitious. If there had been any implication of witchcraft in her house, the state would have taken us from her. It's different now that there are others out there." He shrugged. "So I did what every kid does. I followed her."

"So following people has been a lifelong endeavor?" Explains why I didn't hear him sneak up on me the other day. Bastard.

He didn't answer that and just gave me a look. "I was about twelve, but looked older, so I could be out on the streets and no one said anything. Back then the courts hadn't sanctioned resurrections and life-swaps, so it was very underground. Only the family of the victim was present, and the killer of course."

"You were such a wiseass, even at twelve, weren't you?" The image I had of him at that age was funny, all legs and feet and not quite grown into his attitude yet.

"Yeah. I was a piece of work. Got into more trouble than I was worth. Until the Rangers, anyway." He looked away. That's where his secrets lay, in his past, but here was an opportunity to find out a little more about him.

"Did she have a fit when she found out you had followed her?" I could just imagine. My grandmother would have kicked my ass from here to Sunday.

"Oh, yeah. My ears rang for a week. She could carry on like no one I've ever known." He grinned as if it was a good memory. Having good childhood memories is a sign of a balanced life. "Kinda miss that now." That was good. We usually have too many bad memories from childhood that are stuck in our brains. I never understood why the bad ones always come through first and the good memories are left behind. It would be nice to have that in reverse. If I'm ever elected Queen of the Universe, that's the first thing I'm changing. "I had to clean the chicken coop for three months after that."

"Oh, man." I pinched my nose shut. "Just the sound of that stinks." I released my nose with a giggle, then remembered why we were talking about her. "Do you know how she came to have her powers?" I'd heard stories that were different from mine. People who weren't murdered, but born with the abilities.

"No."

"I wonder if you could have inherited something from her." Could this affinity for raising the dead be passed from one generation to the next? Would Sam develop powers of his own? If he hadn't already, it was unlikely that they would surface now. Dammit.

"I don't think so." Sam maneuvered the car through the desert on the dusty, rutted road with casual ease, his long-limbed body relaxed, yet in control. The jiggling of the vehicle over the ruts was about to shake my liver loose, but he didn't seem to be bothered by it. "There's never been any impulse for me to do what you do."

"You have three sisters, right?" Maybe there was some hope in them. Some traits were passed from female to female.

"Yeah."

"Any of them?"

"Not to my knowledge. They'd have told me."

"Oh." It would have been nice to know that there was someone else I knew well who could have helped me.

"Sorry." He reached out and patted me on the arm once, then returned his hand to the wheel.

"I'm thinking about Roberto's case. I don't know if I have what it's going to take to bring him back. In all of my other cases, I've always had intact bodies. Not as far gone as this one is." Something in me just knew this was going to be one of the toughest cases I'd ever been involved in, emotionally as well as physically. Admitting that to myself, let alone to Sam, is a big step for me. Admitting vulnerabilities only makes you responsible or gets you a weekly date with a therapist.

"Have you checked with the hospital lately? What's Filberto's condition?"

"Same. Brain-dead. Waiting on the court order." Sometimes it takes hours, sometimes it takes days.

"What happens if you can't bring Roberto back?" He gave me a glance.

That was a good question. A really good one. And one I didn't know the answer to. I hated admitting that. In the world of nursing you must know the answers for every question. Saying *I don't know* isn't acceptable. It's no more acceptable to me now than it was then, but I said it anyway. "I don't know."

I just hoped we didn't have to find out. Thankfully, Sam didn't give me any meaningless reassurance to make me feel better. It wouldn't, and he knew it.

Chapter 4

There are days when the past haunts me entirely too much, and this was one of those days. Being around pregnant women unnerves me. I admit it. I should have no problems dealing with the condition of women who are growing new life inside of them, but I do.

It's what got me killed.

I hate thinking that I'm weak and vulnerable when I've worked very hard to be as tough as I can be. Certain things set me off, and seeing a happily pregnant woman on the arm of her police officer husband is what did it today. This is a joyous time for them, but for me, it does nothing except bring back haunting, hideous memories that still have the power to make me shudder.

After they passed with a happy smile and a wave, I closed the door to my office. Usually, I keep the door open unless I'm consulting, but now, I need some privacy to have my nervous breakdown. In an office that sits in the middle of the police station, there is no such thing as privacy. Or quiet.

One by one, I pulled the horizontal blinds and closed

off the windows. Was I hiding? Yes. I'd hide until it's safe for me to step out again. Until then, the memory of my life in the past overwhelms me in sloshes of emotions that build into pounding waves, and I allow it. Crawling onto the small couch against the wall, I tucked my feet beneath me and clutched a pillow to my middle. Closing my eyes, I let the memory, the horror of it, wash over me. I've learned that resisting only puts off the inevitable and gives more power to the pain. If I give it the time it needs now, then life will go on much more quickly.

I had been happily, blissfully, ignorantly, pregnant. My husband hadn't been as thrilled about it as I had been, but I don't think men can ever have the same connection to a baby as women do. Just the nature of how we're put together.

Anyway, my husband, Blake, and I had been headed for divorce when we decided to give it one last go. He'd been carrying on with a woman for several months and had tired of her clingy, demanding ways, so he let her go and went back to his wife, who wasn't so clingy and demanding. Maybe I should have been and things might have been different, but now, we'll never know.

So, giving it the old college try at reconciliation, the husband and I had a nice dinner with requisite margaritas, enough that I became a little intoxicated. Okay, a lot intoxicated, but I wasn't driving, so who cares? And we screwed our brains out all night long. We hadn't done that since we were dating, so we indulged in an all night bang-a-thon.

And I got pregnant. My family was thrilled because I was finally fulfilling my reproductive obligations inherent to any large family that seemed to want to take over the earth, one generation at a time. The playboy-doctor-husband was not thrilled. Although he said he wanted children someday, to him, someday meant years into the future, when he had a more secure practice, blah, blah, blah. What he really meant was *never*. He wasn't the fatherly type who could, or would, be there for his child.

In the old days, T&A's meant tonsils and adenoids. Now it was tits and asses, making them bigger and smaller in that order. There was serious money to be made in elective plastic surgery, and he was going to make his killing now, then retire to an island in the Caribbean and work on skin cancer late in life. Or something equally brilliant.

As my pregnancy progressed and my belly grew, I was happy. Even though the spousal unit couldn't be bothered to come to checkups and ultrasounds with me, I was content in knowing that I was growing a new life I could love and cherish. One that would love and cherish me, at least until the teenage years, and then it would be all over for a while.

Although my growing abdomen housed a new life, and that was good, it also threw my center of gravity off, and that was bad. I was in an awkward stage at the end of my third trimester when the doorbell rang and without thinking, I opened it. I'd been shopping for baby things and had taken a load into the house and was ready to return for another, so I was right there by the door. An unfamiliar woman stood there, and the smile fell from my face when I noticed the gun in her hand. She grabbed me by the shirt and dragged me out of the house toward my car with an open back door just a few feet away. I tried to struggle, knowing if I got into my car I was dead. It was the middle of the day and my neighbors all worked, so screaming wasn't going to help. I had to save myself or die trying.

She clobbered me on the head with something that felt like an anvil, and I collapsed onto the backseat. She shoved my legs in, and away she went with me unconscious in the back. I finally roused, but had no idea where we were or for how long I'd been out. My legs were numb from being folded up in such an awkward position. I had to move, but if I did, she'd know I was awake. I eased my weight up slightly so my legs got some circulation, and they screamed in pain as the blood flow returned.

"Dammit, where is this place?" she grumbled aloud. I heard the shuffling of papers, so maybe she was looking at a map. There was no GPS in my car. If she didn't know where we were, I wasn't going to find my way out of there either. Panic as well as my position was making me dizzy.

She turned off the car and got out. As quickly as I could, I shifted to my back. Not a comfortable position when you have a watermelon in your belly, but when your life was on the line, you coped. She opened the back door and reached in. I kicked out with both feet as hard as I could, and she went flying.

I knew I had hurt her, or at least surprised the hell out of her, but I was certain we weren't done yet. With any luck, she'd left the keys in the ignition, and I could get out of there. I scrambled out of the car as fast as any nine-months-pregnant woman could scramble, which wasn't too sprightly.

"You're a dead woman," she yelled. "Fucking bitch."

She was on her knees and clutched her front. Hopefully, I'd broken a few ribs. I didn't know who she was or why she thought kidnapping me was going to improve her life.

"What do you want?" I tried to slide against the car toward the front door.

"You. Dead."

The words didn't make sense, but as a nurse, I knew that things many people thought didn't make sense. She might have been an escaped psych patient who was on a mission from above or listening to the voices in her fillings. Or just off her medications. In any case, keeping her talking and away from me was my first step to survival. "I see, but why? Who are you?"

"You're the only thing standing between me and Blake."

Oh, shit. She was his mistress, who was supposed to be a *former* mistress. And she was freakin' nuts. Good going, Blake. If I got out of this alive, I was going to put certain of his body parts in the blender.

"Are you out of your mind? What the hell are you doing?" Anger overcame fear for a moment.

"Blake went back to you." The idea that Blake was married to me seemed to have escaped her. "If you hadn't gotten pregnant, none of this would be happening."

Oh, yeah. As if this was my fault. Another sign of pathological nuttiness. Blame everyone else for your personal failures.

"Now, just a damned minute. I have the right to sleep with my own husband. You are the one who doesn't." This was pissing me off. Now that I could see what was going on, I was damned mad and some of my fear wore off, which wasn't necessarily a good thing.

"We were so good together," she said with a wistful tone to her voice. "You should have seen us." She spoke to me as if we were girlfriends sharing secrets. Definite lack of reality attachment.

"I would prefer not to." I didn't need anything else to make me nauseated.

"Bitch." She reached for a large knife on the ground beside her and dove for me. I ducked, but that's hard to do with a big, fat belly. The knife missed me, but the impact of her body against mine thumped me between her and the car. The air went out of my lungs, and I couldn't breathe. A pregnant woman has a hard time breathing to begin with. When one is body-slammed by an insane woman, it's all over.

We collapsed into a heap on the ground, and she clobbered me again. Back then, I didn't know how to fight. Every woman ought to know how to defend herself, and this was one reason why.

When I woke up there was a knife sticking out of my stomach. I screamed, not certain if it was from pain or from the sight of the butcher knife protruding from my body.

The woman obviously intended to cut my baby out of me.

"Stop!" I reached out to the knife. Adrenaline and the heat of a white anger so deep I felt it in my bones surged through my marrow. I was going to remove that thing and stick it into her. I was not going to die. I was not going to lose my baby to this psychopath.

Unfortunately, I did all of that.

She reached the knife before I did and pulled it toward her, my left. "I'm going to take your baby and watch you bleed to death." She laughed, as if she was surprised she hadn't thought of it sooner. "And there's not a damned thing you can do about it."

Clenching my teeth against the pain that penetrated every cell of my body, I felt as if I were on fire and there was nothing I could do about it. Pushing up with a hand beneath my hips, I bore the weight of my body on my left hand and reached for the knife with my right. Breathing was next to impossible, and my chest burned with the need for air. I had to win, I *had* to win. This woman was going to kill me and steal my child. "No." It's all I could manage. "No." She was not going to win. I would not let her win.

Digging deep into a place I didn't know existed within me, I grabbed her hand on the knife and pushed with everything I had in me. Although I'd never hurt anyone before, I was going to kill this woman.

Somehow I got to my knees with her trying to shove the blade deeper into my side. In the movies there always seems to be a lot of noise in fight scenes, but it was eerily silent. Only the groans of pitting my strength against hers broke the night.

Abruptly, she let go, and stood, her breath coming in and out of her in harsh gasps. "You bitch!" Then, she kicked me in the stomach, and I crashed to the ground, the pain incapacitating me. Stars and bright lights swam in front of my eyes and seemed as though they came from all around us. Then she tackled me and straddled my body, her knees forcing my hands down, trapping them at my sides. My strength was fading. I knew it and so did she.

She grabbed the knife with both hands and pulled, spilling everything inside me out onto the ground. A scream echoed off the canyon walls, and I realized it was mine.

"Come here, little one. You're so precious," she said in a sweet voice as she searched for my baby.

"No." Reaching up with one hand, I tried to save him, but I was too weak. My vision blurred, and I was certain shock was overtaking me. Shock isn't such a bad thing. It keeps us from remembering the horrors that are happening to us, and at the moment I welcomed it.

She extricated the baby, and held it up. It wasn't moving and it was purple. "Oh, that's right. I have to cut the cord before it will breathe." Talking to herself, she retrieved her knife, slicing through the umbilical cord. Blood spurted, then she looked at me, as if I had the answer to the stupid thing she had done. "It's bleeding. Why won't it stop bleeding?"

I looked at my limp baby that she held out. I could see that it was a boy, and tears pricked my eyes. It wouldn't have mattered to me. I would have loved a girl just as much. She'd cut the cord close to the abdomen and hadn't tied it off. Now there was nothing left. If the baby could have survived, it would surely now die. It was going to bleed to death, just like me. "Didn't tie... the cord." It was all I could manage as tears for him and for me closed off my throat.

She looked down at the baby and tears flooded her eyes. "Dammit! I worked so hard on this. And now, just look at the mess it is."

My legs went numb, and I knew my end was near. I felt my breathing become labored.

She'd won after all. She laid the baby down beside me, wiped her hands on her jeans, got into my car and drove away, leaving us alone in the darkening desert. I had only moments left.

Pulling the baby toward me, I cuddled him as best I could, tucking the little head under my chin, and I let my tears flow. I sobbed and my baby fell out of my arms.

A light, the brightness of which I've never seen, appeared a few feet away. It wasn't a person, or an angel, though it could have been. I knew I was dying, and who knew what was coming to get me? I wasn't particularly religious. At least until that moment. For a second, I reconsidered what I knew about religion.

And then I took a breath, and it sighed out of me for the last time.

"Come, child." The other-sider, for that's what I have come to know it as, reached out to me. How I knew it was from beyond, I don't know, but I realized it was trying to communicate with me, even though no words were spoken aloud. All I could hear was a loud ringing in my ears.

"No." From above my body, I looked down at the baby, who had never begun to live, and touched it with one finger. I wanted to stay with him. He should go with me.

"He is gone to the source now. Your time here is not finished."

"Yes it is." It ~~was. I knew it. I'd accepted it.~~ Closing my eyes, I waited to be taken too. Waited for that irresistible pull from beyond I had heard about.

"You will go back. The call for help has gone out, and you will be saved."

Saved? How could I be? Did it not see the condition of my body? It was too late now. "No." I looked down at the mess that had been my body. It was almost beyond recognition. I don't know if I said it out loud, but I thought it and the other-sider heard me. My condition was beyond saving.

The being moved toward me, and the glow of it burned through my eyelids and into my brain. I wanted to let go, to leave this plane of existence, but couldn't. Something was drawing me back inside. I felt a pop in my physical body. I don't know how else to explain it, but it was as if someone or something had yanked on me, only I felt it at a visceral level. I had returned.

I began to glow, just like the other-sider. The life force had returned to my body, not floating around as it had been moments ago.

"You will return. You will survive, and you will right the wrongs committed against you, against humanity, and against the universe."

"Who do you think I am, Wonder Woman?" I managed to ask with my mind. Something was changing, something was reforming inside me. I could feel it. Reaching down, I placed my hand onto my abdomen and realized all was not as it had been. Things were returning to my body that had just been on the ground. I didn't want to think about infection or how much dirt was coating my internal organs. Should I survive the injuries, I'd die of septicemia for sure. No antibiotic could cure this.

"You are indeed a wonder. Each step of your life has prepared you for this moment. Your life-threatening wounds are repaired, and you will fully heal, be stronger than you ever were. You will return to your life, gifted as no other." The light that I had thought was bright went nuclear. In that moment, that nanosecond, my life was changed, whether I wanted it to or not.

I screamed from the deepest part of me, and the sound of it echoed off the canyon walls. The smell of wood fires and the murmur of my ancestors crowded my mind. I had been gifted with knowledge from the ancients, and the power of justice. Just as I had come back from the dead, I would assist others to return, to restore the balance of the universe.

Now, I pulled myself out of the musing at the sound of a scuffle outside my door. In a police station, there is always a scuffle of some sort going on.

The clock face slowly came into focus, and I decided my day was over. Though it was early, four o'clock or so, I was whipped. Nothing else was going to get done today.

I grabbed my bag and stood just as the door opened.

"You look like someone beat you with a rock," Sam said. Charming as ever. Where was that damned petrified wood? I could use it about now.

"Yeah, I feel like it, too." Shouldering my bag, I avoided looking into his eyes and shoved my shades on. They protected me somewhat, but he was so friggin' observant that nothing got past him. Damn cops anyway.

"I'm buying," he said and stepped sideways in the doorway to let me pass.

That meant I had to touch him with my body and slide intimately against him, smell that cologne of his that always made me want to forget my mission and lick my way from one end of his body to the other. Right now, I was too tired, and tried not to sense the way his body felt, the firmness of his chest and abs as I slithered past him. "You coulda moved." I threw a glare over my shoulder. With the sunglasses on, it was less effective. Sam wasn't very susceptible to my glares anyway, which pissed me off. I wasn't in the mood, so he was on his own for chow.

"Coulda." He fell into step beside me. "Garduno's?"

It was the one word I couldn't resist. My mouth began to water in anticipation. Guacamole, margaritas and meat. "You're such a bastard," I said and hung my head.

I was defeated already. My stomach ruled my life, and he knew it.

"I am, but that's why you like me." With his hand on the middle of my back, he gave me a playful shove toward the main doors. "Let's eat. I'm starved."

In less than thirty minutes I was surrounded by the things I loved and needed to get through the day: an excellent margarita, a flat-iron steak, rare, and a hot-blooded man across the table. It was a feast for the taste buds and the eyes. Okay, so I didn't really need the margarita to get through the day, but it was a nice touch at the end of a sucky one. And I really, really didn't need the hot-blooded man across the table from me, but boy, the eye-candy factor was too hard to resist sometimes. He was buying me dinner, after all. Who could argue with that?

I know Sam was interested in me in a way I couldn't return. My life was so complicated, it was all I could do to get through it. I didn't need any more complications. So for the moment, I just sat there and let him ogle my body, enjoying the rush of it. I knew he wanted to, and if this was the only control I had over a man, I had to take it. Gave me a shiver just thinking about what it would be like to have Sam naked and pressed against me. I gulped my frozen-no-salt-on-the-rim drink, trying to cool off my brain and the burn in my crotch. Didn't work though. Next time I was having salt. I didn't care what my blood pressure did.

Fortunately, our orders arrived quickly and I grabbed my knife, ready to stab it into anything that didn't move.

"You're the only woman I know who likes her steak bloodier than mine." Sam cut into his meal.

"I feel so feminine and dainty when you say things

like that." Me? Ha. Not even on a good day. After I was resurrected, I burned every feminine thing I owned. Except for that one pretty pink thong with a matching bra. Someday…

"We never finished our conversation the other day," Sam said.

Uh, what conversation? We had so many that got interrupted with phone calls and firearms that I couldn't keep track. Always on the move, always busy doing something for the station or my office, we never seemed to have a moment to allow our brains to catch up. "Which conversation was that?"

"About my grandmother and her job in the underground."

I had to laugh. That's certainly one way of putting it. "Yeah." I looked at Sam. I liked the way his smile sort of slid over his face slowly just then. The man has a face that isn't pretty or handsome, but it is compelling. His hair is that dark, dark black that Latin men have, and his is cut very short. Not quite a buzz, but a little longer. He is clean shaven, but I've seen pictures of him with a 'stache, and it's nice, too. The most compelling part of his face is his eyes, which sort of pull everything together and make it come alive. His eyes were the shade of espresso, dark and fathomless, eyes you could get lost in. Kinda like now.

"Dani?" He waved his hand in front of my face, bringing me back to the present. Doh!

How embarrassing. "Sorry." I cleared my throat and speared a piece of grilled jalapeño. Maybe setting my mouth on fire would keep me focused. "Didn't mean to stare."

"No problem. You just seemed lost for a second." The espresso in his eyes percolated a little warmer.

Yeah, I was lost. In his eyes. It's that damned cologne he wears. I swear there's some sort of chemical in it that puts me in a trance. Kinda like catnip for women. Ugh. Back to the convo at hand.

"We were talking about your grandmother and Roberto's case the other day, weren't we?" Back on track. That's where I feel best, with a job in front of me, a purpose and a mission to accomplish, not just drifting around like those in the nebula.

"Is there another resurrectionist who can help you?"

Sadly, no. "Not right now. I know a few, but not well enough to step into this kind of job." Something occurred to me, though. Something I've been doing just to get the events of the day out of my brain is something Sam's grandmother may have done. I have a computer and the internet, but she had access only to books and papers. I frowned and leaned closer to him across the table. Intent. Assistance might come from the other side in a different form. "Did your grandmother keep any records, any sort of journals, papers, anything about her work? I write some things, keep a journal of sorts, so it clears my brain and records some of what I do in the rituals. She might have done the same thing." That would be a huge bonus, to have information from such a source. I never know if the internet information is legit.

Sam thought a minute, then frowned. "If she did, I don't know of any, but my sisters might."

"She could have had a journal she kept hidden, if, as you say, she was at risk of being accused of witchcraft." If nothing else, I had to have a little hope.

"That's true. She had so much stuff though, something like that might have been overlooked. She was a Depression-era survivor, so she never threw anything away." My grandmother had also survived the Great Depression, and she has a garage full of toilet paper and plastic water jugs. The two things she can't live without. Oh, and soap, too.

"Would you ask your sisters if they found anything like that?" Desperation led me to ask Sam for such a favor. The weight of it got to me sometimes, even with my jovial outlook on life. Even if his *abuela* was dead, at least I might connect to her through her writings. Burton might be helpful, but he's unreliable and difficult to contact. Sam, I know I can count on, no matter what it is. He is a man who keeps his word, keeps promises he makes. I just didn't know why.

"Sure." He searched my eyes, and I wondered if they had returned to their normal color. After eating, my need for protein and blood is satisfied, and externally, I look normal again. Hesitating, he reached out and placed his hand over mine. He knows that touching is difficult for me. It isn't something I can easily control, and I can get sucked into the feelings of the person I'm touching. Occupational hazard. But right then, it was simply nice. "I'll help you any way I can. Sometimes you seem so lonely in what you do, that it takes so much out of you."

There was no other way to acknowledge that very astute observation. "I am, and it does."

Chapter 5

Two days passed and the resurrection order finally came in. We were given the go-ahead to perform the life-swap between Roberto and Filberto. I was a nervous wreck. I wasn't certain I had what it was going to take to make the swap successful. I had no one except myself and Sam to rely on. I kept dreaming of the movie *The Fly,* where the scientist tried transporting an animal and it came through *inside out.* Even for me that's got a high ick-factor.

Burton was no help. The bastard. Sometimes he just annoyed the hell out of me and took the teenager persona entirely too far. He's involved in a skateboard competition today and can't be bothered. *Dude.* I hope he leaves some skin on the sidewalk.

I was on my own. Again. I should be used to it by now, but sometimes, the times I felt most vulnerable, were the times I needed someone, and there simply was no one except Sam, and he could do only so much.

Details, details, details. Sometimes I thought I was going to get sucked into my phone, ear first, as I made arrangements to have Roberto's remains thawed and prepared to travel to the hospital. Then all the hoops I had to jump through at the hospital, I felt like a tiger leaping through flaming hoops and getting my tail singed. Having worked in the hospital system, I should have been used to the flak, but it continues to amaze me that any patient walks out of the hospital alive, because so much documentation has to be done first. Oy!

If I had more time, I'd sick my Korean grandmother, Suzie, on them. She'd get some results pretty damned quick. She's small, but she can be very mean. Maybe that's where I got some of my enhanced traits from. I'm descended from several mixed cultures, of Anglo, Mexican, East Indian, with a little Korean for extra spice. That's makes me perfect for this wonderful melting pot city of Albuquerque. Here, no one sticks out because there are so many different cultures mingled together. It's great. Don't get me started about the unbelievable variety of food here. If I didn't take kickboxing three nights a week, I'd have an ass as big as a sports car.

Finally, things were moving in the right direction, and I called Roberto's parents.

"Now, I know you're going to want to have the whole family there for the ceremony." People reacted better to that word than *ritual*. Too many ghosts and references to the occult regarding the word *ritual,* even though it's a bunch of crap. "It would be better if everyone stayed at your house. Just you and Julio come to the hospital. Normally, it would be different, but we have to obey the hospital rules while we're there."

"Sure, I understand. It will just be us."

I heard the tears in Juanita's voice, the questions that she hadn't asked. This woman's happiness rested on my shoulders, and disappointing her would be painful to both of us. "Don't worry," I said, trying to reassure myself, as well. "Things will turn out the way they're supposed to." I hoped that The Dark entity was going to take a powder tonight. The ritual was going to be difficult enough without adding an unknown threat to the scenario. This was so out of my comfort zone, I didn't really want to think about it.

"My son wasn't supposed to die." She burst into tears, and I felt the burn of them on the back of my tongue, but forced them down. I'd shed my tears long ago.

"I know." I know. Believe me, I know.

After ending the call, I headed out to the parking lot. I had to go home for a while, gather energy, gird my loins and do all the stuff it takes to perform a ritual. The sun was just beginning to head off the edge of the horizon, so I watched for a second or two as the sky turned a deep peach, frosted with magenta hues, as if someone had dragged a spoon through melting sorbet. Lovely. I wish I could breathe those colors inside myself and feel what it's like to be so alive on the inside that the hues are deep enough for others to see on the outside.

When I arrived later, there were fifty people in the hallway outside the ICU waiting room. Could no one follow directions? I was surprised security hadn't tossed out the lot of them.

Sam was already there, looking strong and silent by the doorway of the ICU. Now, his presence was comforting rather than stimulating, which was what I needed. I'm never more vulnerable than when performing rituals, and having him at my back relieves a stress I don't need. My energy and concentration can go where they're needed.

At least the ICU's visiting policy kept most everyone out of the room. I nodded at Sam and pushed open the stainless-steel double doors. Two of my guards came along with me. One pushed a cart covered with a white sheet. Beneath the sheet were Roberto's remains, which I dearly hoped would fuse together using the energy from Filberto's dying body.

There's only so much I can do, and then energy from the source, the nebula, the other side, or whatever you want to call it, takes over. Every resurrection was a little different, so I wasn't exactly sure what was going to happen tonight. With any luck, we'd all come out of this unscathed and the Ramirez family would have their son back. With even greater luck, he'll have no memory of what had happened to him.

Even before the ritual began, I felt the charge of power surging within me. It was like a small pulse growing stronger and stronger, as if something inside me had just awakened and was slowly humming to life. In a way, a piece of me remains dormant until I call upon it.

Filberto's parents were at his bedside sobbing their eyes out. I couldn't help them. No one could. For now, their son was gone. And who knew if I could do anything more than just make that really final?

One of the physicians, Dr. Ernest Cooper, was an older man and one I had worked with in my days as an E.R. nurse. Seems he'd snagged some extra time in the ICU tonight. "Dani, how are doing?" he asked and patted my shoulder. He's been with me on a few cases and knows that since my change, I can't touch his hands the way I used to. He leaned over and gave me a fatherly kiss on the temple.

"I'm doing well." I glanced at the white sheet on the cart and shrugged. He knew what I meant. He'd been around far too long not to.

"I hate to ask, but do you have the paperwork?" I know the man has a job to do, and I'd rather it be him than some physicians I know. Most don't have the temperament for this work.

"Here it is." Sam handed him the paperwork packet, and he removed his glasses to read it. I never understood why some people take their glasses off to read. I have to put glasses on to read. Go figure.

He sighed. I understand the depth of that sigh. It's an unfortunate event that has brought us together. We're caregivers, trained healers, we work our asses off to save people and return them to their lives unscathed. The two primary players in this drama are already dead, but we, the living, are charged with carrying out the task of returning the balance to the way it should be. It's a heavy load to bear, and sometimes my shoulders ache from it.

"It's okay, Doc. We're going to get through this and go have a midnight snack at The Frontier." They have the best home-baked cinnamon rolls smothered in butter ever made. Sign me up for another kickboxing class.

Without a word, his fatigued blue eyes met mine. Time to get moving.

Sam ushered in Roberto's parents, who were understandably freaked out. If this ritual was a success, they'd have their son back and lose a once-trusted cousin in the process. They'd already lost Filberto anyway. If the ritual didn't work, then they stood to lose their son all over again. I could feel the energy pouring off them, and it invaded every corner of the room. Sam slid the glass door shut, closing off distractions from the other parts of the ICU, and closed the curtain.

This was a private party and no one else was invited. A stretcher had been brought into the room, and

I moved the cart carrying Roberto's remains beside it. After removing the white sheet, I looked at what had once been a happy, thriving little boy and was now just a pile of bones. I had to put rubber gloves on to prevent contamination of his remains and prevent me from feeling anything just yet. Totally focused on my task, I moved the remains onto the stretcher.

The pulse that had begun inside me increased in vibration to a hum. This is the time where people usually started to freak out. That's why I hired a few guards to help keep the families focused instead of running away screaming in the dark. I usually perform the rituals in graveyards at midnight, so you can understand why some people run.

Sam unzipped my kit of tools and placed them on the cart. There were several lethal-looking knives, but most were ceremonial in nature. A picture of Roberto, provided by his family, was placed here with several candles. Lighting the candles in a building with a sprinkler system might be a problem, but the ritual can't be done without them. They're white, sacred and specially made by a *curandera*.

I held my hands over Roberto's remains, took in a deep breath, closed my eyes and began to glow.

Power surged down from the universe, swirled within me, and I became the conduit through which the souls passed. Practice makes a perfect resurrection, but the circumstances here were difficult. I had been right—I would need to bleed hard for this one. Even then, I lacked the confidence to say everything would work out the way we wanted it to.

"Peacemakers of the universe, hear me now." My voice rose over the whoosh and noises of the life-support system, the heart monitor and other extraneous sounds in the room. All I could hear was the voice inside me and my heartbeat throbbing in my ears. "Death is bitter, and worse when a child is taken. Tonight, spirits of those beyond, we gather to right the wrong done to this soul. Hear me now and let it be." I took the dagger that had been given to me at the time of my recovery and drew it across my forearm perpendicular to the bones. A line of red appeared and droplets formed. Shaking my arm, I flicked the blood onto Roberto's remains. "Take my blood offering and restore this star to his proper state."

I looked at Dr. Cooper and nodded. It was time to remove the life support from the criminal. Dr. Cooper turned off the ventilator, silenced the heart monitors and removed the breathing tube from Filberto's throat. In minutes the body would die anyway without it, but the ritual hastened the process.

A whirlwind developed inside the room. Paperwork scattered, and the ends of my hair rose up with the energy of it. I touched Filberto's arm with one hand and placed the other over Roberto's bones. Energy filled me, flowed through me, electrified me. Tears filled my eyes as the surge, the power within me, drove everything else from my mind.

Then everything stalled, and I opened my eyes. The energy dropped down through my legs and out my feet. I didn't have enough power to bring Roberto back. Dammit. Filberto was going to die, and Roberto was not going to return.

This was my worst nightmare.

Scrunching my eyes closed, I dug deeper inside myself, searching for the power I needed. But it was no use. I shook my head. Denial wasn't going to help me this time.

"More," I said. "I need more." Panic began to overwhelm the energy surge.

"More what?" Sam called over the torrent of energy in the room. He placed his hand on my shoulder, and I opened my eyes. Then I knew. An image of his *abuela* flashed in my mind.

"Blood."

Juanita rushed forward and thrust her arm toward me. "Bleed me dry if it will bring back my son." Sobbing, she pulled her sleeve back and reached for my blade. She'd slit her wrist and it wouldn't help, then where would we be?

"No. It's not right." I turned to Sam. "It's you. It's your blood I need. Your *abuela* was powerful, and I need the blood of another resurrectionist." I couldn't make the right words come out, but I knew it was right.

"I'm not her." Thank you, Captain Obvious.

"I know, but you have her blood." I hoped he wouldn't make me tackle him.

"Do it." He stepped closer and offered himself to me as no man has ever done. Although he'd volunteered before, part of me was still shocked that he'd stepped up to the plate for me. The color of his eyes was dark, brooding and intense. Part of me that had shielded myself against him eased. This man was going to bleed for me, and I was humbled by the gesture.

I took the ceremonial dagger and sliced it across his right palm, not too deep, but enough to make a pool of blood well quickly in his cupped hand. Next, I sliced the dagger across my palm. This was a man who understood the sacred and understood the need for rituals. The blood of his grandmother, the blood of another resurrectionist, ran in his veins, and that was what was needed to complete the circle here. I needed her power to blend with mine. I sliced our other palms, and we joined hands, mixing our blood, pooling our power together.

The second I touched Sam's hands to mine, the sensations I've always tried to avoid pulsed from him into me. The beat of my heart beat in time with his as our energies melded, becoming one, more powerful agent. I gasped, and Sam's eyes widened as intense heat flowed between us. Snatches of his memories flittered through my mind, and I'm sure he saw parts of my past he never expected to.

An energy I'd never sensed in Sam now surged upward. Unable to look away from his face, I spoke the final words needed to complete Roberto's restoration and return his spirit to his physical body. Calling this spirit to return from the nebula took some doing, apparently. Having been injured so badly in life, the reluctance I felt from him was understandable, but returning him righted the wrong.

"We, together, join our bond and sacrifice our blood for this child. By all that is right, by all that is true, restore the balance." I took a deep breath and closed my eyes, pulling on every ounce, every speck of energy and power in me. I squeezed Sam's hands, and he squeezed mine until they hurt, but it was the final requisite joining our blood cells together to create something bigger, something deeper between us. "Hear me now, and let it be."

A blinding white light glowed in the room, similar to the one that had approached at my dying time. It was a spirit from beyond, and I knew it was Roberto, waiting. His body had reformed and glowed with a beautiful white light. It began to move, and everything returned to its proper place.

Roberto breathed.

At this same time, Filberto's body gurgled out its last breath. His body ejected his spirit as if it were trying to vomit up a large, sticky object. A chasm of darkness opened in the ceiling of the room.

Some of the tension left me, as I knew the ritual was going to be completed the way it should be, and I had not failed. Failure in myself was something I would not accept. Not when so many people depended on me. My death grip on Sam's hands relaxed slightly, but I didn't let go of him. I still needed his strength to hold me upright.

In contrast to Roberto's light, glowing spirit, Filberto's spirit was a dark, nearly black light. Maybe it was an indication of the color of his soul. The innocent are light and clear and wondrous. The evil are nearly black, dense and cloudy.

Drawn toward the chasm of darkness, Filberto's spirit hesitated. I knew it would be punished, and it deserved that for the acts it had committed while in physical form. The spirit would return to the nebula for an undetermined period before being allowed to return to physical form. I don't believe in purgatory, but I do think there are waiting periods for certain souls, allowing them time to think.

Finally, it was gone and the dark chasm swallowed itself, then disappeared with a small pop. I breathed a sigh of relief and looked up at Sam, relieved the ritual had worked.

"Mom?"

Screams and cries filled the room. Juanita and Julio

enveloped Roberto in hugs, kisses, tears and bab-
bled words. My breathing came in quick gasps, and I
squeezed Sam's hands again until his nails dug into my
skin, the pain grounding me in this time, helping me
avoid the pull of the nebula. It's easy to see why souls
want to leave this plane and go there. The pull, the sense
of peace, is overwhelming. The familiarity of the place
is nearly too much to resist, and one that's hard to give
up for the corporeal body and the earth plane.

Tears filled my eyes as I watched the grateful family bundled together. Roberto sat in Juanita's lap and
Julio's arms were around both of them. Tears streamed
from his eyes, and he pressed his cheek to the top of
Roberto's perfect head.

"A pediatrician is waiting to examine Roberto." I
cleared my throat, trying to choke down my emotions.

"Thank you, thank you, thank you." Julio started in
English, then reverted to Spanish. He looked to Sam
for help.

"He says he doesn't have the right words to tell you
how grateful they are." Sam cleared his throat, his
voice deeper than usual, choked with the same emotions swirling inside me. He wasn't as unaffected by
this ritual as he would have liked.

"I know. I know." I released Sam's hands because
his emotions were beginning to leach into my skin.
I hugged Julio, and I thought he was gonna crack my
ribs. "Take care of him and each other. This restores
the balance. So let it be."

"If you ever need anything, I mean *anything,* do not
hesitate to come to us. We will do anything for you,
Miss Wright." He crossed himself and then grabbed
me again into another hug, kissed both my cheeks, then

released me and grabbed Sam. "My family is yours. We'll do anything for you. You have my word." His voice cracked. "Anything."

"Restoring your family is enough." He needed to stop or I was going to cry. That would totally defeat my tough-chick persona.

"What's going on?" Roberto asked and peaked through his mother's arms. "Mama?"

Juanita looked at me, panic in her eyes. She'd apparently not thought of what to tell him. I stepped forward, careful to hide the blood on my hands from Roberto.

"You've been sick for a little while, but are doing much better now." It's the simplest explanation for someone of his age. Kids understand what sick is. His parents could decide what to tell him later, when he was older. I'm older and still don't know if I understand everything. "You're going to go home tonight and sleep in your own bed. You probably won't remember much from your time away from home, but if you do, be sure and tell your parents about it." Counseling is always available to families of the newly resurrected. Families heal, but it takes time. Time they now have together.

"Okay." He closed his eyes and sighed against his mother's chest, his little arms wrapped around her as far as they could go. "I'm tired."

Everyone in the room gave a small laugh, and the tension eased. "Me, too." I was beyond fatigued and was grateful that someone was going to drive me home. I looked at Sam. He looked as bad as I felt. The guards ought to drive him home, too.

Turning away from them, I faced Dr. Cooper. "Thank you." It was all I could manage. After scenes like this, my brain forgets how to operate for a few hours.

"This was a good thing you did, here, Dani." He met my gaze for a few moments, then looked away. "Want to come back to the E.R.?"

I had to laugh. "No way." This is my job now. "This is kind of like E.R. nursing, but with better weapons."

The man chuckled, opened the sliding partition and walked out.

"Why don't you go meet the doctor who'll examine Roberto?" I didn't want Roberto lingering in the area and speculating who or what was under the sheet in the bed next to him. "Dave will take you there."

The group of three followed my guard out of the room, leaving Sam and me alone with a corpse. Did I mention that we have such romantic moments between us? Yeah. This was another one.

"What now?" He was looking down at me, his energy vibration flatter than usual.

"Now we wash our hands." It wasn't the answer he was looking for, but I didn't have one. Instead, I approached the sink and motioned him over. We scrubbed the blood off our hands in silence, then dried them on paper towels from the dispenser.

I dug in my bag of supplies and retrieved a tube of antibiotic ointment, squeezed a bit onto my fingers. "Let me see." I wasn't exactly avoiding his question, but I wasn't tackling it head-on either. We exchanged blood during a ritual. That might do nothing, or it could tie us together forever. There's no way to find out, other than to wait and see what happens.

The wounds on Sam's hands weren't deep, but they were going to hurt a little bit. I rubbed the salve across both cuts, careful not to press too hard, then finished with a one-inch-wide gauze, hooking the thin wrapping around his thumb to hold it in place. Nursing experience does come in handy sometimes. I gave his other hand the same treatment.

"Yours now." The touch of his hands on mine was tender, careful, as if he thought he could hurt me. My hands didn't hurt. They were actually numb. I wasn't sure whether that was good or bad, or made no difference whatsoever. My circuits had probably overloaded and wouldn't reset until after I'd had some sleep. Being unconscious was restorative, as long as you woke up again.

After he was finished, he pressed a kiss to each wrapping. Surprised, I looked up at him. Some of my emotions must have shown in my face, because he gave that sideways smile of his that always lit me up. At that moment, I was too tired to get lit up, but it still warmed me inside. I appreciated the gesture and tried not to read anything into it. Sam was a protector, and he included me in the circle of people he protected. But I couldn't imagine him being so tender with his sisters. "Let's get out of here."

I led the way, and we took the employee elevators to the back door by the loading docks. Facing crowds of family, curious onlookers and possibly the press was not something I could cope with now. Sam would try to shield me as much as he could, but we were both wiped out from this one, and it was better just to deal with it later.

We were on the way to my place when the inevitable happened.

My stomach growled.

"Time for food?"

"'Fraid so." I hate being at the mercy of my stomach, but I have no choice. "Rats."

Chapter 6

Erotic dreams are generally not part of my imagery. At that moment I didn't care what the rule was, I was so diggin' the exception. I knew it was a dream, yet I didn't care. The world could wait for a few minutes while I got off on my nice, safe dream. There's no sex safer than that. Rolling onto my stomach, I dug deeper into the dream.

Strong hands rubbed the small of my back. That's exactly where most of my tension ends up, and the man in my dreams knows it. The sigh that rolled out of me was pure bliss. Pressed against the soft sheets, my nipples tingled, and I was certain an orgasm was on the way. Since I had been celibate for years, it wouldn't take much. Restless, I couldn't stop the moan lodged in my throat. I wanted more of this dream.

The hand of my dream man eased up my sleep shirt, and his skin touched mine. More bliss.

Then the scratch of something unexpected dragged me away from Nirvana. The rough texture of his hand was interrupted by something soft, but different from skin. Strange. Frowning, I opened my eyes and blinked, looked around my bedroom. Everything was the same. Except for the hand.

Whipping around, I turned to the other side of the bed.

Sam lay there, his eyes intense, serious and wanting. Oh, by the gods, how had the man ended up here? I remember passing out over coffee, but that was it.

"What are you doing?" I tried to sound mean, but as turned on as I was, the effort was totally lame.

"I was rubbing your back." He moved his hand upward, then cupped my breast, and it seemed to fit perfectly. My throat tightened and my lungs burned. Breathing would have been helpful. "Now that you've turned over, I'm finding this to be a much better place to touch." Thumb stroking lightly over my nipple that now felt heavy and swollen.

"You can stop anytime you want to." I reached for his wrist. Before I knew what he was planning, he had me on my back, arms pinned to my sides, his hips pressed against mine and his weight holding me to the bed. Fighting him off seemed like a really bad waste of energy, but there was no way I was going to give in to the lust brewing in me.

"I don't want to." Lowering his head, he opened his mouth over my nipple and suckled it through the satin of my shirt.

Men simply have no idea how good that feels or how instantly nipple sucking can turn a woman to mush. If they knew, they'd skip kissing on the mouth and go straight for the nipples. Whoever invented going from first to second to third base was stupid. Women need a long pause at second base before there's going to be any action at home plate.

I am so not a morning person, but this could inspire me to be one. That, and the feel of his cock pressed hot and heavy against me, making me wet in places that hadn't been moist in entirely too long. Morning testosterone levels had something going there. Get a little action in the morning and start your day off right. I'd take a good lay over breakfast any day.

Without a word, Sam released my nipple and moved his oh-so-lovely mouth to the other one. Struggling against him occurred to me again, but I simply couldn't find the resistance. I didn't know why he was there, but at that moment, I didn't care as long as he kept it up. (Well, you know what I mean.)

The alarm clock buzzed, and we both jumped. Sam raised his head and looked into my eyes. I knew this little romp in the park wasn't over, simply delayed.

"We have court in an hour." I hated myself for speaking aloud and breaking the aura of sexual arousal surrounding us. My mouth ached for the first touch of his, but it wasn't gonna happen today. Especially not before I brushed my teeth.

"It won't take an hour." He moved one of my hands to his groin. Through the fabric of his shorts, I felt the hugeness of his erection, and my mouth, as well as other parts, began to water. I remembered sex. I simply hadn't had any since my comeback. That was a long time to go without intimacy, without satisfaction, without the craving of skin to skin, flesh to flesh. The temptation of him was nearly too much, and my resistance wavered a smidge.

"I know it won't take an hour, but parking is a bitch."

Distraction, that's what we needed. "We've got Epstein. She makes Judge Judy look like a puppy."

"This is far from over." He pressed a hard kiss to my lips and left it at that, then pushed off me and sprang up from the bed.

"I know." Like a coward I ran into the bathroom and slammed the door. Only frigid water was going to keep me from unlocking that door and inviting him in. Ditching my nightshirt, and tossing my panties on top of it, I turned on the taps and jumped in.

I screamed. Son of a bitch, it was cold. But it kept my mind off the hot man outside the door. Rushing, I let the water run over my body. The goose bumps were so big, I looked as if I had puckered nipples all over my body. Great. As if two weren't enough already.

A quick rinse, and I was so ready to get out of there. I dried off, wrapped the towel around me and opened the door.

Sam stood there, rumpled and sexy, holding his clothes in front of him. "You screamed?"

"Uh, yeah. Water. Cold." Squeezing past him wasn't going to help my state of turned-on-ed-ness, so I waited for him to move.

"I hope you saved some for me."

That made me feel better. He had it as bad as I did. "I did, but if you scream like a girl, you're on your own."

With a nod, he moved back, obviously realizing the precariousness of touching me again. I stepped past him, and he entered the small bathroom.

I needed clothing and coffee for my armor. What's a woman without her accessories? Just as I reached for the coffee in the freezer, my phone rang, and I silenced the secondary alarm I had set. The Grim Reaper ringtone usually gives me a little laugh. Right then, I didn't care. I was horny and hungry, and that was not a good combination when there was a naked man in my bathroom.

Sometimes the gods were crueler than even they knew.

Somehow we got through that awkward morning-after feeling though we hadn't had a night-before to justify it. Kinda wish we had, but it could ruin our working relationship, and *that* we both needed, no matter how hungry we were for each other. We made it to court on time.

"Your Honor," my lawyer, Elizabeth Watkins, began. I sat behind her, and Sam was beside me. There were quite a few seats taken by people interested in the case, especially the family of the mentally ill killer. He, however, was not present, and I was grateful for that. "We'd like to introduce new legislation that is being presented in other states right now, which will help us toward a decision on the cop-killer case."

"Give it to me." Judge Epstein motioned it forward. The bailiff retrieved it, then passed it along to the old bat for review. She took three seconds to look at maybe the first paragraph, then set it down and folded her hands over it. We were hosed before we even began. She'd already made up her mind before our court appearance.

Dammit. If she's ever killed, I am so not resurrecting her.

"When the legislation is complete you may come back to my courtroom to petition for a reopening of this case, but until then, forget it."

In that moment, I hated her. Or at least her position on the issue.

"Your Honor," Elizabeth began again. I could feel the

frustration pulsing off her. I wanted to reach out to her, to try to stop her, because we were not going to win this one right now, but I kept my hands clenched in my lap.

"Forget it, counselor. There is no precedent in *this* state, and I'm not starting one." She banged the gavel, and that was the end of that. Bitch.

Elizabeth turned to me, anger blazing in her blue eyes. Her hair was blond and done up in a French twist, which only made her eyes more prominent in her thin face. "Dammit. She didn't even listen." She slammed her briefcase on the table and stuffed the paperwork back into it.

"I know. This was a long shot anyway." I sighed and looked at Sam, who looked as irritated as I felt. That made me feel somewhat better, and I choked down my disappointment. Getting hopeful had been just stupid. "This is the process for getting new legislation looked at here. We aren't the first state to have to go through this."

"California and New York have had this in place for three years without one single adverse incident. We're not in the backwoods, and she shouldn't treat us as if we're stupid." I knew Elizabeth hated that. Her husband had always called her stupid. She divorced him, put herself through law school, and when he continued to publicly demean her, sued him for libel. That was a smart woman. She didn't get anything out of him financially, but the humiliation factor was priceless.

"Let's get out of here," Sam said and stood. "I have something to show you. We can go back to the office later." He shook hands with Elizabeth, and we left the courtroom, our quest and our moods thoroughly doused and the morning had only just begun.

As expected, there were cheers and jeers to greet us

on the courthouse steps. Fortunately, I was immune to most of that now. Nothing could compare to what I had been through in my life.

"Come on, I'll drive." I followed him to his truck, his really big four-wheel-drive truck. Don't get any ideas that Sam's got a little winkus or anything. Just this morning, I had had evidence to the contrary. Almost everyone, or every other person, drives a truck in New Mexico. It's like the token vehicle. Never know when you're going to have to haul something, or use the four-wheel drive to get out of a flooded arroyo that two seconds ago was dry. Here, even in the desert, we get floods. A storm in the mountains above Albuquerque can send your feet out from under you thirty minutes later, and you'll be floating down the river before you know it. That's just one good reason to have a truck around here. I stepped up onto the running board three feet off the ground, and hauled myself into the passenger side.

"What are we doing?" I trusted the man with my life and my firearms, but I wasn't certain about my body. This morning's incident had left me a little on edge. I was still aroused to a point the frigid shower hadn't curbed. Buckling up and staying on my side of the truck seemed like a good idea, so I did.

"Going to my grandma's place."

"Elaborate, please. I thought she left the house to one of your sisters."

"She did. The place belongs to Elena, but out of habit, it's always grandma's place." He looked my way, or simply checked for traffic on my side of the truck. With the sunglasses, I couldn't tell. He may have copped a visual feel while he was checking out the traffic. My nipples tightened as if he had.

I straightened and cleared my throat. "Did you find something? If you found journals I'm going to kiss you."

"Actually, Elena found them, so you might have to kiss her." ·

"Ew. Not on your life."

Sam barked out a laugh, and I felt as if we were back to our old snarky relationship. Maybe it really had been a dream. Except that there were two wet towels in my bathroom. Yeah.

"What's in the journals? Did you read any of them?" I hadn't allowed myself to get hopeful, so this was exciting stuff.

"Down, girl. You'll just have to wait."

"Dammit, Sam." I punched him in the arm, even though he was driving. "You're taking all the fun out of having an anxiety attack. Don't make me shoot you so early in the morning."

"Only ten o'clock and you're threatening my life. You're ahead of the game, babe." He pulled onto I-40, the interstate that cuts east to west through Albuquerque. Or west to east, depending on how you look at it. In the western regions of the state lay vast high deserts and Indian pueblos interspersed with an occasional outcropping of the Rocky Mountains. To the east, past the city limits, the interstate winds through the canyons cut from the mountains by ancient glaciers, passes a few small towns, then straightens out in the high desert of eastern New Mexico, the badlands, and on into Texas.

We were headed west, to the old part of town where the earliest of the Spanish settlers created their lives. Not that I'm a historian, but I believe it's important to recognize and appreciate the cultural varieties of wherever you live. Here, it's old neighborhoods and even older superstitions.

After making a series of turns and losing me completely, Sam pulled the truck onto a dirt lane that ran alongside a large, relatively modern house by Albuquerque standards, and parked beside the adobe home. It squatted between a couple of ancient cottonwood trees with gnarled and scarred bark. It looked as if the larger house had been plopped down in what might have been a corral for livestock. A frayed rope, which might have once been a swing, hung from a high branch and drifted, caught by the wind or the push of an unseen hand.

"This is her place. Where I grew up." After cutting the engine, he sat a moment, looking through the windshield at the small house, seemingly lost in memories.

This was perhaps a greater task than I'd understood when I asked for the favor. "You okay?" Although it didn't take a trading of blood to understand he was bugged by being here, something else brewed in me that helped me see something was up.

"Yeah. Just been a long time."

"When was the last time you were here?"

"The day she died."

"Ouch." Guess that should have occurred to me before now. I tend to get a little self-focused at times. Like right now. The journals were right there. Fifteen feet away. I was almost salivating. Please, can't you suck it up a little longer for me? "Sam, if you're not cool with this, we'll figure out another way to get the journals." I was dying inside. There could be something in there about The Dark and how to defeat it. I needed there to be information in there. At some level, I knew there was information there. There could be information about how long I'll live as a resurrectionist, and why I don't get sick anymore. After my recovery the first year, I've never had a cold or been ill in any way. Maybe my immune system has been supercharged too. I just want to know! There could be so much in there that she wanted to pass on, but didn't have the opportunity to.

Or there could be no answers to any of my questions, and I was basing my expectations on a dream.

"Nope." He opened the door. "Elena's at work, so she left them on the table for us."

I followed his lead. If he said he could handle it, it was the truth. Small rocks crunched beneath my boots as we walked across the gravel driveway. The cry of a Mexican jay screeched overhead, the echo of its call ceasing suddenly, as if it had been snuffed out. A foul wind stirred the branches above and a chill fell over me, though it shouldn't have. This wasn't the weather for it. Something lingered here, and I didn't like the feel of it, even though I didn't know what it was. I wasn't precognitive, but something was literally in the wind. Perhaps I was just being paranoid, uncomfortable in this part of town that I wasn't familiar with, but a sensation, an instinct or intuition I hadn't felt before, nagged deep in my gut.

I recalled Burton's warning at that moment. Maybe we really ought to pay attention to that, rather than blow it off as I wanted to. I'd been dead once, so it's hard to fear more than that. At the next stirring of the leaves overhead, I expected to see a monkey that had escaped from the zoo or some sort of giant lizard hiss at us. Weird, but I couldn't shake the sense that we were being followed by some unseen force. I'd have to pay more attention.

"Jumpy?"

I almost jumped at the word. "I'm getting a weird vibe here. I know this is Elena's house, but something is raising the hair on the back of my neck." And twisting that knife between my shoulder blades.

He paused and looked down at me, considering my words, and his hand reached for the back of his neck. "It ain't just you, babe. I thought it was because I hadn't been here in a while." If I had been paying more attention to him, I would have seen the tension in his shoulders, the stiffness of his movements and the subtle alertness, as if he were sending out his own senses. I was glad that he and I were tuned in to the same thing.

"I think there's something here, Sam." I glanced overhead again, convinced we were going to be experiencing a boreal attack at any second. I hate monkeys, and if any had escaped from the zoo I was going to shoot them. The *Wizard of Oz* had scared the crap out of me when I was a kid. And the skeleton monkey scene in *The Mummy Returns* made me want to hide in the closet for a week. Nasty little bastards. Don't get me started on sock monkeys.

I hate monkeys.

The jingle of Sam's keys directed my attention away from my dreadful primate fantasy. We approached the home, which was probably one thousand square feet. And she'd raised four kids in this little place? I suppose they spent a lot of time outside running wild. Knowing Sam, I'm sure that was true.

Sam unlocked the door with an old key on his chain. "Elena never changed the locks. Felt like she was locking grandma out if she came back to visit, you know? The door was always open for us kids, no matter how old we were." He gave a sort of sad, sideways smile, as if he were remembering something bittersweet.

"Does Elena…see spirits?" How does one ask that question without sounding like a kook? Maybe that was the sense I had had outside, but somehow I doubted it. I didn't think his *abuela* was evil, just dead.

"No."

"That's good."

"She hears them."

"Oh." Not good.

"Sometimes she smells them. She swears she's smelled grandma's perfume, especially right after she died." Sam avoided looking at me while he said this, so I couldn't really figure out how he felt about it. Potential primate attacks were still creeping me out.

"Maybe she did come back for a while. I've heard stories of others being visited by the newly dead and fragrance was one of the indicators." Whether he believed it or not wasn't important. I was certain his grandmother did visit until she was ready to go to the nebula. A strong spirit like hers would have had more control than others. She's been around awhile, of that I'm sure. She had all the signs of an old soul. I just wish I had met her.

"She sounds like a wonderful woman."

"She was the best."

"So, you've never told me how you and your sisters came to be raised by her."

"No, I didn't." He gave me one of those sidelong glances I've seen him use on suspects he's annoyed with.

"And I take it you're not telling me now, either, are you?"

"Nope."

Who says I'm not precognitive? One of these days I

was gonna get something out of him. One day I'd figure out how to get Sam-The-Clam to open up.

We stepped into a surprisingly modern kitchen. I'd expected avocado-colored appliances from the 1970s. The house had received an upgrade, and all of the appliances were white. Lacy curtains hung in the kitchen window, framing a wooded view of the land behind the house, bordered by the bridle trail. I could imagine Sam's grandmother on lazy weekend afternoons watching people ride their horses and thinking of times past. As I looked out at the beautiful scene, I could imagine Sam's grandmother sitting here, but I couldn't shake the effects of the evil sludge that tainted my skin. Something was coming for us, but I had no idea what. It seemed that entirely too many bad things had happened in a short time. Could there be some pattern to it? Was it The Dark again? I hoped we didn't have to find out anytime soon.

"Here they are." Sam drew my attention to a cardboard box on the table. It was stuffed with old journals, turned on end, spines out.

There were about a dozen notebooks of varying sizes and types. Some were old black-and-white composition books. Others looked like handmade leather volumes with fragile, yellowed pages in the middle. A fine layer of dust covered their spines.

"I'm almost afraid to touch them." I wiped my hands on my thighs.

"Well, I'm not." He reached in and pulled out about five of them at once.

"Sam!" So much for reverence and respect for our elders and their legacies.

"What?" He gave me such a man look. "They're

books. They aren't going to bite you." He took two, gave me three and sat at the table. "Get started."

"You're such a charmer." I sat opposite him, and opened the first one. Anticipation swirled through me, and I was nearly giddy. I didn't do giddy, but if I had, that's what I would have felt like. Then my giddy bubble burst.

It was written in Spanish. With a sigh, I frowned and ground my teeth together. I was entirely too dramatic sometimes, but now I didn't care.

"What did you expect?" he asked as if he could read my mind. After our blood exchange, maybe he could. "Spanish was her first language, *gringa*. You didn't expect everything to be laid out, did you? You're going to have to work for what you want."

"Dammit. I can get by speaking the language when I've had enough to drink, but not with the written word." My mother is so disappointed in me. She's from Old Mexico, too, and enjoys an affinity for languages that has escaped me, even though I genetically belong to three ethnic groups. My father, who is the sole white guy of the family, attempted to learn Spanish, but always sounded like a backwoods drunk with a bilingual dictionary asking for another round. Perhaps I inherited my affinity for languages from him. *Dónde está la margaritas!*

I tried to glance over the first page, but glancing brought me nothing. Sam was right. I was going to have to work to decipher these writings. Struggling to hide my disappointment, I frowned harder, as if it would help, and focused on the words I knew. Didn't help. Too many holes.

"I'll make coffee. We're going to be at it awhile."

Sam set about the task. I needed the caffeine to sustain my blood. Blood chemistry was a fine balance. I hadn't had nearly enough coffee this morning between rushing from the house and to court. Bastards, messing with my coffee addiction.

Journal entries ran together in front of my eyes after a while. Plodding on, I pulled a small notebook from my blazer pocket and wrote a few things down, but none of it really helped. I was so disappointed.

"There's nothing that jumps out at me." Except every word I couldn't understand.

"Sorry there isn't more here to help you." He waved at the stack of journals spread out over the table. "There are pages and pages of cooking, canning and preserving. I think she wanted to record the old ways, hoping we would use these someday, but we've all gone away from that life." He closed his journal and opened another. "I thought there would be something in this."

"Me, too." More often than not I'm afraid to hope. To hope means risking disappointment and pain. I've had enough of those to last a lifetime. "Would you mind if I took these back to my place for a while?" I could go through them at my own pace and perhaps learn something more, something not obvious to the casual reader. This wasn't going to be an easy discovery. In the end, there might not be anything helpful in here. There might just be her *sopaipilla* recipe.

"Sure. I'll let Elena know." Sam was such a doer and a fixer. Frustration didn't set well with him. I could just imagine him riding hard on his sisters and their dates. Probably made their lives a living hell. That image made me smile, and the knot between my shoulder blades eased a little.

"I'll take good care of them. Promise."

Sam took me back to my truck. I transferred the journals and gave him a quick salute. "Later."

He went on his way, and I returned to the office. I called Roberto's parents to check on them. Juanita didn't answer the phone, so I left a message. I was sure they'd turned their phones off to find a little peace after what they'd been through. I hoped Roberto wouldn't remember a thing, believing that he'd simply been ill. It was easier that way.

Could this incident have been connected to the threat of The Dark? Burton seemed to have no clue how the thing was going to harm me, but maybe it could influence people. The Dark certainly seemed powerful enough to have an effect on people. Could this entity have influenced people to commit atrocities against each other in order to get my attention? I hoped not.

Chapter 7

Distracted by paperwork and irritated I'd forgotten to pick up coffee after Sam dropped me off, I answered my phone without looking at the caller ID. Normally, I liked that nanosecond of brain recognition to get all the cells moving toward the caller.

"Dani." I still can't believe I forgot the damned coffee!

"It's Liz."

Brain function came to a screeching halt. "Did she change her mind?" Oh, this was great news after such a sucky morning.

"What? Oh, hell no. This is something else. I've got a case for you."

"Oh, goody. Another gangbanger who hosed a bunch of his friends?" It would be fitting for today.

"No. A lot more complicated than that." She sighed. Liz rarely sighed like that, so I knew we were in for some serious shit. I was glad I was sitting down. "What is it?"

"A compassion killing."

"Dammit." I ran a hand through my hair, thinking of alopecia again, then rested my forehead on my hand, tried not to anticipate. "Tell me."

"An elderly gentleman killed his wife, who had been suffering from Alzheimer's for years. He shot her, called 911 and waited for the cops. He even took a video of it, so there would be no questions."

"Jeez." Can't imagine the gore.

"He read her medical power of attorney and her living will, said she wouldn't have wanted to be kept alive, and so he took care of what Mother Nature didn't."

"She's going to be awfully pissed off."

"Who, the wife?"

"No, Mother Nature." She's not one to mess with.

"Very funny. Will you take the case?"

We talked about the particulars. He'd plead no contest in court, sentenced to life, no parole and all that. He was ready to return his wife to the living if that was what she wanted, but if she didn't he was content to end his days behind bars.

"I'm going to have to think about this one." The space behind my eyes began to throb. Going blind. Need. Coffee. Now.

"There's going to be a huge amount of press, probably worldwide, on this, whether you take it or not. You're the best one to do it." She paused. "There could be some good PR with the judge, too."

The caffeine headache I had was nothing compared with what this was going to be. "Let's have lunch and talk some more. I'm gonna need a drink for this one."

We met at my favorite lunch spot, kind of halfway between my office and hers. Nice shady trees overhead, great to eat *al fresco*.

"Albuquerque's going to be in the world focus for this one, and so will you. Are you ready for that?" Liz speared a piece of avocado from her salad.

"Hell, no. You're my lawyer. You can do all the PR, nicey-nice stuff, can't you?" Nicey-nice ain't in my bag of tricks, and I preferred to stay behind the scenes, rather than being out front like a cheerleader for the team. I wasn't very good with pom-poms.

"Sure, I can, but people want to know who does the rituals, how does she do them, what happens and all that crap. You know there are more resurrectionists out there who are too afraid to come forward. This could do it. We could turn this into the world's biggest reality show, but we won't." She held up her hand to silence me, knowing as soon as she said those two words I was gonna blow. I hate reality shows. The one I live in is bad enough.

"Well, hell." I swirled my *margarita de oro*. Next time I'd just get straight tequila and a long straw. "There's so much that's appealing about this case, but there's so much that's gonna drive me nuts, too." The PR alone could do it. I understood the need for it. I just didn't like it.

"I know you don't want to be the poster child of resurrectionists, but in this case you're going to have to be. Might even bring some closet resurrectionists out of hiding to help. There aren't enough of you here to present a united front to take on the judicial system." She leaned forward, her blue eyes bright with eagerness and righteous passion for her subject.

She was thin, but well developed, the epitome of a modern, successful woman. Sometimes when I look at her, I just don't know how she could ever have been an abused woman. Then I recall my own previous life and know it sometimes takes an earth-shattering event to bring about change in people.

"I know." I sipped the remainder of the drink and broke off a piece of tortilla chip and stuck it in my mouth, chewing slowly. This restaurant makes the most delicate, homemade chips in the city, and I adore them. Doesn't matter how full I am, there's always room for one more chip.

"Look at it this way—it could bring your business more recognition, more legitimacy and frankly more money. You can't do everything pro bono, like that kid's case. It's great for the PR, but screws your budget all to hell. You have operating expenses, and security doesn't come cheap." Reality check.

"Brings out more protesters, too." They've begun showing up lately. One here and one there, but eventually they'll get organized. There are the pro-lifers scaring people at family planning clinics, and we have the anti-deathers. Both ends of the spectrum are now covered. Yippee.

"Dani," she said with a slight reprimand. "Nothing's perfect."

"You're right. I know." I hate that. I perform the resurrections because they're the right thing to do and they right a wrong, not because I get piles of money for them, or immense recognition. I perform resurrections because the balance of the universe is truly in jeopardy. I owe the other-siders for returning me here instead of letting me die by violence. As I now knew, those kinds of acts only fed The Dark and gave it strength. In the early days of my recovery I had hated them for returning me, but time has soothed that pain to a dull ache, and for the most part I understand my purpose here.

"I had to take the Ramirez case. I couldn't not." Squirming in my seat a little, I fidgeted, not wanting to go into explanations.

"I know. There are cases that call to you, and you have to heed that call. That's what made you a good nurse, a loyal friend, and what's making you a great resurrectionist." She reached out and patted the back of my hand, then picked up her water. She knows some of my quirks and respects them, just as I respect her right to check each and every one of the five locks on every door and two on every window and the security system of her house four times before she can fall asleep at night. Some things we can't change about ourselves. We just accept them, figure out how to deal with them and move on.

"I'll take it. Who's funding it?" She'd mentioned budget, so I figured someone had to be putting up the cash for it.

"He is."

"What? He's funding his own life-swap?" This was a first and a rare surprise. Little surprised me anymore, but this was a shocker.

"He's ready to die. He has no quality of life, no family and few friends. He wants to go, if coming back can heal his wife."

Put like that, it sounded simple. When things sound that simple, they rarely are. "I gotta talk to this guy." Was he a nut job looking to go out in a blaze of glory, or could he truly be what he said he was? People rarely were.

Liz gave such a Cheshire cat smile, that I was beginning to think I'd been set up. "Good. We have a three o'clock appointment at the jail with him and his lawyer."

I had to admire her bravado. I laughed and for the first time all day, felt a little joy seep back into it. "What if I'd said no?"

"You wouldn't. Who else was going to do it?"

"Really." As if.

She grabbed the check and I let her. Next time I'll grab it. I finished what was left of my drink, then added sweetener to the iced tea I had also ordered and guzzled that down too. I'll take caffeine in just about any form today.

Surrendering my weapons, even if it is for a good reason, makes me itchy. I don't want to have to depend on others to defend me should the need arise. Given the situation, that we were meeting with an elderly man in shackles in the middle of the county jail, I should have relaxed, but I didn't. There was more to this case than I knew, and my radar system was whooping it up in my gut. It wasn't just the bean burrito I'd had for lunch, either.

Liz shook hands with the lawyer, but I refrained. The only lawyer I touch is Liz. "Mr. Vernon." I resisted the urge to call him Mr. Vermin, which was what he was. He took the most absurdly horrific cases there were to be had. Drug dealers, rapists and murderers were his norm. Don't know why he was on this case, other than for the publicity.

Introductions to the prisoner, Harold Dover, were made.

"What's your offer?" Vernon asked and placed his forearms on the table, laced his carefully manicured hands together and waited. I never trust men who have professionally manicured hands. I don't know why. Too much the perfectionists, I guess. Usually they're far from perfect, but like to keep up the illusion. My ex-husband was that way. Deliberately deceptive, so my hackles were up already.

"Our offer?" Liz scoffed, leaned back in the chair and extended her legs in front of her and crossed her ankles. All she needed was a cigar, and she'd look like a CEO in a bad movie. "I'm not the D.A. We're here to listen to *your* offer."

"Don't listen to him, ladies. He's an asshole," Mr. Dover said. He was gray of hair, of course, since he was in his eighties. Though soft around the middle, his arms looked strong and so did his hands. He wore silver-rimmed glasses, nothing special. Clear, intelligent, amused blue eyes connected with mine. I smiled. I was gonna like this guy. Too bad I was gonna have to kill him.

"So what's your deal, Mr. Dover?" I asked. I know I'm supposed to be silent and let the lawyers duke it out, but I've never been the silent type. Opening my mouth has gotten me into a lot of trouble, but keeping silent hasn't kept me *out* of trouble either. Go figure.

"Please, call me Harry. My deal is that I'm done here. I've murdered my wife, and she deserves to come back to life."

"No regrets?" Curious.

A fleeting look of what could have been regret passed his face, then was gone. "I just wish I hadn't had to act."

"I see." I leaned forward, unconsciously mimicking the same posture as Vernon. Ick. So I placed my hands under the table on my lap. "You do realize this is no guarantee, right? There are rules about resurrections. You have to go through the psych eval first. We'll also consider your wife's disposition and mental state."

"She'll be better then, right? She'd be...normal again?" Eagerness and hope oozed out of him in a rush, as he clung to one thought. If she were better, it was all worth it.

I had to look away from him for a second and think how to say this. "Unfortunately, no. She would return to her former mental state with the dementia intact. The resurrection won't remove any medical conditions." Sad, but true. There were entirely too many high expectations by the family of the waiting-to-be-resurrected. They got the person returned to them. That was it, but for most families, that was enough.

Harry deflated. The eagerness, the positive energy surrounding him, simply vanished. Damn.

"She wouldn't be better?" Though he asked me the question, he looked at his lawyer, who simply shrugged. The idiot didn't want to admit to his client that I was the expert here. I just love when that happens.

"No, I'm sorry. As you know, she was suffering. I can't in good conscience return her to a suffering state. What I can do is wake her up a little and ask her what she wants. That will satisfy the law and my conscience." I reached out to touch his shackled hands on the table. I wasn't supposed to touch the prisoner, either, but I wanted to read him. Some people, even the elderly, are master deceivers after a lifetime of practice, and the only way I can know for sure is by using my senses.

The second my skin contacted his, I was yanked into the death scene. He had been so calm, so sure in his convictions, I knew he was telling the truth, and I released him. Any more contact would pull me away from my control, which I will never give up. "Harry, I need to do some research, and then we'll go in front of a judge. It's not a simple request you've made." Not a slam dunk by any stretch.

"I thought it would be all right. She didn't want to live that way." He shook his head, and I hardened myself against the emotion in his voice. "We made a pact years ago, since it was just the two of us. We were going to look out for each other." He glanced down and cleared his throat. "I promised to protect her."

I stood, unable to bear any more. "We'll be in touch soon."

Liz followed me out the door, and I recovered my weapons, which made me feel much better. Once you're used to being your own personal security system, being without any part of it is like going out without earrings. Such a naked feeling.

Thinking is easier for me when I'm hitting something. Kickboxing is not just exercise. It's fitness for my mind. Saturday mornings are my favorite classes. Tom Ju, my instructor and owner of the gym I belong to, works my ass off, gives me time to work the body and the brain without asking me about my job. Focus is the key, focus on what's right in front of me.

Right now what's right in front of me is a very muscled instructor who doesn't give any regard for my gender or station in life. He tries to beat the crap out of me, and I give him the same treatment for half an hour. Exercise should always be this much fun. Otherwise, what's the point?

After a hot shower, I was ready to face the day, and it was only 10:00 a.m. What to do on a Saturday? Before I left the gym, I checked my phone. Something was nagging me, and it wasn't the muscle in my ass I pulled on that last series with Tom. My phone is a lifeline to my schedule. If I lose it, I'm hosed. What at first had been a complete annoyance has now become a way of life. I am so lame. A techno-babe.

The sound of skateboard junkies heading my way made me step off the sidewalk. I looked up, expecting to see Burton, but it was just a bunch of nameless kids whooping it up, and they sailed by.

"Waiting for someone?"

Startled, I flashed around and let Burton have it. I knocked him off his feet with a right-handed shoulder punch that hit him in the center of his chest. He landed on his ass in a heap. Fortunately, my phone was in my left hand or I could have crushed it. They are so fragile. "Dammit, Burton! When are you going to stop doing that?"

I reached down and helped him to his feet. For his advanced age, he's really not very smart.

"That hurt." He rubbed a hand to his chest and looked at me, shock in his eyes.

"Oh, shut it. It did not. I can't hurt you."

"If I had been truly human, that would have hurt. How about that?" He grinned.

"Fine, but you should know better than to surprise someone who has just left a martial arts studio." Duh.

"Oh, right."

"What do you want?" I stuck my phone back into my purse. In case I needed to whack him again I'd have two hands free.

"The other-siders have been observing the compassion-killing case and would like you to take it without hesitating. They are old souls who wish to return home."

Who says I can't shoot the messenger? I have a gun, and he deserves it. "I'm not hesitating. I'm considering all the angles, and since when do they get to tell me what to do?" That always makes my claws come out.

"Uh, since they're responsible for returning you." He directed his gaze away for a second, as if he were listening to someone speaking in his mind. "They are old souls who are tired and need to return home to the nebula to rest and join their energies with the others. This fight with The Dark has only begun, and they are needed at home."

"I am grateful, but the decision must be mine to make. As always." Free rein on earthly decisions is mine and always has been.

"Dude, I know. I'm just giving you the information."

I'm so not a dude and despise it when I'm called one. My *chi-chis* may not be very large, but they are there, and they work just fine.

"Although they wish you not to take unnecessary risks, this one is vital to the old souls."

"Thanks. Now go annoy someone else. I have work to do."

"On a Saturday?" He tossed the skateboard down and was off again.

Yeah. There was never truly a day off for me. I had journals to decipher. The thought of asking my mother to assist me in the translation occurred, but that meant I'd actually have to see her and get a lecture I didn't need. A pain shot through my head, reminding of my caffeine quest. I'd think about the mother bit. Sam could always help me. He was easier to deal with than my mother, and better-looking, too.

I went home, got the journals and my Spanish-English dictionary and headed to the coffee shop.

In about an hour I was ready to tear my hair out. This so wasn't working. There was information here, and I knew it. I was going to have to call Sam a lot sooner than I'd anticipated.

"Where are you?" I almost screeched into the cell phone.

"None of your business, and why are you calling me on a Saturday?" He was in as foul of a mood as I was. Not a good time to ask a favor, but I live dangerously.

"Starting over. Hi, Sam, whatcha up to today?" The brightness of my tone was enough to make me want to hang up on myself.

"I'm gonna puke if you keep that up. I liked surly better."

"Fine. I need help." How's that for surly?

"Like I didn't know that."

Bastard. I could almost hear him laughing in my head, but keeping me humble was part of his job. "With the journals, I meant."

"I figured you'd be calling me instead of your mother. Dinner, tonight. You feed me, I translate for you."

"Done." He was so easy. Apparently, so was I.

"Six. Steaks on the grill, your place. Rare."

The line went dead. I pretended as if I had ended the call just to make myself feel better and shoved the phone into my pocket. I checked my watch. Time to get moving and get shopping. The kind of meat I had in mind ideally should be marinated for twenty-four hours, but I didn't have that kind of time now, so I was gonna have to pound the hell out of it with a hammer. That ought to make me feel better.

* * *

Sam arrived looking as if he'd stepped right from the shower, put jeans and a T-shirt on, ran his hands through his hair and got into his truck. Yummy. I love a man with good grooming habits.

"Where's the food?" He walked past me into the kitchen. He'd been to my place dozens of times, so it wasn't as if he didn't know where to go.

"Yeah, come on in, why don't you?" I slammed the door with a flair, just because I could, and followed him. I needed a beer, too, so I got out a couple of cold beers, quartered a lime, tossed a squirt into each bottle, then handed him one.

"Moving."

"What?" I blinked. It's rare that I'm caught off guard, but I had no idea what he was talking about.

"When you called, you asked what I was doing. I was moving my sister's house full of stuff. She bought a new house, and of course, being the only male of the family with a pickup, I get to help." He shook his head and muttered something ugly in Spanish. That I understood.

"Lucky you. Now you get to kick back, drink a beer, have a steak and help me."

I turned away to check the meat, and Sam slapped me on the ass. "Get me some food, woman. I'm hungry."

Yet another shocker for today. "Did you just…" Incredulous, I looked at him and gave him the stare I usually reserved for souls that were about to head to their graves permanently.

Sam laughed and sipped his beer as the look in his eyes changed to something I couldn't quite read, but might have been a flash of desire. I shook my head and headed into the kitchen. I gotta work on that stare.

His immunity to it was growing or our relationship was changing, big-time. Not that it would be bad, but it would certainly be different.

Later, after a few more beers, a belly full of steaks with grilled green chilies on top, and *calabacitas,* a side dish of corn and squash with green chili and cheese, we finally dug out the journals. I hoped I wasn't placing too much faith in something I wasn't certain would be of help, but for a woman to have preserved journals like this, something of great importance had to be contained in them.

"I've placed them in chronological order, I think, but double-check." I gave him the first one, pulled a chair beside him and got out my notebook and pen. There was no way I was going to remember all of this stuff, so I had to take notes.

"Let's go outside. It's a nice night." He stood, took the journal and the beer with him.

"I'll put on coffee first." Always gotta have that damned coffee. Someday I'll wean myself off, but at that moment I was ready to drink it straight from the pot with a curly straw.

My house was down by the river. It was originally a caretaker's house in the back of a horse property, but the land had been divided some time ago, and I got the little cottage-size house. I loved it. Massive trees surround the property. There's no garage, but there was enough sun protection from the trees, and winters here are mild enough most of the time so I don't really need one. Evenings outside in the small yard are what make this place so worthwhile. The original owner had laid a flagstone patio big enough to have a party on, so I put a wicker set of furniture out there and called it good.

Of course, Sam headed straight for the hammock strapped up between a couple of trees, and flaked out. I had strung little white holiday lights around the perimeter of the yard, so it was festive as well as functional. I think I read that in a decorating magazine in a hardware store somewhere. Move over Martha.

Right now, all I could do was wait until Sam found something I could use.

Okay, so I admit it. I'm not a very patient person. I took the second journal outside with me to slog through, gave Sam a giant mug of coffee that matched mine, sat at the table and tried to work on my translation.

After being watched for several minutes, I couldn't take it anymore and glared at Sam. Hmm. He was engrossed in the reading and didn't look up from where he swayed in the hammock.

Weird.

But I couldn't settle down. Something kept bugging me, as if some perv was watching me undress. I looked over at Sam, the only possible perv in the area. His jeans remained zipped, both hands on the journal.

"You getting it, too?" he asked without looking up.

"Yeah." Sometimes we were so tuned in, it was scary. I was beginning to think the blood exchange had made us more in tune to each other. I positioned myself sideways in my chair in case I had to move quickly. My gun was in a shoulder holster today, so it was handy. Sam was armed, but didn't have his usual open display of firepower.

He closed the journal and stood. "Got any more coffee?" Though his eyes were keen and assessing, his voice remained casual.

"Sure. Come on in."

He pretended to stretch, and I stood too, waiting, watching, anticipating. My nerves were taut, straining and about to snap. Dusk was hovering, just minutes away. We'd be dead if we were attacked outside in the dark, and Sam without enough weaponry.

Sam took one step toward me and gave a nod to the trees overhead that began to shake violently, as if something had been poured out of the sky onto them. Mummy monkeys, I knew it! My worst fear brought to reality in my own backyard.

The sound, like the advent of a hard rain coming on, approached. The sky blackened, and the wind roared.

"Dani, go!" Sam raced hard toward me and nearly flattened me into the back door. Splatters of black rain hit, sizzling as it pounded the patio. This storm hadn't been there moments ago. I got the door open, and we burst into the house and slammed the door shut behind us. It was one of those heavy metal security doors, but had a window made of double-paned bulletproof glass. Nothing was getting through it. Not even the skeletal monkeys pressing their ugly little faces to the window. I was gonna have nightmares for sure.

"Get out of my yard!" I hit the glass with the heel of one hand, but they just turned away and headed for the trees. The things were really monkeys, devoid of flesh, and they were ripping my beautiful, lush yard to shreds. How could my greatest fear from childhood have manifested so hideously? The only answer was The Dark had invaded my fears and fed on them. Somehow, The Dark had been inside the place where I keep my fears locked away, and I hadn't even known it.

"What the hell is going on?" Sam caught his breath beside me and looked out the window. All we could do was watch as a herd of evil, skeletonized monkeys tore branches from the trees, ripped the shrubbery from the ground and bent my patio set into shapes it wasn't meant to be bent into.

"I have no idea. I had the same feeling when we were at your grandmother's place. Like we were being watched, and all I could think of was the monkeys from a horror movie." I looked up at him. Concern and confusion filled his dark eyes as he looked into my face. He looked at me as if I held the answers, but I didn't. We were lost in this together. We needed each other more than ever. I trusted Sam, but this was a whole new level we were heading into.

"There's been something going on since the Ramirez resurrection, hasn't there? Like someone's deliberately watching us and throwing things in our path." The tension in his shoulders changed, and his energy focused totally on me now.

"I feel it, too." I felt more than the danger outside the house now. There was danger circling between us, closing the gap.

His eyes searched mine, nearly pulled me into some deep place where you dance naked and pull the petals off daisies. I couldn't go there ever again. But I would consider a place where we were both naked and entwined in certain positions to achieve mutual sexual satisfaction that we had not yet explored. *That* I could get into. I let my gaze drop to his mouth and watched as he talked.

"Don't look at me like that." His eyes darkened, and his voice thickened.

"Like what?"

"Like you want me to touch you."

The heat of his breath fanned my face, and I didn't

need any help in the heat department. Tension flared between us, grew taut, and I swallowed, wanting to stay in the moment.

"Sam, I…" I watched his mouth as I salivated in anticipation.

He leaned closer. "Tell me what you want."

Chapter 8

The man had a mouth that I'd like to have wander all over me. But not now. We had Mummy monkeys to contend with.

"I say we shoot them all." I was in the mood for it, too. Sexual frustration of this magnitude didn't sit well and needed some sort of outlet.

"Like that's gonna work against supernatural spirits from the underworld, or wherever the hell they're from." Sam snorted and took his shirt off over his head in one swift move. Obviously it didn't set well with him either.

"What are you doing?" My mouth had gone dry at the sight of his smooth, tawny chest. Although I had seen many a chest as a nurse, this one had me intrigued.

He held up the shirt. The back was filled with holes. If, indeed, something can be filled with empty spaces.

"It wasn't like this when I got here, babe. That rain burned. Didn't you feel it?" He turned me around to inspect my clothing.

"I felt something, but I didn't know what it was."

Now, I was pretty certain it was his assessment of me that burned, not the friggin' rain.

"You have a few spots on your shirt and the back of your jeans, but I think I got the worst of it." He balled his shirt up and tossed it into the trash.

"The hell with the shirt, how's your skin? Turn around." His skin was covered with tiny wounds, and I cringed. "Oh, Sam! You need to shower and get that stuff off you." If raindrops burned holes in his shirt, they could burn holes in his skin. "I don't know what to put on them, though. Antibiotic ointment?"

"Baking soda and water." He turned around.

"How do you know?" I was the nurse here.

"It feels kind of like a bee sting, right? I read in the journal about an episode where she treated an ailment like this. She didn't mention acid rain when being attacked by Mummy monkeys, though. I extrapolated." He shrugged. "Can't hurt to try, right?"

"Smart-ass. Get in the shower, and I'll mix up some goop."

Burton and the other-siders had never mentioned anything like this. The frustration level I thought I had before was nothing compared with this.

I got the baking soda in the ugly box that couldn't decide if it wanted to be yellow or orange, and poured a bunch in a small bowl, then added some water and mixed. I added more water, then got it too soupy, so I had to add more baking soda to even it out. Guess it wouldn't hurt. Caveman chemistry at its finest.

I heard Sam leave the bathroom as I stirred the goop at the sink. "I used your scrubber thingie. Hope it was okay."

"Sure." I gave the stuff one last stir and turned toward Sam. "Christ!" I nearly got a case of whiplash trying to stop quickly.

"Nope. Just me," he said with a very male grin.

"You're standing there naked and aren't expecting me to say anything?" Tremors that had managed to remain hidden now found their way to my brain and turned it stupid. My salivary glands screamed in anticipation of taking a big bite out of him.

"What? I'm covered." He reached for the precarious knot of the towel around his hips. "But if it bothers you…"

"Nice try." With a smirk, I regained some of the sass and confidence that had momentarily evaporated. "Turn around and show me your ass."

"Gladly." Sam flicked the knot and dropped the towel.

"Sam!" I screeched and clutched the cereal bowl to my chest, spilling some of the goop down my front. "What are you doing?" The tone of my voice was unnaturally high, and I sounded like a teenaged girl who had gotten her first good look at a naked man. I wasn't far from it at the moment. I'd never seen Sam naked and wasn't sure I ought to be seeing him in such a state now. It could make our professional relationship a bit precarious. Interesting, but precarious.

"Oh, come on. You're a nurse. You've seen plenty of skin." He turned his back to me, and I swallowed.

"What? Skin?" Was I supposed to be doing something? I looked at my hands and saw that I held a cereal bowl. What was that white stuff on me? Oh, yeah. Sam's injuries. I looked up at what had once been flawless skin that had turned angry red, but at least wasn't as bad as his shirt. "The shower helped. I was afraid it was going to eat holes in you, but it's just red now." I wanted an excuse to touch him. I needed an excuse to touch him. Now.

Regaining control of my libido and my tongue that hung out of my mouth, I dipped my fingers into the paste and applied some to the speckles on his shoulders. His very defined, broad shoulders that I wanted to surround me. The muscles beneath my hands bunched, but other than that, he held still like a good little patient.

Continuing on to the marks on the center of his back, I applied the paste again, then down farther on his hips, then his nicely sculpted buttocks. Ooh la la. Mama needs a new pair of shoes!

The skin and muscles were firm and warm beneath my fingers. I licked my lips and swallowed. I hadn't had my hands on any man's buttocks in such a long time. I hesitated, trying to control the lust that seized me. I was a professional. I was a trained nurse.

I was so drooling over his ass.

"Dani?" He leaned both hands on the table and parted his feet. He looked as if I were about to frisk him. Sweat formed on my upper lip, and I licked some of it away. An image of him naked, hands cuffed overhead to the wooden slats of my headboard, hit me with an almost painfully vivid picture. A shudder passed through me, and I remembered to breathe. I wanted to reach out to him.

"Are you in pain?" I frowned, hating to hear the answer.

"Yes." The word hissed from between clenched teeth.

I grabbed another beer and gave it to him. "This might help. I have tequila or whiskey if you want." Frankly, the thought of a shot of tequila was extremely appealing right now. Anything to put out the fire smoldering inside me. If I didn't get it under control, Sam was going to be experiencing a sexual assault at any moment. As he chugged the beer, I reached for the tequila. I already had the limes cut, so I licked my hand between my thumb and first finger, and sprinkled it with salt.

My hands shook so badly I got salt everywhere. I drank straight from the bottle. Half the liquid drizzled down my neck and into my shirt. I was so not a shot drinker. Coming up for air, I bit into a lime and gasped as the flames shot higher. Note to self: never toss alcohol onto a smoldering fire, of *any* kind. "Oh, gods, that was good." I blew out a long breath and gasped for another one.

Sensing Sam's presence beside me, I looked up. He was standing there, all male, and naked, and gloriously aroused.

"Did that help?"

"It's not that kind of pain." He grabbed me by the shoulders and held me facing him. He leaned over and pressed his tongue to the skin over my breasts bared by the V-neck shirt I wore. He licked upward, cleaning up the tequila spill I made. I was paralyzed. I couldn't have moved if I had wanted to, and I certainly didn't want to anymore. I wanted Sam with everything I had in me, and he was in obvious agreement. The feel of his tongue on my skin was exquisite and made me want more of it. He roamed his way over my jawline to my mouth. My heart raced, staggered in my chest. My breathing was uneven in anticipation of more, more, more. I wanted his mouth. I wanted to taste him. But he didn't kiss me.

He licked the remaining salt from my hand, raised the tequila bottle and guzzled. I watched the muscles in his throat work as he swallowed, spilling much less of it than I had. With a wet slurp, he released the bottle from his lips and returned it to the counter. Apparently, he didn't need the lime.

He cupped my face in his hands and licked the excess salt from my lips and then swallowed, as if he were taking a part of me down inside him. That was the most erotic thing I've ever seen, and I was lost to him. Tipping his head back, he growled, deep in his throat, as if I were the most wonderful thing he'd ever tasted. When he looked at me again, I knew we were in serious trouble. Neither of us was turning away. Neither of us wanted to move. I don't think either of us could have.

Maybe it was the blood we'd shared or the emotions of our shared cases, but I sensed things in Sam I hadn't before this moment. Maybe he was just more open to me now standing naked in my kitchen. I didn't know, but I wasn't going to destroy whatever was going on by moving, or speaking. I craved him with every resurrected cell in my body and knew he felt the same. Unmasked desire sparked off him and torched something deep inside me, some female part that needed this moment. With him. Only him. I needed Sam's hands on me, his skin against mine. I needed to be a woman again for just a while, and I knew Sam could take me there. I trusted him. My defenses broke.

"We've been circling this moment for a long time," he said.

"I know. I know." It was a truth I couldn't deny.

My hands didn't know what to do with themselves as we stared at each other, so they drifted down and landed on his hips. The full contact with his skin was something I'd forgotten about trying to avoid. The instant I touched him, rockets of desire filled me, and my knees buckled from the power of it. I actually cried out from the intensity of feeling, emotion and unbridled desire scorching the air between us. If lightning had erupted inside the house, I wouldn't have been surprised. The vibrations were from somewhere deep inside him I hadn't known existed. He'd blocked them from me, and I hadn't even known it. I felt like an idiot standing there with my mouth hanging open, but I'd had no idea the depth of his wanting of me. And it was intensely arousing.

It reflected mine for him, that I had somehow, insanely, managed to suppress until this moment. There was much of myself that I didn't want to reveal to him. I had scars inside and out. I didn't know if I would ever be prepared for a man to see me naked again. The visible scars were evidence of my fight to the death and of my struggle for survival. The hidden ones, no one would ever see. Would seeing my physical imperfections douse what was going on between us? There was only one way to find out, and I had to trust Sam as I hadn't ever trusted any man.

"Don't fight it." He drew me closer. "I don't want to fight it anymore, either." Looking down at his cock, hard and straining toward me, I could find no deceit in his words, or his erection.

What could I have said? Let me rephrase that. What could I have said that wouldn't have been an outrageous lie? Denying what was going on between us had been amusing for a while, but now, there was no more denial I could rely on. He'd stripped it away as swiftly as he'd stripped away the towel, and he was as vulnerable as a man could get.

I looked at his mouth and finally, thankfully, he kissed me. He still had my face cupped in his large, gentle hands, and he pulled me to him by my face. Oh, the man knew how to use his mouth. Surprisingly soft, his lips covered mine, and he eased his tongue forward. Since my mouth had already been hanging open, this was an easy task. Responding to the silky softness flared my need from desire to outright lust.

A moan began deep inside me and surged upward. He touched me as if I were a precious thing, and at that moment, I felt it. For once in my life a man touched my soul. He opened his mouth wider and devoured me. After that, things got really hot, really fast.

My hands, the hands that had avoided touching Sam's skin for so long, now roamed over every inch of him that I could reach. Pulses of energy surged from him into me through my hands. Images of me, as he saw me, flooded my mind. He'd pictured me naked more than once, and his desire for me was overwhelming. He tucked me into his shoulder and leaned me back over his left arm. I was in a foggy haze of desire, and I knew nothing except for the feel of him against me and filling my mind. His right hand left my face and drifted down to my ass. His splayed fingers dug in and pressed the front of my crotch against his raging erection. I was so lost to him. My feminine body that had been dormant for years now pulsed to life. Surges of desire filled me. I was wet and ready for him.

Then, I really don't know what happened next, but it was good. Oh, it was so good. I was lost in him, simply lost to his touch, his taste and the smell of him. There came a point where there was no separation between us, and I'm not talking about the physical. It was almost as if we had fused our spirits together to form one being.

He broke away from my mouth and kissed a hot trail down the front of me. Tequila still dampened my front, and my nipples were cold and wet and so hard I thought they were going to tear a hole in my bra. He raised the hem of my shirt and used his thumb to drag the lacy bra down, revealing all of my B-cup glory.

"You are so beautiful." He watched his thumb turn my nipples to rigid points.

What can I say? When a man calls you beautiful, take him at his word, especially if he's standing naked in your kitchen. He leaned over and took one nipple into his mouth. If this type of torture were used on women, the secrets of the world would be revealed in short order. I adored this man and what he was doing to my body. The rest of the world could take a number.

A bowl of oatmeal was more stable than my legs at that moment. While his mouth was busy, so were his hands—working at the front of my jeans. I wanted this man inside me. Or at least I wanted one very specific part of him inside me.

Then I realized if he got the jeans off me, he would see the scars I'd worked so hard to hide. They were hideous, and I did everything I could to hide them. His breathing came in harsh gasps as I clasped his wrists. Unable to put words to what I was feeling, I turned my face to his, and he rubbed his forehead against mine. Tenderness oozed out of him.

"I know, Dani, I know." He pressed his mouth against mine. "I'll keep your secrets."

I released his wrists and opened the damned jeans myself! It was such a relief to shove that zipper down.

With a quick movement, he slid his hands inside the back of my jeans and cupped my bare bottom. In seconds, my jeans and panties were in a pile on the floor.

Sam picked me up, then parked me on the counter. I had to clutch his shoulders for balance, and the skin connection deepened the desire between us. Each finger that made contact with his skin pulsed with the heat of his emotions and shot into me, driving his energy directly into my body. He scooted me to the edge of the counter that was surprisingly level with his hips. I hadn't noticed that before. He stood between my knees, and my legs seemed to remember what to do. They wrapped around his lean hips and tugged him closer. Oh, yes. That was right. "I want you inside me, Sam. I need you, now."

Groaning, he held me against him and kissed me as if he couldn't get enough. His arms strained with the effort to hold me still, his cock inching forward into my soft and highly sensitized flesh. I was dripping with moisture, and my feminine sheath ached for him to fill it.

"I don't want to hurt you." Precarious restraint directed his movements as he dug his trembling fingers into my hips. He knew that it had been a long time since I'd been with a man.

"You won't," I whispered against his lips and kissed him, teasing my tongue forward into his mouth, and luring him toward me.

Sam sheathed himself deep inside me. My head snapped back at this intrusion, and I gasped at the welcome fullness of him. Digging my nails into his shoulders, I had to hold on or I was going to explode.

Sam stilled, except for his breathing. "You're like a

fist around me, so tight, so firm." He stroked my hair back from my face. "You're exquisite."

A rage of desire swept through me, and deliberately I placed my hands around his shoulders, pulling him against me. Tension, the really good kind, pulsed through me. The fullness of him satisfied something that had been lacking and I hadn't even known it. I hadn't had a lover in years. Now I don't remember why I resisted. Sam stretched my taut flesh to the max, and he began to move.

With each surge of his flesh deeper inside me, we became more deeply entwined in each other. There was a connection between us that somehow fused us. We were joined physically, and something emotional had taken over.

I dug my fingers into his shoulders, relishing the feel of his bunching muscles beneath my hands. "More." It was all I could manage. I needed more of him, harder, faster, deeper. He moved us against the door, and used his chest to support me. With his fingers clutching my hips, he let go of any restraint. Oh, by the gods, I needed this. Each movement hit just the right place. My flesh was on fire. Shots of electricity raced from my center, and I was nearing the rocket stage of the evening's program.

Sam's harsh breathing in my ear told me he was close, but at that second I didn't care. The next time he surged into me, I shattered. I dug my nails into his shoulders and screamed. I'm not normally a screamer, but at the moment, there wasn't a damned thing I could do to stop it. Not that I cared, either. Pulses of pleasure erupted. Jets of pleasure surged, and my sheath flexed, clamping down on Sam's cock. The longer he kept up the pace, the more drawn out my orgasm. Sam's cries joined mine, and together we found what we both needed.

Finally, the spasms of my body came to an end. We slid down to puddle together on the floor, gasping for air. At that moment I was really glad I didn't have a wooden door.

Sam lay back on the tile floor and dragged me with him. I flopped over his chest and listened to his ragged breathing and the erratic tempo of his heart. The pounding of my heart finally slowed, and I was no longer in danger of having a heart attack from excessive sexual stimuli. Then I realized he was lying on his injuries, and I tried to get up, but he prevented me from moving away. "How's your back?"

"Perfect. Yours?"

"Oh, I'm good." I smiled against his skin and closed my eyes. "Do you know what we just did?" I was incredulous. We'd just breached every professional barrier in existence.

"Yeah." I felt the rumble of a laugh begin in his chest. "I think we're going to do it again, too."

We spent the remainder of the night in my bed, naked and getting to know each other in a way we never had before. I crawled over every inch of Sam's body, and he did the same to me. The first time we made love in the bed, he turned on the lamp, and I wished he hadn't. As he kissed my breasts and worked his way down my body, I tensed, waiting for him to see the scars on my abdomen and run screaming from the room.

Instead, he kissed each rib beneath my breast on the left side and eased over my abdomen. With a tenderness I hadn't known know he was capable of, he kissed each scar, each stab wound, each imperfection that would never go away and was forever a part of what made me who I am. Tears formed in my eyes as I watched the way he moved over me, the way he touched me with his gentle hands. This man worshipped my body as it had never been before.

When I said he crawled over every inch of my body, I wasn't kidding. He moved down and opened his mouth over my flesh, and I nearly imploded from the hot feel of his tongue on me. Nothing compared with the feel of his mouth or the silken strokes of his tongue. The stubble of his light beard was an extra tactile bonus.

Sam was an incredible lover and took me further sexually than I'd ever been. I never knew such intimacy was possible. He filled me up and gave a part of himself to me that he can never have back. It's mine, and I'll treasure it no matter what happens between us. Some part of my heart that had been forever wounded healed a little beneath the care in his hands. I didn't want to love anyone, but with the connection between us, I was beginning to realize I might not have a choice. Something was changing for us both.

We woke up Sunday morning in a tangle of sheets and limbs. I think I was mostly at the foot of the bed, my head on his lap. I was mostly lying on my stomach, and I was exhausted. Happily exhausted and used up, I sighed. I opened my eyes, groaned and contemplated calling 911 for emergency assistance to get to the bathroom.

"You okay down there?" He hadn't moved, so I figured he was in no better shape than I was.

"Yeah." I cleared my throat because my voice sounded as if something had crawled inside and died.

"Yeah. I'm good. Need coffee and steak." I turned my head and came face-to-face with an erection. "Uh, what's that for? I thought we solved the problem of inflation last night." Or was it this morning? "Do you need an ice pack for that?" I thought of the stupid commercials on TV for male enhancement pills. Sam certainly didn't need them. "You know, men sustaining an erection for more than four hours should seek medical attention." At least that's what the commercials said.

"I did. You're a nurse, and you handled it nicely."

I shifted my focus to his face. "I did, didn't I?" For some reason, I was really pleased with myself.

Then the phone rang and shattered the moment. I could actually reach the phone without having to move much, so I grabbed it out of habit. "Hello?" I listened for a nanosecond before squeezing my eyes shut. It was my *mother* calling entirely too early for a Sunday. I returned my head to Sam's lap and refocused on that enticing erection waving like a flag in front of my eyes.

"Things are cool here, Mom." Sam chuckled, but his eyes had turned dark and wanting when I touched him.

"Is someone there?"

Was someone here? "Yeah. I'm having a breakfast meeting with Sam."

His grin widened, but he remained silent. I adjusted my position so I could hold the phone with one hand and clasp his cock with the other. His grin faded and so did mine. "Have a good time, Mom. I gotta go or we're going to be late."

I clicked the phone off and tossed it onto the floor.

"Late for what?" he asked and his eyes drooped to half-mast as he reached for me. "Did I miss something?"

"Yeah. This." I crouched on my knees and opened my mouth over him. He was soft and silky in my mouth, and I swirled the tangy taste of him around with my tongue. Gripping his shaft firmly in my hand, I went down on him and didn't let up until he begged me, in a strange mixture of breathless English and Spanish, to stop. I love it when a man begs, especially when I have him where I want him. Moving forward, I straddled his legs and rose up on my knees. He reached for my hips and drew me closer. With my hips tilted forward, I sheathed him deep. We both cried out at the perfection of the movement. The ease with which he slid home assured me this joining between us was right. I was sore, but it was a good kind of sore, and my hips began to move back and forth, drawing out the pleasure for us both. I leaned back on my hands and clasped his knees. One of his hands moved between my legs, and his thumb stroked my clit in time with my hip movements. I was sweating. I was breathing hard as the tingles of pleasure quickly built in my pelvis. Each touch of his thumb on my flesh took me closer. Each stroke of his cock sealed my fate.

Releasing any semblance of control, I gave my body to Sam and the sensations raging between us. My hips moved faster as I strained toward release just seconds away. With his flesh filling me and rubbing against all of the right places, I crashed. Pulses of pleasure overtook me and spasms rocked my body. I clamped down again and again, milking everything I could from him. His fingers dug into my hips and pulled me down hard onto his shaft. I felt the response of him deep inside me.

Unable to remain upright, I drooped forward, totally wasted, onto Sam. He wrapped those amazing arms around me and squeezed me tight. I couldn't talk and neither could he. We were simply saturated in each other. Then we slept again, content.

Chapter 9

We spent what was left of the day, after a massive breakfast, reading the journals and trying to discover any hidden secrets in them, but there was nothing obvious. I have one of those industrial-size coffee carafes that's usually reserved for funerals or catered events, and I filled it with strong black coffee. We were going to need it for the rest of the day, and I just didn't feel like driving to the coffee shop this morning. Go figure. Didn't know if I was even capable of it today. There were always a few pounds of superior coffee beans in my freezer, so I used some of them now.

Since Sam's shirt was in the trash, I gave him an old shirt that looked better on him than me. It was from a martial arts competition and everyone had received the same outrageously large size. He filled it out better than me, but it was still too big for him. When we went outside to inspect the damage from last night, I was furious. My beautiful yard and private sanctuary had been destroyed by those foul creatures. "Fucking

Mummy monkeys." I wanted to shoot something, but the little bastards were nowhere in sight. If they came back tonight, I was going to dynamite them if I had to.

Sam looked down at me, a bemused expression on his face. "Where in the world did you learn to swear like that?"

"ICU nursing." I shrugged. "It was a matter of self-preservation at the time, and I never lost the habit."

"You could embarrass some of the career military men I served with." He shook his head in amazement.

"Ah, you're just jealous I cuss better than you." I elbowed him playfully in the ribs.

"I am. I am." He returned to the hammock and opened a journal.

After a few minutes, the words began to make a little sense with the help of my high school translation book and an online application from www.babelfish.com. The words made sense, but putting them together into a context that applied to our situation took more finesse than I could muster.

"Hey, here's something." Sam motioned me over.

"What, what, what?" I felt like a kid who had just been given a birthday surprise.

"It's vague, but it does reference a dark being. I wouldn't call it an entity, but that's the feel I get. I think this thing has been hanging around for a long time."

Puzzled, I tried to read over Sam's shoulder, but it still looked like a salsa recipe to me. "Anything else?"

"I'll just read it. 'By the truth, by the right, by the power of the chosen will the being be driven back.'" Sam looked up at me. "It doesn't say defeated, just driven back or away."

"Hmm. Makes me wonder."

"What?"

"The chosen. Is that just me, or is it referring to other resurrectionists?"

"Doesn't say." Sam looked down. "I'll keep reading."

I returned to my spot at the table and sipped my coffee, hoping that the caffeine would inspire me to suddenly understand Spanish.

It didn't.

The day was glorious. We spent our time as lovers, discovering each other. A touch here, a glance now and then, and a quick brush of the lips. We were living in a balloon that was rapidly losing its air. Time was running out for us, and we both knew it.

"Tomorrow is coming too quickly." Sam looked down at me as he leaned against the counter. We'd come in for more coffee and were reluctant to leave the cocoon of the kitchen. "We have to go back in the morning." He tucked my hair behind my ears, then slid his hand behind my neck, inching me toward him. I tipped my face up.

"I know." I didn't like it, but he was right. "I know."

"You have to know that our personal relationship has changed, but our professional one has to remain the same or they'll pull me off liaison duty, and I don't want that." He was intense. "I don't trust anyone else to protect you."

"What about Romero? He's pretty good with a gun."

"What?" Intense, every muscle in him clenched. Testosterone oozed from his pores.

"Or how about Westlake?" He wore thick glasses and was confined to desk duty.

"He couldn't shoot his way out of the men's room." I was teasing him, but he wasn't buying it. He clutched me tighter. "The only person I trust to protect you is me. Don't forget that, Dani. Don't ever forget that."

I tilted my head to the side and held his gaze. "Why is that?"

"No one but me." He dropped his gaze to my mouth, and I had the feeling he wasn't just talking about protection. Taking a chance, I placed my hands on his face, wanting to connect with this warrior. I wanted to know what went on inside him, what made him so fierce.

"Tell me why. Why only you?"

Terror filled him. Each breath, each pulse drove the panic further. I felt it throb into my hands, and I almost pulled away. The feelings were so intense. Looking into his eyes, the memory was right there, nearly on the surface, but he pushed it away again before I could pull it out. Something had happened to him. He'd never forgotten it and never forgave himself for the aftermath of it. He was young and people had died. I wished I could help, but the image snapped away, and I dropped my hands from his face.

"Listen to me, Dani. I'm the only one who can protect you. We're connected like never before." He couldn't put it into words any better than I could, but I knew what he meant.

"I know." I felt as though I kept saying that over and over, and I was. I smiled and felt a little sad inside.

Evening had begun to gather on the edges of the horizon and pushed in on us. Pressing a tender kiss to my mouth, he parted my lips with the tip of his tongue. He explored my mouth gently and didn't take the heat any further. Then he lifted his head.

"I'd like to stay awhile and see if the Mummy monkeys return at dusk."

That made me smile. "I'd appreciate it." After all, he has bigger guns than I do. I licked my lips and drew away when my stomach began to clench. I didn't want to get too distracted. We had to end this thing between us now. Neither of us was prepared for more. I'm not sure we were prepared for what had already happened. "I'm wondering if it was a one-time thing or what. I'll ask Burton about them."

"Burton? What could he know?" Sam frowned and drew back.

Dammit. What a dumb slipup. What was I going to tell him? "Yeah, Burton." I sighed. I was going to have to tell him at least some of it. He deserved the truth. At least as much of it as I could tell him. "Grab your cup and sit down." I added a little more sugar to mine. I was going to need it. We sat at the kitchen table, and I kept an eye on the yard. "Burton's not quite what he seems."

"He seems like any dumb-ass skateboard junkie. So what else is he?" Sam sipped his coffee, but kept his sharp gaze on me. I'd not slip anything past him. Not just because of the new level of intimacy we now shared, but because of the blood we had exchanged.

"He's a messenger, sort of my liaison between me and…" How did I explain them? The other side, the source of my powers, spirits?

"What?"

"You're not going to believe me, so I don't quite know what to tell you."

"Try me. I've seen a lot of things I never thought I'd believe."

"Do you trust me, Sam?"

"Of course."

The answer was too quick. I leaned forward, pressing him more than I'd ever done. "I mean really trust me with everything in your soul, know I would never deceive you."

This time he paused before answering, and I knew he meant it. "Yes."

"You know something really bad happened to me in the past that gave me the scars on my stomach." I hated even mentioning them. "I was kidnapped, and my child was cut from me."

Surprise and sorrow entered his eyes. "I didn't know that was you."

He squeezed my hands, offering me a silent support I needed. "Well, I truly died back then and something happened. It wasn't simply a light from the other side, but a presence appeared and fixed my body so I would survive and sent me back with a mission." I watched his eyes. He wanted to tell me this was all bullshit, but he didn't. He knew me and knew I wouldn't feed him a bunch of crap for no good reason. And he carried the blood of a resurrectionist in his veins.

"What happened?" The emotion in his voice almost made me cry with relief. He believed me. Until now, I hadn't realized how important it was for him to believe me. No one else knew my whole story, and it was a relief to share it.

"I was restored to a living status, rescued and survived. My mission is the resurrections. You've never asked questions about how this all started or anything. You just took the job as my liaison. You have no idea how I appreciated that. I didn't know if I could have answered any questions at the time."

"You were new at it, and I had a little information

from my grandmother's experience." That's why he'd fit so easily into the role.

"Anyway, Burton is a very old being who comes in the guise of what you see. He brings information from the other-siders. It's not like I can call them on my cell. When Burton is in physical form, he carries one, but it only seems to work one-way. He calls me."

The rise of the wind drew our attention to the window and the trees beyond. They moved and swayed in the breeze like usual. "I don't get any weird vibes from out there, do you?"

Scanning the yard through the window, he shook his head. "No. Seems like it's going to be okay tonight." He looked down at me, his glance bouncing off my mouth, then returning to my eyes. "Call me if anything changes. And I mean anything."

Always the protector. Sam had his secrets that went as deeply as mine. Someday he'd share them, but for now, pushing him wasn't going to help. One day he'd have no choice.

"Yeah, I'll call." I thought it unlikely he'd get here in time to help me go target-shooting for monkeys.

Then he stood, and our time together as lovers came to an end. Nervous and jittery, I walked him to the door. He faced it for a moment before turning back to me.

Without a word he reached out to me. With a gasp I reached for him, too. He pressed me against the door with his body, and I was so grateful for the hard feel of him against me one last time. His mouth was hungry for me, and I dug my hands into his hair. There was more desperation than passion in the embrace, as if we knew this was the end, and we could never return to that status of newly found lovers again. Though our status lasted only a day or so, I would miss it, and I knew he would, too. Asking him to stay any longer would just put both of us in more pain.

Finally, he pulled back, and I opened the door. "Call me." I knew that meant to call if anything weird happened, like the monkeys returning, or worse. I also knew if I called him to be my lover again someday, he would be there.

"I will."

Whoever invented Monday morning meetings, especially the mandatory kind, should be shot, drawn and quartered, their entrails flattened by a road paver. Having to be somewhere, awake and pretending to be interested at the revolting hour of 7:00 a.m. on a Monday, is a violation of the Geneva Convention. I don't care that we're not at war. My right to sleep until sunrise ought to be protected by something, other than my 9 mil. Glaring at the officer in charge wasn't helping, so I rose slowly and filled my coffee cup. When I turned around, Sam was sitting in my chair against the wall and closest to the door for a quick getaway.

Now was not the time to have a hot flash for the man, so I chose to lean against the doorjamb. Standing was a better option at the moment, since my tender parts were getting the raw end of the deal on a folding metal chair. Unfortunately, standing so close to Sam, his fragrance and his energy continued to draw my attention away from the mesmerizing topic. Whatever it was.

My cell phone rang and the Grim Reaper got a chuckle from the guys.

"Hello?" Trying to whisper in a meeting only draws more attention to you, so I stepped into the hall.

"Dani, it's Liz. I know it's early, but can you come to my office?"

I glanced at the stuffed conference room and considered my desire to return to it. "Uh, sure."

"Bring a box of coffee. You're going to need it," she said and hung up.

"Okay, then." I returned to the conference room and crouched beside Sam with a groan. The muscles in my thighs screamed in protest. I'm a kickboxer in good shape, but the kind of sexual antics I'd engaged in over the weekend used an entirely different set of muscles, and they didn't like it one bit. I looked up at him, motioned him closer. "Liz has something going on. I gotta go. Take notes for me, will ya?"

He smirked. "Sure."

"Thanks." I rose like an old woman with an arthritic back, then got the hell out of there.

Half an hour later, I had my bucket of coffee and entered Liz's office. "I'm here. Where's the fire?" I parked the coffee on a side table beside her own silly and insignificant drip brewer that cringed in the presence of real java.

"We're good to go with the Dover case." She sat behind her desk all perky and enthusiastic. She's one of those early-morning people, and I'm surprised our friendship has lasted as long as it has. I do want to smack her sometimes for being cheerful so early.

"Really?" I plunked down into the chair across from her desk and gave an involuntary groan.

"You okay?" she asked, concerned. Did I mention that she's bright and observant?

"Yeah." I adjusted my position and tried not to move too much more. "I worked out a little extra this weekend."

"Oh." She turned her attention to the files in front of her. "I thought you were going to say you spent the weekend having hot monkey sex with a certain sexy police liaison."

"Don't mention monkeys." I shivered with revulsion at the memory of them. I told her about the Mummy monkeys, but kept the rest to myself.

"Are you okay? They didn't attack you, just your yard?" Concern emanated from her.

"Yeah. Want to go shopping for new lawn furniture with me?"

"Maybe, but not now. Dover wants to bring his wife up from the freezer. How soon can you do it?"

I thought a second and couldn't come up with any conflicts, but checked my phone calendar anyway. "I'm good. I could do it as soon as tomorrow." I needed a night to rest after the weekend I'd had.

"The sooner the better, I think." She sighed, rested her hands on her desk and laced her fingers together.

"What am I not going to like?" I'm always suspicious when people take poses like that.

"Press release." She let out her breath in a rush of air and held up her hand to keep me from screaming at her. "I'll be there with you. I'll give the release myself, but you must be present, and you'll have to take a few questions."

"Oh, no. No freakin' way." My mood went from slightly sour all the way to vinegar.

"This is essential PR, and it must be done. The resurrectionists have a lot of supporters out there, but this case is going to hit a lot of people in different ways. We have to be very clear about the intentions of Mr. Dover and our intentions in bringing back the wife."

"Why?" I crossed my arms and pouted like a two-year-old. Liz was making me do something I didn't want to, and I hate that. She's one of the very few people who can make me do things without sticking a gun in my back.

"Because if it works, we can use the attention to get a decision on Vassar and Liebowitz."

I narrowed my eyes. Those were the two cops who had been killed by the schizophrenic patient. More than anything, I wanted to know what was going to happen. They were good cops with families who suffered without them. Every month I received emails from the wives inquiring about the status of the case, and I hated to disappoint them forever. That niggle of morality kept coming up, making me hesitate yet again. I wanted them back, but could we do it ethically and morally? I didn't know, but if this case helped set that one to rights, then I would do what I had to do whether I liked it or not. I narrowed my eyes at her.

"Anyone ever tell you you fight dirty?"

"All the time, but I never believe them." She laughed and waved her hand as if such an idea was preposterous.

"You might consider starting." I scooted forward in my chair and instantly regretted it, as my gluteus maximus screeched. I cringed again.

"You really overdid it this weekend, didn't you? Poor thing." She clucked her tongue in sympathy. "Why don't you go get a massage?"

I didn't tell her that I'd had a massage, inside and out. "I'll consider that."

"At least soak in an Epsom salts bath." She snapped her fingers and nodded. "Those old home remedies are the best sometimes."

"Yeah." I nearly choked. One of those old home remedies was what had gotten me into trouble in the first place. Baking soda and water, smeared all over Sam's back. I would never look at one of those ugly orange boxes the same way again.

"So, when are we going to do this dirty deed?"

"Three o'clock this afternoon."

"What?" I started to hyperventilate. "Why?"

"They can have it for the evening news. We'll set up an interview with Dover, so he can say his piece, then off to thaw out the Mrs. and ask her what she wants to do."

"Christ almighty—"

"You'd better watch your mouth around the cameras." She gave me a stern look and pointed her finger at me. "You need this, and the public support, or you'll never move forward. None of you will. Resurrectionists have made great strides in the past fifty years, but public support isn't where it needs to be. Above all, the safety of the resurrectionists comes first."

"I know, I know." I shot out of my chair and tried not to scream. "I just hate being on center stage." I paced her small office, and she let me do it in silence. We've known each other for only a year or so, but in that time, we've become very good friends, a friendship that began with mutual respect for surviving brutal experiences. Survivors recognize each other and form bonds that no one else can understand. "The restraint, I mean. Makes me feel like I've gone back to being Blake's wife."

"I know, sugar, I know." There was that sympathy again. "But you've grown quite a lot since that previous life, as have I. We've moved on, we've become stronger for our experiences, and we are never, *ever* going back." She came across the room, somehow managed to appear to glide on her stilettos over the carpet, and placed her hand on my shoulder. "You can do it. What's ten minutes out of your life? You can live with that, can't you?" She removed her hand and went back to her desk. "Now get outta here. Go have a massage or go to the gym." She handed me a card for her masseuse. "Be back here at two-thirty, and we'll go together."

I took the card from her, grumbled the entire way to my truck. I stuck the card into the cup holder on the console. I didn't know what to do with it. Having someone touch my body, even in the most innocent of ways, so recently after the way Sam had touched me, wasn't something I wanted. I'd erased the smell of him off me in the shower, but remnants of his touch lingered on my skin, and I wanted that to last as long as possible.

That meant I needed to hit something.

Two hours later, I collapsed on the mat beneath Master Tom.

"You're off today." He reached down and helped me to my feet.

"Yeah. I got something I have to do that I really don't want to do." I could admit that to him. He'd understand, make sympathetic noises, and I'd feel better.

"Resistance will get you nowhere. Is it a one-time thing?" He gave me a hand, then hauled me to my feet.

"I think so." Gods, I hoped so.

"Then just do it. Putting so much energy into the

resistance takes away your energy for other things."
He grabbed a towel from his bag and wiped his face.

"I hate having to do things I don't want to." Always
had, always will.

"Don't we all?"

"I suppose." I parked it on the bench against the wall
for a minute to get hold of myself.

"Here." He handed me a key. "Go sit in the steam
room and sweat out whatever's bugging you. No one
else is going to be in there, so put on a towel and drink
a liter of electrolyte water."

"Thanks."

"Let me know if you need anything."

"Sure." I undressed, wrapped a towel around myself
and went into the sauna. I set the timer for ten minutes,
pretty sure that's about all I could take. Jets of steam
filled the room, and in thirty seconds I thought I was
going to die. Hot air scorched my lungs, and I coughed.
After a few seconds the discomfort eased, and I was
able to relax on the wooden bench. I closed my eyes,
as secure as I could get in there, and tried not to think.

I must have fallen asleep or passed out. Although I
didn't remember falling asleep, I startled awake.

It's in the yard.

A voice spoke very clearly in my ear, but I knew I
was alone. "Is someone here?" The voice wasn't someone I recognized, so maybe it was just from my imagination or my semi-dream state. It was hardly surprising
I'd fallen asleep, due to the lack of rest I'd had over the
weekend. If I dreamed, I didn't recall it. Just the voice.
A woman's voice. *It's in the yard.* Whatever the hell
that was supposed to mean.

The timer had stopped, but I didn't know how long

ago. Securing the towel around me, I opened the door. "Holy mother of Christ, it's cold in here." The AC was on in the building, and my skin nearly took off back into the sauna. Needless to say, I dressed quickly.

"Here's the key." Still shivering, I gave it back to Tom.

"How was the steam? Clear your head?" He stowed the key on a hook by the door.

"Yeah. I think." I frowned, wondering about that voice I heard.

"Something wrong?"

"Frankly, I'm not sure. I think I had a hallucination in there."

"You should have had more electrolyte drink first. Did you have any?" He glared at me, suspicious, and he was right. I'd forgotten.

"Uh, no."

"See, there's your problem. You can't take direction from anyone, even when it's good for you." He rambled in Korean, swiveled his desk chair around and opened a small refrigerator, pulled out two drinks and gave them both to me. "Drink them. One now, one in an hour, then two liters of filtered water."

"Thanks. What do I owe you?"

"Nothing. Just go do your thing you have to do and come back in a better mood."

I had had a free sauna and now two drinks. My day was beginning to look up. "Okay. Watch for me on the evening news." I stuffed one bottle into my bag and opened the other one. Kiwi-strawberry. Yum. A little sweet, a little tart, just like me.

"That's all you have to do? A press conference?" He laughed. "I can't believe they're going to let you and that mouth of yours on the news. They do have ratings, you know."

"Maybe they'll save it for the late edition." I cringed and shuffled out the door.

Chapter 10

I looked pathetic on camera, like some hostile Asian bodyguard in a bad martial arts movie. Black looks good on me and hides an abomination of sins, but in this instance, I looked skeletal. Fabulous. Here's the great resurrectionist, who looks as if she's just been brought back from the dead. Again.

I flopped back on my couch and wanted to ignore the phone, but I sat up and read the caller ID. If it was another reporter, I was gonna unplug the damned thing. But it wasn't, and I picked it up.

"Hey."

"Hey. Saw you on the news tonight," Sam said, and I could hear the slight rumble of laughter through the phone. With fiber optics these days, you could hear things you really ought not hear sometimes.

"Not my idea at all." Way not.

"I could see that. Liz did a good job."

"That's why I keep her around. If I depended on my PR skills, my business would have been dead in the water long ago."

"You were fine. You looked serious and respectful, and no cussing on camera."

That made me smile. "Thanks."

There was a small silence between us that wasn't quite uncomfortable, but might have been a yearning we both knew we couldn't give life to.

"Well, I'm going to head to bed." I tried not to think of him there, but the fragrance of him lingered on my sheets.

"No more monkeys?"

"None so far." I hoped to never see those little bastards ever again. I was about to hang up when something weird happened.

"Dani?" he asked when I paused. "What's wrong? I can feel it."

"I don't know yet, but something feels wrong in the house." I stood. A fine mist of blue-black smoke hung in the air. Something definitely wasn't right. "Smoke."

I hung up and ran to the kitchen, because that's where most fires start. Somebody always forgets something on the stove. But this somebody hadn't forgotten anything. That left the barbecue outside, but that hadn't been on since Saturday night. I could see it from the kitchen window. A fire raged in it.

"Dammit." I yanked open the door, ready to charge outside when instinct hit me. My gun was in my hand before I was even conscious of it. I'd almost committed the same blunder that had gotten me killed once. I wasn't about to do it again. That shook me more than the fire blazing away in the barbecue.

Backing up, I slammed the door and locked it. Someone or something was out there. The Dark. I hadn't felt the force of it until I opened the door. My cell phone was screaming at me. I'm sure it was Sam, and that blasted ringtone only added to the chill inside me.

"I'm here." I kept my voice low, not quite a whisper, and I hunkered down in a corner between the cupboard and the back door.

"What's going on? I'm on my way." It was Sam. I could hear the roar of his truck in the background.

"I don't know. Be careful. It's not monkeys, but something is out there and it feels…bigger. Badder." What could be worse than Mummy monkeys? Was this The Dark trying to get my attention again? If so, I was shaking in my shoes, and I hadn't even seen it yet.

"Call 911 on the house phone and then leave the line open."

"Sam—"

"Do it!" The line went dead. I didn't know if he'd hung up or if there was interference in the cell system. I flipped it to vibrate and shoved the phone into my pocket. If I needed it again, I didn't want it to be across the room from me. I flicked the kitchen phone onto speaker and dialed 911, briefly told the operator I thought I had a house fire and needed the fire brigade, but couldn't stay on the line. See? Tom was wrong. I can *so* take direction. Someone just needs to light a fire under me first.

Some people get the shakes during a crisis, some people cry and can't function. I become silent, very focused and deadly. I shake later. Whatever lurked out there was stalking me, and I was never going to be taken down unprepared again.

I moved to the wooden bread box on the counter and eased it open. Bread-schmead, my extra weapons are in there. Why have a broom and dustpan when you can stow a gun by the fridge? And a little derringer for close work should the occasion arise. I stuck that firecracker in the back of my waistband.

The crystal amulet around my neck warmed and pulsed red tones. It's never done that before. Great. I was just a beacon in the night, an illuminated target for anyone who cared to shoot me, but I wasn't taking it off. Ever.

I'm here.

What the *hell?* The words were a whisper in my mind. This was the second time in a few hours I'd had an auditory hallucination. I didn't know how or why I heard the words, but I knew Sam was waiting for me to open the door. I backed up through the kitchen and to the front foyer. Of course, I had a security window, and I took a look through it, just in case I really was losing my mind. I could barely make him out with help from the streetlight a few yards away. I didn't want to turn on the front light and blind him, or alert whatever was lingering outside that we were now opening the front door and it could trot right on in.

There are few home maintenance chores I do, but keeping the front lock and hinges lubed was one of them. The bolt slid back without a sound. Sam turned the knob and pushed. He eased inside, gun ready, then closed the door, and I locked it again. Thankfully, he didn't try to take over the situation, or I'd have had to shoot him, too.

He looked at me, and I inclined my head toward the kitchen. He moved to one side of the doorway, and I took the side opposite. I motioned to the window so he could see the fire in the barbecue.

"Smells like incinerated chicken."

"I didn't have anything in there that could catch." I was baffled.

"Is anyone there?" The 911 dispatcher's voice came through the speaker.

"I'm here." I glanced at Sam, and he nodded. "I don't think we need the police any longer, thanks." I didn't disconnect though.

Sam eased the back door open, and we made our way out. The smell coming from the barbecue was an odd mixture of ozone, charred hair and fried chicken. Maybe the monkeys were tired of being vegetarians and wanted to party.

Trying not to get too distracted by the obvious, we moved closer to the target, but still kept an eye overhead. The night was still. Still, not in a way that's just pleasant with no wind or bugs, but in a creepy way where you knew something was coming for you. Any second. The hair on the back of my neck raised and an instinct I hadn't known I had clenched in my gut.

Foul didn't begin to describe the smell of the new breeze blowing through the yard. Whatever it was hovered above the tree line. If black could glow, then this black being certainly did. It was like a glob of gelatinous energy. I didn't know what the hell it was, and I was pretty certain I didn't want to find out, either.

The crystal amulet around my neck glowed from red to a gloriously brilliant white, brighter than a welding torch. It blinded me, and I panicked. "Sam!" Whatever was out there was going to kill me, and take Sam along with it.

"I can't see!"

Hideous noises roared from the back of the yard and

every hair on me stood up. It was like nothing I'd ever heard before, as if something was being torn into bite-size pieces while it was still alive. If evil truly existed, then it was in my yard.

"Cease your interference." The voice boomed, pushing away any other sound.

I nearly dropped from the noise and clamped my hands over my ears. Had I really heard that? "What?"

"Cease your interference and the balance will be restored."

Oh, I get it. "Trying to scare me into stopping the resurrections?" Though I was temporarily blinded by my amulet, I wasn't stunned stupid, too. This was the troublemaker from beyond. "Oh, just bite me." Showing your enemy fear only empowers them. Though I was shaking in my shoes, I couldn't allow The Dark to see it.

"You are indeed formidable." It laughed.

Seriously? It was laughing at me? "You sent your monkeys to destroy my yard, didn't you?"

"Indeed."

"When I get my vision back, you're dead!"

"What you fear will manifest. This is your only warning. Cease."

With that, the being or whatever it was, faded into the back of the yard and disappeared. My limbs started to shake. I was more vulnerable than I'd ever been. I didn't know what the hell was going on.

Oh, gods. *Sam.* "Where are you?" I called out for him, and he pulled me against him. I kept the gun down at my right side and clutched him with my left hand and arm as if I was never gonna let go.

"What happened?"

"The light blinded me." I opened my eyes and things

began to take shape again. Trees and objects in the yard all had a white halo around them, as if I had looked at a camera flash too long. I hoped my retinas weren't fried. Being disabled was not in my agreement with the other-siders. We were so going to amend my verbal contract.

"It's your crystal. It's glowing like a solar flare."

I clutched the piece in my hand, but the light still emanated from between my fingers, engulfing us inside it. It was brilliant enough to reach every area of the yard and eliminate the shadows. Nothing could hide in that sort of illumination. Not even the evil thing I had seen.

Damn. "The door. I left the door open." Great. If something was out there, I just gave it an invitation to waltz right into my house.

Before we secured the house though, I had to see what had been burning. It did smell like chicken, sort of. I looked into the barbecue. Someone had toasted a small animal to get my attention. Surely there were better ways of doing that. Coulda been a cat. Coulda been a squirrel or a raccoon. I gave a full-body shiver and sent healing energy for the unfortunate critter.

Now that my vision had mostly returned and the auras I saw were fading, we returned to the house just as sirens cracked open the silence of the night, and the fire trucks showed up.

"Dammit. I should have called them off sooner." I hated for them to make a wasted trip. The smell of smoke was thicker in the air, and I then realized something was happening inside the house, too. House fires smell different from other fires, and I looked through the kitchen to the table.

The journals were smoldering.

They were still in the box, but the stench of ozone

and smoldering papers touched the air. "No!" I holstered my gun and took one step toward the box on the table when the whole thing went up in flames as if someone had dumped gasoline on it. There was actually a whoosh, and my hair blew back from my face. The heat of it made the skin on my face feel tight and crinkly, as if I'd been in the sun all day.

I cringed and turned away from the sight, and felt Sam's hand at my waist, guiding me away from the area. "Let's get out of here. We'll secure the house later."

"But the journals!" I looked back and the flames had shot up to touch off the curtains that seemed to melt against the window.

"They're gone." We both knew that what was in them could never be recovered. That thing out there in the dark didn't want us to finish the translations. That only proved to me there was something important in them we needed. Without a choice, we dashed out the door into the waiting arms of the firefighters.

In my previous life, I would probably have wrapped up in a blanket, sobbed on the driveway and watched my house go up in flames. Now I stalked back and forth and cursed with every breath I took. Amazingly, some of the Korean phrases my cousins had taught me as a kid came back now.

Glaring into the night, I watched as the firefighters extinguished the flames. I hated the violation of my home, what had been my sanctuary. Not by the firefighters, but by the blight that had entered uninvited. I'd have to perform a smudging of the entire place to rid it of the stench I knew would remain long after the dark energy had left. White sage is a sacred plant in the Southwest, and I know where to find it wild. That's the best kind, to pick and dry your own for your rituals. Always makes them more powerful. I was gonna need every bit I had on hand to purify my space.

"It's contained in the kitchen, Miss Wright." The chief, Andy Gonzales, gave me the report. "Seems to have stayed on the kitchen table and the curtains." He scratched his head. "Don't know why."

"Thanks, Chief. When can I get back in?"

"Not tonight, that's for sure. Sorry."

"Dammit."

"You really don't want to be in there tonight. Smells like hell."

"It smelled like hell before the fire started," I said and thought of the thing in the yard. It smelled as if it had come straight from some unclean place.

"Yeah. My wife's always finding something nasty in the back of the fridge. You probably just had something go bad." He scribbled on a clipboard, then handed it to me. I signed the paper, and took a copy.

"Go get your stuff, then we'll secure the house once you're out," he said.

In a few minutes, I had gathered my essentials: the guns and ammo from the kitchen, a toothbrush, sweats and clothing for tomorrow. Just about all a woman like me needed. And my pillow. I have a fierce reluctance to use any pillow except my own.

The fire trucks pulled away just as I closed the front door. The night seemed unnaturally quiet and dark after the sirens and lights faded.

"Want to stay with me tonight?" Sam asked.

"Uh…" How to answer that question.

"No strings, Dani. Just a place to bunk for the night." He took my gym bag and carried it to my truck.

He had read my mind. Dammit. There was no peace for me anywhere tonight. "I'm staying at Elena's. She's out of town for a few days."

"Sure. If you think she won't mind."

"Nope. Let's go."

I followed him in my truck.

Restless and agitated, there was no way I could settle down to sleep, so I dumped my stuff on the couch. Without a word, he grabbed two longnecks from the fridge, opened them and handed me one. "Hell of a night."

I looked at the clock on the microwave. "And it ain't over yet." It was just after 1:00 a.m., and I was wide-awake. That's what adrenaline and endorphins will do for you. "You tired?" I asked him, wondering why we were staring at each other when we smelled like hell-fire and were covered with soot.

"Nope. I'm gonna take a shower. Join me if you want to." He took a long swig of his beer and gave me a longer look, then moved away down the hall.

O-*kay*. So much for no strings. He didn't need them. All he had to do was toss me a look like that and my nipples puckered all by themselves. Traitors. My body had been sexually turned off until the other night with him. And now look at it. As hot and horny as a teenager with a new box of condoms. Yee-*haw*.

For several minutes I tried to focus on the event that had gone down at my house. I really tried to keep my mind off Sam naked and wet and fully aroused in the shower, water sluicing down his shoulders and back. Really. I did try.

It was the longest ten seconds of my life.

Then my mouth went dry. I was certain it was from simple dehydration, so I guzzled down the rest of my beer. It wasn't enough to get me drunk or even buzzed, so no worries that I was going to do something I normally wouldn't have, because I'd done just about everything with Sam already.

Except for a shower. Somehow we had missed that.

The sound of the shower drew me down the hall. Part of my personality is an insatiable curiosity about many things, life in general and what one particular naked cop looked like all wet.

Steam escaped through the narrow opening of the ajar bathroom door. Steam. It jogged a faint memory of my time in the steam room, but I didn't want to think about it at that moment. A fresh-and-clean smell wafted from the bathroom, and I had to admit that my hair and clothing held on to the gross fire smell. Sweat formed between my shoulder blades and broke out on my knees.

I pushed the door wider. Rats. Elena didn't have a nice clear shower curtain, but something opaque that distorted the view.

That meant I was gonna have to get a lot closer.

I pulled the shower curtain back about a third of the way. I knew it was steam in the shower, but I felt as if the sizzle between us had finally created real smoke. Time would tell whether there was anything else there.

"You have too many clothes on for a shower." He turned his face toward me. Oh, the man was gorgeous, all hot, and wet, and naked. Better than my imagination. My very own aphrodisiac that was legal and wouldn't make me fat.

"I wanted to inspect your back. Make sure there isn't any infection after the black rain exposure." If that wasn't a lame excuse, I didn't know what was. It was more see-through than the shower curtain.

"I've been meaning to make an appointment for a follow-up."

I removed my smelly shirt and dropped it on the floor. "No need for that, now." Modesty seemed like an overrated use of energy right now. Reaching behind me, I snapped the bra clasp open and it recoiled like a broken slingshot. The jeans and panties weren't much trouble.

After years of celibacy, it seemed I was making up for that lost time in the span of a few days. Now that my body recalled what it was to hunger for a man again, it wanted more, more, more.

Stepping into the shower, I was enveloped in a cocoon of heat, and steam, and hard muscles. Sam snapped the curtain closed and opened his mouth over mine. The smell of smoke permeated the air. It had to have come from my hair.

I pulled back with a frown. "I stink. Sorry." I reached for the shampoo, even though it wasn't mine.

"Wait." Sam took the bottle from my hands. He poured a dollop into his hand and returned the bottle to the shelf. Sensing his intention, I tipped my head into the spray and saturated my hair, then turned my back on him. The hot water blasted my nipples, and Sam thrust his hands into my hair, scrubbing and sudsing until the odor of smoke was gone.

His fingers massaged my scalp, and I closed my eyes to enjoy the sensation and to avoid any dripping shampoo. Now would not be the time to have my eyes burned out by hair care products.

Sam took half a step closer to me, and his cock brushed my buttocks. What a delightful feeling, to know he was as turned on by me as I was by him. Abandoning the scalp massage, Sam opted for a mammary gland manipulation. His hands fit my breasts, and he tweaked my nipples between his thumbs and fingers.

I turned and dragged his head down to mine. Sam's hands stroked me nearly everywhere, cupping my ass hard. My skin was alive from his touch and the stimulation of the water.

Making love in a shower is no easy task, but Sam handled the situation beautifully. He pressed me against the tile wall and I wrapped my legs around his hips. I was gonna have bruises tomorrow, but right now I didn't care. I just didn't want to have to explain a fall in the shower to paramedics. With his face against mine, his chest pressed to mine, he eased the shaft of his swollen cock into me. Hissing at the pleasure of him inside me, I nearly came at that very second. Plunging in and pulling out, Sam set up a reckless pace. Clutching his shoulders, I cried in his ear, "Take me home." And he did.

Naked, we slept curled together in the guest bed. Guess I didn't need my jammies after all. I dreamed about steam. It choked me, tried to strangle me. Then I realized Sam was draped over me in his sleep, holding me tight against him like a body pillow.

"Sam, wake up. You're crushing me." I tried to elbow him, but he woke too quickly and grabbed my arm.

He woke, but didn't move, just alert and tense, then he looked down at me. Inky darkness filled the room, but dawn was just creeping over the edge of the Sandia Mountains.

"What?"

"You're crushing me." I gave him a light shove. "I need my lungs back."

He accommodated my request, but didn't go far, just raised his weight up off me with his hands. "I meant before that."

I thought a second. "Before that, I was asleep and dreaming I was being choked to death."

He rolled all the way to his back. "Guess I was dreaming, then. I heard a voice." With a sigh, he eased me to his side. "We have a few hours yet. Go back to sleep."

I let my head rest in the hollow of his shoulder and stretched my left arm across his middle, my hand in full contact with his skin. The sensations were warm and comfortable coming from him. That didn't bother me in the least, but it made me wonder about where our relationship was going. Were we going to be sex buddies or was there more going on than we knew about? At the moment there were no answers, so I closed my eyes, a sigh on my breath. We slept that way until morning.

I cruised by my house to make sure everything was okay. I wanted to wait for the insurance adjuster, but couldn't. My stomach and dead people waited for me to fulfill their needs.

My cell was still on vibrate and scared the shit out of me when it rang. It wasn't one of those fancy text-until-your-thumbs-fall-off types, just a regular, sleek flip phone.

"What?"

"Down, girl. It's Liz. We still a go for the Dover case tonight?"

I'd wanted a night off, but last night hadn't been in the cards due to the fire. The feel of the atmosphere around me was a growing pressure that I couldn't stop.

I was tired, but I could do the ritual, especially since Sam could loan me some energy when I needed it. "Let me check my phone again." Nothing. "Can you get him here before nine?" I paused and sighed. "We'll need to check with the wife, and it ain't going to be pretty."

"Yeah, I know." I heard her sigh on the other side. "She's been on ice, so she ought to perk right up, right?"

Perk right up. Yeah. With half her face missing. I wondered how the hell I was going to talk to her and ask her if she wanted to stay on this plane or go home to the nebula. Not that I had a *Resurrections for Dummies* or *Idiots Guide to Resurrections* book I could reference. Maybe I ought to write one for the others out there like me. That would generate some PR that Liz couldn't argue with.

"Call me when she's ready. Me and Dover's ass-wipe lawyer need to be there."

"Will do." I laughed at her apt description. "Liz, do you realize you made a joke?"

"Yeah, I'm hanging out with you too much." The line went dead. I switched the damned thing from vibrate back to my hackle cackle.

This wasn't going to be an easy case, and I ought to prepare more this afternoon. I tried to call Sam to let him know the schedule. He didn't pick up, so he was either busy or ignoring me. As he had no reason to ignore me, I knew he was busy, so I left a message. We were professionals and weren't going to let a little fantastic fornication get in the way of business.

Time to eat, so off to the Cooperage I went for a slab of rare prime rib. Seconds after I ordered, Sam called. "Hey, I'm gearing up for tonight. Can you make it? It's the Dover case. Nine o'clock."

"Yeah, where are you now?"

"Cooperage."

"Be there in ten." The line went dead. What was it with people hanging up without giving a proper sign-off? I might be abrupt, but that's just plain rude.

So I chowed down on the salad and waited for what I really needed. Less than ten minutes later sirens neared, and I wondered what was up. Since my life change and hanging out with cops, I've been acutely attuned to the sound of sirens.

Then Sam charged to the table and I knew what was up. He sat, picked up my glass of water and guzzled the entire thing, reminding me too well of how he had downed the tequila the other day. Down, girl.

"Thanks. I'm fuckin' starved." He motioned the waiter over. "Give me whatever she's having." The waiter nodded and headed to the kitchen. Sam peered at me. "Your eyes look okay, so what's the deal?"

"I needed flesh." Then I looked up at him, the inference clear. Of course, he sat there with a self-satisfied amusement on his face, and I had the good grace to blush. Slightly. Over the past week, I'd certainly had enough of *his* flesh, but it wasn't the right kind to sustain me for a ritual. I gave him a look. "You know what I mean. Gearing up for tonight. Needed the extra load of protein and stuff."

I said *stuff* because the women at the table next to us were getting a little too curious. Though I have to agree, Sam makes a stunning table companion with his dark looks and commanding presence, they needed to mind their own business. It wasn't jealousy that crawled onto my back. Really. I'm certain it was just irritation at the disturbance. With a dark blue, nearly black blazer thrown on over those impeccable shoulders to cover his gun, he did indeed make fine eye candy.

But this was business. Totally business. I gave the women at the table a glare, and they looked away. Some people *were* susceptible to my glares, and that made me feel better.

"Do you practice that?"

"I do. Keeps the masses at bay, and I have fewer questions to answer." I chowed down a few bites, then told him about tonight. "Liz is going to have Dover and his lawyer at my office at nine. The wife should be ready by then."

"Sounds like a typical procedure. Why are you indulging in an extra dose of protein?" He speared a delightful-looking piece of flesh and smeared it in the steak sauce.

"Tonight's gonna be a giant energy suck, I can feel it already." I shrugged. "After the weekend, then the fire and that dark thing in the yard, I've got a bad feeling. I just want to make sure I've got enough juice to make it happen." I sighed. "It feels like there's one thing after another bombarding me and taking up a whole lot of my attention and energy. Makes me wonder if it's on purpose. If The Dark is going to make serious trouble for me. For us."

He glanced at one of his palms. His were healed, as were mine, but I knew he was thinking about when we had shared the blood for the Ramirez case. "I can help out again if you need it."

"I might. The last one kind of freaked me out." I wondered now about what the dark thing had said about my fears. If anyone died because of me or was injured because of me, I didn't know what I'd do. That was my greatest fear, and I think it knew it. Looking at Sam now, I knew I had to protect him if I could, but he certainly wasn't going to like it. He's the ex-military army Ranger cop who's decided to be the protector of the universe.

"Yeah, but you dealt with it, handled it, and everything worked out okay. Have you heard from that family?" The confidence coming off him was stunning. He truly believed in me and my abilities.

"Yeah. Once. Everything's cool with them. The boy's back in school, and has no memory of the event." I shook my head, amazed at the ability of children to bounce back from situations that would cripple an adult. I looked at the remaining food on my plate. It wasn't that my appetite went, but the reason I do what I do is because there are so many selfish people in the world. That hits me between the eyes now and then.

"You did a good thing, Dani. If the family paid you tenfold, it wouldn't have been enough. They have their child back, and that's more precious than you can imagine." His voice cracked. Family was very important to him. He'd lost his at some point and had never recovered. The intensity of him nearly glowed.

"I know. Believe me, I know." But I didn't know why *he* thought that. "What's that about?"

"Nothing." He clenched his jaw, and a flash of rage I'd never felt from him roared between us. Something was up with him, and I tried to reach out mentally to see what it was. I was either not good enough, or he blocked me from reading him. Again. His jaw worked for a second. "Just…you're not the only one with a past."

I dropped my gaze from his. That was the most he'd ever given me. Someday he'd tell me, or he wouldn't.

Whatever it was, was obviously still painful and raw. Pushing wouldn't make that go away, so for now, I remained silent. Another time and another place.

"I know."

Chapter 11

"Who said there could be cameras here?" I nearly screeched. I hate that sound in my voice. It means I'm expending too much energy on things out of my control.

Liz pulled me aside. "This was my idea. If the judge can see the ritual and the results you get, she might sort out the cop-killer case."

"Dammit, you should have told me." I hate surprises. I mean really hated them. It's all about control, I know. "I need to be ready for stuff like this."

"Simmer down, Dani. All you're going to do is your usual thing. There is simply one extra person with a camera."

"And a light system to rival Isotopes stadium." That's our resident minor league baseball team. Popcorn and beer anyone?

"It's not that bad." She gave an exasperated sigh. "If the lighting isn't right, we won't have the best images for the judge."

I could see her point. I just didn't like it. "Okay, but

if he gets in my way, I'm not going to be held responsible for anything that happens to him."

"Agreed."

Sam approached after Liz returned to the camera guy.

"I know you're not okay with this, but try to settle yourself, focus on what's in front of you."

"You're in front of me." It was a small attempt at a joke, and Sam did smile.

"The case, babe, the case." A quick surge of emotional energy pulsed from him to me.

"Okay. Okay." I closed my eyes and took a deep breath. There are times when I feel silly doing the things I do in front of others. It's kind of like having an orgasm with an audience. I was just waiting for the judges to flash scorecards.

So I stood with Sam shielding me while I prepared myself, which I knew was his intention. Ever the protector. He had such strength and I wanted to know where it had come from. But not now.

My ritual items had already been prepared and were lying on a red silk scarf beside the recently thawed corpse of Edna Dover. Liz, the camera guy, Stan, Mr. Dover and Vernon waited in a corner of the room. All were silent and anticipation hung heavy in the room. The only thing not ready at the moment was me.

So I focused on the crystal amulet hanging around my neck and took in three or four deep breaths. My eyes opened halfway and I gazed at, but didn't focus upon, Sam's chest. The power in me simmered and then sparked through my veins. It permeated every molecule in my body and electrified my blood. Although my blood was already a living organism within me, now it became almost sentient.

Noise in the room fell silent, or the bubble of protection I created around myself pushed everything except the necessary elements away. After a nod from me, Sam moved away. I was ready.

Generally, I wear jeans, boots, a T-shirt and a blazer. For tonight I had felt a need for a ritual outfit more congruous with ceremony. So I had chosen a red kimono-style silk jacket. The pants were drawstring, made of silk that whispered across my skin. I was also barefoot, needing to connect as much as possible with the earth, though we were in the basement of the building in the cryo lab. It was close enough.

Reaching out, I pulled the drape back from Edna's face and tried not to react. Her face was a mess, so I wasn't sure how she was going to answer any questions. I walked a circle around the gurney and focused my energy, my concentration, on Edna's body and pulled my power from deep inside. I began to glow. Power drawn down from the universe, enhanced by my amulet, blended with the strange mix already inside me and fed by my connection to Sam. My body was the conduit through which the souls passed, but for now, I simply needed information from Edna.

"Peacemakers of the universe, hear me now. Help me free the soul of Edna Dover. Tonight, spirits of those beyond, we gather to right the wrong done to this being. Hear me now, and let it be." A blood sacrifice is always required to open the portal between the worlds, but this night, it didn't need to be a big one. The dagger that had been given to me at the time of my recovery lay on the red silk and I took it, drew it across my forearm.

A line of red immediately appeared. Shaking my arm, I flicked the blood onto Edna's body. "Take my blood offering and awaken, child of the universe."

I held my hands over Edna's body, let them hover about six inches or so away from her chilly skin, covered by a sheet for modesty. The first sign I had of some success was a twitch beneath the sheet.

"Edna Dover, spirit of the universe, I command you to rise and speak. Your eternal future and that of your mate requires this action." If you don't use the proper language and instruction, the dead simply don't know what to do.

I had to admit, it was creepy. The corpse sat on the edge of the gurney, and the sheet fell away to puddle at her hips, revealing her body that was entirely too thin to have been healthy in her life. She had been wasting away, as Dover had said. It took a few seconds, maybe half a minute, for her to blink her one good eye and focus on me.

"Are we speaking to the spirit of Edna Dover?" I always had to make sure, just in case some mischievous spirit had somehow made it through to jerk me around. Under the influence of the ritual, they could not lie.

"Yes."

"Edna Dover, you are required to speak only the truth."

"About what?" She tilted her head, focusing intently on me.

"That's my Edna," Harry Dover said from the other side of the room.

Edna sat up straight and took in a gasping breath. She had seen Harry.

"Your husband is accused of murdering you. We can

return you to a state of physical being should you wish, but the spirit known as Harold Dover will be sent to the nebula and be no more on this plane." I know it's a lot to ask of a newly undead to process that, but on some level they understand.

"N-o-o-o-o!" she roared. Yes, she actually roared, because my hair blew back from my face. With that response, I was guessing she required no further explanation. "It's *not* true."

"Your mate has been convicted of a heinous crime on this plane. The choice is yours whether to return to a physical state, or to return in the nebula."

"We promised." The *s* came out like a hissing sound because the soft palate of her mouth was missing, but I understood her. At a deeper level, I understood what she meant, but had to clarify for the others and the damned camera.

"You promised to take care of each other and protect each other? Is that correct?"

Edna nodded.

"You do not believe that Harold committed an act of violence against you, but saved you by terminating your physical body so your spirit could go to the place beyond where it yearned to go?"

She hesitated, and her attention wavered.

"Is that correct, spirit of Edna Dover?"

"Yes-s-s-s."

"Do you wish to remain on this plane and return to your previous state?"

"N-o-o-o. Send. Me. Home."

Turning to the others, I tried to focus on them and not the brilliant lights searing my eyeballs. "Seems she's pretty clear about not wanting to come back." With that,

I had fulfilled my part of the bargain, to ask and allow her to make her own decision.

"I told you," Harry said. It wasn't said with a smug attitude, but with the conviction of one who was certain at the depth of his soul.

"I know, Harry, but there is still the law on this plane to consider. You have two options, stay and live your days in jail, or go with her now." Although I'd never made that offer to anyone else, the words just came out of my mouth as if I'd channeled one of the othersiders. Hmm. Maybe that was part of my recent upgrade. I knew I could do it, I knew I could release him with a minimum of fanfare.

Harry glanced from me to her and tears filled his eyes. "I can go with her now?" Liz clasped her hands over her face, her eyes wide, and the cameraman's eyes widened, as well. Dover's lawyer stood stone-faced, and I couldn't decide if he was frozen with fear or he had messed his shorts. I turned back, expecting to see the corpse ready to attack.

Instead, what I saw nearly broke me.

Edna's corpse leaned forward, her arthritic and gnarled hands stretched out to Harry. She wept, and silent sobs convulsed the cadaver. "Let's…go…home."

Harold staggered forward, still shackled, and he reached out to her as much as the restraints allowed him to. "Don't worry, darling. I'll take care of you. I promised."

Those words brought tears to my eyes, and I glanced at Sam. These people, spirits, were so at odds to the relationship that I had had with my ex-husband, and I wondered what would happen between Sam and me. Could we find something even close to the commitment they had made? Harold was so dedicated to her that he even killed for her. Would Sam do that for me? The men of Dover's generation were dying by the thousands every day. They'd been through wars and depressions and knew what suffering was. Things that we who were born past the 1960s had little experience with. If we had hardships, they were usually of our own making. Sam stood strong and his presence reassured me. If there was a man I could count on, it was him. But I didn't know if I could give back to him what he needed.

These two had suffered and survived together. Who was I to keep them apart now? I focused deep again and clasped my crystal. I don't know why. Maybe I was hoping it would give me answers or could somehow connect me to the other-siders who had more knowledge than I did. I pushed aside my feelings, my emotions about my own life that had fallen into a deep, dark chasm long ago. What was important was the right now in front of me. This was the right thing to do. I knew it and they knew it. Make it so and let it be.

"I will return the spirit of Edna Dover as is her wish. Does the spirit of Harold Dover wish to return to the nebula now?"

"Send me home." He spoke to me, but his focus remained on Edna. There was nothing except love glowing from him. This man had done what he believed was in the best interest of another. Though the act on this plane was wrong, the intention was pure.

"Be at peace. Together you will return to the nebula." I picked up my dagger again. The feel was cool against my skin for a second, then it heated against my palm.

Edna returned to a prone position and closed her eye. The guards released Harold, who climbed onto the gurney beside her. I didn't want to pick him off the floor after he was dead. I wasn't in the mood for a herniated disc.

"Miss Wright?" he asked.

"Yes?" I approached and looked down on him as I had looked down at many patients in the past.

"Thank you for this. You don't know how much I appreciate it."

"It's my pleasure, Harold."

"Don't ever stop. We need this." I knew he meant more than just Edna and him. The balance of the universe had to be restored or humanity faced destruction. With dark forces like those I'd encountered running interference, my job was going to get harder. Other resurrectionists had died trying to balance the good against the evil. I couldn't give up, ever.

His eyes were bright with emotion and something else, maybe gratitude, but that certainly couldn't describe what I felt from him. There was something I couldn't interpret unless I touched him. "You are the only one who saw my plight for what it was. Thank you." Reaching out, he clasped my hand and kissed the back of it.

In that second I knew what he had been hiding from me at the jail.

He was dying. He was full of cancer. That's why he'd acted when he had, before he didn't have the strength. Sympathy nearly gushed out of me, but I choked it back. If I lost control now, I might not be able to go on with the ritual. My heart ached for the choice he felt he didn't have.

"Be at peace. I'll see you again, spirit of Harold Dover." I believed that. We souls had spent eternity roaming back and forth from this plane to others. There was an infinity to explore out there.

"Let nothing stop you." After that, he removed his glasses, folded them, and tucked them into the pocket of his shirt and relaxed. "I'm ready."

"Spirits of those beyond, open the doorway for these friends who wish to return to you." I sliced the dagger across my palm and shook the blood over both Edna and Harry. The droplets hit each of them. I held one hand toward them and one hand toward the roof. The portal inside me opened, and I closed my eyes in order to view the other-siders better.

"Our friends are welcome to return."

"Hear me now and let it be." I spoke the words that would encourage the spirits to move through me and seal the portal until the next time. I didn't have to tell them what to do. They knew. This was their home, and they gravitated toward it as small orbs of purple-opalescent colors that evolved and shifted and changed.

They were visible to the naked eye as they rose from their bodies, then shot to the ceiling. That's when things went truly wrong.

Darkness exploded and blanketed the doorway just as the souls entered. In a flash of light, it was all gone. All I saw was the other-sider and my crystal glowing like a freakin' strobe light.

"What the hell was that?" I focused on the other-sider.

"The Dark has taken them." There's never any emotion from the other-siders. I'm not certain if they're capable of emotions as humans know it, but there was distress or something coming from the being.

"Why would it take them? I thought it just wanted

to mess with me." I sensed it was related to The Dark being in my yard, but I didn't want to believe it. This was so out there, I didn't want to be a part of it, but like Harold, I was feeling I had little choice.

"The Dark. It has taken the spirits. They are the eternal stars of the universe and The Dark is taking them."

"And you didn't feel a need to tell me about this? Why would it do that?" My head was about to explode from the unanswered questions boiling in it. I was hyperventilating and stars appeared in my vision. If I didn't calm down I was gonna barf or pass out. Either was unappealing in front of witnesses.

"We had hoped it would return to the nebula as it should have, but it is growing more powerful. With each capture of eternal stars it grows more powerful." The being glowed gloriously bright, but it didn't seem to affect my vision. "Danielle Wright, spirit friend, you must help us." Its vibration hummed at a higher level, and the hairs on my arms stood out.

"I thought I was already doing that by restoring the *balance*." I wasn't out here knitting booties.

"Your efforts have not gone unnoticed."

"Well, thanks for *that* vote of confidence." Sarcasm was my deal, not theirs.

"Your inner strength and power grows daily. So does your confidence."

"I'm not here for a self-esteem boost. I'm here to help, because I *need* to help." Whatever was in me wouldn't let me walk away, but I was not sacrificing anyone for their cause. The innocent spirit of my child was enough. No more.

"We are aware."

"Then help me. I don't know how to help if this entity is more powerful than the other-siders." If it was, we were so cosmically toasted.

"We have sent you assistance."

"Yeah, Burton's incredibly helpful." I refrained from snorting. That wouldn't earn me any eternal brownie points.

"You are not alone. Look to your allies, and your source will be revealed."

Give me a break. Why does every question have to be answered with another friggin' riddle? You'd think after so many thousand millennia these beings would communicate better. I know, I know. I've read the parables about struggle, and I *hate* every one of them. No one said life was going to be easy, but does it have to be so damned hard sometimes?

With that bomb dropped on my head, the portal snapped shut and the ritual ended. The light of my crystal faded to its usual color, and all energy fell out of me in a long, tired sigh. My eyes closed and darkness seemed to swallow my brain. Sam caught me. As off balance as I was at that moment, if I had tried to walk under my own power, I would have landed on my face. How nice for the camera.

"You okay?" Sam held one hand on my shoulder, the other at my waist, pressing my weight against him.

I blinked a few times and nodded, trying to clear my head. "Do you believe that?"

"Believe what?"

"What just happened, what the other-sider said." Hadn't he been listening?

"Dani, we didn't hear anything. There was a big flash of light, and everything was quiet for a second, then you fainted."

"I. Did. Not." As if. He, of all people, should know better.

"You did. You were going over backward." He squeezed my shoulder and a surge of comfort pulsed into me. "Your eyes rolled back."

Ew. Definitely a neurological sign of loss of consciousness, though. "Didn't you hear what it said about The Dark?"

"It all happened in about half a second." He nodded to the others, who watched us, then leaned closer to my ear. "I heard it in my head, but to the others, nothing happened."

"Got it." I pulled away from him. I took a deep breath and braced myself to face the others. But first, I checked on the bodies of the Dovers. Edna was still a mess. Harold, however, was a different story. When some people died, depending on their physical condition and disease processes at work, they turned various colors after death. By the time I saw most people, they were either a waxy yellow with a hint of green, or purple. Harry looked as if he had simply gone to sleep and quit breathing.

I respected Harry for his choice. I wondered if I would have made the same one. "That's it then. I'll do the pronouncement for Harold."

"You can't do that, Dani. It's a conflict of interest. Or it appears to be anyway." Liz moved forward and motioned the cameraman to come with her.

Huh? Since when? "I'm a deputy medical examiner, certified by the state of New Mexico to attend deaths and make the pronouncements. I do it all the time." Then I looked at Vernon, who had a smug look on his face. Now what? Something else was up, and if I did the pronouncement of death, then I was not going to like it. Call it gut instinct, or whatever, but I didn't want to make this guy's day, so I listened to Liz. She didn't even have to argue with me this time. "Okay. I'll call the medical examiner, and they can take it from here." I looked at the rat-face lawyer, wanting to sneer back at him, but at the moment I didn't know what I would be sneering about, so I resisted. "What's your problem?" All I needed was an excuse, and I'd smack him. However, I did put down the blade in case the urge to use it overwhelmed me.

"Be in my office tomorrow morning at ten." Apparently, Dover's death meant nothing to him, because he was rocking back and forth from the balls to the heels of his feet. At least some part of him had balls.

"Why?" I didn't want to be anywhere except my own bed at ten. We were nearing 3:00 a.m. now, and I was beat.

"For the reading of the will."

"Whose will, and why would I need to be there?" I was more confused than ever. Someone take pity on me and just answer a question in a straightforward manner, pretty please?

"Dover's. He left everything to you."

Why don't people ever do what you ask them to? That's all I want, just stick to the rules and everything will be fine. Take Harold Dover for instance. All I wanted was the fee I usually charged, to cover expenses, my time and expertise, with a little left over for a pedicure and a laser hair removal. I'm getting tired of shaving my legs.

Unfortunately, I was sitting in his lawyer's office.

Sam and Liz were with me. Sam was supposed to keep me from assaulting the guy, and Liz was keeping me from doing something stupid, such as giving it all back. Both of those options would have been quite satisfying for a moment or two, but in the long run, bad for business.

I still wanted to call him Vermin, because with those small dark eyes that watched everything, he looked quite ratlike. I knew if I turned my back on him for a second, he'd pull a hunk of baby Swiss out of his desk and start nibbling. "The estate is roughly worth three million dollars," Vernon said without preamble.

"Three mill…?" I was stunned. "What am I going to do with all that?" I turned to Liz, cool as ever. Sure. It wasn't happening to her. Sam's brows twitched once. He knew better than to wisecrack me at the moment. Good man.

"We're going to set up an endowment. This is going to make headlines everywhere, Dani, and there may be others out there who might also like to contribute to your work." Liz adjusted her skirt that had ridden up. Vernon's eyes lingered a little too long on her. Rat bastard. "This doesn't benefit you personally, just the business."

"Thank the stars for that! What the hell would I do with that kind of money anyway?" I know, you think that's totally stupid, but truly, too much money has ruined many lives of people who weren't prepared for it.

"We'll set up a meeting with an investment guy I know. Don't worry."

"Thanks, Liz." I stood. Meeting over.

"Keep in touch, Miss Wright," Vernon said and handed me a business card. I took it, making sure I didn't touch his fingers. Who knew what kind of vibes I'd get from that guy? *Ick.*

We left the office and opened the door to pure chaos. Someone had alerted the media about our meeting. We were assaulted on all sides by camera flashes, people shouting at us and others throwing insults. "Come on, Dani, give us a minute," one of the reporters called out.

"Hi, Mike." I paused on the steps, and Sam nearly ran me down, but managed to keep us from embarrassing ourselves in front of the cameras. He stood behind me until he caught his balance. He was so close that I felt his gun pressing into my butt. At least I think it was his gun.

"We hear you're a wealthy woman now, Miss Wright. Will you now perform resurrections without the support of the state?"

"Now, where'd you hear that? I'll be continuing on as usual."

"You know my sources are protected. Is there any truth to it?"

"I'll continue to perform resurrections as long as the requests fall within current guidelines." Deep breath in and long breath out. I'd talked to the press just a few days ago. I could do it again without having a coronary.

"We'll keep you posted. Right now we're on our way to another appointment," Liz said. Sam took each of us under his arms and escorted us away from the gawkers and press. Trying to go down the stairs together was awkward, but after a few seconds, we arrived at his truck, and he released us.

"Jeez. Of all the—"

Three shots popped and a window on Sam's truck shattered. It was the middle of the damned day! Glass grazed my cheek. Getting out of bed so early had been a righteous mistake. I dropped and rolled under the truck, not caring if I was hit by a car on the street, but I was not about to be shot in the back by a coward. Whoever it was. With my right hand I pulled the gun and scraped the back of my hand on the pavement.

"Sam! Liz!"

"Stay under the truck," he said. From where I was, I could see him crouched by the front tire.

"Where's Liz?"

"She's with me," Sam said. She didn't reply, so I was certain he'd shushed her. Then I realized something else was wrong as the crowd scattered. The gunman was getting closer. Surely someone had called 911 by now. I focused on the guy who was trying to kill us. This was taking protest a little too far. I rolled again, coming out from under the truck at the tailgate.

"Come out, come out, wherever you are." A man with a singsongy voice called to us and every hair on my body stood out. There was something so sinister in the intent in opposition to the sweet voice, it gave me more creeps than I already had. I didn't recognize the voice and wasn't about to stick my head out to try to ID him.

Then I heard what I never wanted to hear again. The sound of someone trying to breathe through blood in their lungs. Someone was hit, bad. I didn't know who it was. I might be able to help if I could get out from under the damned tires, but the gunman was getting closer.

Footsteps approached, then hesitated. I got a look at a pair of scuffed loafers. And jeans. Not helpful. "Where are you, my little lamb chop?" Who the hell was lamb chop? It wasn't me, and it certainly wasn't Sam.

Liz.

No! This wasn't going to happen. I wouldn't, I couldn't let a spirit die because of my work. Dammit, I should have listened to the warning from The Dark, but how was I supposed to do that and live with myself? I crawled toward the passenger side of the truck and was able to scoot around the right rear tire, then duckwalk toward the front. I heard him moving around the front. Sam was gonna put a bullet in his brain the second he made the corner. If this asshole had hurt Liz, I wanted him alive so I could pound him into the ground myself.

The raspy breathing sounds grew louder as I approached the front of the truck. My stomach clenched, but I pushed it down.

"There you are, darling," he said. "I've missed you."

I came around the front. "Stop." The halt-or-I'll-shoot thing doesn't work for me.

Liz sat, legs sprawled out in front of her by the back tire. She looked like a rag doll that had fallen over and lost a shoe.

"Go ahead, shoot me," the guy said and raised his gun toward Liz. Before I could even think of blinking, a cannon went off behind me, and the guy dropped.

Sam surged forward, and kicked the guy's pistol out of reach. "Dani, you okay?"

"Yeah." I rushed to Liz, knowing that Sam was going to handle the dude on the ground. "Liz!" I tried to sit her upright again, but she was unconscious. "No, no, no, no, no." I tried to shake her. "Liz, wake up." Desperation clawed at my insides.

I holstered my gun and shot into E.R.-nurse mode. Once an E.R. nurse, always an E.R. nurse. First, I had to see how injured she was. Maybe it was just fright or a good scare, and she had simply fainted. As she turned from a sickly pale to a ghastly gray, I knew she was dying. Her head was okay, nothing in the neck, but blood pooled between her legs and puddled beneath my boots. I ripped open her shirt, heedless of her modesty. As soon as I clasped the fabric, I knew she was bleeding out. The blouse squished in my fingers. When I tore it apart, bloody splatters flew in all directions.

There was a hole, right over her left chest wall. It didn't look like much, but some bullet wounds don't. It was about the size of a dime with jagged edges. It gushed like a raging river. Her aorta or another major vessel was gone. My breath came in short gasps, almost matching her dying breaths.

I clenched my teeth together and tried not to scream. If I started, I'd never stop. "Liz. Stay with me, girl, stay with me." I pressed the palm of my hand to her wound, and that was a mistake. Her pain became mine, but how the hell else could I stop the flow of her life onto the pavement? The only thing I had was my hand.

Sam hovered close to me. "Help's coming. How is she?"

"Dying." From the tone of his voice a second ago, he already knew what I was going to say.

"If anyone can save her, it's you." He placed his hand on my shoulder and squeezed. He tried to push energy to me, but the emotion of it would undo me, so I pushed it back. Dammit! This had to be more influence of The Dark. It was fucking ruining my life, and I wasn't going to let it. Nothing was going to stop me from bringing Liz back. Nothing. Not even an unseen foe from the beyond. Somehow, I would find a way to defeat it, starting with resurrecting Liz.

My lips trembled and tears filled my eyes, dripping down to mingle with the flood of blood. I was so not a tough chick at the moment. "Liz, I'm going to save you. I'm going to bring you back. Don't worry." I whispered what I hoped were soothing words to her that I knew she would hear on some level.

My worst fears were coming true, and The Dark was winning.

She died in my arms.

Chapter 12

For the rest of the day, I was in a numb fog. I felt as if I was walking through chest-deep water. Of course, we had to give statements to the police. Several other people were injured, but only Liz had been killed. I didn't know whether to be thankful or outrageously pissed. The gunman was her damned ex-husband, Jerry. He'd never been this aggressive before, so I wondered if The Dark was somehow manipulating him, egging him on. Thankfully, Sam hadn't killed him, so there was a chance for resurrection and life-swap. Having known Liz as I did, she would have wanted the resurrection. Dying like this was not in her makeup, especially not at Jerry's hands. She'd worked too hard to get away from him and would never have wanted him to win.

When I was certain nothing more could be done for Liz, I removed my hand from her chest, and held her, leaning against Sam's truck. I vowed to bring her back to life as well as the justice she deserved. Every victim like Liz deserved justice. The violated part inside

me screamed for it for every woman, child or man who
had been murdered. Every cell in my body vibrated at
a new frequency, fueled by the atrocity playing out in
front of me.

One paramedic crew looked after Jerry and whisked
him away, lights flashing, sirens blaring to the hospital. Yeah. His life was gonna get saved. Until I took it
from him.

Sam approached. I stood and dropped the blanket. I
didn't even look at him, just started walking. "Get me
out of here."

"Gladly."

We walked side by side away from the scene and
caught a cab back to my truck, parked at the police station. I didn't want to go inside, to see the sympathy and
feel the grief hanging around the office.

"Move over," Sam said and shoved me across the seat
from the driver's side to the passenger side.

"This is my truck, dammit."

"Yeah, and I'm driving it." He held his hand out,
and I reluctantly slapped the keys into it. If anyone else
had said that, I'd have stuck my fist up his nose. But it
was Sam, and I trusted him with my life, my firearms,
my body and now, apparently, my truck. In silence we
drove to my place.

"Everything's gone to hell, hasn't it?" I mumbled
aloud as he pulled into my driveway. Crime scene
tape was an obnoxious yellow color. Now, it fluttered
brightly in front of my door. The insurance adjuster had
been there and made his assessment, but I still probably
ought to find a hotel. First, I needed a shower.

"Pack a bag. Enough for a few days."

"Why?"

"We're getting out of town. I'm on forced leave for a few days, and you need to rest after today." He turned off the truck, and we went inside. It didn't take long to shower and pack a bag. I had my weapons in one already, and I stuffed a bunch of crap I probably didn't need into another.

"Where?" I didn't much care.

"Zuni Mountains. My uncle has a place out there we can use."

Two and a half hours passed as we drove west on Interstate 40 in silence. Just west of Albuquerque there's a whole lot of nothing. The road cuts right through red rock canyons, then an Indian reservation, Laguna Pueblo. After that it's just miles of high desert until you reach the small town of Grants. It had been a boomtown at one time for uranium mining. Now, the old miners were glowing in the dark. They're dying of cancers related to uranium exposure, thanks to our government. When will we ever learn?

We headed south on a two-lane road that began to climb from around sixty-five hundred feet up over the Continental Divide to over seven thousand feet. Made my ears pop. Then down past the blown-out cauldron of an ancient volcano. The edge of it was still visible as we moved around the curves of the road that seemed to hug the land and move with it, instead of plowing through it like the highway.

Past El Morro National Monument we turned again, and by then the sky had turned a dusky shade, somewhere between purple and lavender with peach swiped over top. Sort of like melting ice cream, instead of sorbet this time, but without the calories.

Eventually, just as darkness draped its inky cloak

over us, we pulled into the driveway of a modest adobe house. I stood in the doorway, not quite sure what to do with myself, so I shoved my hands into the pockets of my blazer and discovered my cell phone. It hadn't gone off in hours. I pulled it out to check for messages. None and no service out here either. There was a goddess.

Sam busied himself bringing firewood in, and he built a fire in the kiva in the corner of the living room. A kiva is an adobe fireplace built into a corner of the house, with an oval mouth where the wood burns. Cedar, mesquite and juniper are mostly what are found around here. "Tell me what you need. Wanna get drunk? It's too dark to go shoot anything now, but we can in the morning." The man knows me too well. Maybe that blood-exchange thingie hadn't been a good idea after all.

Anger and the need for revenge burned inside me and needed an outlet or it would feed on me. I felt as if The Dark was now influencing me. By causing my friend to be killed, it stimulated the harsher side of me. By putting horrific cases like Roberto in front of me, it tried to shake my confidence and my resolve. Now that I realized this, I was more determined than ever. With Sam as my partner, we could be invincible. Slowly, I raised my eyes to his and found a tiny measure of energy pulsing to life. "I need to hit something."

"Why am I not surprised?" He removed his jacket and gun, tugged off his boots and socks, and scooted the coffee table out of the way.

"What are you doing?"

"A little sparring might improve your mood."

"My mood is fine." I clenched my teeth together, trying not to make that sour face my grandmother does when she doesn't want to take her medicine.

"Doesn't look like it to me." He poked me in the shoulder.

"Fine." I tore off my jacket and tossed it on top of his while he circled me. The man was sneaky, and he had military training, so I watched him closely as I shed the shoulder holster and the knife sheath on my left arm. And the derringer tucked somewhere you don't want to know about. The boots were last, because they were the hardest to get rid of. I bent over and pulled them off, tossed them and my socks beside the couch. "Is your uncle going to mind if we wreck his house?"

"We aren't going to wreck it. We're just going to burn off a little energy." He crowded me, arms at his sides. "Hit me."

"No." I couldn't just smack him. That wasn't fair. Backing up, I tried to get away from him, but he kept pushing me.

"Come on, Dani. I can take it." He bumped me again and knocked me back a few feet, but I recovered quickly. "Show me what you got, baby."

He'd already seen what I got, but that was a whole different kind of sport.

"Get away from me, you Neanderthal." I twisted to the side, but he anticipated and blocked me. Probably learned that shit in the military. And I thought I was gonna spar with *him?* I was out of my mind.

"What are you afraid of, *chica?*"

"Not you." I ground my teeth together. He was not going to get to me. I could hold my ground. I didn't care what kind of training he had. I had been dead and survived.

"Think you can't handle me? Think I'm too much for you? Without your gun you're nothing, and you know it."

He was trying to piss me off. Though I knew this intellectually, emotionally was something else. The fire in me burned brighter.

"Fine." I came at him, but he was quick, and I wasn't trying very hard. We'd never sparred together, so neither of us knew what the other was capable of. I had my suspicions that Sam was going to take me in more ways than one, given the height and weight difference. But I was pissed. At the universe, The Dark, the othersiders, but mostly at myself for not saving Liz. Anger can be very motivating. Or it can work against you. I was betting that it was going to do things for me. Anger boiled somewhere deep inside me like the ruptured volcano we had passed. I just hadn't blown yet.

"Come on, baby, I can take what you got, whatever it is." He bounced lightly on his feet, but kept his hands loose in front of him, and I looked for an opening. "You're such a girl."

That did it.

No one, not even Sam, called me a girl and got away with it. I went at him, kicking, jabbing, anything, but he pushed me easily away with a patronizing smile plastered on his face. Dammit, he was having fun, enjoying it too much.

"That all you got?" He came after me and had the unfair advantage of long arms and legs. With my height I almost held my own, but he had a reach I couldn't defend against. Each time I attacked he pushed me off. When he attacked I lost ground, and I sensed he was holding back.

Dammit. I was *such* a girl. Unable to penetrate his defenses, I groaned, and punched out from pure frustration.

I hit him right in the nose. He recoiled and bent over, grabbing his face. My anger vanished. Shit. I hadn't really meant to hurt him. If I broke that beautiful nose of his, I was gonna pay a plastic surgeon to put it back.

"Oh! Sam, I'm sorry. Are you okay?" I put my hand on his shoulder. I was such an idiot sometimes and let my emotions get the better of me. "Let me see."

Slowly he turned, then straightened. There wasn't a mark on him. "I'll show you mine if you show me yours." Before I knew it, he had me on my back on the floor.

I gasped, outraged. "You *cheat!*" Squirming, I struggled to free myself from his grip, but he only held me tighter. I hadn't known he was that strong, or I would have never engaged him in a spar. "Get off me."

"No." He took my hands and shoved them over my head. Just like that. So much for self-defense classes. I want my money back.

"Get off me. I'm not kidding." I was so not kidding, but I was so stuck.

"Make me."

Oh, I *hate* when people say that. I always feel compelled to try. Just as I was back in grade school getting into fights with boys on the playground. I grew up with boys, and the only way I knew how to communicate with them was by giving them a good wallop. That usually got their attention. Now, struggling, I gave everything I had left to Sam, but he didn't freakin' budge. Oaf.

"Give up?" he asked and trapped my legs with his.

"Never." I never give up. It's what had kept me alive. Never mind *want,* I'm going to *demand* my money back for those self-defense classes. They obviously had taught me nothing.

Renewed struggling on my part simply resulted in a massive erection on his part. This was not going as I had planned, so it was time to change tactics. "Sam." For a second I stilled to catch my breath. My heart was racing, and I wasn't sure if it was from the struggle or something else looming inside me.

"All you have to say is 'surrender.'" He grinned, knowing that word was so not in my vocab.

"Never." Struggling again was useless, but I tried anyway. All I succeeded in doing was grinding my crotch into his and making him grin wider. "I hate you!" Chest working too hard, I gasped for air and glared at him. I would not say the word. "I am *not* a girl."

He gave a low chuckle and allowed his gaze to trot down over my chest and back up over my face. "You certainly are not a girl. You're all woman. Every last inch of you."

The light in his eyes turned from playful to wanting. I allowed my gaze to drift down to his mouth, which had moved closer to mine. His nearness was intoxicating. Who needed tequila when Sam was around? I took a deep breath that left me in an unexpected, erratic rush. I was *so* not doing the emotional scene. I wasn't, I wasn't, I wasn't. It just wasn't me, but tears pricked my eyes and overflowed down into my ears anyway.

"Let it go, babe. Just let it go." His gentle voice unlocked the dam of frustrated emotions inside me.

"I can't," I said, my lower lip wobbling anyway. "I don't cry." As the emotions of the day overwhelmed me,

I did indeed cry. Sobs choked out of me, and I made sounds I had never made before.

Liz was dead. Two eternal stars had been captured. Was The Dark behind Robbie Ramirez, too? The Dark wanted to force me to stop my work, but I couldn't. If I didn't give in, was Sam next?

Sam released my hands and legs and simply held me as I cried. Rolling over, I pressed my face to the cool tile floor and let it go.

Curled against my back, Sam held me loosely in his arms. Spanish words of comfort flowed out of him and soothed me, as did the gentleness of his touch. So many times in the past week I'd needed him, and he'd helped me, but other than satisfying his sexual needs, had I really extended myself to help him the way he helped me now? He had hurts that burned him deeply. Could I ease his pain? I didn't know.

Thankfully, it was mostly dark, except for the light from the kiva. I turned and sat. Sam sat, too. With only the firelight for illumination, I was glad it hid my messy face. I tried to brush the remaining tears away, but new ones simply replaced them. Without a word, Sam gathered me against his chest, and I let him. I was sort of sitting on the floor between his legs, leaning into his chest, and his arms curved around me. He soothed me, and rocked me, and for once, I didn't argue. I trusted him more than any man I'd ever known, and more than my libido was falling for him. Allowing him to hold me felt really good. No one had held me when I returned from the dead, and this embrace was an indulgence I rarely made.

"Better?"

"No." The headache behind my eyes was throbbing

already, as if someone had stuck a screwdriver through my left eye. Raising my hand to his cheek, I turned his face to mine. The soft sound of his voice created a hum in my blood that had nothing to do with soothing. "Thanks." I gave him a soft kiss he accepted, and my blood warmed. I guess it was the contact of my palm with his skin that did it. For a moment I'd forgotten about guarding my palms against the contact. It could have been the emotional outburst, but whatever it was, I needed it. I needed Sam.

Sam cupped the left side of my face with his right hand. "Things are different between us since we shared the blood." He stroked his thumb over my lower lip, and I tasted salt on my tongue.

"I noticed." There was no denying that. Even when he wasn't inside me, he was inside me.

"I feel you in me, in my mind, sometimes. Faint, but you're there." He brushed my hair back from my face with his fingers, then tucked the mass behind my ear. It was such a sweet gesture, and the tears nearly returned.

I could only nod, as the experience had been the same with me. "I need you now. Can you feel that?" Clutching his shirt in my fist, I pulled him toward me.

"Yeah. I feel it. I need you, too. Like I've never needed anyone." He lowered his head and kissed me. Eagerly, I parted my lips for him, the taste of him. The silken glide of his tongue against mine turned the emotion of the day into the rapture of the night.

Soft and slow, he kissed me, seduced me with this mouth, and lowered me to the floor. My trembling fingers tugged at his shirt, and he pulled back long enough to whip the garment off. His gentle hands eased the hem of my shirt up and off, then worked the front-hook clasp of my bra. I love front-hook bras for this very reason. Whoever invented them ought to get a Pulitzer. Tenderness drove every movement, and he sucked my nipples. There's a little-known neurological highway that runs between a woman's nipples and her clitoris. Sam must have been aware of this secret, because he used it so well. He'd obviously paid attention in anatomy class. Some women have been known to orgasm from nipple stimulation alone, and I was well on my way.

The rest of our clothing fell away as we undressed each other, touching, teasing, relearning the shape and feel of each other. He was a sight to behold as I lay back, and he moved over me. The firelight illuminated his face, but left shadows of mystery. I wanted his weight on me, I wanted his sweat dripping on me, I wanted him buried deep inside me. I needed it. I needed him. Now.

I parted my legs and reached for his erection, guiding him to my center. He was hot and hard in my hand, and I stroked my thumb over the peak of him. He was ready and so was I. Sam eased into me. Parting my feminine flesh, he joined with me at last, and I sighed as he filled me, filling parts of me I hadn't known were empty.

"Surrender," I sighed into his mouth. The fire that had just raged within me now burned slow and white hot. He kissed me again, and there were no more words between us. I tightened my legs around him, pulling him deep. The fire flared brighter inside me, flashed to a critical point. The fire in the kiva sparked, and then I did. The quick wave of pleasure took me, caught me by surprise, and I gave in to it. It crested and crashed, dragging me under with it. My cries were smothered beneath Sam's mouth, and soon his cries mingled with mine. Together we came, pulsing to a rhythm shared by the ancients that only deepened with the night.

"You didn't let me finish." Sam raised his head.

"I beg your pardon." I wiggled my hips. "I believe you finished quite nicely."

"Not what I meant." He remained joined with me, but eased some of his weight up with his hands. "When I said I could hear you in my mind sometimes."

"Oh, that. How silly of me." A flaming orgasm just makes me giddy. So sue me.

Now, he eased back and settled beside me. "Like when you opened the portal at the Dover ritual and I heard the other-sider speak to you."

I sat up, reluctantly coming back to the real world, and curled my feet under me. Being naked in front of Sam was no longer so frightening. And it was still quite dark, so my scars were mostly hidden.

"The others were there and nobody else saw or heard anything." He shrugged. "But I did."

"Do you know what this means?" Reaching out, I stroked my hand down one strong shoulder and over his arm. Little sparks flashed from him to me, but they were only pulses of good feelings.

"No, do you?"

"Hell, no. But I'm hoping that together we can learn more about what's going on. You have cop instincts I just don't have, and I have an unfortunate learning experience that you don't. Together we might be able to pool our power and take back the eternal stars." Oh, this was exciting stuff! The Dovers might not be done for just yet.

Sam paused for a second, looked away from me, then back. "About that unfortunate learning experience. You told me about how you died." He stroked a hand down my back and rested it on my hip, as if he liked the feel of my skin beneath his. "Do you think it would help for me to know all of the details?"

That was a change of topic I hadn't expected, and I swallowed down the anxiety that immediately tried to surge up my throat. It was my turn to hesitate. I looked at him, considering. "You ask me to share my secrets, but I don't know any of yours."

He pulled back. "Nothing about me will help save the Dovers."

"How do you know? This universal imbalance didn't just start with me. It's been going on since time began probably."

"I've probably done more to harm than balance the scales," he said and looked away. He was withdrawing. I felt it inside me, and I reached out to him.

"Don't leave me, Sam. Don't leave." Panic flared, but I shoved it down. "We're together for a reason. I know it."

"I'm not going anywhere," he said, but his jaw was still clenched, eyes guarded.

"If I've overstepped my boundaries, I'm sorry." I shoved a hand through my hair, wanting to push him a little. "There's so much about you I don't know. We're off balance, and I'm beginning to realize there needs to be balance in any relationship."

"Ask me whatever you want, but it won't help." He clenched his jaw and a muscle twitched in it. Although he hated that I was asking, he would answer me, tell me the truth about him. For now, that was enough.

"Will you tell me about your pain someday? I know

you have it. I feel it inside me sometimes, but you always push it back."

The look in his eyes pulled me in. There was pain there and also relief. Sharing a story takes the sting out of some things.

"Yes."

I've shared more with this man than any other. He knows me better than anyone, knows me as well as I allow anyone to know me. There are some secrets that are mine alone to keep, but he knows me.

This moment, this request from him, although not couched in those terms, was about trust. Did I trust him with my past, with what could get me killed? I did, but did he trust me?

He did. I know he did, but some pain is too deep to ever recover from.

We sat entwined in each other, still naked, but warmed by the fire. So I told him everything. The kidnapping, having my child cut out of me, his death, my death, and then meeting with the other-sider who healed me.

"You know pretty much the rest. Survived, hospitalization and recovery, then focused on weapons training, martial arts and opening the business." I shrugged. Some of it seemed too long ago. "It made me a completely different person than I had been." There was no shame in any of it. No apology for who I had been or who I am now.

Sam cupped my face in his hands and made me look up him. He was so intense, so serious, and I was surprised at the ferocity of him. A flash of memory that I knew wasn't mine surfaced. Firefight in a jungle. Bombs screeching overhead. The weight of another slung over my shoulder. More death than one could imagine. For a second I was sucked into the noise and assaulted by the smells, then Sam's voice brought me out of it. "I will never, *ever* call you a girl again."

"If you do, I'll bust your ass. No one calls me a girl and gets away with it." I gave him a playful slug in the chest as the memory faded. Protecting my hands against touching him again, I kept a loose fist. Not that I'd have hurt him anyway. He's such a rock.

"You have my apology."

"Apology not necessary, but accepted." I stood and stretched. Sitting on a tile floor for too long makes my bones ache.

"Oh!" Turning, I stared at him a second. Something just occurred to me. "Do you remember when I stayed with you the night of the fire? We woke up dreaming early in the morning."

"Yeah. What about it?" He stood and stretched too. So he wasn't impervious to physical exertion or hard tiles either. Good to know.

"You said you heard something, and I thought I had too. I didn't tell you." I grabbed my jeans and stuck them on. "I had an auditory hallucination when I was in the steam room at the karate studio."

"A hallucination? Was there something funky in the steam?" He pulled his clothing on. "Incense gone bad or something?"

"No, weirdo. I guess I fell asleep. A voice woke me up, saying 'it's in the yard.' Any idea what that could mean, supersleuth?" Now that I was dressed, I was feeling a little more snarky and back to my usual charming self. Maybe a good cry and smokin' sex helped my

disposition, though I could have lived without the crying part.

"None."

He opened the front door.

"Are we leaving?" I was confused. We'd just gotten there.

"No. Just going outside for a minute."

O-*kay*. Pausing for a second, I pondered whether to
follow or give him some space. Eh, I voted going outside. Danger was my middle name, and I kick personal
boundaries in the teeth.

Two steps out into the driveway my breath lodged in
my throat, and I halted. The nubs on my legs stood out.
Sam stood there casually looking up at the sky. However, the spectacular view overhead stunned me stupid.

"Oh, wow." I stood there with my mouth hanging
open. "That's the most amazing thing I've ever seen."

"Thank you."

I nearly choked and tried not to snort. "Not you. The
sky, you egomaniac."

"Oh." He walked closer to me and admired the view,
as well. "I'd almost forgotten how close the stars are
out here."

"Do you think the other-sider was right? That the
stars are being taken by The Dark? I mean, if you believe the stars are souls that come and go." How can
you tell if there are fewer stars up there?

"I don't know what I believe about that, but having
heard the other-sider tell you about The Dark, I'm inclined to believe it."

My grief over the journals and Liz extended to him.
"I'm sorry I got you into this." So many people had
been hurt or killed because of my work. Had I gotten

careless, or too cavalier, or had the world taken on a more sinister tone?

"If I hadn't wanted to share my blood with you, I wouldn't have. It's not your fault, Dani. None of this is. I was raised by a resurrectionist. I know the score. I chose to help you, and I would choose to again." He put his arm around my shoulders, and the gesture was a comfort.

"Thank you." The sky drew my attention again as a series of stars dropped from the inky sky and plummeted toward us. I almost reached out to catch them. "I wonder if those are the souls coming back."

"If we choose to believe the other-siders, you could be right. If we choose to only believe science or religion, you're wrong, and we're witnessing a meteor shower." After a pause, he continued. "Maybe we can help them."

"I hope so." Leaning against Sam, I watched as more stars fell. A sense of peace came over me for a moment, as if I were in the right place at the right time, and I knew my purpose here. For once, all felt right with me.

And then it was over.

Chapter 13

A spectacular light glowed behind us, and we turned. Why was I not surprised to see an other-sider there? "Hello." Freaking out when they arrived was just a waste of energy, so I stopped doing that. Then two more appeared, and I reconsidered.

"We greet you, Danielle." This was a little different, seeing them out here and no Burton in sight. "Your suppositions are correct. What you view are the souls of our brethren returning to your plane. They also chose, as did Samuel, before coming to this plane." Their focus moved away from me, to him.

Though I didn't hear a voice aloud, I felt it vibrating inside my mind, communicating to us. Sam was definitely in on this conversation. "How can we help you?"

"Balance is being destroyed by The Dark. It has chosen to steal the souls returning to the nebula. If it is not stopped, the universe will go dark."

Uh-oh. That didn't sound good for any of us. "How are we going to stop that from happening? That's way out of our league." We were so small compared with what they were talking about.

"Continue the work you do, and we will help."

"You can help me by sending someone to help me." That sounded odd, but they knew what I meant.

"The soul beside you was sent to you. Do you not find him helpful?"

For a nanosecond I pictured us in a naked clinch. Now I *know* that wasn't what they meant, but yeah, I found him *helpful*. "Thank you." Humility in front of eternal beings could only score me some brownie points, right?

"The blood inside him carries that of another like you."

"Yeah, we figured that out already." Thanks, *abuela*.

"More blood sacrifice may be required to fulfill your mission."

"No. Absolutely not." I was not sacrificing Sam to further the cause. "I will never sacrifice Sam or any of my friends again. Why can't you…people, or whatever you are, bloody well just answer a question when I ask?" I shoved my hand through my hair. "What does, 'it's in the yard' mean? Someone from the other side spoke to us, trying to give us information. I know they did, but we can't figure it out by ourselves."

"Do you not wish to learn?" No judgments, just a simple question. They were so unemotional.

"Not right now, I don't." Frustration doesn't even begin to explain it. I'm out here trying to learn my craft. There is no resurrectionist library to reference. I'm almost alone. Even as much as Sam helps me, he isn't a resurrectionist.

"Your crystal is a guide. It is not simply decorative."

"I gathered that when it nearly blinded me."

"Dani," Sam said through clenched teeth and nudged me. I'd forgotten he'd never seen them before and was probably freaked out.

"Sorry." So much for humility. For me, it's fleeting, just like my charm. I took a deep breath and let it out slowly.

"The wisdom you seek is there between you." One of them held out an appendage that couldn't rightly be called a hand or arm, but something dangled from it. "The choice has always been yours, Samuel. Take this amulet and wear it. It will join your soul with Danielle's when you choose to make it so."

Without hesitation, Sam took the amulet from the other-sider. He's such a man, so responsible, so good. So wasted on me. He placed the pendant around his neck, but nothing happened. That was a relief. It was just a crystal shaped like a helix, kind of a double corkscrew made of quartz. Just like mine.

"It's not doing anything." He looked from the pendant to the other-sider.

"When you choose it, it will bond you. For now, it is dormant." Now that just explained everything, didn't it?

The other-siders eased back from us, and I sensed they were about to go.

"We can't do this." Someone had to tell them, so it might as well be me. "We just can't do what you ask of us. It's too much. Why can't you do it on your own? I'm plenty busy with the first mission you gave me." I thought about Liz, and my heart cramped.

"We are aware of your dedication to Elizabeth. If our efforts had been fruitful, we would not wish to enlist your assistance."

"If you can't figure out how to stop it, how the hell do you think I'm going to? And how do we retrieve the Dover souls from The Dark?" I'm not that smart.

"Our council of old souls is meeting to assist in their recovery, but those questions do not have answers at this time."

"Figures."

I felt a shift in the energy coming off them. It wasn't a good feeling, either. "You can't give up. If you've taught me anything since my return, you've taught me that."

"That sentiment is one of benefit to you."

"But not to you? How can you say that?" I was about to tear my hair out over this.

"The future is not set, and we have hope, but The Dark is a strong force."

"You are stronger." Of that I was certain. I refused to think otherwise, or I'd never succeed at any of this.

"The struggle is not over. The future is not set."

Sam raised the amulet, then let it drop against his chest. "Thank you for this."

"We feel your sentiment is genuine, Samuel, and we will gift you now."

Another uh-oh. When I had been gifted by them, I became a resurrectionist. What did they have in mind for Sam? RoboCop?

"Do not worry, young star." It spoke to me. "Do not fear for this one. All is well. Samuel will be able to hear you now when you call to him. The communication between you must flow both ways to be balanced."

Whatever was flowing between us was already powerful, but I'd take better communication any day. Then, in a snap, they vanished like falling stars in reverse, and the night returned to its previous state of tranquility.

"Wow." Reaching out to Sam, I held his amulet in my fingers. It was cool, nothing special right now.

"I'm just glad I didn't have to be eviscerated to get mine," he said and looked wide-eyed at me. Mr. Innocence, my ass.

Unable to stop it, a laughing snort found its way out of me and a coyote yipped in reply. "You're such a dork sometimes. You have no idea how lucky you are." No freakin' idea.

After admiring the night and its glory for a while longer, we went into the house and slept until the sun could be ignored no more. We spent the remainder of the day brainstorming what to do about Liz and Jerry. Sam made some calls to get an update on his condition. He'd live.

Long enough for me to kill him.

Who says there's no job satisfaction anymore? This case will give me tons, and I won't even charge Liz for it. After the endowment from Dover, I can afford a gratis now and then. Though she charges me for her legal services, this is different. I want her back. I need her back. She's part of the team that's going to bring justice to the cops and their families, to the people who need the service Sam and I provide. She gives voice to the people whom no one can hear. They need it and it's part of the paradigm that will bring balance to the universe. We need the good to counter the evil. That has been going on since time began and can't end now because The Dark has its panties in a twist.

After two days away from Albuquerque, I wanted to get back. We made the trip a lot livelier when we were coming out. The respite was good for both of us.

Sam had to face an internal investigation about the

shooting, and I had to get an order to resurrect Liz. Although Jerry wasn't in charge of her estate, I wasn't sure if her parents were, but they would be the logical choice. While discussing other people's deaths, we'd talked about the end of our lives in general terms. After a few conversations and knowing the way she felt about Jerry, I was absolutely certain she'd want the resurrection.

"Want me to drop you off at the station?" I asked Sam. On the way back, I drove. How very modern of him.

"Sure. I have to see when I can get my truck out of impound. There's at least one window to get replaced."

I touched my cheek, but the small wound had healed. "Keep me posted." I pulled up to the curb, and he got out, but left his gym bag on the floor. Appearances. If anyone saw us, he didn't want them to think we'd been together all weekend. Appearances make a difference in how the men treat me, and what they think of Sam. If they think Sam is banging me, their respect for him will go down the toilet.

We were back to being professionals once more. Without a word, he walked up the stairs to the P.D., and I didn't stick around to watch him go inside.

I had a spontaneous appointment with a certain rat-face lawyer who was going to help me, whether he liked it or not.

My truck requires a full-size space, so I had to park it down the street a few blocks from Vernon's office. As I approached the curb where it had all gone down a few days ago, I shivered, then clenched my teeth and looked away. But I could see in my peripheral vision that the blood had been cleaned up and the curb was in its usual state.

The farther I walked, the faster and more determined

I became. I charged up the stairs to Vernon's office. If he hadn't alerted the press, Liz would still be alive.

Who knocked when they were in the mood I was in? I barged straight past the receptionist.

"Hi, Vernon." He was alone, and stood. Panic made the whites of his eyes show, and he began to sweat. Good.

"Now, Miss Wright. What are you doing here?" He held his hands out as if to ward off an evil spirit. In the mood I was in, I wasn't far from it.

"I've come to collect, Vernon."

"What, the inheritance? It'll be locked up in probate for a while I'm afraid." He dropped his hands and rubbed them on his slacks. I could smell his sweat. Must be one of my enhanced traits.

Making myself at home, I strode to the small refrigerator, grabbed a soda and sat in the plush chair across from him. "That's not why I'm here."

Suspicion appeared in his eyes, but also keen curiosity. He knew I was up to something, but had no idea what. "Then enlighten me. Why are you here?"

"I want Liz back, and you're going to help me."

He gave me that patronizing look that men who thought they were superior acquired, and I knew he was going to say something totally stupid and condescending. So I was ready for it.

"Liz is dead."

See? I knew it was going to be stupid. "I know, you idiot, she died in front of me." I wasn't going to tell him that she died while I held her and felt her spirit slip away while I sobbed in the middle of the street. Deliberately, I set my soda on his desk. An unblemished mahogany desk and not a coaster in sight. Too bad. "If you hadn't alerted the press to our meeting, none of this would have happened." At least I was pretty sure of that. The Dark's powers were growing, that was more obvious every day. I believed that it could influence people into doing things they normally wouldn't, but with a little encouragement from the dark side, who knew what it was capable of? "You're going to help make it right."

"What? I am not." A frown just pinched up his rat face even more.

"Shall I call Mike and ask who sent the press a tip? You know he loves to chat over coffee. It was you or someone in your office, I know." I whipped out my cell phone for added drama. That made him pause a second, and I knew I had him. "I want a court order to resurrect her, and send Jerry to the 'yard."

"I can't do that." The man's eyes nearly popped.

"You're gonna."

"How? It's not my area of practice."

"I don't care. You're going to help me set this to rights."

"Jerry is guilty, has admitted it, so there's little to argue about." At least that confession made things somewhat easier to bear, but I worried about how The Dark was influencing this situation and how pervasive it could be.

"No court battle?" he asked.

"No. Just the life-swap."

"No judge is going to agree to that so soon." He shrugged. "At least no clean one."

"I'm sure you can find one that will." I shifted my position so my blazer drifted away from my body and the gun was clearly visible in my shoulder holster. His gaze went exactly where I wanted it to. That is, after he had a good look at my chest. I knew the second his gaze shifted from my breasts to my gun. No threats were exchanged. I didn't have to threaten him. He looked at me again, and swallowed. Carefully. New respect emerged in his gaze, and he nodded. I wouldn't hurt him to get what I wanted, but he didn't know that.

"I'll see what I can do." The tone of his voice dropped, and I knew I had him for sure.

"Do that." I stood and picked up the soda, then dropped a business card on the desk. "You've got twenty-four hours to make this happen." That was ridiculous, even I knew that, but he didn't know that I knew that.

"There's no way—"

"Find a way." I left and took the stairs down. Elevators are death traps, and I don't need that today.

The medical investigator's office is located behind University Hospital between the law school and the heart of the University of New Mexico. The hospital itself is massive. It's a regional trauma center with a burn unit, and now it boasts a world-class cancer treatment center. The ME's office is a low, nondescript building, but it's a very busy nondescript building.

After signing in and asking to speak to Dr. Allen Goodman, the physician who runs the place, I paced the waiting room. Eagerness pulsed through me. Three days usually have to pass before authorization for release of the body is obtained, so I had plenty of time to get Liz's body to my cryo storage bunker. We'd spent two in the Zuni Mountains, so we were good. It was Monday, early afternoon.

"Hey, Dani. How can I help you?" Dr. Goodman arrived and ushered me out of the locked waiting area. Everything's locked, every entry, every hallway and closet. Even the bathrooms required a code to get into them. Made me wonder if you needed one to get out.

"I've come about Liz. Elizabeth Watkins."

"Oh, yes. Sorry about her. A terrible shame." He shook his head and clucked his tongue.

It wasn't a shame, it was a freaking *crime*. But I nodded and played the grieved friend, which was what I was, even though I had other intentions.

"I didn't do her autopsy, but let's get her paperwork and see what's going on with her." Dr. Goodman carries a load of administrative duties as well as performs autopsies. All of the names are recorded in various places, but the easiest way to find one is by looking at the dry-erase board behind the clerk's desk.

Dr. Goodman made that curious *hmm* sound all physicians learn somewhere. He squinted at the board from behind wire-rimmed glasses, then flipped through the first few sheets on the clipboard.

"What is it?" I was getting a sneaking suspicion I wasn't going to like something.

"She's gone. Been released to the funeral home. For cremation."

"What?" I grabbed him by the lapel of his lab coat. I had to, or I was going to keel over. "No. Look again." If she's been cremated already, there will be no bringing her back. There's no way that Sam and I, even with our power pooled, could overcome that kind of challenge.

"Dani, I'm sorry." He put down the clipboard and patted my hand. "Mortuary picked her up two hours ago."

"What? Which mortuary?" I was freaking out. Had her parents lost their minds? Or were they so grief-stricken they weren't thinking right?

"Autopsy was done on Saturday and the body released to her family this morning. Dani, I'm sorry." His eyes were wide and his brows raised. He looked a little scared.

"When's the cremation?" If it wasn't too late, maybe I could get to her family and convince them I could help. Liz obviously hadn't communicated her final wishes to them. Probably because she never dreamed Jerry would kill her. If I couldn't get to them, Vernon would have to get a court order to stop it. What would that be? A stay of cremation? I didn't know, but I had to get out of there fast.

"Cremations are done at night, and it's Streamline Services down on Fourth Street."

"Thanks, Doc." I tossed him my visitor's badge and dashed out the loading dock entrance, pulling my phone out of my pocket at the same time. I raced around the building to my truck. Think, think, think, dammit.

Though I drove through sixteen red lights, the chase was futile. I got nowhere with the mortuary. The watchdog secretary at the front wouldn't give me anything. So much for professional courtesy. I send them business all the time, but could they give me one shred of help? No.

Against company policy to give out information. If you're not family we can't help you, don'tcha know?

Sarcasm was just oozing out of me. I hate it when I have to be nice to get information out of people, when reaching over the desk and choking it out of them would be so much simpler and more satisfying. Of course, the bulletproof glass the woman sat behind had been an issue.

Jerry.

He'd know the information I wanted. Jumping back

into the truck, I headed back through the same sixteen lights to University Hospital. This had been my hospital once. I knew all of the stairwells, the shortcuts, the staff entrances and the back ways around it.

Until construction had screwed everything up. Dammit. I was going to have to go in there like a civilian. I stopped at security for a visitor's pass. They were new guys and didn't recognize me as a former staff person, so I made sure my blazer covered my gun. I have a carry permit, but security guys get overly excited when they see a visitor carrying weapons. Don't need that today.

I asked for Jerry, but he wasn't listed. Sam had put two bullets in him three days ago. Unless he died of fright, he was still here. There was a DNI status that VIPs could be admitted under. So could wastes of human flesh, for their own protection. Do Not Identify. No information about them was to be made public, not even that they were in the hospital.

"Since I'm here, I might as well eat. Where's the cafeteria?" I accepted the visitor's badge and clipped it to the chain on my crystal.

"Nice piece," the guy with Roy on his name tag said. "Guy was in here a bit ago with one just like it."

"This is a one of a kind. No one has one like it." Idiot.

"You got ripped off, lady, 'cause there was a guy wearing one just like it." He snorted, obviously thinking I was the idiot. We'd see about that. "Take the elevator down one flight, then follow the yellow brick road to the cafeteria."

Sometimes I just can't help myself, and one day it's going to get me into trouble. I widened my eyes and gasped. "Like, OMG, you have a Yellow Brick Road, just like in the *Wizard of Oz?*" I flipped my hair back and gave a brilliant smile to ol' Roy. "Are there, like, flying monkeys, too? That's *s-o-o-o-o-o-o* unsanitary."

"Uh, no. There are just yellow tiles *painted* on the floor. Just follow them, and you'll get there." He frowned and considered my mental capacity. "I think."

I nodded and blinked a few times, as if I were having difficulty processing that information. "O-o-h. I get it." I turned and walked away, leaving Roy more confused than ever. Some men are just meant to be tortured.

Shoving through the door to the stairwell beside the elevator, I paused. Had Sam been here? He'd know how to find Jerry. I paused on the landing below and pulled out my phone to call him. No bars. No cell phone service inside the hospital. Too many electronic gizmos in one place interferes with cell service. Was I actually going to have to do it the old-fashioned way and find a landline to call him on? OMG indeed. If he were still in the hospital, he wouldn't get the call anyway. Dammit.

Then something the other-siders had said jolted my brain. They had said our communication abilities were enhanced now. So, could I just make a *cerebral call* to Sam? Oh, this was just too weird, but I had to try. Time was running out.

So, did I just think of him or actually say his name in my head? *Sam? Sam, are you here?*

I waited a few seconds, but there was no returning call in my mind. I was such an idiot for believing in this. At least I was an idiot alone in the stairwell.

Just as I reached for the door to the first floor to let myself out, it opened.

Sam stood there.

"I know it's a relatively small city, but how is it even remotely possible that you're standing there?"

"You called me, didn't you?" He stood to the side to let me through.

"There's no cell service in the hospital." See what he had to say about that as I led the way toward the cafeteria.

"In my mind. I heard you in my head, Dani."

He said it as if it was something I did every day. I shook my head. Wow. Maybe balancing things was going to be possible, if this was any evidence. Maybe Sam and I together had something special that could defeat The Dark, or at least put its panties in a twist. We needed those damned journals though to prove it. "What I mean is, doesn't this even seem remotely freaky to you?"

"Yes, it's extremely freaky to me. I keep wondering if I'm going to wake up from a head injury or something."

Stopping in the hallway that was flooded with staff coming and going, I pulled him to the side. I gave him the details about the pending cremation.

"Do you know where Jerry is? What floor, what unit?" There are so many different types of units for different types of patients scattered throughout the hospital, we'd never be able to track him down.

"He's on the pediatric ward."

"Peds? What the hell is he doing there?"

"Who's going to look for an adult prisoner with guards in the children's ward?"

"Who, indeed?" Not even I had thought of that one. I patted him on the arm. "Glad you have connections. Let's go."

"Dani, you just can't go barging in there." I ignored the amusement on his face.

"Watch me."

* * *

Or not.

I charged toward the elevators, away from the pediatric unit, steam fuming from every orifice, and Sam standing silently beside me. The energy coming off him was so I-told-you-so, he didn't have to speak it. By now, he knows better.

The guard outside Jerry's door was like a Hispanic version of Mr. Clean. Big, bad, bald. There had been no getting past him with or without credentials. Rather than getting myself arrested and becoming totally useless, I left.

"Now what?" Sam asked.

"I'm going to have to steal a body, and you're going to help me."

"I can't believe this." He shook his head. The doors to the elevator swooshed open. Sam and I squeezed out as others squeezed in. There is no courtesy at the doors of elevators. "I've done a lot of unsavory things in my life, but never something like this." I'd have to ask about that unsavory stuff later.

"It's the only way to save Liz." Desperation made me ask, and I felt the resistance of him in the confined space as well as within my brain.

"Surely there's another way."

"If there is, I don't know it. I need you with me on this. I can't do it without you." Needed as I never needed before.

"I know, but we've got to figure out a way around this."

"You're my liaison. You're supposed to help me."

"Not by breaking the law."

"Dammit, Sam. Are you saying you won't help me?" The breath huffing in and out of my chest turned painful. I felt as if I'd been shot in the chest, too. As Sam's anger flared, so did mine. I felt the waves of pain coming off him. The painful waves of a memory flitted at the edge of my mind. A memory that wasn't mine.

"I made a promise, and I don't break my promises." He clenched his jaw. The stare he gave me almost made me want to cringe. He'd never looked at me like that before, let alone refused to help me. I wondered if The Dark was now influencing him.

Flashes of a jungle scene moved like a scratched film in my mind. The weight of another body across my shoulders tried to push me to my knees, but the weight of a promise was stronger and kept me moving. One foot after another I trudged with the weight of a friend on my shoulders. I had to save him. I had promised.

Though a firefight surrounded us with little chance of anyone surviving, I rushed through, my breath wheezing in and out. *I promised. I promised.* The mantra rang in my mind, drowning out the danger around me. After what seemed like an eternity, I made it safely to the bunker and collapsed under the weight of my friend.

I had kept my promise.

Then I snapped back to the present and some of the steam went out of me. This was Sam's secret, Sam's memory, and part of what burned inside him.

Chapter 14

I touched him on the chest over his heart, unable to put into words the effect his memory had on me. Now was not the time anyway for softer emotions, and I refocused on the task at hand.

"Well, I'm out of ideas. If you have any I'd love to hear them." Furious, frustrated and hungry, we left the hospital. We had to find a place for me to eat or I was going to turn into a psychopathic monster.

Sam walked with me to my truck, and we headed toward a diner, conveniently enough, in the general direction of the mortuary.

"Did you get your truck back?" I asked after I had mowed through about half my steak and three glasses of water. I was on overload and needed more energy than I ever had before. Or at least that's what it seemed like. Something was building. Something was coming to a head, and we were going to be in the middle of it. Maybe we were already in the middle of it and didn't know it. I just hoped we all came out of it alive.

"Yeah."

"When's your review?" There was no question of if, but when he could get back to work. If anyone found out he helped me steal a body, it wasn't going to go well.

"Tomorrow, noon."

"Good. That should buy me enough time to figure out what to do. Vernon should have the court order by then, and we should have Liz back by Friday night. Cool." I was hopeful, if not delusional, that this was all going to work out the way I wanted it to.

"There's a lot of *shoulds* in there." Sam's eyes were guarded as he watched me. He had a burger and ate more slowly than me.

"Don't bother me with details. By now you ought to know what my life is like, right?"

"I should." He shook his head, but I didn't know whether in disbelief at me, or that he was going to help me despite his claim to the contrary. "Do you have any idea how you're going to do this?"

"There's one last thing we have to check first before we commit any felonies. Where are Liz's effects?"

"Probably still at the station, unless her family picked them up." Now that was something I hadn't thought of.

"If I could just talk to her parents, maybe I can convince them to stop the cremation. I'm certain she'd want the resurrection, but I don't know if she's ever talked to her parents about it." I was certain that when Liz divorced, she'd returned her powers of attorney to her parents. There was no way she'd leave things in Jerry's incapable hands.

"I can get you in to look at her possessions. Her phone is probably there with the numbers plugged right in it."

I nearly threw myself across the table at him. "Sam. If you can get me in there, I'll kiss your feet."

He laughed and his eyes glowed hot for a second. "You don't have to go that far down, but I'll get you in." He pointed to my plate. "Finish up. Change of shift is the best time to do it."

"Forget it." I stood, tossed some money on the table. "Dinner's on me tonight. Let's go."

We arrived at the station just before 6:00 p.m. Change of shift is when mistakes are made, no matter what industry you're talking about. People either try to pass things on to the next shift because they want to go home, or get pissed because they catch whatever it is and have to actually go to work the second they're on duty. Not just cops and clerks, but nurses as well. Change of shift is also when most patients are found dead in their beds.

"Hey, Martinez," Sam said, greeting the cop at the desk. They spoke for a moment in Spanish, then he introduced me. I was polite and subservient, just the way I had been raised, but had long since overcome. Sometimes playing a cultural ace helps. It might be wrong, but I would do just about anything to get hold of Liz's phone.

As I said before, my life's in my phone and so was hers. After a short search, Martinez brought out the small bag of items that belonged to Liz: her jewelry, her purse and a notebook. I could see through the clear, zippered bag that there was no phone, and I wanted to cry.

"Thank you, Sergeant Martinez." Holding Liz's belongings, especially her stupid purse, renewed my grief, like stirring a pot of dust that nearly choked me with its dry taste on my tongue. I opened her purse and nearly fainted. There it was.

"So, I heard you just had a baby, right?" Sam said to Martinez, who broke out from ear to ear in one of the proudest new-daddy smiles I've ever seen.

"Yeah. He's two months old." Already the man was reaching for his wallet. "Wanna see some pictures?"

"Sure." Sam nodded and turned his back to me. "Bring 'em out and let me see that boy."

I knew he was giving me an opportunity, and I stuck the phone into my pocket. After looking through the remainder of Liz's purse, I realized there was nothing else helpful in there. I did see her driver's license, and it didn't indicate organ donation. Thank the stars. If her organs had been harvested already, there wouldn't be any way of returning her to a living state. Time was not our friend, and with each passing second she was wasting away and turning to dust. I had to get her to the cryo room as soon as possible and just hoped to hell that The Dark was having a nap.

After zipping the bag, I pushed it back across the desk. "Thank you, Sergeant Martinez. I appreciate your help." I hesitated a second, not certain what made me want to ask. "Can I see the pictures, too?"

"Oh, yeah. Sorry. I get so excited sometimes, my manners walk off without me." He turned the picture in his hand toward me. It was him in civilian clothing, his wife, who looked beautiful, and the baby, who was only a few weeks old, so chubby his eyes were nearly lost in his round little face.

"He's adorable." Seeing pictures of babies shouldn't make me uncomfortable or make me wish for one of my own. Sometimes it does, but now I was just happy for him.

"Thanks. I think he looks like me now." Martinez grinned again and scrunched his eyes up.

I had to laugh. "He sure does."

"I'm sorry about your friend," he said and returned

the pictures to his wallet, then picked up the bag with Liz's items in it. He scrawled in the ledger, signing the items back in.

I dropped my head. Sam turned, putting his arm around my shoulders, and brought me up against his side. I knew it was for show, for Martinez's benefit that I was a grieving friend, but Sam's touch comforted me more than he knew and probably more than I was willing to admit.

Once we were at the truck, I turned on the phone, or tried to, as the battery was dead. There was only enough juice to flash that there was no juice. Fortunately, I had a universal charger and it fit. One thing had gone right, but in the grand scheme of things, it meant little.

Flipping through the numbers, I came to the emergency information, but it was my number. I didn't know whether to be pleased or disturbed.

"Did you find it?"

"No." Frowning, I kept scrolling to the Ms. Mom and Dad. There it was. "Got it!" I pushed Dial and waited for someone to pick up.

"Wait. Hang up."

"No. I've got to talk to them." Was he nuts?

"Listen. How freaked would you be if someone called you from your dead daughter's phone?"

I hung up. "Shit. I hadn't thought about that." A shiver crawled over me. "You're right."

I opened my phone and dialed the number that was in Liz's phone. Waiting, waiting, waiting, no answer. "Dammit." Voice mail. "What does the universe have against me today?" Nothing had gone right, and I felt the influence of The Dark bearing down on me with every incident that had prevented me from taking possession of Liz's body.

"Do I even want to try to answer that?"

"No." I tried the number again and got voice mail again. This time I left an urgent message.

"Wouldn't her parents want her to be resurrected?"

"They aren't in my camp of supports, from what Liz has said. Although they'd want their daughter back, they wouldn't necessarily want her this way." I leaned my forehead against the steering wheel. "It's weird. We can't wait on them."

Although Albuquerque is a city spread across a large land mass, you can get to many places pretty quickly. Most of the city is set up in a grid pattern with few one-way streets, the exception being right downtown. You can also drive forty-five miles to get from one side of the city to the other. It's a long way over the river and through the desert. Fortunately, for the moment, we were near where I wanted to be. Fourth Street. There were some savagely good restaurants down in this part of town. My thoughts weren't on food for a change, but on kidnapping. Or more correctly, body snatching.

I pulled up to the front door of the mortuary facing Fourth Street. It's a small business area. Car lots, burger joints and a most excellent rubber stamp store. Everyone's gotta have a hobby, right?

Sam got out, closed the door and joined me on the sidewalk. I was as close to a nervous breakdown as I'd been in years. Later. I didn't have time for it.

"Do you have a plan?" He tugged on the front door, but it was locked.

"No." Disbelief and denial warred within me. I grabbed the door with both hands and shook, but it didn't budge. "If you want to go, you can." I had to release him from helping me. It just wasn't fair to ask him to do something that violated his beliefs, even if it was for Liz and for me.

"You could have told me that sooner. Now I have to walk home."

I nodded and closed my eyes. I wanted to scream, to cry, to bash my head against the wall, but none of it would help and would only give me a righteous headache.

The light touch of a breeze lifted my hair, and I tucked it behind my ear. In seconds, a raging, black whirlwind developed between Sam and me, and we dove in opposite directions. Generally, dust devils and whirlwinds are harmless and far away, but this one landed right on top of us, as if sentient. It was strong enough to suck the fillings out of my teeth. I pressed myself into a doorway, and Sam dashed to the truck. "Hold on to something!" Screeching over the vortex wasn't helpful, so I screeched in my mind. Rocks, dust and pieces of debris pelted me, and I turned my face into the corner. I hoped Sam was faring better.

What I hadn't realized when I stepped into the arched doorway was that I had trapped myself with no escape.

The whirlwind pressed in on me. Air filled with dirt and the stench of death consumed the space around me, creating a vacuum that made it impossible to breathe. My body was flattened against the hard adobe surface. Gasping, I tried to suck in a breath, but the wind forced my lungs nearly flat. Struggling against the wall, I tried to draw a breath and felt my reserve of air being forced out.

"You are no foe to *me*." An oily, dark voice reverberated around me.

The Dark.

I'd let myself be vulnerable, and it had taken full advantage of my lapse. If I died tonight, it was due to my own stupidity, my own arrogant belief that I could defeat this entity on my own. It could obviously suck the life out of me anytime it wanted to, but apparently taunting me was more fun. Moving my hands up to cup my mouth and nose was impossible, and I couldn't breathe. Spots of black appeared in my mind, and any remaining energy was fading. The only person who could possibly help was Sam. With his strength, I was stronger. With his nearness, I would survive.

Sam. Sam. Sam.

Thinking of his name and the power we shared together was all I could manage. He was close, and I felt him getting closer, but the wind kept him from pressing forward. Guns were of no help. Only by our personal power would we defeat this entity. I didn't need any journals to tell me that.

Then the pressure against me vanished. I fell backward as I sucked in a big lungful of dirty air. Then Sam's arms were around me, helping me to the ground as I coughed and gagged and gasped for air.

"Dani! Are you okay?" The urgency, the concern and the outright fear in Sam's voice penetrated my fog.

"Friggin'…Dark again." Turning, I let him help me sit again, and my lungs finally felt as if they were going to inflate. "What happened?" At least no monkeys this time.

"All I could see was a damned black shadow holding you in the doorway." Sam yanked me into his arms. He shook and trembled. He was as freaked out as I was. "Oh, my God."

"It's okay. It's okay."

"I can't lose you, too." He squeezed me tighter, and I heard him in my mind. *I won't lose you, too.*

"How did you get through it?" That was a miracle.

"I don't know. I grabbed the amulet in my hand, charged toward the doorway, and it vanished."

Standing with his help, I steadied myself and he wiped some of the grit from my face. "Wow. That was something I never expected."

"Me, either." Although he released me, I still felt the vibration of him from a foot away. He glanced down and then stooped, picking something up from the pile of dirt in the corner.

"What's that?" It looked like a book had blown in with the debris.

"It's one of *abuela's* journals." He gave me a look of utter shock tinged with hope. "I'll be damned. Look at this."

Taking the leather-bound volume, I could see it was singed and burned all around the edges, but the leather had resisted the heat of the fire. Another good reason to use natural leather products. "It *is* one of her journals, but why?"

"Maybe The Dark thought it would flaunt its power over us, but something obviously went wrong."

"Obviously." I snorted. "We're more powerful together. When we pool our energies, something happens. It knows this and is defenseless against it." I held up the journal. "Your *abuela* knew it, too. There's something in here, or it wouldn't have kept this one." I opened it and looked at the foreign words lining the pages. "We have to figure this out, Sam. We have to use the information she left for us. It's her legacy, and it shouldn't be forgotten."

"It won't be." The tone of his voice dropped and the emotion surging off him brought tears to my eyes. My warrior, so strong, so true in his convictions, was going to help me defeat this entity.

I clutched the journal to my chest and looked at Sam, the emotion of the day almost overwhelming me. "We're a force to be reckoned with. I know it."

He planted a hard kiss on my mouth. "So does The Dark."

The lighting in this area was crap, but I opened the journal anyway. The lights from the truck were still on, so I held the journal into the beam. Thumbing through the first ruined pages, I stopped at a place where the words were still legible, but again, in Spanish. "Help me out. Can you see anything off the bat?"

Sam leaned over my shoulder, trying to read, then he took the book from me. Frowning, he read, shook his head, but said nothing.

"Well?" Patient, I am not.

"It's something, but makes no sense. Like it's in code or something. Just talking again about daily tasks, but in a very weird way. Like using things as weapons or defenses. *Put grape jelly in the windows to protect from external threats.* Now that makes no sense."

"Grape jelly?" Did she have an allergy to strawberry? "That is weird." I knew I wasn't going to figure it out tonight. I put my hand over Sam's and he looked up, the frown still in place and surges of frustration wafting off him like the blaze of a blowtorch.

"It'll take more time than we have right now to figure it out."

He nodded and a muscle in his jaw twitched.

I took another deep breath, determined to get back to the quest that had brought us here, though deciphering the book was high on my priority list. "We've got to get to the mortuary. We've been delayed long enough." Although less than twenty minutes had passed, it felt like a lifetime. The way Sam charged into The Dark humbled me more than I cared to admit. I owed him so much.

"I won't ask you to jeopardize your job any more than you have, but I need help to save Liz." There was only one person who could do that, and I had no way of contacting him.

Reaching to my chest, I clutched the amulet in my fingers and squeezed. The other-siders had said it was not merely decorative, and Sam just proved it. I shut my eyes and pictured Burton. *Burton, I need your help. It's an emergency.* I said the words in my head, not seriously believing he would show up, but after the communication with Sam, who knew? I opened my eyes. There was no preemptive skateboard sound preceding Burton's arrival, and we were alone on the street.

I closed my eyes again and took a deep breath. I had a death grip on the amulet. *Burton! Get your ass down here!* I screeched inside, digging deep within myself to a place that I rarely had to go. This was for Liz, not me.

"Jeez, *chica,*" Burton said. "I heard you the first time."

I jumped. He stood behind me holding his skateboard and rubbing one ear.

"Burton," I breathed, scarcely able to believe he was there.

"You called. I came. Where's the fire, dude?"

"Inside, right now. They're going to cremate Liz,

and we have to get her back." I let the *dude* comment slide, this time.

"I guess there really is a fire." His eyes popped wide.

All I did was blink, and we were inside the locked mortuary. I don't want to know how we got there. I was just glad we were. "I don't even know where to look."

"This way." Burton moved in his lanky, long-legged lope to a door I hadn't seen. He spoke a word I didn't understand, and the door opened without setting off any alarms. Curious.

Burton leaned against a counter and pointed to the middle locker on the far right row. "There."

"Thank you, Burton. I'll never be able to repay you for this. If we get out of here without getting arrested, I'll do something for you. I don't know what, but I will." I handed my keys to Sam. "Will you bring the truck around?"

He took the keys, but paused. "Are you asking me to assist you in committing a felony?"

"Uh, no. Not technically. All I'm asking you to do is move my truck." I hated to ask, but I did anyway. "These are dire circumstances."

"I know. If you're letting me drive your truck twice in a week, things are definitely out of control." With a sigh, he left the room via the loading dock. I didn't know if asking him to help would bring us closer together or drive us apart.

My heart was racing, was beating away, and I didn't know if it was from relief at having arrived in time, anticipation of getting caught or the thrill of getting away with it. "Can you fix the paperwork trail, the computer entries and all that?"

"Already done."

"But how?" He hadn't moved from the counter.

"The mind is a powerful tool if you use it right." He grinned and looked like such a kid again that I could only shake my head.

"You're gonna have to sign me up for that class."

Trembling, I opened the door to the drawer where her body was kept and pulled back the sheet to look at her. Just in case. But this was her body, so lifeless, so pale and empty. By the end of the week I hoped to have her back to her usual state of consciousness, filled with life and energy. For now, we had to get her out of here.

Burton and I eased her onto a stretcher. I closed the door and turned around, expecting to see someone calling the cops, but we remained alone. He pushed the gurney to the dock entrance, and I opened the doors. My truck sat there. Sam stood beside it. The lump in my throat I'd tried to choke down for days tried to crawl up at the sight of him. I owed this man so much.

We eased Liz's body, still in a bag, into the bed of my truck and shut the tailgate. I took a step back and cursed. It looked exactly as if I had a body in the back of my truck. We weren't going to make it without being seen by either a cop or some nosy person who just *had* to call 911.

"Don't worry, *chica*. No one will see you." He sort of waved a hand toward the truck and for a second it glowed. A shield had been placed over the truck as well as Sam and me. To others, we were invisible.

"Thank you again, Burton. Remind me to buy you a gift certificate to the skate shop."

He tossed his board onto the sidewalk and jumped onto it. With a wave, he disappeared into the night.

Despite my hands reshaping themselves into claws

on the steering wheel, gray hairs sprouting and new wrinkles appearing between my eyebrows from glaring at all the people who decided they needed to be in front of me, we made it to the lab without incident.

The second we closed the door to the cryo tube, my hands shook. Then for some reason the ligaments in my knees melted away. What had once been my cast-iron stomach now quivered as if I'd had a hefty dose of Mexican jumping beans. Or maybe I had parasites. I drank the water.

It was only when my lungs began to burn and holes appeared in my vision that I knew I was in trouble. I opened my mouth, but nothing came out. Trying to catch Sam's attention before I hit the floor was apparently also impossible. I was in a dreamscape, all the colors and shapes melted together, and whatever consciousness I had left me in a rush. The last thing I remember was an overwhelming need to sleep, so I closed my eyes, not caring that I was vertical and sleeping upright wasn't in my skill set.

A vision of Sam racing toward me, his blazer flapping, was the last image I recall before the neurons in my brain went on strike.

Someone had stuck a screwdriver through my left eye and drove it straight into my brain. Unable to open my eyes, I raised my hand to remove the screwdriver. I didn't care if I lost an eye. I had to remove that spear from my head.

Hmm. Curious. I patted my face. No screwdriver. I extended my senses outward and discovered I was lying down and there was a cool washcloth on my forehead.

Moving, attempting to sit up, renewed the screwdriver pain, and I groaned.

"Dani. Thank God." There was movement, and I recognized Sam's voice. "Are you okay?"

"I don't know." I fluttered my eyelids, trying to see. "The light." It pierced my brain.

Sam dimmed the light, and I could open my eyes. I was on the couch in my office. "What happened?"

"You fainted." He knelt beside me again.

"Quit saying that. I did not." I was made of sterner stuff than most people. Fainting is not what I do. I might check out for a while, but I do *not* faint.

"Well, you did this time." The muscle in his jaw twitched. The man was more upset than he let on, and I tried to comfort him in my mind, but he pushed me away, more irritated than he wanted to admit.

"Maybe it was something else." I wanted it to be anything else. Low blood sugar, high blood pressure, electrolyte imbalance, nail fungus. Anything.

"When was the last time you ate?" I could hear the recrimination in his voice and was sorry I had put it there.

"With you. Whenever that was. I had a busy day. What time is it?"

"Almost midnight."

Shit. "Uh, about ten hours ago, maybe more."

"Dammit, Dani. You know better. You need to feed whatever it is inside you, or you're going to faint again." A tremor shot through him and into me.

"I told you, I don't faint." I sat up and fought against the tide of vertigo that wanted to send me horizontal and make a liar out of me.

He said something nasty under his breath, but I heard it in my mind. "Let's go."

"Go? Where?"

"To get you a bloody steak." He stood and assisted me to my feet.

"But Liz—"

"Isn't going anywhere. She's safe and secure. Let me see to you, Dani. For once, let me take care of you."

Something in his voice made me look up. We stopped in the doorway of the office and stood there for a moment. Time ceased to move forward, or at least it slowed down for a few seconds. He'd been scared. That's why he was angry. Men like Sam don't do scared. They break things instead of admitting they suffer a weakness. I was apparently Sam's weakness. I just hope he hadn't broken anything while I was out.

Chapter 15

After we ate, Sam took me home. We hadn't spoken much during dinner. I was too ravenous to make polite conversation and rather than saying something stupid, I remained silent. Shocking, I know.

Doing the cop thing, Sam stalked around my house checking doors, windows, closets and behind furniture. At the moment I was glad for his company and for his guard-dog attitude. I was too hosed to do any of it myself, though I followed the same routine every time I'd been away from home. Being murdered will do that do a person.

Sam removed my jacket from my shoulders, took off my shoulder holster and checked my gun. After that, he squatted at my feet and tugged off my boots. "Come on." He took me by the hand.

I must have been tired, because I didn't protest any of this. If I were feeling myself, I'd be tossing him out of my house and yelling at him for being bossy again. Strangely enough, I was glad he was there. If left to my own devices, I might have simply stood in the living room and not remembered what to do.

We entered my bedroom, and he left me for a moment. The sound of the taps running drew my attention, and I realized he was fixing a bath. I looked down at my soiled clothing, the grit that filled every crevice, and wrinkled my nose. I was a mess and should be hosed off in the yard. Seconds later, the fragrance of my body wash filled the room. I love lavender. Stimulates the mind and refreshes the soul. If there was a heaven, that's what it would smell like.

He removed his blazer, but kept the shoulder rig on. Reaching out, he gripped the hem of my shirt and tugged it over my head. Next was the bra, the jeans, socks and finally the panties. I stood naked in front of him, but there wasn't a spec of desire in his eyes. Apparently, I'd lost my touch or he was still pissed.

Silently, he led me to the bathroom and put me into the tub.

The second my feet hit the water, I wanted to melt away, to give up my bones, flesh and skin to become one with the bubbles. I groaned out loud, closed my eyes and sank beneath the water as far as I could go and still breathe.

Sam chuckled, and I opened my eyes far enough to watch him. "Good?" He closed the toilet lid and sat on it.

"Exquisite." I dragged in a long, beautiful breath and sighed it out, settling down into the decadent luxury of the perfectly hot water. In a few minutes Sam moved, but I didn't open my eyes to see what he was doing.

The scent of him, spicy and masculine, alerted me to his nearness. Speaking would have broken the spell of the moment as I opened my eyes. His sleeves were rolled up, and he was kneeling beside the tub, a washcloth in his hand, and I immediately guessed his intention. Am I sharp, or what?

Dunking the cloth beneath the water, he soaked it, then took the bottle of body wash and squeezed entirely too much onto the cloth, then set the bottle aside. Beginning at one hand he scrubbed with a gentle touch, worked his way up to my neck, then down to the other arm, beneath each breast, down my abdomen, which was blessedly covered by bubbles, and then the rest. After he finished with the top portion, I leaned forward and let him scrub my back. There's nothing that feels as good, or almost nothing, as having the skin and muscles tended to by someone else.

Nothing in his touch, his gaze or his demeanor told me he was after anything more. I think this was just his way of coming down off his fear. "Sam?"

Silently, he looked at me and there was tension around his mouth, between his eyes and in the stiff way he held himself. I wish I'd noticed this earlier, but earlier I was just recovering from a light coma.

"Will you tell me about it? About your grandmother and what happened to your family?" Though he blocked the majority of those memories from me, I felt the pain of them now and then. At times such as now when his emotions were raw, I could sense the pain he'd kept to himself for way too long.

I swallowed down the nameless emotion wanting to rise up from my gut to choke me. This man had saved my life more than once, and I'd saved his a time or two. Now, we were connected by much more than shared job interests. The least I could do was help him with grief he had run from most his life. He needed this, and I wanted to help. I needed to help.

"No. It's in the past, and I want it to stay there."

"You know as well as I do that the past never stays where it belongs." A maelstrom of emotion sparked off him and nearly electrocuted me in the tub. I jumped at the ferocity of his pain. "Tell me. It will help."

"I can't," he whispered. The tone of his voice dropped with the pain he couldn't speak. Sadness and grief poured off him. The strong muscles in his throat worked as he swallowed down the pain.

"Will you show it to me, then? Let me see it?" He knew I could do it, could read his memories. He just had to open himself in order for me to see them. If he shared them this way, it would ease his pain. "Please, just show me?"

"Dani—"

"You once told me you'd keep my secrets. Won't you trust me with yours?"

Without a word, he closed his eyes and leaned toward me. This proud man of mine was lost. He didn't know how to put the pain behind him. He could only push it away when it threatened to consume him. After all the things we'd been through, all the passion and the pain we'd shared, we were closer than ever, but this one thing kept him from reaching out fully to me. I needed him more than he could possibly know, and I wanted him to be free.

After shaking most of the water off, I gently placed the heel of one hand on his forehead and let my fingers drop over the top of his head. The story unfolded as if Sam were telling it to me out loud.

Gunshots shattered the night and panic burned in

my chest. Hysterical screams, babies crying and dark voices mixed together. Leaving the safety of the bedroom wasn't the smartest move, even at age twelve I knew that, but someone had to do something.

My mother screamed in terror, and her cry was cut off. I opened the door only a crack, but it was enough to see the bodies of my parents on the living room floor. A dark figure stood over my father, cursing his name, cursing his family, cursing his blood. "Now you know what it is to bleed," the man said.

I must have made a noise, because the next thing I knew I was on the floor with a gun in my face. A stranger held me down and shoved a pistol in my mouth.

"Stop it! We're not killing no kid." Another voice spoke from the shadows. One of my sisters woke and began to cry. Then another one cried out. If even one of them got up, they'd all die.

"Let's go. The job is done." The man sitting on me was dragged away by his companion.

Panicked and hysterical, I crawled to my father, who lay gasping on the floor. One look at my mother, and I knew she was dead. Those beautiful eyes of hers would never again sparkle with laughter. My sisters would never be held by her again. Tears fell down my face and a pain raged in my chest. Pain shot through my head as I leaned over my father.

"Papa? Papa!" I shook him and wanted him to wake up.

"Sammy?" My father's voice was a whisper, and I collapsed beside him.

"I'm here, Papa." My voice sounded small, like a little child's. I wanted him to stand and make it all go away, to tell me to wake up from this nightmare I was in.

"Protect the girls." He took in a gasping breath as he tried to give me the message most important to him. *"You're the only one who can take care of them,"* he said, and I vowed then that nothing would happen to the people I loved.

"I'll get help. I'll get help!" Tears blinded me, and I couldn't see the numbers on the phone. *"I'm calling."* Gasps choked out of my body and I couldn't breathe. I couldn't think.

"You're the only one," he said in a rush. Reaching out, he clasped my arm. *"Sammy. My little man. Protect them. Always."* Papa's hand fell away. I knew he was dead. I ran to the neighbor's house for help. Help came. But it was too late.

Sam shuddered as he came out of the vision. This explained so much about him, and why it was such a painful story to tell, why his heart broke every time he made a promise.

Tears filled my eyes and rushed down my face. I broke the contact with Sam's forehead, and I fell out of his memory. "Why?"

"One or both of them witnessed something, a robbery or another serious crime, and could identify the perpetrators. That's all I can figure, because they were good people." Sam sat back on his heels. "Back then they didn't have any protection as witnesses." He reached out to stroke my face, the pain in his eyes almost tangible. The energy coming off him was black and heavy, and I wanted to console him, but there was nothing that would take away this pain. "That's when *abuela* came from Mexico to take care of us."

"I'm so sorry." There were no words to tell him how deeply I felt his pain. Nothing, not even time, would heal those wounds. Time only softened the point of the dagger.

"I know." He wrung the washcloth out and hung it over the edge of the tub. Reaching behind him, he dragged a towel from the metal rack and stood, holding it out.

"There was nothing you could have done to save them."

"Who knows." He shrugged again and looked away. He blamed himself, but I now understood why he took the protection thing to such a degree. The only thing he could do was take care of his sisters. It was a vow he'd never broken and had expanded to include me in the circle of those he protected. I couldn't blame him. He wasn't just being bossy. By not protecting me, he was breaking a vow that made him part of who he was.

"Thank you for sharing that with me." I touched his cheek, and the ache dulled to a throb. "I know it hurts, but you aren't to blame, and you kept your promise."

"Let's get you out of there." Conversation was over for now. This was as much as he could give me, and I accepted it. I stood and accepted his ministrations to dry me, put on a nightshirt and put me into bed.

"Go to sleep now." He tucked me in, and I let him, but reached out and took his hand.

"Stay. Please."

After a moment's hesitation he removed his boots and lay down beside me. Turning toward him seemed natural, and the heavy sigh he emitted made me think that some of his pain had eased. I hoped so. I didn't want him to hurt so much. My eyes closed and I drifted away, powerless to do anything else. My body had betrayed me despite my will. Guess I was still human after all. Sometimes I wondered.

* * *

When I woke, ten damned hours later, I sat straight up in the bed, blinked a few times and did the only thing I could do. Ran straight to the bathroom and peed like a racehorse. A woman's bladder was not made for long-term storage.

The smell of freshly brewing coffee drew me downstairs like an addict to the opium dens of long ago. Frankly, I think caffeine's a better deal and a hell of a lot less expensive. You don't have to hide your caffeine addiction either, because all the other addicts were right there with you cheering you on. Coffee, anyone? I felt as if I was drifting on a cloud of caffeine, drawn in by its lure and promise of immediate satisfaction. Yeah.

Sam stood in the kitchen, looking all rumpled and sexy. Barefoot, he looked as if he'd just pulled his jeans on, halfheartedly zipped them, forgot about the button, tossed on his button-down shirt and left it. My mouth was kind of like his shirt. Hanging open.

Weak as I was, that was not the first thing I needed to see after a ten-hour coma.

"How are you?"

"Starved, caffeine withdrawn, stupefied by you standing there and about as grumpy as a cat in heat." I turned with my cup and glared at him.

"Back to normal then?"

I nodded and couldn't prevent the grin from hitting me. "Pretty much."

"Glad to have you back, babe." He laughed and raised his mug in salute. I clinked my mug with his and sipped. Okay, rest was over. I was back, and we were a team again. Time to get moving.

"We got a body to resurrect and a life-swap to perform."

* * *

The paperwork was in order. Vernon, the little rat bastard, had done it. Now I knew he was afraid of me. I felt a laugh, similar to my evil ringtone, making its way up out of me, but I resisted. Gloating could wait until later. Oh, by the gods, this was going to be a good day. I could feel it in every tingling little neuron throughout my body.

Sam had gone off to do what he had to do for a while. Yesterday had been the last of his three days of administrative leave, and today who knew what was going to happen. For now, I was on my own, and that's the way I usually like it, though I did feel a bit as if I was missing something. Last night had changed things between us. Seriously. We hadn't exchanged any bodily fluids, but I felt closer to Sam than I ever had.

Ten seconds later, the day seemed to explode with activity. Noon came and went before I had a chance to lift my head and go get food. If I didn't eat, there would be no ritual tonight, and Liz would have to wait another day. I raced to the nearest carnivore café and got what I needed. Minimal fanfare sometimes is all that's required to get the job done. Kind of like why women buy vibrators. No muss, no fuss, gets the job done and you don't have to compliment man or machine.

"Vernon," I said into the phone. Scooting aside the petrified hunk of wood, I shut my office door. "We'll do the resurrection at midnight. Have Jerry here by eleven-thirty. We'll take him to the 'yard after I bring Liz back."

"I'll make the arrangements." Something in his tone made me suspicious. He normally wasn't so agreeable.

"What's going on, Vernon? There'd better not be a single screwup in this."

"I don't anticipate any, Miss Wright."

I frowned, suspicious. "Then what's wrong? You don't sound like your usual self." That was polite, wasn't it? I left out the smarmy part.

"Let's just say I'm having a deep philosophical issue at the moment and leave it at that. I'll see you tonight."

"Fine." Anticipation hummed through me, so I didn't care what kind of philosophical issue he had going on as long as he got the deed done.

Two o'clock. Ten whole hours to fill. Dammit.

My phone rang. "Wright."

"It's Sam."

"Hey."

"I need your help."

"Sure. What kind?" Anything for this man.

"Come to Elena's and bring a shovel." The line went dead.

Cripes. Couldn't anyone just say goodbye anymore? I turned off the phone, then got a shock to my system. Hot damn! We were going to look for the missing journals. I didn't know whether that was a sense from Sam or just brilliant deduction on my part.

I arrived, shovel in hand, to find Sam walking around with a metal detector. Watching a man hard at work had always been an endless source of entertainment for me. I don't know why. Doesn't matter the type of work, from digging ditches, to neuro surgery, when a man is in his element and focused on what he is doing, I'm fascinated. Maybe that just means I'm easily entertained.

"Whatcha doin'?" As if I couldn't see.

"Fishing, what do you think?"

Uh-oh. The frown between his eyes gave away his frustration level, and I got a weird vibe from him. He'd obviously been at it awhile before he called me. "Catching anything?"

"A pile of change. A bunch of old toy cars, some of which were probably mine. A few nails, odds and ends like that."

"Did you think you'd find the journals with that thing?"

"Yes." His mouth tightened for a moment, and he kept his eyes on his work. He'd become nearly as obsessed as I had, though we now had one journal to work from that had the seeds of useful information in it. "She had to have put them in something to protect them from the weather, time, someone finding them. I remembered seeing her out here at night, but she always said she was checking food she was fermenting."

"Oh, gross." Don't get me started about fermented foods. "Do you know how long Clostridium botulinum spores live?" I didn't wait for him to answer because he didn't know what the hell I was talking about. "For-freaking-ever. You're probably going to find some pot of dead raccoon that's been there for twenty years and stinks to high heaven."

Sam shot me a glare. "I don't think so. I think she was hiding her journals so we couldn't find them."

"Smart woman. What kid would go near that smell?"

"Not us. That's for sure."

"Okay, think about her, how she would have secured the journals from you kids, animals and people who would use them against her, yet still be available for someone to use at a later date."

Sam stopped and considered that, though he didn't

look at me. "She'd have had to have a box made that was metal, had it buried or buried it herself. She was tiny, but she was strong. And she'd have had to have convenient access to it."

"Was there anything that used to be here that isn't anymore? A chicken coop, a barn." I searched my mind for anything. "Old cars, old furniture, a workshop of some kind. A spring house, a root cellar, a bomb shelter."

"Bomb shelter?" At that I got the first inkling of a shift in mood from him.

"I'm reaching here, just trying to think of things." Brainstorming ain't perfect.

Sam shook his head. "I can't think of anything. She didn't like a lot of mess around, said it made us look poor. We were, but she said we didn't have to look it."

I laughed. "I think I would have liked her."

Finally, he raised his head and looked directly at me. "Together, you two would have been unstoppable."

"Kind of like you and me, now, huh?" A lump formed in my throat, and I swallowed it back down where it belonged. "How did she die?"

"Breast cancer. About five years ago." He began to pace with the detector again.

"I'm sorry, Sam."

"It's the way the world works. I'm just glad she didn't suffer."

"Yeah. Me, too." There are definitely worse things than dying, and suffering was one of them. "Maybe one day I'll see her eternal star."

Sam gave a nod.

"How old is this house?" I asked as something occurred to me. We were near the Rio Grandé River, where many homes had irrigation rights. Channels were built alongside these properties and diverted river water for residents to use for farming. Not very long ago everyone in this area had farmed and raised animals. Some still did.

"Probably late 1800s. It's been updated over and over, so it doesn't look as old as it really is."

"I assume that it was hooked up to the city water at some time." Hmm. This was giving me ideas.

"Of course." Sam looked at me and grinned.

"A well," we said together.

Sam put the metal detector down and strode right to me. Without a word, he grabbed me by the shoulders and planted a hard kiss on my mouth. "You're the smartest woman I've ever known."

Not giving me time to bask in the glow of that, he released me and strode across the yard toward the far end of the property. It was long and narrow, rather than being a square the way many properties are these days. This place had once accommodated farmland and livestock away from the house, closer to the source of the water.

Not needing the shovel, I dropped it and ran after Sam. We were going to find the remaining journals, finally! I caught up to him. He stood with his hands on his hips looking totally disgusted. "Now what?"

"Sealed over. With cement." Now that we were more connected, his language was starting to resemble mine. Weeds and thorny things had grown up around the site, hiding it from the casual observer. Sam had found it only because he knew it was there.

"What?" Shocked, I stared dumbfounded at him. "Why?"

"Until now, I'd forgotten. When that baby girl fell down an old well in Texas, Grandma freaked out." He cursed. "Of course, we were always playing on top of it, so she had the damned thing closed off."

Disappointment nearly broke me. "If her journals had been there, surely she moved them before sealing the well." I'd been so sure we'd find them, I'd never considered anything else. "Well. Hell. Couldn't she have had it closed off with a lid that opened?"

"What would be the point of sealing off something you could open?" he asked with a raised brow.

"I don't know." Raking a hand through my hair, I sighed, more bummed than I wanted to admit. Though I had started out believing today was going to be great, now it was going down the tubes.

"That would have been a good hiding place." The afternoon had begun to wane. Shadows grew behind trees and overhead in the great cottonwood trees I was sure Sam had climbed as a kid. I gave a shiver, remembering the skeletal monkeys, and my attention rose upward.

The remnants of an old tree house filled the crook of one tree. Wooden steps that had once been nailed securely into the tree now hung precariously. There was a flat platform that had served as the base, and two of the four sides were still intact. There was no roof, but what kid needed a roof when you were in a tree house? "That yours?"

"What?"

I pointed up. "The tree house."

He paused and a nostalgic look covered his face. "Yeah. That was mine. With so many girls around, I needed a place to call my own."

"Your very first bachelor pad. Doesn't look like anyone's used it for years."

"Elena's kids are hooked on computer games and crap like that. The simple things are entirely beyond their comprehension. Unless it's hooked to a computer screen, they don't get it." He had a curious expression on his face, as if seeing the thing triggered memories. "I had a lot of good times up there."

"I'll bet you did." I could almost imagine him playing army up there.

"Had my first kiss up there." With a grin, he hooked his thumbs in the waistband of his jeans.

"How old were you?" Intrigued, I wanted more information. I knew so little about his life before we met. He was a man of mystery and secrets, and I wanted to know all of them.

"Ten, I think. Bernice Alvarez." He snorted a laugh. "She was the only one who could climb trees well enough to get up there. I added the steps later."

"Show me. I think I can climb as well as Bernice Alvarez." I removed my blazer and hung it over a low branch.

"Dani, this thing is so old, I don't think it's safe anymore."

"Come on. Where's your sense of adventure?" I leaped up, caught a branch and pulled myself up. Chin-ups were in my workout regime, but I hated them and struggled to bring myself upright. Sam gave me a lift into the tree. I think he just wanted to handle my ass.

"Okay, but if you get up there, just don't hit me."

"Why would I hit you? This time, I mean." I could think of a lot of reasons, but not at the moment.

"After I kissed Bernice, she slugged me one. I fell out of the tree and broke my arm." That made me laugh, and I nearly lost my grip. I finally caught my feet on a branch and heaved myself up to the base. It was too small for me to fit into so I leaned over and looked into the space.

The laugh stopped.

Sitting in front of me, hidden right out in the open, was a small metal foot locker, about the size of two loaves of bread and twice as high.

"What's wrong?" He caught the change in me right away.

"I think I found the journals."

Chapter 16

"What do you see?"

"A metal box. Beat to hell, but intact." I tried to balance myself on a branch that would support me and reach in at the same time. Finally, I was able to grab one of the handles on the side of the box. As I dragged it toward me, it scraped and bumped and then hung up on the nearly rotted floor of the tree house. I almost had it. Reaching out, I scooted it closer to me, and I grabbed the handle more securely. Tremors shot through me as I touched it.

"It's heavy. Can you reach up for it?"

"Yeah." Sam stood beneath me, and I pulled the box over my lap, then gripped a branch with one hand and handed him the box with the other.

And the branch snapped.

I didn't have time to scream or even take a breath. One second I was on the branch ten feet up, the next second I was on the ground, on top of Sam, on top of the box, on top of a pile of toothpicks that used to be a branch.

Sam grunted, and I rolled off him with a groan. "Are you okay?"

"Yeah." His breath wheezed in and out of his lungs. He crawled to his hands and knees, trying to catch his breath.

In the meantime, I eyed the box that had popped open. "Keep breathing, Sam. Just keep breathing." Eventually, the paralysis of the diaphragm causing the suffocating feeling resolves. It's only a few seconds; it just feels like an eternity.

Pushing aside the mangled and rusted lid, I nearly screamed. "It's them. It has to be." Trembling, I pulled one of the leather-bound journals from the splinters. I was trembling from excitement, and my gaze flashed to Sam.

He'd turned over and was sitting on the ground now. At least his coloring had returned to normal. "Let's see." He held out a hand for one, and I gave it to him, knowing he was still going to have to translate.

Oh, please, please, please, let it be them, I muttered. *Abuela, I need your help.* Clasping my hands together, it was as close to a prayer as I could get.

Sam cracked open the book and began to read. In seconds, he grinned. "It's them. This is what we need. I'm sure of it."

Launching myself at him, we fell over and landed in a pile in the dirt. "Oh, thank you, Sam!"

"You're the one who found them." He looked up at me from his prone position.

What I felt coming off him unnerved me. There was tenderness and respect, but there was a need, an ache that I hadn't expected, and I looked deeply into his eyes, as if I could see into his mind and his heart. I no longer needed my hands in full contact with him to read him. Something in my heart cramped, and I wished for things that could never be between us. I was falling for him in ways that would only hurt us both.

He was a protector and that was great. He was also dedicated to family, and that was something I could never give him. Having had my uterus severely damaged in my attack, I was told by doctors I would never carry another baby. Too much scar tissue. Although it disappointed me, I thought it had been a good thing at the time. Until now. Until I fell in love with Sam. He was so about family and connections that not having children would pain him forever. He should be bouncing babies on his knee someday, pacing the floor with a sleeping child on his shoulder and loving a woman who would complete him. I couldn't do any of that, and I wouldn't stop him from finding that happiness with someone else. I loved him too much to stand in his way.

"I don't want anyone else, Dani." His voice was a whisper, and a shock wave echoed through me.

"How could you…"

"I know, Dani. I know." He pulled me down to him and opened his mouth over mine. Resisting occurred to me, but I'd become less interested in pushing away things I wanted. Someday soon, I'd no longer be able to have Sam as a lover. I could feel our time together coming to a close. We'd still be partners in the professional sense, but we couldn't be intimate the way we were now. This was only a respite. At least that's what I tried to convince myself. I parted my lips to the searching quest of his tongue. I wanted to milk every bit of pleasure out of our arrangement while we could. Once it ended, we'd never be able to go back.

I raised my head and looked at him, as if he had the answers to questions I didn't even know how to ask.

"Come inside with me." The yearning in him matched that bubbling up within me.

"Sam—"

"Don't pull away from me. Not now." He pressed a hard kiss to my mouth. "Not yet. I'm not ready."

I didn't know what that meant, but he'd never asked me for anything. Could I deny a request I stood to benefit from? I wasn't very self-sacrificing. He heard the answer in my mind and rolled me over, pressing me into the ground. There was desperation now rising up between us.

He stood and helped me to my feet, then picked up the journals. Urgency filled every footstep as we entered the house. He set the box down, locked the door behind us and reached for me. Though his mouth was the driving force setting the pace, his touch was gentle, reverent, and I settled into the feel of him.

"I need you." And I did. How I could admit that and walk away from him, I didn't know. But for now, I needed him, and I wanted to fulfill the need burning within him.

He eased my jeans open and dragged them down. Pressing kisses to my breasts, my abdomen, my hips, Sam worshipped my body and I began to quake inside. The heat of his mouth seared my core, and my knees nearly buckled. Thankfully, I was leaning up against the wall. A whimper of need left me as the searing texture of his tongue touched my flesh. Cupping my bottom, he tipped me into his mouth and pleasured me. In seconds I was ready to explode. With my hands holding his head, I could only hold on as he took me to the edge and flung me over it. Spasms of intense pleasure erupted, and in that moment I knew I loved Sam beyond all else.

I knew I couldn't, that I shouldn't, but I did. Here was a man who deserved so much more than I could give him. For now, I could give him the pleasure of sharing my body. I urged him up to me, and with trembling fingers I released his erection into my eager hands. I needed him to know the pleasure he'd given me.

He pulled my right leg up around his hip and eased into my flesh. The groan of pleasure echoed in my mind. This was what I could give him. In my mind, I spoke. *Take me, Sam. Take me the way you want to. Don't hold back.*

Withdrawing from me, he spun me around and pressed me down onto the table, leaned over me, his breath hot in my ear. "This is what I want."

Arching my back, I wasn't going to protest as he eased the length of his shaft inside me. He filled me in a way that stirred new sensations. Though I'd just had an orgasm, when he reached in front of me to touch my flesh, I knew I was going to have another one. My body no longer seemed to be something that I controlled, but something I had given over to Sam's hands. He moved in and out of me, drawing out every bit of pleasure for us both. Faster and harder, each movement brought us closer to the brink. Any second now, we were gonna blow.

Gasping for breath, I clutched the sides of the table and held on while Sam did what he had to do. When his fingers dug hard into my hips I knew he was close, and for some reason I opened myself up more fully to him mentally, allowing myself to feel him, feel his pleasure and the sudden release. His orgasm became mine, and together we scorched the air around us. Then he collapsed over me and pressed me into the table. Unintelligible Spanish words flowed out of him. I didn't know exactly what he said, but I was sure the content had to do with being sexually fulfilled in that moment, and it made me smile. I was so there, too.

After we had our senses together again, I covered my face with my hand. "Your *abuela* would be ashamed of us. We find the journals then fornicate like a couple of teenagers."

"She'd have laughed her ass off."

"Really?" I was relieved, but surprised. People of her generation were a lot more conservative than me.

"She was no prude. How could she be and still be a resurrectionist?"

"Really?" That made me feel a lot better and more connected to Sam than ever.

Thunder rumbled outside, and I looked out the window. Black, ominous clouds threatened to rain down on us like nothing we'd ever seen. As Sam joined me at the window, I knew this night was far from over. We had a job to do, and it wasn't going to be easy. Bringing Liz back was only the first step of many that would be required to push back The Dark, if only temporarily.

"What do you think that's all about?"

"The balance. We're doing something right The Dark doesn't like. It's trying to scare us. Like the monkeys and the whirlwind." The Dark had it in for me, for us. I looked at the way the trees trembled, nearly bent in half by the breeze. That had been me once. Trembling at the slightest ill wind, but not anymore. I was stronger with Sam by my side.

"The next time it might not play so nice."

"Nice? The whirlwind nearly sucked the life from me."

"I know. That's why we need to get at these right away. I'll take them to my place and start interpreting before the resurrection tonight."

"Okay. Let's get out of here before the monkeys come back."

Finally, the hour arrived. Liz was ready, I was ready, and so was Sam. Over the past few weeks he'd turned into my go-to guy in so many ways. I was depending on him more than I ever had, which made me wonder about that teeny little blood exchange of ours. Would I be able to manage without him, or were we more connected than ever? Was it even possible for me to let go of him?

The buzzer to the outside door rang and the guards ushered in more guards with Jerry in tow. Vernon was with them and hung back just a little. The look in his eyes wasn't as amused as it had been the last time we were in this room. Must be the philosophical issue he'd mentioned. Maybe he was finally coming around to our side.

"Bring him over here." I motioned to a spot close enough to Liz's body, but far enough away from me that his toxic energy didn't touch me.

Tonight, again, I'd made a change in my attire. For whatever reason, I felt the ceremony demanded it. I wore a red silk robe. With Liz's death, something inside me had changed. Maybe I was having my own philosophical issue.

Barefoot, I moved to Liz. I moved slowly, reverently. Made me look ethereal, I guess, because Jerry's eyes widened when I eased past him, and he turned a sick shade of green. I pulled the sheet back from Liz's face. She was perfect and beautiful, just as she'd been in life.

I raised one hand to the ceiling and placed one hand over Liz's forehead and began the ceremony. There was no reason to delay.

"Hear me now, guardian spirits of the west. We implore you to return this child, wrongly taken, back from the light. We seek your guidance and knowledge, to right the wrong done here. Return the spirit Elizabeth Watkins and restore the balance." I cleared my throat as overwhelming emotion began to claw its way up my throat, and I let the tears flow. It was right. "In her place, we send the fallen star, Jerry, who ended her life. Hear me now, and let it be."

I never knew quite how the other-siders would arrive. Sometimes they just appeared. Other times there was a great gust of wind inside the room, and other times a sprinkle of what looked like glitter, but was probably stardust. Tonight, the stardust appeared in an arc from the corner of the room, widening into a stream of glittering lights. Out of the light stepped an other-sider, then two more. Lately, they seemed to come in threes. More power, I guess.

"Thank you, friends. We are honored by your presence. Elizabeth was brutally and wrongly murdered. Her killer stands before us, and will be given over to make amends for his crime against her and against humanity."

"We have heard the honor in your cry for help. We, too, wish to restore the balance."

With those words, I picked up the sacred dagger. It vibrated in my hand. Off duty it was quiet, but during a ceremony it vibrated with life, almost sentient. I sliced it across my left forearm, perpendicular to the bones.

Accidentally hitting a vessel and bleeding to death right now would ruin my day. A red line appeared as soon as I slid the blade over my skin. Holding my arm over Liz's chest, I allowed my blood to drip onto her.

The atmosphere in the room changed. The heaviness lightened, somehow came alive. No one moved, no one spoke.

Sam's presence behind me was a comfort. Closing my eyes, I drew on the strength and energy he was sending my direction. I drew on the strength of a promise. I, too, had made a promise to Liz to return her, and my conviction now was as strong as Sam's. Maybe it was the new connection between us, or just the friendship we'd developed, but whatever it was, I needed it right now.

"Spirit known as Elizabeth Watkins, return now to this plane. We seek to right the wrong done to you." I took a deep breath as I felt her presence returning from the nebula. The energy of the room sizzled with her presence, and the other-siders glowed brighter. Tears overflowed my eyes, and I let them fall. Sometimes being tough just takes too much energy.

Reanimating a corpse is no easy task. Reanimating one that is your friend is monumental.

The signs are subtle at first. The coloring comes back into the face, neck, and upper body. I suppose it's like the cardiovascular system shutting down at death, only in reverse. Some people return with a huge gasping breath, sucking in oxygen as if they'd never get another breath. Others simply open their eyes and take in breaths as usual, as if they're awakening from a deep sleep.

Liz was the gasping kind. She took in that deep, deep breath full of oxygen, awakening her cells and setting them on fire again. She opened her eyes, blinked several times, looked around the room and finally focused her vision.

She was royally pissed.

Liz was a smart woman, and she knew exactly what had happened, why she was in her current state of undress, covered by only a sheet, and in a room full of men, one of whom was her ex-husband sporting shackles. Yeah. She put it together more quickly than your average undead. A woman scorned *and* a woman murdered is not someone you want to have focused on you.

"You," she hissed, looking at Jerry. *Looking* was probably the wrong word. Shooting poisoned spears that would explode with flesh-eating bacteria would be a better description of what her eyes looked like.

It was quite amusing.

Now that the bulk of the drama was over, I settled in for a good show. Unfortunately, I didn't have any popcorn. She tried to sit up, but couldn't quite manage it, so I helped her to swing her legs over the edge of the gurney and balance while keeping her covered. "Easy, Liz. You don't have your legs under you just yet."

"I'm going to have more than that under me in a few minutes." Hopping down, she draped the white sheet around her like a toga, then grabbed the dagger from the table. "I'm going to have two hundred pounds of asshole under me." She charged forward, but I grabbed her by the waist and held her back. As entertaining as it would have been to watch her carve Jerry into bite-size pieces, I couldn't let her. I'd just rectified one disaster. I didn't want it undone thirty seconds later.

"Hi, Liz." Jerry stood there, his eyes glittering, from what I wasn't certain. They certainly weren't unshed tears of joy clinging to his eyeballs. He was probably scared shitless. I was just glad I didn't have to wash his shorts after this.

"Hi, yourself, you prick. What did you do to me?" Trembling with rage, she marched forward as if she were the queen of England, and I let her go. Minus the dagger.

"I had a bad moment." He shrugged, as if that explained it. "Got drunk, followed you and put a bullet in your back."

The gasp she drew nearly sucked the hair off my arms. I swear, I could feel the vacuum of it, and the air in the room shifted directions. "How could you?"

Jerry's gaze shifted to Sam. "I was actually hoping you'd kill me." The disappointment in his expression was clear.

Sam simply grinned and looked at me. "I know better."

Good man. Well trained. I should keep him around.

"Coward," Liz said. Her right hand curled into a fist, and she coldcocked Jerry in the nose. His head snapped back and blood spurted from both nostrils. He screamed like a girl and dropped to his knees, then fell over and hit his nose again. Shackles. Oopsie.

Way to go, Liz. She did *not* hit like a girl. Someone had taught her a few things about fighting dirty. Hmm. We'd have to chat later.

"Somebody help me," Jerry whined from the floor, but no one moved.

"Guys?" I drew their attention. "Help him into the van. We're going to the 'yard in a few." My security guys hauled Jerry to his feet, and Liz went after him again, but Sam grabbed her this time. She was much stronger now with the power of righteous indignation firing to life inside. Didn't need extra powers to understand that.

The other-siders drew my attention by speaking into my mind. "We are complete." They disappeared in a fraction of a second, and I turned back to Liz.

"I've got some clothing for you. If you want to go to the 'yard with us, that's fine. Otherwise, I'll have one of the guys take you home."

"Are you kidding? I'm seeing this through so I can spit on his dead carcass."

Okay, then, decision made. I handed her a bag with loose clothing in it and a pair of slip-on shoes. Her autopsy scars would begin to heal as soon as Jerry's soul departed, but until then, they would hurt like hell. "You can change in the locker room." I led her out and watched as Sam, not my security, hauled Jerry to his feet. Now that was interesting. Maybe he was taking special interest in this one since he had taken Jerry down. Or he felt what I felt, and needed to extract a little vengeance of his own.

I was okay with either one.

Liz changed, and I assisted her. We'd never been real girlie-pals, but now, it didn't matter. I was a nurse, so naked bodies didn't bother me, and I'd seen just about every kind of scar there was, hosting a multitude of my own. When Liz turned away from me to drop the sheet, I knew she was freaked about the Y incision in her body. It extended from both collarbones, met over her sternum and extended down past her navel.

"It will heal and fade. Please don't be ashamed in front of me." I wanted to reach out and hug her, to give her some of the strength that I had needed when I'd returned.

"It's hideous." She hung her head, and I heard the

tears in her voice. "I know you say it will heal, but what if it doesn't?"

"There are some wonderful plastic surgeons in town whom I can refer you to if necessary." Excluding my ex-husband. Not referring a dead dog to his practice.

A sob ripped out of her, and she collapsed onto the wooden bench beside her. She turned away from me, and I felt waves of shame rolling off her. The shame in this wasn't hers to bear.

"You are not to blame in any of this." I sat beside her, wanting to reach out to her, wanting to comfort my friend. Absolution wasn't my job, but I wanted to assure her nothing she had done had brought about this incident. She knew I had scars, too, but she didn't know how extensive mine were. "It's not your fault."

"I married the bastard in the first place. I knew I shouldn't have, but sometimes you start believing the garbage people feed you." Tears dribbled down her nose and landed on her hands.

"I know. I know." Now, I eased her back against me and held her in my arms for a moment, making full contact with my palms on her shoulders. The contact seemed to soothe her, and her tears faded. For some reason, it soothed me, too. "You're stronger than you know right now."

"Thanks." She pulled the sheet up and wiped her eyes with it.

"Let me show you something." There was no shame in me. No fear, no guilt. Some things just were. I finally understood that. Standing, I parted my robe, and revealed my abdomen, which was scattered with lines and scars in all directions. Some were surgical scars from the multitude of repairs I'd undergone, some were the result of having my baby cut from my belly. None was pretty. They would never fade completely.

"Oh, Dani." Her tearful eyes looked directly at me for the first time since we'd entered the locker room. "I had no idea." Her gaze dropped to my abdomen again, and she reached out to touch me. We'd never had such an intimate moment before, but two women who are scarred inside and out overcome many barriers when they connect.

"We have a lot more in common now than we used to."

"Yeah. Kind of sisters in suffrage." She dropped her hand, and I closed the robe. "What an exclusive club to belong to."

I laughed. "Maybe we need a secret handshake or something."

"Yeah." With a deep breath and a long sigh out, she collected herself, pulling herself together. She was going to be okay.

"Let's get the hell out of here and finish it. I need a drink." Did I ever.

"Amen to that, sister. Amen to that." She slipped her feet into the sandals, and we returned to the lab.

Chapter 17

The ride to the 'yard seemed longer than usual. Liz and I rode with Sam in his truck, giving me a shiver of remembrance when I realized the last time we were all together in it was the day Liz had been killed. Weird, freaky and full circle. Isn't that how life works sometimes? If you don't laugh at the weird stuff, you'll end up in the loony bin ripping the wings off of flies.

Closing my eyes, I allowed my energy to percolate, to brew, to grow and re-create itself. My part in this energy show wasn't over yet. I still had to put Jerry in the ground.

Fear, especially the mortal kind, does strange things to people. It turns the wicked suddenly moral and the nonbelievers righteous. It turned Jerry an odd shade of green. Chartreuse, I'd say.

Without preamble, I began the ritual. "Now, I finish it." With the sacred dagger vibrating in my right hand, I raised both arms skyward. I called on different spirits to complete the ceremony and take the spirit of

Jerry away. We weren't playing nice anymore. "Angels of death, come to me now as we turn over the soul of this criminal."

As each resurrection is different, so is each life-swap. The sound of an ancient, rusted door screeching open flowed over the 'yard and through me. Shivers broke out on my flesh, and I tried hard to control them as whatever-it-was ruffled my robe. Instinctively, we all react the same as the stench of rotting flesh touches us. I knew it was here not to take us away, so I relaxed as the spirit of whatever-it-was whooshed past us.

A black robe, tattered at every edge, covered the thing that glided across the desert toward us. Jerry began to hyperventilate. "No. No. I. Didn't. Mean. It."

"We offer you this soul to pay for the crimes it has committed on this plane."

The being, death, whatever-you-wanted-to-call-it, bypassed Jerry, and stopped in front of me. O-*kay,* this was new. It had never engaged with me before, just taken the murderer with its appendage and moved off. *Fetid* was the only way to describe the smell coming off it. As a nurse and a resurrectionist, I've smelled my share of vile things. Try an anaerobic organism in close quarters some time.

This odoriferous creature put them all to shame, and I resisted the urge to pinch my nose shut. Breathing through my mouth didn't help. Just added a nasty taste to the stench. I *so* needed a mint.

"Yes?" I didn't quite know how to address a being from the underworld.

"Spirit known as Danielle Wright. You restore the balance."

I guess that was as much of an acknowledgment or

thank-you as I was going to get from this good ol' boy. "As do your kind." Honestly, I didn't now if there were others like it, or what, but somehow, there had to be.

"The Dark will be defeated. By your convictions it will be defeated."

Shocked at that tidbit of information, I blinked several times as the soul taker remained in front of me, but what the hell did it mean? I alone had to defeat The Dark? Was I seriously the only freakin' person in the universe who could do it?

"Tell me how. I need information, help that's stronger than me." I was ready to scream at so many cryptic messages from the universe.

"None is stronger than you. Join forces with your allies to strengthen your power. Allow the power to join you. The underworld also wishes for your success."

"Seriously?"

"There is none more powerful than what you are tonight."

The stench was too much, and I took a step back. The creature took that as a sign our conversation was over, as it moved off in Jerry's direction. I had to complete the ritual before I freaked out and forgot how. I raised the dagger of vengeance, prepared to slice my arm again. "Blood seals the pact between us and closes the portal between the worlds."

"Wait!" Liz cried.

Oh, gods. "You're not having second thoughts, are you?" I paused with the blade just inches from my skin. Now *I* was starting to hyperventilate.

"Oh, no." She stepped forward and held her arm toward the dagger. "This one is mine. I want to be the one who sends him to hell."

Now, I no longer believe in hell in the traditional sense, but as another realm where souls exist. If she chose to believe in it as hell, that was fine with me. "I accept your gift of blood." Before she could change her mind, I sliced her arm.

One quick stroke of the dagger opened a small wound in her arm. She jumped and gave a surprised gasp. I spoke the words, she spilled the blood. We were true sisters in vengeance.

"Take this spirit with you now and leave this plane. Hear me now and let it be." The words sealed Jerry's fate.

The dark being moved toward Jerry, who now cried like the coward he was. I had no feeling for him. He'd sealed his fate.

I simply sealed the portal.

The dark being oozed across the ground. Rather than stopping, it mowed him over, encompassing Jerry's physical body into the gelatinous goo that it was. Jerry fell over, screaming as the life force was sucked out of him, gurgled, then his voice fell silent, his body twitching, jiggling, slowing, as his brain died without the soul to operate it. Though he had appeared somewhat green upon our arrival, he now was so pale his body appeared devoid of blood. Maybe it was. Who knew. Maybe the thing that had come for him had sucked it from the body for a midnight snack.

"Balance has been restored. Hear me now and let it be." Those words ended the ritual and sealed it permanently. The spirit known as Jerry would never return to this plane. The thought occurred to me at this moment that it might now be possible to resolve the psyche-patient-cop-killer case now. If the underworld was willing to work with me and obviously approved of what

I was doing, this case might take a turn for the better. Sometime it had to end, if only to ease the misery of their families.

Turning away from the sight of Jerry's body, I let the men do their thing with it. The lawyers and guards from the prison ambled off talking about getting a drink on the way back. I'm sure they needed it. I ushered Liz back to Sam's truck, and we headed to her house. She had given me a spare set of keys, and I used them now. Hers were still in the P.D.

It was kind of freaky, I have to admit, walking into her house. It felt as if it had been in mourning, too. All of her plants were dead. Except the succulents and cacti that required little attention and were their usual thorny selves.

But it was the energy, or lack of it, that struck me the most as we entered the two-story condo. It was a person's presence that made a house a home. Now that Liz had returned to it, it was filling up again, breathing life into itself and sighing that it was now complete.

The first thing Liz did was go to the kitchen and pull out a bottle of tequila and three glasses and pour us each a shot.

"What, no lime?" Sarcasm is just a side benefit I don't charge my clients for.

"Sorry, chick. I've been dead for a week and didn't have time to shop." She smiled at me. "But I do have salt." She reached into the cupboard and got down the margarita salt. We licked our hands, dabbed salt on them and raised our glasses, clinking them together.

"Welcome back." I blinked away tears that wanted to erupt. I looked at Sam, who held my gaze and gave a nod. He was as emotional as I was, but controlled it better.

"Thanks for bringing me back." The look in her eyes

was heartfelt and serious and something I couldn't stand for very long without making a smart-ass comment. Not wanting to spoil the moment, I licked the salt and the others followed suit. Tossing back the most excellent tequila I'd ever had on an empty stomach may not have been the wisest move, but was better than Liz's decision to partake, since she'd had no sustenance for a week. I saw stars when I swallowed, and I swear fire blazed out my nostrils.

"Holy mother of god, that's good." I needed a bottle of that for myself. I sucked in a breath and clutched the counter. I looked at Sam, and he simply wiped the back of his hand across his mouth, his eyes locked on me. I knew he was remembering the last time we'd had tequila in a kitchen and the aftermath of it.

Gulp.

Liz slammed her glass on the counter, and I jumped. "I need a damned shower."

That made me smile. I really was going to have to work on a gift bag. "Go ahead. I suspect you'll sleep for twelve hours after that. Don't expect to be back to your old self in a snap. Take a shower, get something to eat, and I'll call you tomorrow evening." It was approaching 4:00 a.m. now, and we all needed some sleep. "We'll get out of here."

I hugged her, and she clung to me for a few seconds.

"Dani, thank you. I'll never be able to repay you for this." She pulled back and sniffed.

"Will you be okay tonight, or do you want me to stay?"

"I'll be fine since Jerry's gone for good." She gave a nervous laugh. "I might actually be able to sleep in peace now."

I was happy to give her that. "Rest up. You're going to need it."

Sam and I left her alone and got into the truck. For a few seconds, I relaxed my head back against the seat and closed my eyes. I could feel Sam's attention on me and turned my head toward him, but kept my eyes closed. "What a weird night."

"That's one way to put it." His voice was very close to me and searching for that place inside me where we connected. I knew he wanted me. There was a new intensity about him I hadn't felt before. Something I almost recognized and needed from him. My heart was aching for him. All I had to do was reach out.

I opened my eyes and his face was inches from mine. Raising my hand, I cupped his face. "Take me home."

He did.

"I'll walk you up."

Fatigue overwhelmed me, and all I could do was nod. He would have whether or not I agreed, so it was easier than disagreeing and trying to be the tough girl. He knew better anyway.

After his prowl around the house, he was satisfied. "Do you want me to stay?" He stood just a few feet from me. The night was almost gone.

"I need a shower before I can think of anything else."

"Go ahead. I'll wait."

After a hot shower and scrubbing every inch of me, I left my hair damp and combed straight back from my head. I wrapped a light robe around me. Barefoot, I followed the smell of coffee to the kitchen and found Sam at the table. He'd removed his blazer and gun, rolled up the sleeves of his shirt to the elbows and leaned back in a chair. I was glad he was comfortable enough in my kitchen to make his sexy self at home. I bit my lip. Seeing him like this was getting too good to walk away from. I had to end it between us for his sake. I couldn't be what he needed.

Reaching down into a place I hated to go, I searched for the conviction that the soul eater had spoken of. My conviction was going to get me through these next few moments. It was the *only* thing that was going to get me through.

Getting closer to him, I felt that hum between us vibrate faster, and my conviction began to wane.

"Find everything okay?" I stopped in front of him, letting the fragrance of my soap and shampoo flow over him. I knew it did, because the light in his eyes changed.

"Almost."

What, was I out of sugar?

He tugged on the belt of the robe and eased it free. The act of opening the robe, of sliding the fabric against itself, freed something that had been tied up in me. I don't know what it was, but I knew at this moment another level of feminine power opened up inside me.

The knot popped free and the sides of the robe parted, yet remained on my shoulders. He eased the robe open and bared my body to him. The quick brush of his hands against the skin of my abdomen sent a sharp pang of desire through me. This is what I wanted. This is what I needed and would never be able to have again. For this moment only, I would allow myself to savor one last moment with Sam.

The skin is the largest organ of the body and is filled with a gazillion nerve endings. It feels everything and transmits those sensations to our brains for interpretation. At the moment, I was interpreting lust.

"Beautiful," he whispered. "You're just beautiful."

At that moment, I felt it. Tingles and surges of moisture flooded my body as Sam reached for me. My amulet hung from its chain between my breasts. Seconds ago, it had been only as warm as my skin, but now it glowed hotter as Sam's breath blew across my skin. When he leaned forward, his amulet swung free and glowed amber. This was the first time I'd noticed it change color.

He opened his mouth and took one nipple inside, teasing it, tugging, as his hands clasped the curve of my waist and drew me closer to him.

Resting my fisted hands on his shoulders, I allowed him complete access to me. What woman in her right mind was going to push a man like Sam away? As he worked at my other breast, I worked at his shirt and pushed it off. I wanted to see his skin, to feel that large expanse beneath my hands. He shrugged out of the shirt and parted his thighs to bring me closer. The amulets pulsed brighter.

He always seemed to shake me up, and I wanted to do some shaking of my own. Leaning back in the chair, he gave me access to what I wanted. Breathing no longer seemed important, but I did it anyway. My heart raced, fluttering wildly in my chest as I drew down the zipper and opened his jeans.

Now that I had what I wanted, I looked into Sam's eyes. I'm certain the need, the want, the desire I saw there was reflected in my own eyes. I could never hide my emotions and didn't see any reason to now.

"More."

Sam raised his hips up, and I dragged his jeans down to his knees. Then I reached for his mouth and parted my lips over his. Tongues and teeth and hands ranged everywhere. Sam eased me onto his lap and I straddled his legs, hooking my heels on the back of the chair. His cock was positioned so that when my flesh parted, it rubbed against the right place. I was so wet, so ready for him one last time.

With his expert hands, he clasped my bottom and pulled me tighter against him. The feel of his rigid shaft nearly had me gasping for air. Nothing was as important or as perfect as his touch, his fire, his erection. Clutching my hands to his shoulders, I urged him on. Moans and groans and little cries of pleasure burst out of me. Every nerve ending in my body was on fire. Every place Sam touched was imprinted with the feel of him, the taste of his mouth against mine, the scent of him locked in my brain. Rocking my hips back and forth against him, I nearly exploded, but I held back, wanting to take us as far as we could go. When his breathing became as restless as mine, I knew the time was right. I reached between us and straightened his erection, torturing him with my moist flesh. There is no anticipation like that of hot sex, and we were dripping with it.

His eyes glazed over, and his fingers dug into my hips. I took him inside me.

His amulet glowed supersonic. And so did mine.

Sam threw his head back, gritting his teeth against the tide of primal pleasure that washed over us. I felt the pleasure he was feeling inside me, the pressure, the heat, the wild animal of sex in him that wanted out.

"Dani." I heard his voice in my ears and in my mind. I was unable to resist the heat or the emotion joining us together. Devoid of thought now, I clutched him to me. I had no control and didn't want any. The prelude to an orgasm is kind of like tightening a spring. Each touch, each lick, each sensation winds that coil until it can no longer tolerate the pressure and it blows.

That's what happened between us. Each movement brought us closer together until we were reduced to one body, one mind, one flesh searching for the same release.

I bit my lower lip as my coil sprang open. Digging my fingers into his shoulders, I held on as spasms of carnal pleasure overwhelmed me. My legs trembled, and I curved forward, my head bowed as each pulse rocked through me. His fingers dug into my hips as I felt the orgasm rip through him. This time, I screamed, and Sam came apart in my arms.

The aftermath was nothing like I'd expected. After we recovered a bit and could speak rationally, I pulled back and looked at him. He was hot and sweaty and very satisfied-looking.

"What happened with the amulets?"

He cupped my face and pressed his forehead to mine. *I love you, Dani.* I heard it in my mind.

"No." I tried to pull back, but he wouldn't let me, and I wasn't working that hard. They were words I wanted to hear, but couldn't let him say. "Sam, you can't."

"Yes. We're bound to each other. I love you, and I know you love me." He lifted his face skyward. "Hear me now and let it be."

I remembered the conversation in the mountains with the other-siders. *When Sam was ready, the amulet would speak.*

"They won't let you work with me if we're involved." Concerned, I searched his eyes, but found no uncertainty. The conviction with which he spoke shook me more than anything. "This has to end."

"I agree." He clenched his jaw and a muscle twitched there. This was the hardest thing I'd ever done, and my throat closed against the emotions I couldn't voice. I loved Sam, but I had to give him up. I loved him with my entire soul, and that's what scared me. I was so in charge, so in control of my life. Would loving Sam this much change who I was? Would I still be in charge of my life, or would every decision revolve around how it would affect Sam?

"I'm sorry." My voice cracked and my vision blurred. The place in my chest where my heart lived fractured. This just wasn't going to work, no matter how much I wanted it.

"I'm not."

"What?" It was a whisper in my mind.

"What stops is the pretense. What stops is not claiming you as mine." He cupped my face in his hands. "I love you more than my damned job."

"I won't let The Dark hurt you, Sam. It wants me and the worst thing it can do is hurt you." That was my ultimate fear, and The Dark knew it.

"It's my choice and I choose you, Dani. The Dark we'll deal with together." He took a deep breath. "I feel you inside me every day. If we're not together, I feel like something's missing, like I forgot my underwear. Something's just not right."

I snorted a laugh at that. "I kinda like you commando."

"Be serious. We are one, you and I. I love you, and I know you love me." He pulled me against him, the intensity of him almost overwhelming. "You don't have to say the words because I feel everything inside you."

There was truth in his eyes. A truth I couldn't hide from. Not any longer.

"Will I have no secrets from you?"

"I don't know. I only know we have to work it out because unless I'm with you, I'm only half what I used to be." He held the amulet up between us. It had dimmed to a light golden hue. "I won't go back to what I was before, only half-alive."

My amulet matched his and I knew there was no other choice for us. We were destined by the stars above. Maybe we had known each other in another life on the other side. Becoming earthbound could have erased the memory of that other life from us, and it's taken until now for us to find each other.

I hugged him tight. Control? Did I really need it that badly? Wasn't there enough room in my life to share with Sam? A smile began in my heart and expanded outward. I knew there was. I just had to let it be. "If anything happens to you—"

"Nothing will happen now. We two are one and the other-siders will protect us. The Dark will be defeated. The balance can't be righted in one lifetime, so we'll have a long, long time together."

That supersonic light I'd never gotten used to appeared behind me, and I flashed around. An other-sider hovered there, glowing unnaturally in the confines of the house, but for the first time I was able to look directly at its colors, all mixed into one.

Er, can anyone say *awkward?* We were still half-naked.

"You are indeed correct, Samuel. The other-siders will provide information and assistance, but the two of you, joined together as one spiritual being, will be able to defeat The Dark in time. It has gone into hiding now with this new development of your joining. It will refocus and return more powerful than ever."

"So how are we going to defeat it, if it's more powerful?"

"You will lead a group of beings like yourself, and together the power of you will win. The most important step is joining with Samuel and accepting his power as your own."

Sam and I looked at each other. Yes, I had to agree that with our powers joined, we were more than we had been as individuals.

Then, the other-sider disappeared. There was a reprieve now. I felt it in the universe and I felt it between Sam and me. We could connect as never before.

The glow that began in my amulet filled the inside of me. Now that Sam and I could be together, there was no reason to resist. I opened the door and fully allowed him inside my soul.

"Sam. I love you in a way I have never loved anyone." I accepted him for who he was, scars and all. He accepted me, with all my faults, all my scars, and loved me anyway. The best thing I could ever do for him was to let him love me the way he wanted to. I accept that now, too.

He pressed his forehead against mine, and I felt the truth in him. I was enough.

I would always be enough for him.

"You have to do one thing for me." He pressed a soft kiss to my mouth.

"Anything." Did that just come out of my mouth? Boy, I was easy. A flaming orgasm, and I'd agree to anything.

"Marry me." His voice had softened with the emotion of that request.

"What? We've been together for millennia, I'm certain. We don't need a ceremony." Who needed a ceremony when you were an eternal star? Seriously.

"For our earthbound families, we do. They don't remember the beyond, so for them." The passion and the love in his eyes was my undoing. I'd do anything for this man.

I was silent for a few seconds, digesting this. He was right. Doing things for others generally wasn't my gig, but this time he was right.

"You know I'm right."

I glared, but there wasn't much heat to it. "Are you going to do this the rest of our lives?" I hate mind readers. They think they're always right.

"Absolutely." He grinned and any resistance I thought I had melted away.

"Once in a while you've got to let me be right, okay?" I stroked his face, loving the feel of him, the texture of his skin, and I was no longer afraid of the sensations.

"I will."

Whatever he thought he was going to say got lost somewhere as we raced up the stairs to my bedroom. The universe would just have to wait on us for now.

My work, my mission to restore balance, had only begun, and there was time. There were many roads still to be paved for me, for others like me, so that we could exist together beside others in the normal world. We had a job, a mission, to right the wrongs committed against man in this world. I owed the other-siders something for saving my life and sending me back, so I would carry on. I owed them for putting Sam in my path and making him strong enough to resist my efforts to push him away, too. I've learned to reach out to those around me rather than trying to protect everyone on my own. I can't do that, but together we can be stronger than we ever were individually.

Though the weight of the world sometimes rested on my shoulders, with Sam, anything was possible. I had felt the power of him, the impressive personal strength he carried, and with us together The Dark would be defeated. We had pushed it back as surely as his *abuela* had years ago. With new information in the journals, with Liz reborn to our cause and with the power humming within all of us, we would win. The future wasn't set. Not even the other-siders could predict the outcome, so there was hope. There was always hope.

For now we would train, draw strength from each other and build a life together that nothing, not even forces from beyond, could destroy.

* * * * *

Discovering he's a father of a newborn, rodeo cowboy
Theo Colton turns to his new cook, Ellie, to help out as
nanny. But when Ellie's past returns to haunt her,
Theo's determined to protect her and the baby…
but who will protect his heart?

Read on for a sneak peek at

A SECRET COLTON BABY

by Karen Whiddon, the first novel in
The Coltons: Return to Wyoming miniseries.

"A man," Ellie gasped, pointing past where he stood, his
broad-shouldered body filling the doorway. "Dressed in
black, wearing a ski mask. He was trying to hurt Amelia."

And then the trembling started. She couldn't help it, despite the tiny infant she clutched close to her chest. Somehow, Theo seemed to sense this, as he gently took her arm
and steered her toward her bed.

"Sit," he ordered, taking the baby from her.

Reluctantly releasing Amelia, Ellie covered her face with
her hands. It had been a strange day, ever since the baby's
mother—a beautiful, elegant woman named Mimi Rand—
had shown up that morning insisting Theo was the father
and then collapsing. Mimi had been taken to the Dead River
clinic with a high fever and flulike symptoms. Theo had Ellie
looking after Amelia until everything could be sorted out.

But Theo had no way of knowing about Ellie's past, or the danger that seemed to follow her like a malicious shadow. "I need to leave," she told him. "Right now, for Amelia's sake."

Theo stared at her, holding Amelia to his shoulder and bouncing her gently, so that her sobs died away to whimpers and then silence. The sight of the big cowboy and the tiny baby struck a kernel of warmth in Ellie's frozen heart.

"Leave?" Theo asked. "You just started work here a week ago. If it's because I asked you to take care of this baby until her mama recovers, I'll double your pay."

"It's not about the money." Though she could certainly use every penny she could earn. "I…I thought I was safe here. Clearly, that's not the case."

He frowned. "I can assure you…" Stopping, he handed her back the baby, holding her as gingerly as fragile china. "How about I check everything out? Is anything missing?"

And then Theo went into her bathroom. He cursed, and she knew. Her stalker had somehow found her.

**Don't miss
A SECRET COLTON BABY
by Karen Whiddon,
available October 2014.**

Available wherever

⊞ HARLEQUIN®

ROMANTIC suspense

books and ebooks are sold.

Heart-racing romance, high-stakes suspense!

HRSEXP0914